"Knowing you won't be there...it's
woke up at about two in the morn
looked around my bedroom which is nothing special...I've got a litt
one-bedroom apartment. There's my little computer, my little brand-
new bookcase which I put together myself...And just this terrible,
terrible sinking feeling: I don't ever want to leave this. I'm given so
much comfort by this strange little room which is nothing special
whatsoever. But it's me. I can't imagine leaving it behind."

Will The Circle Be Unbroken?
Justin Hayford (as told to Studs Terkel)

for Amy, Zuzu, Mom & Dad

Building Heaven

Andrew Osborne

सच्चिदानन्द

Lost Pilgrim

Press

Portions of this book were previously published as a work-in-progress in the Unitarian Universalist Psi Symposium Journal (Fall-Winter, 2007-2008)

ISBN 978-0-9968613-2-8

Cover photo © 2007 Marie-Lan Nguyen/Wikimedia Commons, cover title design by Jana Christy

Published in the United States by Lost Pilgrim Press

www.lostpilgrimpress.com

The ancient Egyptians postulated seven souls.

*Top soul, and the first to leave at the moment of death is
Ren, the Secret Name...*

*Second soul, and second one off the sinking ship is
Sekem: Energy, Power, Light...*

*Number three is Khu, the Guardian Angel.
He, she, or it is third man out...depicted as flying away across a full
moon, a bird with luminous wings and head of light...*

Number four is Ba, the Heart, often treacherous...

*Number five is Ka, the Double, most closely associated with the subject.
The Ka, which usually reaches adolescence at the time of bodily death,
is the only reliable guide through the Land of the Dead
to the Western Lands...*

*Number six is Khaibit, the Shadow, Memory,
your whole past conditioning from this and other lives...*

Number seven is Sekhu, the Remains...

The Western Lands
William S. Burroughs

Morning. I'm awake. I'm still here. Intravenous feeding time. The plump white nurse adjusts the feeding tube without a glance in my direction. The overhead fluorescent lights are still flickering...flickering...*flickering*...

...ignore it, ignore it, *think*...

Fives. Five fives. 5:55:55.

I can't move. Okay.
...hello?

...*HELLO?*

...I can't speak...

...what's happening? What happened? Okay, *think*...

...hospital room. Private room. The plump white nurse – Mary. Her name is Mary...I've seen her twice...three times. Just now, last night, yesterday morning. And before that...

Fives. Five fives. 5:55:55.
Dancing, digital, yes...

...I remember...

SEKHU (*The Remains*)

There were two Marys on the coma ward at Cedars-Sinai: Big Mary, the ward administrator, was all thin lips and petty tyranny, while Little Mary resembled nothing so much as a cartoon mole: sweet and nearsighted, timid and sexless, muttering "Oh dear, oh dear, oh dear" whenever she felt overwhelmed or under the gun.

"So I hear ol' Herlinger woke up."

Little Mary chirruped in surprise, startled from her reading, and looked up to see the tall black orderly Ray leaning across the counter of the sixth floor nurse's station. "Oh, what? Yes," she replied, capillaries flushing pink as she tucked her book away a little too quickly. "Well, actually, no."

"No?"

"I mean, he spoke, but it didn't make sense."

Ray shifted his weight, trying casually to steal a glimpse of Little Mary's book. "So what'd he say?"

"Mr. Herlinger?"

"Yeah."

"He said *five*."

"Five?"

"Mm-hmm. Yep."

"That's it?"

Little Mary adjusted her thick glasses, pushing them tight against the bridge of her nose. "Well, he said a few other things, but that was the only word I could really understand."

"So you were there when it happened?"

Little Mary's head bounced a quick nod. "His vitals went haywire yesterday just after you left...y'know, like a seizure or whatever? Anyway, I got there first and he was muttering something, as if he was talking in his sleep. Then he said, very clearly, '*Five*.'"

"Huh," Ray said, yawning like a cat. "So what'd the doc say?"

"He wasn't sure *what* to think...I guess it's pretty unusual for patients to speak after so long in a vegetative state."

"How long..."

"Since he came in? Well..." All at once, Little Mary lowered her voice dramatically, so Ray was compelled to lean closer. "...that's kinda the *weird* thing. I checked his file, and *guess* how long he's been here?"

"Tell me."

"Five years, five months and five days *exactly*."

Ray smiled. Weird hospital stories and gossip were a shared currency between them, a hobby to break up the monotony of their days on the ward. "*Five*, huh?"

"Yeah. Kinda spooky."

"I hear that," Ray mimed a shudder, only half playacting: Herlinger gave him the creeps, for real. Not so much the scarred wreck of the man himself, but what he represented – a lightning strike of tragedy Ray didn't care to think about.

"So what else been goin' on?" he said, eager to change the subject. "What's the word around the campfire?"

Little Mary shrugged. "Nothing much exciting."

"Yeah? How 'bout you? What's up? What you readin' there?" Ray probed, hand striking with sudden precision to snatch the book she'd been hiding in a quick, casual motion. *"1001 Baby Names?"*

Little Mary's lowered gaze and violent blush instantly told Ray he'd miscalculated. Sometimes he'd catch her reading gooey romance novels, and he liked teasing her about it – but this was different, more personal. It was no secret she loved babies, and was forever angling for a transfer to the maternity ward. But whether she'd ever have a child of her own, he knew, was a different, more painful subject.

Fortunately, she had a ready response: "Oh, well... Elphaba just had puppies, so..."

"She did? Congratulations!" Ray smiled, feeling the awkwardness pass. "You're a grandmother!"

Little Mary laughed, feeling it too. "Yeah, right, some grandma...I'll be giving most of 'em away..."

"Oh, yeah? Maybe you could hook me up with something for Baby Joyce...what are they?"

"Dachsund-beagle. I call 'em deagles...they're supposedly real good with kids."

"How many you got?"

"There were nine in the litter, and I'm keeping two."

"Emiko and Erzsebet," Ray suggested, opening to a random page in the baby name book.

"Hey, I like those...what do they mean?"

"Let's see...Erzsebet is 'consecrated to God,' and Emiko...'blessed, beautiful child.'"

"Ooh, that's a good one. *Emiko,*" Little Mary said, committing it to memory. "And how's about *your* beautiful child? Joyce?"

Ray flipped to the "J" section. "Joyce...*merry.*"

"That's so perfect!"

A big grin of tiny teeth flashed in the mental photo album Ray carried everywhere. He loved his daughter so much it was almost painful to think of her when they were apart, separated by the hours of his long hospital shift at Cedars. Every morning he dropped her at Happyland Day Care was a desperate act of faith, every night when he retrieved her a joyful thanksgiving. He wasn't a religious man, but he *was* superstitious, which accounted for his dread of Herlinger, as if tragedy were contagious.

"Let me see," Little Mary said, reclaiming her book, flipping it to: "Ray, *wise protector...*"

"More like blind piano man," Ray replied, modest. "Or anyhow, that's where Mama Wyatt got the name. How 'bout you? What's it say for Mary?"

Little Mary turned to the appropriate page, read and scowled. "Bitter."

Ray just laughed in surprise. "Oh, now, that can't be right..." – but before he could reach for the book again to check, the elevator bell rang at the far end of the hall, causing both their heads to snap instinctively towards the sound as sliding doors revealed Big Mary and Dr. Ku, stepping onto the floor.

"Now *there's* a bitter Mary," Ray whispered, winking to Little Mary as he made himself scarce, heading away from the elevators towards the employee lunchroom.

No one used "Big" or "Little" around the Marys – it was, rather, just a handy way of distinguishing them in third party conversations or lunch orders, as in "I've got Little Mary down for a tuna melt...does anyone remember what Big Mary wanted?"

In person, Little Mary was always just Mary, while Big Mary was usually referred to as ma'am or Ms. Barnes or Nurse Barnes or occasionally Nurse Ratched. And, whereas Little Mary was liked but generally taken for granted, Big Mary had somehow managed to secure a fairly unassailable position in the hospital's political rigging without being particularly well-liked by anyone.

"...so you basically have no contact information for Mr. Herlinger other than legal, correct?" Dr. Ku was saying as he stepped off the elevator.

"And the insurance reps," Big Mary confirmed, fingering the file in her hands.

"Would the lawyer know how to reach anybody with more of a *personal* connection? It might help with the cognitive recovery."

"We're still waiting for a call back," Big Mary said, pausing by the nurse's station to ask, "Anything new on Mr. Herlinger?"

"No change since this morning," Little Mary reported. Her counterpart continued on without a second glance, quickening her step to match Dr. Ku's long strides as they made their way to Herlinger's room.

His eyes were open, staring, as they entered. Big Mary was unnerved in spite of herself, releasing a tiny gasp as Dr. Ku approached the patient's bed, seemingly unaffected by the lizard stare, the mottled skin, the frozen expression of horror and despair. "Mr. Herlinger, I'm Dr. Ku, this is Nurse Barnes...can you understand what I'm saying?"

Herlinger was silent for a moment, pupils flicking back and forth, lips quivering, before he finally rasped a single word: "...*five*..."

"That's very good, Mr. Herlinger, but I need a more specific response to let me know that we're communicating. Can you try that? Can you say anything else?"

"...five..."

"Okay," Dr. Ku continued briskly, removing a penlight from the breast pocket of his white hospital jacket. "I want you to watch the light, follow the light..."

Herlinger closed his eyes.

"Mr. Herlinger...*Pete*."

Big Mary checked the patient's vital signs, reported no change. Herlinger's eyes remained tightly shut, lips pursed, teeth clenched.

Dr. Ku watched him for a moment, then reached for the dense patient file. "He's been here five years?"

"Going on six..."

"And no eye, ear, nose, or throat trauma in that time, including the original incident, correct?"

"Not to the best of my knowledge."

"So, no sensory degradation apart from the paralysis, no articulation issues," Dr. Ku said, delicate fingers skimming the file. "We should get Dr. Jeglinski in to confirm that, and schedule a new CAT scan..."

A sharp intake of breath drew their attention back to Herlinger, and Big Mary was the first to notice the strained expression, the single tear of sorrow or frustration squeezing out from the corner of his left eyelid. "His lips..."

The steady beat of the heart monitor sped its tempo as Dr. Ku watched Herlinger's mouth quiver and pulse. "He may be aphasic...Mr. Herlinger, can you hear me?"

"...five...sin..."

Herlinger's voice disappeared again, but his mouth continued, struggling. Big Mary remembered something and shifted to the doorway, calling Little Mary into the room. "You've had some experience reading lips, haven't you?"

"My grandfather was deaf. I'm a bit out of practice, but..."

Big Mary steered her towards Herlinger's bed. "That's okay, do your best."

Dr. Ku stepped aside at Little Mary's approach. "His speech abilities may have atrophied, but he's definitely saying something."

Little Mary leaned close, watching for sibilants and bilabial fricatives, goading her dormant skills to match the faint sounds of the patient's breath with the motion of his lips and tongue. "...five...sin..." Herlinger wheezed. "...where..."

"There were...five of us...in the car, where..." Little Mary translated. Herlinger's eyes snapped open again, staring desperately into the twin windows of her thick prescription glasses as she concentrated on his words and finally understood: "There were five of us in the car...*where is my family?*"

REN (*The Secret Name*)

I know they're gone. I just need to hear the names.

Father. Mother. Wife. Son.

If they were alive, somebody would have mentioned them by now.

I just need to know what happened. I remember only...

...flashes: driving in the rain, digital numbers on the dashboard...

...5:55:55...

...evening, my wife beside me, my parents in back, flanking my son, Pete Junior...

...my eyes flick to the rear-view mirror. Pete, Jr. smiles in reflection. My wife, Karen, screams in terror...

...eyes forward, too late. A black, onrushing form...

...a Humvee in my lane, blinding headlights through the windshield...

...one last moment, all of us together, then...

...IMPACT, airbags – mine "saves" me, Karen's kills her. Screaming: my son, my parents, Detroit steel. My son, dead. My wife, dead. My parents, dead. My body, dead.

Of course, this part survived, my thinking part, trapped in useless flesh all puckered with bed sores, poked with needles and catheters.

I'm some kind of miracle to them, all the doctors and gawkers who parade by my bed like museum tour groups, poking and prodding and scribbling notes. They tell me it's miraculous I survived the crash in the first place. They tell me it's miraculous I recovered from a vegetative coma with my faculties intact. They tell me I was unconscious five years, five months and five days.

But they won't tell me where my family is.

I wish I knew.

KHAIBIT (*The Shadow*)

Karen paced the driveway, seething with impatience as Pete futzed endlessly through his neurotic stations of the cross inside their modest Valley home, running from room to room checking and double-checking window and door locks and God knew what else while his son and parents waited, yawning, crowded together in the back of the Herlinger family's sensible blue Ford Focus.

"All right, I'm coming!" Pete called, appearing briefly in the open front doorway of the house before dashing back to the kitchen to make sure the stove was *really, really* off (so the house wouldn't fill with gas and explode in their absence) and the refrigerator was *definitely* running (so the pork chops inside wouldn't go bad and give them all trichinosis).

Karen sighed and climbed into the passenger seat to wait. "What's taking him so long?" Pete's father asked, not unkindly, from his perch behind the driver's seat.

"Your son is a little obsessive-compulsive," Karen sighed, locking eyes with Bob Herlinger's gentle, steady gaze in the car's rear-view mirror. "In case you hadn't noticed."

"Better safe than sorry," Pete's mother Tilly chirped, instinctively defending her darling son in put-upon tones as Karen and Bob communicated telepathically through the mirror: *we both know where he gets it, don't we?*

Bob smiled at Karen's pretty blonde reflection, then lowered his eyes to the *Popular Mechanics* in his lap.

"Grandma, have you ever seen a Giganatosaurus?" Pete Jr.

asked, apropos of nothing, adorably and inexhaustibly five.

"A Giganto-saurus?" Tilly twittered in the kind of patronizing kid's show voice that made Karen's teeth itch.

"GIGANATO-saurus."

"Why, I'm sure I've never heard of such a thing! Sounds like a *monster!*"

"It's not a *monster*, it's a *dinosaur*," Pete, Jr. explained in the sardonic, eye-rolling tone he'd learned from his mother. Then, with the patient kindness of his father and grandfather, he said, "But I see how you could make the mistake. Dinosaurs *look* like monsters. In fact, dinosaur means *terrible lizard...*"

"No!"

"Yes. In fact, I'm pretty sure I told you that before."

"You did?"

"I think so. But anyway, I don't think I told you about Giganatosauruses."

"And what can you tell me about Gigantic-sauruses?"

"*Giganato*saurus," Pete Jr. corrected her, matter-of-fact.

"How do you know so much?"

"I read," Pete Jr. shrugged, continuing his lecture. "Giganatosauruses were even bigger than a T-Rex."

"That's pretty big."

"Yes."

"But do you know what's *even bigger*, Petey?"

"Sperm whales."

"And, uh, do you know what's even bigger than..." Tilly tripped awkwardly over *sperm*, to Karen's silent amusement, pronouncing only "...*whales?*"

Pete Jr. quickly scanned his memory before declaring, "Nothing's bigger than a *blue* whale, except maybe the Bruhathkayosaurus, but scientists aren't sure about that one yet."

"Well, *I* can think of something *bigger* than *both* of those."

"Really?" Pete Jr. asked, curious. "What?"

"*God.*"

Karen instantly spun around in her seat, annoyed at Tilly's heavy-handed attempt to bring the conversation back to religion, as usual, when Pete Jr. dropped the bomb: "Oh, but that's just a myth. We don't really believe in God."

Pete's parents had just arrived from Kansas the day before, and the ride from the airport had been dominated by Tilly's glowing report of their recent interstate pilgrimage to "Pastor Ted" Haggard's church in Colorado Springs. Raised Catholic, she'd only recently converted to Evangelical Christianity, much to Bob's chagrin.

"She just won't shut up about it," he'd warned Karen at the baggage claim and, in fact, only a pointedly diplomatic segue by Pete had managed to prevent open culture war between his mother and wife...but now the fight he'd been hoping to avoid had finally erupted.

"*WHAT* did you say?" Tilly gasped, eyes bugging wide as her son clambered into the driver's seat.

"Ready to go?" Pete asked, cheerfully unaware of the increased barometric pressure around him.

"*Do you know what your son just told me?*" Tilly hissed as Pete, Jr. blinked around the car in fear and confusion, uncertain what had touched off his grandmother's anger.

"Tilly, please..." Bob tried, without hope of success.

"He said *you don't believe in the Lord*!" Tilly continued, proving her husband correct. "He said God is a *myth*...a *five year old boy*!"

"Well, he *is* very bright for his age," Karen offered, for her father-in-law's benefit.

"Honey, please," Pete scolded, without rancor; then to his mother: "Can we talk about this *later*?"

"What's wrong?" Pete Jr. asked, trying to understand the situation.

"I don't know what your *mother* has been telling you," Tilly said with a poison apple smile. "But God is NOT a *myth*. Without *God*, you wouldn't be here..."

"Tilly," Bob repeated, more serious this time. "Please. We have a long trip ahead..."

"Why aren't you supporting me?" Tilly shot back, aggrieved.

Bob seemed to have an answer that he didn't want to speak aloud, so Karen supplied the words instead: "*Because it doesn't concern you.*"

Pete winced as his mother swelled with righteous indignation, seemingly ready to burst, then abruptly changed gears to a tone of quietly menacing accusation. "My *concern* is for his *eternal soul*..."

"Oh, give it a rest," Karen nearly laughed, exasperated and bemused.

"Don't you speak to me like that, young lady."

"And don't *you* tell me how to raise my son," Karen shot back, turning fully around in her seat again to look Tilly in the eye. "Believe it or not, there are people in the world *who don't believe everything you do.*"

"Agreed," Tilly replied, suddenly and strategically beatific. "But it doesn't make them *right.*"

And with that she fell silent, staring pointedly out her window, though everyone knew it was hardly the end of the matter.

REN (*The Secret Name*)

Motion, light. The hospital...I'm still here. The plump white nurse is changing my catheter, none too gently. Daylight streams through the window.

At first I don't understand. The Korean doctor was just here at the foot of my bed, scribbling notes. I remember darkness outside, *60 Minutes* on the t.v. across the room, suspended from the ceiling.

Time has passed. I don't remember falling asleep, I don't remember dreaming. The space between my last thought and this moment simply disappeared without marker, as if...

My last thought. It takes a moment, but then I remember. My last thought was a wish.

My second wish.

I remember now...

...the accident, the chaos of light and terror, then darkness. They tell me it was *years* of darkness. Five years, five months, five days.

Fives. Five fives. 5:55:55.

I saw the numbers in the darkness. My first thought upon waking from my long sleep, my first memory...and something more.

The numbers brought me back to the car, the night of the accident. The memory brought me back to myself. Yes. I heard the flickering of the overhead lights, then slowly my vision cleared and I saw the room...*this* room. The plump white nurse was there, adjusting the feeding tube without a glance in my direction.

I tried to speak. She didn't hear me. I wished for a voice, and finally spoke...

...five...

She heard me. My wish came true. My first wish, first of...

...five...

Five wishes.

I have five wishes from...*where?* Some mystical quirk of numerology, I suppose, an underlying code, fives instead of sevens lining up a cosmic jackpot...I don't know. I can't be sure.

But they're mine.

Five wishes, five for the five who died: Karen, Petey, my parents, me. It's all I have now. Five wishes. A big responsibility. And from what I know of wishes, they must be worded carefully, exactly. I've already wasted two: one to speak, and two...

...oh no...

...in sudden horror, I realize what it was that I wished for, my second wish...*to know where my family went*. "Where are they now?" I wondered, followed by a wish to know.

And then...nothing. A void. For untold hours, my consciousness disappeared, ceased to exist, until my body, this physical tether, brought me back.

The implications are monstrous.

I wanted to know where my family went and the answer is oblivion. The woman I loved, our child, my parents – they exist now as recollections and moldering bones and nothing more. Their *souls*, if ever such existed, are absent from creation; they tread neither the earth as spirit nor the heavens as angels.

Even to have learned they were in *Hell* would be an improvement over *nothingness*...

...but no, their souls have simply been *erased*, utterly and eternally, and when I die, it will be as if they *never existed*...

...and when the Earth dies, all of human existence will finally reveal its true purpose, *utter futility*...

...*FUTILITY!*

I choke on the annihilating darkness in my heart like a drowning man, gasping for a breath of hope...

...and then my hope arrives.

SEKHU (*The Remains*)

Ray didn't know what to say to his daughter. Her little dachsund-beagle puppy, the one she called Weinie, never opened its eyes that morning. The little runt body was cold.

"I'm sorry, Baby," Ray sighed, eventually. "I guess...I guess he was just too good for this world."

"What do you mean?" Baby Joyce said, big eyes wide in fear and confusion.

"I mean..." Oh, God, Ray thought, realizing his daughter had never heard the cliché about being too good for the world before, had never had reason to acquaint herself with its meaning. At five years old, she barely understood the concept of the world outside South Central, let alone the greater sprawl of Los Angeles surrounding them and the oceans and continents and stars and moons and planets beyond that. Let alone death. And now Ray had to find a way to explain the Great Mystery in twenty minutes, before daycare.

"Okay, it's like this," Ray said, packing apple slices and Melba toast and tiny squares of American cheese in Tupperware for his daughter's midday snack. "Remember when your Talking SpongeBob stopped talking?"

"Yes," Baby Joyce said, rubbing sleep from her eyes.

"Well, that's what happened to Weinie. He just broke."

"Can you fix him?"

"No," Ray smiled sadly. "I wish I could."

Baby Joyce considered this for a moment, then smiled back at her father and said, "That's okay. I still love him, even if he's broken."

"Put on your shoes," Ray said, cleaning up the breakfast dishes, wondering if Little Mary had any other puppies left.

After dropping Baby Joyce at Happyland Day Care (really just a three bedroom ranch house full of toys and Disney discs and neighborhood latchkeys, overseen by a kindly old widow named Indrani Jones, who used to run with the Black Panthers back in the day), Ray doubled back home to dispose of Weinie's body, chucking the carcass in the dumpster of a 7/11 he passed on his way to Cedars-Sinai.

"You're late," Big Mary said as he emerged from the hospital locker room in his orderly scrubs.

"Family emergency," Ray mumbled, avoiding eye contact, hoping that was the end of it. He couldn't afford to lose the job, not with his coke-whore ex-wife threatening a custody fight over Joyce. No way. But for once, Big Mary let the matter slide without some vague threat or high-handed remark, and Ray hurried off on his rounds quickly, lest her temper shift.

An hour of bedpans and sponge baths followed before Ray tracked down Little Mary in the employee cafeteria to ask if she had any more puppies. "Weinie's dead."

"Oh, honey, I'm sorry," the pudgy nurse said, patting his arm. "Was Joyce upset?"

"She will be tonight," Ray sighed, creaming his coffee. "She thinks Weinie's broken...but she's got lots of broken toys she still plays with...I don't know what she'll do when she finds out I tossed Weinie in the garbage."

"You didn't have a little doggie funeral for him?"

"There wasn't time...besides, Joyce don't know from funerals. She don't know the difference between alive and dead. That's why I was hoping you maybe had some more puppies."

"Gave 'em all away," Little Mary shrugged. "How old is Baby Joyce again?"

"She'll be six in October."

"Don't worry...she can handle it. Just tell her Weinie's in Heaven."

"She'll wanna go visit him," Ray said, anticipation of his daughter's reaction already knotting his stomach. "She doesn't understand about death. Shit, I don't understand it my own damn self."

"So maybe just explain that death is the opposite of life."

"Yeah, well, I'm not all that sure I understand *life* any better," Ray yawned, sipping his bitter hospital coffee.

The staccato click of heels on linoleum drew their attention to Big Mary, coming up fast behind them. "Mr. Herlinger needs a sponge bath," she said without stopping, conspicuously brusque.

Herlinger was awake. Fixing the orderly with his filmy gaze, he gurgled, "...*nothing*..."

"What's that?" Ray said, even more uncomfortable in Herlinger's presence now that his least favorite patient had risen undead from his long coma, hissing out madness in cracked, sepulchral tones to anyone who would listen.

"I had five wishes...I wished I knew where my family was, and then...*nothing!*"

"Okay, Mr. Herlinger, calm yourself down."

Ray wasn't in the mood. Moving as quickly and efficiently as possible, he sponged the patient's scarred, blotchy flesh while a glistening bead of sorrow trickled down Herlinger's face. "My family is gone...nothing remains...no soul, no God, no hope..."

"C'mon, now..." Ray sighed, empathy dissolving his discomfort, fumbling for words of hollow consolation as he mopped tears from the invalid's cheek with a wadded paper towel. "...you don't know that."

"*BUT I DO KNOW!*" Herlinger croaked, hysterical, froth in the corners of his mouth.

Ray felt a sudden flash of panic, desperate to contain the situation before Big Mary appeared in the doorway, furious with him for upsetting her miracle patient. "For God's sake..."

"*THERE IS NO GOD!*"

"*Shut up!*" Ray snapped, riding a surge of adrenalin. "You don't know that, okay, man? You're upset, you're outta your head, talkin' all this crap..."

"No! I had *five wishes...*"

"There's *no such thing!*"

"You're *wrong!*"

"All right, fine, whatever," Ray conceded, relieved Herlinger had at least dropped his volume. "You made a wish and it didn't come true."

"It *did* come true. It showed me the *only* truth..."

Ray moved slowly towards the door, hoping the invalid would stay calm until he was safely out of the room, off the ward, and punched out for the day. "Yeah, well, at least you got a few *more* wishes, right? That's more than most people can say."

Herlinger gasped, his expression shifting unnervingly from despair to euphoria in a matter of seconds. "You're right...yes, of *course!*"

"Should I get the nurse, Mr. H.?" Ray asked cautiously, backing safely into the hall. "You need anything, or we cool?"

"I have what I need," Herlinger replied, quiet again. "Thank you."

"Awright, then...lights on or off?"

"Off, please."

Ray doused the lights.

After Herlinger, Joyce was a piece of cake. Weary from his workday, Ray commuted home in a state of anxiety, bracing himself for an emotional scene that never materialized.

"Where's Weinie?" Joyce asked upon her return from Happyland, dashing back and forth between her room and the kitchenette where Ray was microwaving burritos, a special treat.

Taking his daughter's tiny brown hands in his own giant paws, Ray knelt down to her eye level and said, "I'm sorry, Baby...Weinie had to go to Heaven."

But instead of tearful demands for the return of her broken dog, Joyce merely smiled, curious, and asked, "Why are you sorry?"

"I just thought...uh...you'd be sad," Ray said cautiously.

"Heaven's not sad," Joyce giggled, kissing him on the chin.

The drama hit at 2:00 a.m.

Baby Joyce woke screaming in the middle of the night, calling for her mother, calling for her dog. Ray dashed into her room and turned on the light, kneeling beside her, stroking her cheek, trying his best to settle her down.

"Where's Mommy?" Joyce cried.

"Mommy's far away, Baby, you know that."

"Where's Weinie? I want him back!"

"Ssshh...hush, now," Ray whispered. "Weinie's up in Heaven with Grammy Bette, keepin' her company."

"R-really?" Joyce sniffed, calming down now that her father was beside her.

"Really."

"Is she feeding him chocolate? Chocolate is bad for him."

"No, she ain't feedin' him chocolate...Grammy Bette knows better. She's feedin' him steak."

"He likes steak," Joyce yawned, clutching her father's arm like a blanket.

"I know."

"Tell me more."

"Sure, Baby Joyce," Ray smiled, and started building Heaven.

REN (*The Secret Name*)

And when the Earth dies, all of human existence will finally reveal its true purpose: utter futility.

...but then Ray, the orderly, reminds me of the wishes.

The wishes!

Maybe there's no Meaning of Life, no God, no Heaven, but I still have three wishes, and that's enough. I have a purpose. I know what to do.

Should I spend a wish to know the mind of God? No...after all, what good would it do me to discover there is no God, or that God exists but that He is capricious or mad or otherwise little concerned for my welfare? What if the Meaning of Life has nothing to do with humanity at all?

No, too metaphysical. I don't need meaning, I don't need answers...only eternity: I want to continue. I want to be happy. I want to be.

My thoughts trigger an old Talking Heads track in the jukebox of my subconscious about Heaven being a place of repetition and nothingness. I've known the song for years, but never truly understood the lyrics until now: Heaven is my family in the car before the crash. Heaven is my wife beside me, my son and parents in the back seat...enjoying their company, forever. No destination, no sorrow, no end...Heaven.

And if there *is* no Heaven, then I'll damned well create one...but for who? Only the good, the pure, the righteous? Who am I to judge? And who am I to determine paradise?

There's only one fair answer: *everyone* goes to their own blue heaven, *everyone* lives forever.

With eternity to play with, I hope the rest will somehow work itself out.

So...

I wish for an afterlife, as of now, where every soul that dies or has died or will die from now until forever shall go to create an everlasting paradise of their own choosing, the entirety of said domain to be commonly known as Heaven, which I may visit at will prior to my own death, amen.

KHAIBIT (*The Shadow*)

The hours following Pete, Jr.'s innocent blasphemy were thick with Tilly's silence as Pete navigated Route 1 towards San Simeon, the ruined destination of their newly impossible attempt at a relaxing family vacation together.

Pete hadn't seen his mother since his move to the West Coast and, more importantly, since *her* move to Christian fundamentalism, and the breadth of the gulf that had widened between them in the meantime was disorienting. Tilly had always been a formidable presence with her Medusa's mane of silver-black curls and the sheer glittering will of her gaze, but until Karen, he'd only ever been on the right side of that indomitability, shielded and protected by it. Now, though, he felt like a siege army facing the impressive battlements of a onetime ally, wondering how the defenses he'd relied upon in happier days could be turned against him in the bloody savagery of all-out war.

It was only recently that he'd come to appreciate how much Karen reminded him of Tilly in her strength and resolve and how it was this similarity, rather than superficial differences of generation or background, that had always kept the two women in his life at a tense distance from one another, two queen bees, twin lions on the veldt. At five, Pete, Jr. was already an unmistakable product of this vital maternal lineage, while Pete grew increasingly passive with age, more like his father than he'd ever cared to admit.

Yet ultimately it was Bob who broke the stalemate, brokering a truce between Karen and Tilly while Pete was escorting Pete, Jr. to the bathroom at a rest stop just south of Santa Barbara. "You know," he said, in the quiet, hypnotic tones of a drowsy snake charmer, "we don't have to settle this today, and we *certainly* don't want to upset little Petey..."

"No, of course not," Tilly said quickly.

"No," Karen agreed.

"But you can't shelter that boy forever," Tilly admonished. "Sooner or later, he's going to have to learn to think for *himself*."

"He *does* think for himself," Karen flared.

"No, darling," Tilly smiled, arch. "He thinks like *you*...cynical, doubting, *atheist*..."

"Hey, just because he's not brainwashed..."

"But he *is* brainwashed..."

"Ladies," Bob sighed, ineffectual, as Tilly resumed her advance: "...you liberals always think you're so open-minded until you come across an idea you don't like..."

"Okay, hold on...number one, I'm *Republican*..."

"You are?" Bob asked, surprised.

"*Moderate* Republican," Karen stipulated. "But that doesn't mean I just toe some party line. Pete's a lawyer and I'm a scientist, so believe me, we don't accept or reject *anything* lightly..."

"Except God."

Karen sighed. "No, Tilly. I was raised Baptist, Pete is still Catholic...but after a lifetime of education and experience and...and *common sense*, we just don't believe in the Bible as literal *fact*."

"And that's what you've conveyed to your child, that God is a *myth*..."

"Petey just realized..."

"Petey is *five*," Tilly exclaimed. "A very *smart* five-year-old, yes, but he's still just a little boy, and you're his *mother*. He's going to *believe* whatever *you* believe, and if you say there's no God..."

"We never taught him that," Karen argued. "We told him some people believe in God and some people think it's a myth..."

"And *naturally* he agrees with his *parents!*"

"We've never told him what to think!"

"Haven't you?" Tilly sighed, infuriatingly serene. "Petey trusts you and loves you. Whatever you say is *gospel...*"

"He didn't believe us about Santa," Karen volleyed back. "We tried giving him that whole song and dance, and he basically called bullshit..."

"Please, there's no reason for that kind of language..."

"It's just a word," Karen started, then: "Okay. Sorry."

"That's all right, dear," Tilly said, patting her daughter-in-law's arm in a gesture of harmony neither of them believed. "But what *I'm* saying is, my life in Christ is very important to me, and it's something I'd like to be able to share with my grandson..."

Karen's first impulse was to say, *"I told you, I don't want you brainwashing my son with that crap,"* until it occurred to her that any such response would only reinforce Tilly's theories about her alleged liberal hypocrisy, so instead she merely smiled, "Fine. But don't say I didn't warn you."

Pulling out of the rest area, Pete was pleasantly surprised by the peaceable mood that had somehow settled over his family while he and Pete Jr. were in the men's room. Meeting eyes with Bob in the rearview mirror, he was relieved to see a slight nod from his father, a code between them meaning not to worry, things had been resolved.

Karen spotted the silent exchange as she studied Bob in the mirror of her passenger-side visor, watching as the older man turned his eyes to the rolling coastline outside his window. She was glad Pete had inherited his sharp features from his mother and his soft demeanor from his father, instead of vice versa. Her father-in-law was not a handsome man – slightly cockeyed, with a Roman fuzz of silver hair and the round, placid features of a tortoise – yet she was exceedingly fond of his gentle manner, droll wit and low, soothing Great Plains accent. He'd barely registered the first time they met, at the rehearsal dinner for her wedding, and she'd mistakenly assumed then what most people thought when they met him: that he was a henpecked, friendless milquetoast chained to a shrill gold-digger who'd only married him for a share of the Old Money prestige of his family's Kansas City estate...

...all of which might well have been true at one point, but Karen had learned over time that Bob drew advantage and a strange kind of pride from being underestimated, using anonymity to camouflage his true feelings and stratagems. That he possessed secrets, Karen had no doubt, although what they were she could only speculate.

But she was certain of two things, at least, after several years of quiet observation: the first being that, no matter what the dynamic at the start of their relationship, Tilly had clearly grown to rely on Bob's quiet strength and companionship, seeming to need him a lot more than he needed her. As for the second thing...

"Petey, sweetie, can I ask you something?" Tilly squeaked,

launching a fresh campaign against her grandson's skepticism. "You know so much about dinosaurs, I was just wondering if you could tell me where they came from?"

"Sure!" the boy replied brightly. "They evolved from single-celled organisms in the primordial soup billions of years ago."

Atta boy, Petey, Karen smiled, proud.

Tilly let the reference to evolution pass, depriving Karen the satisfaction of her reaction as she continued, "Okay...and what came before that?"

"I don't know," Pete Jr. shrugged, idly flipping the pages of his dinosaur book.

"Well, let's think...was the Earth here before the dinosaurs?"

"Why, yes, of course," the boy replied in a sing-song chirrup of amusement.

"So where did the Earth come from?"

"Hmm," Pete Jr. said, head cocked to the side in a pantomime of deep thought. "Let me see...oh, yes, I remember now. It was formed in the Big Bang."

At that, Karen and Pete exchanged blushing smiles in a moment of shared pride for the little professor they'd created. My God, she thought...had they ever been so smart?

"Pete?"

It's Karen's voice. *It's Karen's voice.* Where am I?

"PETE!"

I'm standing in the garden behind my house...wait...

...I'm *standing*...

"Oh, thank God...thank God...thank God..."

Karen runs towards me, throws her arms around me... she's crying...I'm crying...we embrace for hours, maybe days. It doesn't matter. We're both free of time and we know it. The full measure of despair in my soul has transformed itself into joy and doubled, tripled, exploding exponentially into elation and relief.

"Where's Petey? Where's Pete, Jr.?"

Karen turns around and he's there, our boy, smiling innocently...then, with a giddy shriek of delight, he launches into the air, disappearing like a rocket up, up, up into the perfect blue sky.

"PETEY!" Karen yelps, alarmed.

It's a startling sight, until I realize what I'm seeing: it's Petey's Heaven, too, the weightless, jungle-gym paradise of a five-year-old boy. "He's fine," I laugh, taking Karen into my arms...

...*arms*...

I'm standing, I'm talking, I'm holding my wife...no Heaven could be sweeter, when suddenly I realize...

"...this is *your* Heaven."

"What?" Karen says, nervously eyeing the sky for signs of Petey.

"I'm still alive," I say, piecing it together, as much for myself as for Karen. "I didn't consciously choose to visit...*you* summoned me. I'm part of *your* Heaven..."

"I...I don't understand," Karen replies, disoriented. "I was in the car...you, me, Petey, your parents...I remember the crash..."

"And then?"

"And then I was *here*," she says, looking around at our surroundings, a simulacrum of the house we shared, the garden she tended, the life we'd loved.

"And do you know where *here* is?" I ask, gently.

Karen nods slowly, scanning the yard and garden around us. On closer inspection, it's not *exactly* the house we lived in (seconds ago in her memory, years ago in mine), but has the shifting inconsistencies of dream architecture: the trees are incandescent with the red-orange autumnal foliage of my wife's New England childhood, but the garden is bursting with the lush vitality of California's endless summer...the house is exactly the shade of blue Karen always preferred (before I covered it over with aluminum siding) and the above-ground pool my wife had settled for is now the inground pool she always wanted.

"None of this is real," Karen says, uncertain.

"It's as real as anything is real," I explain. "It's your vision of Heaven, the place where you're happiest..."

"So, we really are dead," she marvels, confirming aloud what she already knew instinctively.

"*You* are," I say quietly. "You and Petey, my folks..."

"But not you."

"No. Not yet."

"Then what are you doing here?"

"Near as I can figure, you summoned me...you wanted me here and I'm here. Heaven is whatever you want it to be."

"So you're not *really* here?" Karen says, confused. "You're just a figment of my imagination?"

"No, it's really me."

"But you're not dead?"

"I gave myself the ability to visit."

"Huh?"

I explain about the wishes. Karen is duly impressed.

...*boom*...

We both turn abruptly towards the sound, which seems to issue from the forest behind the house...

...**boom**...

"What is that?" Karen asks nervously, eyes widening as the sound grows louder and closer. "I hate thunder...why would there be thunder in Heaven?"

"I don't think it's thunder," I reply, uneasily scanning the woods for the source of the...

...*BOOM*...

"I don't like this," Karen exclaims, gripping my arm. "If this is my own private Heaven, why am I scared?"

"It's not private," I say, just as Petey emerges from the forest, knocking trees aside like splintering curtains...

...at least I assume it's Petey...

"Jesus CHRIST!" Karen screams.

...Petey was going through a dinosaur phase at the time of the accident...

"*WHAT THE FUCK IS IT?*"

...and I can easily see how a five-year-old, empowered to fashion his own paradise, untethered by the concept of restraint, might transform himself into a 500-foot Tyrannosaurus Rex, just for the fun of it. After all, what are the quiet pleasures of home to an imaginative, frenetic child, especially when compared with the joy of sheer destruction?

"PETEY, NO!" I cry, too late. Karen shrieks as a monstrous foot STOMPS down, crushing our beloved home into tindersticks.

And then, another unexpected development...fighter planes: Nazi Messerschmitts in tight formation, arcing high overhead, then circling back, diving, swooping low in a disciplined bombing run....

BOOM! The T-Rex screams in pain and surprise as the explosives detonate, and now Karen recognizes the cry: "PETEY!"

The monster falls in broken agony, howling pathetically as bombs rain down and flames rage up, charring our little patch of Heaven into the blackest pit of Hell. I shriek as my skin burns, Karen begs for help, pleading to God, to Christ, to me...

...and I wish it away, I wish it all away.

SEKHU (*The Remains*)

"Heaven."

"Yes," Herlinger cackled the next morning, happier than Ray had ever seen him.

"You went to Heaven. Last night."

"Yes!"

"And now you're back."

"Well...yes."

Ray laughed; he couldn't help it. Shaking his head as he fluffed Herlinger's pillow, all he could say was, "Man, I dunno what the doctor's been slipping into your I.V., but save me a little next time, okay?"

Herlinger fixed his milky gaze on Ray and said, "It was the wishes..."

"The wishes...right..."

"In fact, it was you who reminded me I held the power of salvation in my grasp." The invalid smiled. "That's one of the reasons I came back...to thank you."

"Well...you're welcome."

Herlinger continued, explaining how he'd used two of his wishes to fashion and then refashion a Heaven where none existed before. "Maybe there is no Meaning to Life, no God, no higher purpose...but that doesn't matter now. I realized if I wanted to see my family again, the only way to reclaim them from oblivion was to create my own eternity...and not just for them, but for everyone. *Everyone* goes to Heaven now, *everyone* lives forever."

"Everyone?" Ray asked, playing along with his least favorite patient, enjoying himself for once. "Hitler? Judas? Charlie Manson? You're tellin' me they all get a free ride?"

"Who am I to judge?" Herlinger replied, peaceful. "Naturally, there were some problems in the first version..."

"Wait, wait...the *first* version?"

"My first version of Heaven," Herlinger nodded, head bobbing on a paralyzed body. "To be honest, it was a bit of a botch..."

He closed his eyes and sighed, bemused. "But I did better with the second one..."

Ray stood listening, captivated. He'd never realized insanity could be so entertaining. "You're saying you're on Heaven 2.0 already? Since last night?"

Herlinger cocked his head to one side in his own paralyzed version of a shrug. "Not much else to do around here...besides, it doesn't take long to wish. You just have to be *very careful* with your wording."

"So what'd you wish? How'd you fix it?"

"I simply arranged it so that all who die, have died or ever will die shall pass into a paradise of their own making, as gods of their own realm, with total freedom to satisfy the desires of their own soul, yet no power to harm or control a sovereign spirit outside their own consciousness who does not desire to be harmed or controlled, the entirety of said domain to be commonly known as Heaven and which I may visit at will prior to my own death, amen."

"Wow." Ray blinked in amazement. "What are you, a lawyer or something?"

"And a law professor...used to be, anyway."

"So, uh...how'd that work out for you? Heaven 2.0?"

"It's beautiful," Herlinger gasped, eyes suddenly wet with emotion.

Drawn by unexpected impulse, Ray placed a hand on the invalid's shoulder. "I'll bet it is..."

"I'm heading back tonight," Herlinger whispered now, smiling. "My last wish."

All at once, Ray felt something give inside, a surge of emotion so unexpected and strong he backed away from the hospital bed, embarrassed.

But Herlinger just continued to smile, and Ray felt his voice crack as he nodded back at his new favorite patient and said, "Don't waste it, man."

REN (*The Secret Name*)

"I'm heading back tonight," I say. "My last wish."

"Don't waste it, man," the orderly says, nodding to me as he leaves the room.

Ray. His name is Ray. He's not a bad man. He's done his best to keep me comfortable in my infirmity, even though I sense he doesn't like me very much. I can only imagine how he sees me, these pathetic earthly remains. I look forward to meeting him again in Heaven, in my *true* form. I look forward to easing the transition when *his* time eventually comes to an end.

As my time has ended.

The overhead lights flicker. I smile a farewell...

...and then, slowly, unexpectedly, the smile fades and I realize: I'm nervous. I've seen Heaven, I'm eager to return, but still...I've never really died before.

The feeling, if not the circumstance, is familiar. I've always been a nervous traveler. In my old life, before the accident, I could barely leave my house without completing certain obsessive rituals: closing windows against rain and burglars, unplugging unattended appliances, checking and double-checking that locked doors really were locked and, finally, muttered prayers in precise, exact language: "Dear God, please keep my family and my house and the contents of the house safe while I'm away from them, thank you, amen."

Forgetting any part of my neurotic routine was usually enough to force me back to check – were the burners completely off? was the house filling with deadly gas? – lest I worry across the entire span of my absence.

Leaving life is the same. Is there any last minute business to complete? Everyone I really cared about is gone, but there are still people who know me...former colleagues and distant relatives I might want to contact one last time...

...or not. From what the doctors tell me, no one's been to visit in years – and besides, I have nothing in particular to say to Cousin Julie in Virginia or Aunt Lurancy in Connecticut or Dr. Philbrook, my old department chair at Pepperdine. If they want me, they can find me in Heaven.

Yet what of my obligation to humanity in general? Not that I crave fame or praise for my actions, but surely it would soothe the world's anxiety to know, once and for all, that death is, really and truly, *not the end...*

...but then again, who would believe me? Ray certainly didn't. The world, after all, contains no shortage of holy men with glowing reports of paradise. My feeble voice would soon be lost in the great miasma with no particular effect on the ultimate, unchangeable reality that *everybody dies, and everybody goes to Heaven.*

So why this anxiety?

Perhaps it's nothing but the paralysis of possibility which strikes any artist when faced with a blank canvas. Should I plan my paradise ahead of time or just make it up as I go along? How shall I design it, what should I include? And then, a sudden realization: *how do I protect my Heaven?* After all, as my previous experiences have shown, there will certainly be those in the afterlife who glory in chaos and destruction.

True, they'll have no real power to cause harm, but a sudden chill of instinct cautions me on the brink of my uncertain journey, reminding me how little I know of the complexities ahead, the Pandora's Box I've thrown wide. For, while Heaven may well be my creation, its inhabitants are not.

I lie awake for hours, considering the implications of my previous wish, my blueprint for eternity, pondering the design, probing for loopholes or disastrous flaws of conception. *I still have one last wish*, I think. I could save it, store it away in case of emergency. That would, of course, be the responsible thing to do, the prudent course of action. *I'll eventually die anyway*, I think. No need to waste the power of my final wish to hasten such an inevitable process...

...but, in the end, impatience trumps prudence and I wish for an end to my long confinement, my loneliness, my regret and sorrow. I wish away the monotony of seclusion, the humiliation of bedpans and catheters. I wish for arms and legs, I wish for Karen and Petey. I wish for Heaven.

I wish I was dead.

<u>SEKHU</u> (*The Remains*)

The drama hit at 3:00 a.m.

Alone in his room, Herlinger's eyes rolled back in his head and his heart monitor flatlined.

"Oh dear," Little Mary cried, jumping up from her lonely post at the night desk. "Oh dear, oh dear, oh dear..."

A pair of residents, Cuban and Jamaican, barreled into Herlinger's room with a crash cart, firing up the paddles. The Jamaican tried CPR, then the Cuban zapped the invalid's heart: "CLEAR!"

KHU (*The Guardian Angel*)

Utopia is waiting.

And, with a thought, I am there, leaving my pain behind. No floating above my hospital bed, no tunnel, no bright light. I merely wish for death, and I am dead, back in my Heaven, soaring through cerulean skies, looking down on my wife in her paradise, the home we shared, the life we lived. She waves from the garden she loves, then smiles as our son, the Tyrannosaurus, stomps and snarls and does no harm.

I'm flying. I don't remember any conscious decision to fly, or indeed to return to Karen's paradise, for that matter. I was thinking of her, naturally, how I couldn't wait to see her and Petey again. And, I suppose, I had some preconceived notions about spirits flying around the afterlife – indeed, I saw Pete Jr. blast straight up into the sky on my first visit.

Yet my last conscious thought was only this: *I wish I was dead.*

I am troubled and cannot say why. I should be ecstatic, turning blissful loop-de-loops in the air, but I'm not...and the mere existence of my anxiety only *deepens* my anxiety, for how is it possible to reconcile this creeping disquiet with the eternal bliss of Heaven?

Something is wrong, something I didn't anticipate in my conception of paradise. I feel it, yet cannot explain it consciously. But...

...wait...

...*consciously*...yes, of course...the answer to the first part of the equation reveals itself with a lightning flash of clarity. My desire to return here to Karen was subconscious, as was my impulse to fly. I wanted both things, but I did not deliberately *will* them.

When I visited Karen before, I was still alive and it was *she* who brought me into her own private nirvana. I had been planning to return after my death, of course, yet I'd assumed there would be an interim point, a blank slate where I could determine my own preferences for the afterlife, and...

...my *God*...what's happening?

All at once, I am plunged into...*nothing*, a void, limitless and total, akin to some cosmic blackout, except I find myself not in darkness but rather an indescribable absence of light and substance which is somehow infinitely more terrifying. Were it not for the fact of my own consciousness, basic principles, *I think therefore I am*, I would assume that I had merely hallucinated my visions of Heaven...that it had never existed, there was no afterlife and my soul had been annihilated...

...but I'm still thinking, I'm still here, I am...

...*think*....

...and then I realize: it's happened *again*.

I was contemplating how I'd *expected* a void, an entry point upon which I could build my eternity, and now here I am. *I wanted this.*

Remarkable – and intimidating – for it seems in this Heaven of mine, reality can be shaped and reshaped by subliminal whim as readily as conscious design, a circumstance I had neither imagined nor predicted. Clearly, I must be cautious and precise in my thoughts moving forward, alert to my own feelings and the unexpected vicissitudes of this realm, for already this Heaven of mine is not the state of bliss I was expecting.

There's anxiety here. I've felt it. I'm feeling it now.

There's also fear, panic, confusion, and if these emotions are possible, then...

PETER

...a familiar summons, not exactly a voice, but clearly recognizable...

...my father, requesting my presence and...

...by the merest thought I am with him.

"*Dad...!*"

Except that it's not. Not exactly.

"...Dad?"

We're standing by the marble columns of William Randolph Hearst's San Simeon estate, overlooking not the Pacific but rather Atlantic City, circa 1950. And everyone is naked. Naked *men*, as far as the eye can see, all with perfect bodies and giant cocks, surfing and swimming, sucking and fucking, laughing and dancing and strolling the Boardwalk.

Everyone is naked *except*, thankfully, Dad and me. I'm in the L.L. Bean plaid and khaki I wore to San Simeon that last day with my family, the same outfit paramedics sheared from my body to "save" me all those years ago.

Dad, however, is *not* wearing the same thing he wore at San Simeon. Dad is wearing a sparkling red gown, tiara, 6-inch heels and a Miss America sash across a voluptuous hourglass figure – disconcerting, but gorgeous.

"Hello, Peter," he (she?) says in a husky contralto. "It's good to see you again."

"It's good to see you, too, Dad."

"Actually, I prefer Raquel."

"Raquel. Sure," I say, grinning now the initial shock has worn off. After all, tits or no, Dad is still Dad. I recognize him, despite the startling exterior, the outward shell. There's a logic to it, a certain inevitability.

Raquel suits him.

"*Fuck me! Yeah, boy, git it...git it...dig for gold!*"

Startled, I glance over at an orgy of giant black men and tiny white rednecks behind us, on and around an elegant Venetian fountain. "Forgive me," Dad blushes, grasping my arm with satin-gloved fingers. "I've been indulging my own predilections for so long now it seems that my sense of decorum has just atrophied completely..."

The phrasing strikes me odd: *for so long now?* Then, before I can finish my thought, Dad says, "Come, we'll talk in my palazzo."

In the flash of a word, I find myself perched on the balcony of a Tuscan villa, basking in the spectacle of an impossibly beautiful view of the Mediterranean with icebergs and pyramids on the distant horizon, illuminated by disco globes and comets. "So," my father says, in a more familiar voice. "Is this easier for you?"

I turn and see the man I remember: short, homely, unflappable. I realize, all in a rush, how little I appreciated him in life, how much I've missed him. "Dad..."

We embrace for a long time, and it feels good. "Welcome home," Dad says. "Can I fix you a plate?"

Strangely, I do feel hungry. "But we don't really need to eat here."

"Oh, no, of course not," Dad replies, leading me within the palazzo to a mahogany table laden with fish and fowl and cakes of all description. "Some never do, especially the Ancients. Personally, I still enjoy the sensations of tasting and swallowing, even if the hunger is Delusional."

He watches me as he says this. I've just devoured an éclair – the creamiest, most delicious éclair in the history of the world, as far as I'm concerned – and I'm feeling a little less hungry when his words suddenly register: "The hunger is delusional."

"Yes."

"I'm not really hungry."

"Why would you be?"

I stare back at my father's watchful gaze, his patient expression. He's teaching me, in the manner he employed when I was a child: never lecturing, but rather positing observations, then waiting for me to draw some conclusion.

"I'm hungry because I expect to be," I reason. "I'm used to it. Just like I'm used to seeing you as I remember..." I indicate his appearance with a flourish. "...when in reality, you're...what? A busty redhead?"

My father laughs, his voice husky again as his exterior shimmers and shifts to the voluptuous curves of Raquel. "Does it bother you?"

"No," I say, honest if bemused. "But, so, then...what? You were a woman trapped in a man's body all along?"

"Something like that," she says, running a hand through my hair. "I always loved you, of course...and your mother, in my way. But the rest...the rest was always a lie..."

"It must have been hard for you, all those years."

Dad shrugs. "I grew up in a different era. Repression was our birthright. We all deceived ourselves constantly, pretending away our differences. So ridiculous...it's hard for your generation to understand."

"And what about Mom? Does she..."

"Understand?" Dad offers a sad little smile, a sigh, a shake of the head. "No, of course not. She's a simple, God-fearing woman. She doesn't want to understand. Not yet, anyway. Maybe in time, and there's plenty of that."

"I should go see her."

"You should. But Peter..." Dad grips my arm again, locking me into the quiet resolve of her rain-colored gaze. "...you can't fix everything. Remember that."

I nod, uneasy. Dad smiles again, embraces me, invites me to come back soon. "Sinatra's doing a set with Billie Holiday at the Tropicana later tonight, if you're interested. I'll save you a dance."

"I'd like that," I say, bracing myself for the trip to Mom's.

One impulse and I'm with her, crushed within the twisted steel frame of the accident that claimed her mortal life, drenched in blood, surrounded by corpses: my father, my son, my wife, my own pulverized body. I step outside the grim tableau as she prays to Jesus and screams in perpetual agony.

"MOM!" I cry. "NO! STOP! You can make it *STOP!*"

But she refuses to listen, clinging to her unshakeable convictions, waiting for Christ to end her suffering and transport her to a Heaven where my father remains what they'd agreed to pretend, sanctified in the surety of her superior moral values, safe in the knowledge that sin has been punished and all the queers and deviants were roasting forever in Hell.

It's almost more than I can bear. "MOM, *PLEASE!*" I scream, but I don't know how to help her if she'd rather cling to her last moment of earthly pain than admit the universe is different than she imagined, if she chooses suffering over acceptance.

I consider dragging her from the wreck, forcing her out of her delusion, until I remember the strictures of my afterlife design: that none should have power to harm *or control* a sovereign spirit outside their own consciousness who did not desire to be harmed or controlled. "You can't fix everything," my father said...

...yet surely I can't leave my own mother in Hell, not even a Hell of her own making. Knowledge of her suffering would always spoil any paradise I might create for myself, just as my father's Heaven transformed hers into damnation.

Then I realize the alternative: oblivion. No choices, no pain, no feeling at all. There would never be a suitable Heaven for everyone...some would always suffer by the pleasure of others...

...is that why there was no afterlife? Had there been a God and a reason all along?

I have no wishes left.

Good Christ, what have I done?

SEKHU (*The Remains*)

"It wasn't my fault!" Little Mary said, for at least the dozenth time in as many hours since Herlinger flatlined. First, she'd said it, unbidden, to the Cuban and Jamaican residents who responded to the patient's heart monitor alarm while she'd flustered in a panic at the night desk, knowing there was nothing she could do to help, yet determined to make clear that she'd done nothing wrong. Later, she'd reconfirmed her innocence to the residents, to Big Mary, to Dr. Ku, and to anyone else who would listen.

Now she was repeating her tale of blamelessness to Ray in the employee cafeteria, yet remained unable to shake the feeling that Herlinger's death was, indeed, in some way, her fault. "I'd been checking his vitals at regular intervals, same as always...I'd just been in his room twenty minutes earlier and he was fine."

"I'm sure he was," Ray said, knowing she was upset, trying to calm her down.

"Maybe I missed something, but I really don't think so..."

Ray placed a hand on her shoulder, looking straight into her eyes, the way he did with Baby Joyce whenever she needed a solid dose of reassurance. "It wasn't your fault."

"I know! That's what I keep saying to everyone!"

"Sometimes people just die around here," Ray continued. "Everybody knows that. Nobody blames you...'sides, I'm pretty sure ol' Herlinger *wanted* to go. He was at peace with it."

But even as Little Mary nodded in agreement, she couldn't shake an irrational sense of failure, a habitual self-loathing all too easily exploited by Big Mary in her own quest for someone to hold accountable for the death. The head nurse was several yards away, talking with Dr. Ku by the elevators, and Little Mary cringed every time her supervisor shot accusing eyes in her direction.

"Ms. Barnes blames me," Little Mary said, miserable.

"Nurse Ratched blames the world for being born," Ray scoffed. "Don't let her mess with you. People like her get ahead by always pointing their fingers at somebody else. Herlinger was a big deal 'cause he was unusual. Folks wanted to study him and ask him questions, and now all they got is an autopsy..."

"The autopsy says he died of 'natural causes,'" Little Mary acknowledged quickly. "Which means they don't really *know* what happened..."

"Exactly," Ray smiled, patting her chubby arm. "So chill. You did all you could for the man."

"I guess," Little Mary yawned, gathering napkins and dirty silverware onto her tray as she rose to depart. "Anyway, I should probably get outta here before Ms. Barnes asks me to work another double shift. I'm so tired I can barely see straight."

"Yeah, go rest," Ray said, rising with her. "And don't worry 'bout Herlinger or Nurse Ratched...you just need a good night's sleep is all."

"A good afternoon's sleep, you mean," Little Mary laughed, trying to be cheerful. "I'm back on the floor at midnight."

"Jesus," Ray said, taking her tray. "I don't know how y'all do it."

Little Mary shrugged. "I just do it."

"Ain't that the truth."

When Little Mary left work for the day, the bald guy from
Operation Rescue was out front as usual, clutching his poster-sized
blow-ups of bloody fetuses and calling, "Mommy, please don't kill
me!" to any young woman he saw heading towards the entrance of
Cedars-Sinai, whether she was there for an abortion or not. But as
soon as he saw the chubby nurse in her unisex scrubs, he instantly
wailed, "MURDERER!"

The day he'd first appeared on the sidewalk in front of the
hospital, several weeks earlier, Little Mary had actually taken one of his
pamphlets and talked with him for several minutes, explaining that she
herself was a pro-life Catholic, to which he'd replied "Hypocrite! You
call yourself a Christian and work in a concentration camp,
perpetuating the Holocaust of the Unborn!"

His words had scorched her, because it was an issue she'd
wrestled with: though she had nothing to do with abortions,
personally, she nevertheless worked in a place where they were
performed with sickening regularity, just six floors below her.

Lives, extinguished, day after day.

And whenever Mary thought of them, as she often did, they
always had the same face in her mind...

...bloody, torn and unloved...

...*the face of the first life she'd failed to protect, so many years before.*

Of course, she'd prayed and sought guidance from her priest

about the job at Cedars, even received his blessing for the greater good she could accomplish there.

Nevertheless, she'd sympathized with the Operation Rescue man on the first day he'd appeared.

"I really understand how you feel," she'd conceded. "And I gave it a lot of thought when I first took the job here...but then I figured I had to consider all the babies who *were* born, and grew up and got sick and needed help...and even though the hospital does this one thing I don't approve of, they're still *saving* a lot of people..."

"Oh, so you're a *good* German," the Operation Rescue man had sneered in disgust. "*You're* not a murderer, you just *work* for murderers and turn a blind eye to the Holocaust right under your nose..."

"I'm not a murderer!" Little Mary had snapped back defensively.

"Tell that to God when he casts you into the Lake of Fire!" the bald man had snarled in response. "Try rationalizing your sin when demons are tearing out your tongue by the root!"

"You're just ridiculous," Little Mary had said before walking away, exasperated. "People like you are an embarrassment to the whole pro-life movement."

"MURDERER!" the bald man had shouted that day – and every day thereafter – as Little Mary did her best to ignore him. Unfortunately, she couldn't avoid him completely, since her bus stopped across the street from his encampment and Little Mary refused to give her nemesis the satisfaction of forcing her to switch routes.

She'd thought about buying a car, which would enable her to enter and exit the hospital undetected through the basement garage, but had vetoed the idea for a number of reasons. For one thing, she'd always been a nervous driver, especially in the endless street fight of L.A. traffic, and worried she'd wind up like Herlinger one day if she got behind the wheel (especially after one of her all-too-frequent double shifts at the hospital). Plus, she didn't mind the bus: the long commute from Cedars to her one-bedroom condo in Pacoima gave her a chance to catch up on her sleep or her reading and even, occasionally, to strike up conversations with her fellow passengers.

But the other reason, the secret reason she didn't buy a car was financial. Not that she didn't have enough money to afford a decent vehicle, but rather that she was saving every penny for her child.

So far, she hadn't told anyone about her impending motherhood – and, indeed, she wasn't even pregnant yet – but she had vowed to herself as early as adolescence (and with increasing despair and resolve throughout her lonely twenties) that if she wasn't married by her thirtieth birthday, then she would somehow find a way to raise a child by herself, since motherhood had always been the one, unswerving ambition of Little Mary's life.

Now, at 31, she'd overshot her goal by a year and knew it was time to get serious. Originally, she had planned to adopt, but after months of frustration, the obstacles facing single women in her tax bracket came to seem too daunting, and so instead she began to investigate sperm banks, plopping down fifteen hundred dollars for a trio of inseminations that had yet to produce a single day of morning sickness.

Nevertheless, Little Mary remained optimistic. As the doctors at the San Fernando Valley Reproduction Center in Tarzana had reminded her time and again, it didn't always happen the first (or second or even third) time, no matter what the nuns at Saint Elizabeth's Parish School had told her.

Elphaba was nursing her daughters Emiko and Escaflowne when Little Mary came through the door of her tidy, cramped condo with a cheerful, "Hello!" The tiny brown deagle pups scampered over to her, nails clicking on the hardwood floor, then hurried back to their mother, torn between conflicting desires for love and nutrition.

Little Mary had napped on the bus and was still feeling drowsy as she peeled off her sweaty pink hospital scrubs and switched into the comfy cotton Winnie the Pooh pajamas her Cedars Secret Santa had given her for Christmas. The single window in her bedroom was blacked out with fabric to accommodate her third shift daylight sleeping habits, making the cold blue display of her cell phone that much brighter as she plugged it into the charger by her futon bed and noticed she'd missed a call.

Dialing her voice mail, she heard an electronic announcement of a single waiting message, followed by Ray's voice saying, "Hey, Mare, it's me...I don't know if you care, but Dr. Ku was just telling us how ol' Herlinger ain't got much in the way of close relations anymore, so the hospital chaplain's gonna hold a service for him at the Interfaith Chapel tomorrow at nine. I'm off then, but I thought I might swing by with Baby Joyce...if you're interested, maybe I'll see you there. A'ight, peace!"

"Oh, that poor man," Little Mary said aloud, for the benefit of the dogs, sitting down heavily on the futon. At the sound of her voice,

Emiko and Escaflowne rushed into the room, then circled immediately back to their prone, lactating mother in one continuous lap.

Little Mary laughed at the sight of them, and it was only then she realized she was crying. "Poor, poor Mr. Herlinger."

Wiping her eyes, she left a message for Ray that she would definitely meet him at the chapel in the morning, and would bring homemade cookies for Baby Joyce if she was allowed to have sweets. Then, sliding down to her knees, the plump nurse clasped her hands and bowed her head, squeezing her eyes shut as she had before bedtime ever since she was a little girl, and prayed for her family and her friends and Elphaba and the pups, finally ending with: "And dear Jesus, please bless poor, poor Mr. Herlinger...he was a sad and lonely man, so I hope you have accepted him into your Heavenly Kingdom and will grant him love and peace forever and ever..."

...but before she could say "amen," the earthquake hit like a tidal wave, collapsing the foundations of her cheaply constructed building and the five stories above her, crushing Little Mary flat.

KHU (*The Guardian Angel*)

I feel it before I hear it, a seismic disturbance in the very molecules around us, a tingling in the fibers of my being...*a presence*...

Then I hear the trumpets, high and glorious, blending and expanding into the infinite voices of what can only be a Heavenly choir.

And finally, *light*...a supernova, so bright I no longer see the darkness of night, the highway, the corpses or the twisted steel of the accident that claimed my family. All I see now is Mom, fallen forward on her knees, gazing Heavenward in joy and astonishment.

Following her gaze, I see the Light and the Way incarnate, and cry aloud at the sight of the Word Made Flesh, Christ the Messiah descending from the clouds, arms wide, purple robe fluttering. His voice is gentle, yet pulses through my being like electroshock voltage: "Arise and sing, my child...for thine is the Kingdom of Heaven..."

"Oh, my Lord," Tilly weeps, rising from the mangled frame of my crumpled Ford Focus straight into the air to kiss the hem of the Nazarene's vestment. "Sweet Jesus, take me..."

"In my Father's house are many mansions," Jesus smiles. "There is one prepared for you now, Tilly, for you have been washed in the Blood of the Lamb."

"Yes, Lord, yes!" Tilly cries, following Christ through the air towards a whirl of clouds, vortexing open to reveal a massive pearlescent gate. I follow, too, fascinated and curious, yet vaguely skeptical as it occurs to me that what I'm seeing, for all its divine majesty, is just a little too theatrical, sort of like...in fact, *exactly* like...a

Sunday school depiction of Heaven.

Mom's version of Heaven.

I smile in dawning comprehension as Jesus glances back at me and winks, steering Mom's angelic form towards the golden kiosk of a kindly, white-bearded gatekeeper who can only be St. Peter. "Matilda Thompson Herlinger," he greets her, reaching out to guide her descent as she touches down on a ledge of cloud like dense cotton candy. "Rejoice, for thy name is recorded in the Book of Life."

I land beside and behind my mother as St. Peter withdraws a dark, leather-bound tome from the folds of his long white vestments, opening it to display Tilly's name, etched on vellum in the illuminated calligraphy of a medieval manuscript. Below her name, there are others: my father, my wife, my son, myself.

Tilly smiles, relieved, as her finger traces down the page, then she turns and smiles, tears still glistening in her wide, joyful eyes. "God is merciful," she says to someone behind me, in a tone I recognize from a thousand earthly arguments, the tone of a woman who has proven her case but was raised not to say, "I told you so."

Though I guess right away who the comment is intended for, I am nevertheless startled when I glance back and see Karen, Petey, and my father all standing behind me, beaming beatifically. "God *is* merciful," my wife replies in a humbled, awestruck voice that shocks and disorients me with the sudden, certain knowledge that the Karen-esque figure uttering the words cannot possibly be my wife. The woman I married would never give Tilly the satisfaction of admitting that God's mercy was the only thing saving her from the fiery pits of Hell, not even here on Heaven's threshold...or, rather, Tilly's *mental image* of Heaven's threshold.

Besides, I've just left Karen back in *our* little corner of Heaven...haven't I? Petey was there, too, rampaging around, and my father was in his palazzo...yet at the same time, here they are, standing with Mom and me and Jesus and St. Peter, all reading their names in the Book of Life beside the Pearly Gates...

...it's confusing, but I think I'm beginning to understand...

Then, with a trill like rain on bells, the Pearly Gates swing inward to reveal a glorious firestorm sunrise of light across an infinite horizon, reflected in the endless crystal prism of a glistening sea of glass.

"...*beautiful*..." escapes my mother's lips in a single, orgasmic burst, tears streaming from her eyes as her "family" gathers around her in eerie tableau, frozen in blissful, perpetual adoration of the Lord. Unnervingly, I see a simulacrum of myself beside her motionless form, while Jesus gently tugs me backwards away from the scene and into the surrounding fog of white, fluffy clouds until we hang suspended in the middle of endless blank nothing, the only distinct figures in a limitless void.

"She'll be alright now," Jesus says in Dad's voice as an instant, fluid transformation remakes the Messiah into the buxom redhead of my father's inner preference.

"What...what just happened?" I say, though I suspect at least part of the answer. "Why did Mom stop moving like that?"

"Time is relative," Dad shrugs. "Along with everything else...like most things here, it's simple and confusing at the same time, but I'll do my best. As I said earlier, your mother is and always has been – and, one expects, always will be – a simple, shallow woman. I apologize if that sounds harsh or blunt..."

"No," I say, because I see no reason to pretend otherwise.

"There's a term here of fairly common currency... *Delusional.* It means essentially what you'd expect, except that we tend to use the noun form, as in: your mother is a Delusional. And by 'we' I mean those of us who consider ourselves Realists...although, again, such terms are simple and confusing, since delusion and reality are so inextricably twined, as any Realist will tell you."

Now there are two images in the white void before me, like comedy/tragedy masks: my mother, at the moment of her death, screaming in perpetual agony, and Tilly in bliss, staring endlessly through the Pearly Gates at the moment of her faith's confirmation. "You see the similarities, no doubt," my father continues. "When she died, Tilly's consciousness entered this astonishing realm of limitless possibility...and, like so, so many, she instantly and completely rejected it, choosing instead to exist in the agony of her last earthly moment of 'certainty' forever."

"But this place, this 'Heaven,' can be anything for anyone," I say, uneasily defensive of my creation. "If Mom thought she was a good Christian, which I can only imagine she did, why didn't Jesus come for her the second she died? I mean, I'm guessing He's not exactly the 'Pastor Ted' Easter pageant version..."

"Not exactly."

"...but the actual, historical Jesus *IS* up here somewhere... right?"

"We'll get to that later," Dad says with cryptic placidity. "The

- 61 -

point is, like most so-called *reasonable* people...myself included...you put too much stock in *reason*. Your mother's entire belief system was based on clashing realities which could not possibly co-exist in any rational configuration of existence. She could not, for example, love me as the dutiful, Christian husband I was and simultaneously hate me as the sinful, deviant transsexual I also was...so she merely rejected the piece of the puzzle that didn't fit, believing me to be a quote-unquote *normal* heterosexual male despite all evidence to the contrary. For the sake of tranquility, I did my best to aid and abet her Delusional version of 'reality,' playing my part in the fiction of our marriage as, just now, I played my role in our little Sunday school pageant of Tilly's ultimate salvation. Deep down, I can only imagine she realizes the artifice of it all, but it's what she needs, and so I provided it, because...and this is what I was getting at...she simply can't and couldn't do it for herself. Not yet, anyway. Maybe someday. Who knows? But until then, until she can imagine what comes next, what she actually *wants*...well, I guess she's happy enough just believing she was *right*...″

I stare at the twin images of Mom before me, digesting my father's words. "But this place, this afterlife...as far as I can tell, it operates on subconscious desires as well as conscious. If Mom was expecting Jesus to come for her when she died...why didn't He?"

"Because most of what happens here, whether consciously or subconsciously, is nevertheless an act of creation. Of *choice*. Once again, it's simple and confusing, because it's so difficult to pinpoint the source of that creative impulse... symphonies poured from Mozart's quill, though he did not consciously summon them, nor could he deny them. He might have refused to acknowledge the music in his soul, he might have lain down his pen and refused to commit the notes to the staff, but the genius of the symphonies would nevertheless continue to *exist*, if only subconsciously, in memory or regret of what might have been. In my own case, I was physically a man but subconsciously a woman...Raquel, my ultimate creation... *myself*...and though I spent most of my life trying to deny that creation, it would not die, it would not be subsumed into the preferred reality of my wife, my community, the times I lived in." Dad smiles, proud and bashful, delicate hands running up and down womanly curves. "And so, when I died, I found myself inhabiting the creation I had tried so hard to erase from existence."

My father's masculine form momentarily replaces Raquel's hourglass symmetry as he says, "But consciously or unconsciously, I can only create myself and my surroundings to the limits of my own imagination and will. So, for example, since I never saw *Casablanca*..."

"You never saw *Casablanca*?" I gasp, as shocked by this revelation as anything I've experienced since the whole foray began.

"Never got around to it," Dad shrugs. "Still haven't. And *since* I haven't, I can only conjure a version of the movie based on the bits and pieces I *have* experienced over the years...hearing about it, flipping past a scene on television, that sort of thing ..."

And suddenly, we are standing in a smoky, sepia-tinged black and white approximation of Rick's Café American where, three paces to my left, Rick himself is lighting a cigarette and telling his piano player to "Play it again, Sam."

"He doesn't actually say that," I comment to Dad, who – unable to resist the sleek forties fashions – has morphed back to his feminine form again, if only to wear Ingmar Bergman's hat. "In the movie, I mean...Bogart never actually says that line."

"Really?" my father drawls, lounging back against Sam's piano. "Well, there you go, then...my point exactly. I never saw *Casablanca*, so my version is just that...*MY* version of something I'm only guessing at."

"Yes," I say, taking a scotch on the rocks from the tray of a passing waiter. "But there IS a real version of *Casablanca* out there...you could watch it if you wanted to. Are you saying there's no *real* Jesus to come meet Tilly?"

"The *Real* Jesus would have terrified her," Dad replies. "But the point is, Tilly was unprepared to imagine her *own* version of paradise and she was hazy on what she was *supposed* to think Heaven was like...she's a woman who always thought and believed whatever society told her...so from the moment she died 'til now, she's essentially been waiting for instructions. And she's *still* waiting."

"But," I say, afraid of the answer, "...is she happy?"
"Oh, sure," Dad says with a reassuring smile. "Ecstatic."

"She's happy just staring through the Pearly Gates at a bright light?"

"Not just *any* bright light...God. Or, rather, the anticipation of God, which for Tilly is more or less the same thing."

"So Mom's surrounded by facsimiles of her family..."

"...which are real to her..."

"...trapped in one endless, continuous moment, waiting to see God...and she's *happy*?"

"Well, she's not *trapped*...she can do anything she wants,

anytime she wants...but for now, she's savoring the moment, soaking in it. There are souls I've encountered who seem willing to remain in a single moment of bliss forever...and, of course, there are those who choose the other extreme..."

Dad fixes me with her feline eyes, waiting to see if I understand.

"They choose pain," I say.

"Consciously or subconsciously," Dad nods, rising, her sleek white '40s costume tinged red in the firelight suddenly visible through the sepia windows and doorways of our imaginary Moroccan saloon. "Burdened with ultimate freedom, not *everyone* chooses Heaven..."

There is nothing but flame and darkness outside the windows now. Memories of sweat plaster my clothes to my skin as I hear screams through the open door, mingled with the scent of charred flesh, scorched hair, and sulfur.

"Look," my father says, pointing through the doorway. "Watch. But please don't cross this threshold...there are too many things you don't understand yet."

The heat isn't real.

I will myself cooler, but the *illusion* of heat is nearly overpowering. The stench is nauseating, the screams are terrifying.

My fear is real.

I stand. Rick's Café is empty save for myself and my father now. I don't want to see what he's about to show me.

Hell. It can only be some fire-and-brimstone version of Hell, as bogus as Tilly's Heaven, but no less real for the poor, wretched souls within, self-condemned to unspeakable torment for their sins, true or imagined.

Dad beckons again, angel wings like twin feathery harps sprouting from her back. Step by step I move towards her, fighting a deep, primal urge to flee. And slowly, the Inferno comes into view through the doorway, a strangely familiar vista of jagged cliffs and molten rivers, geysers of indigo flame shooting up towards a dark ceiling of stalactite fangs drenched in blood. Howling naked sinners of all shapes and sizes writhe on glowing hot coals and bob in streams of lava, like extras in some lurid, Technicolor vision of damnation. I feel my anxiety recede: the scene is diabolically uninspired, a nightmare not my own, a bad Ken Russell movie.

But the cries of agony and regret are heartbreaking. While the hellish imagery seems borrowed, common, the sinners themselves are distinct, each face a matchless galaxy of hurt. And then, to my alarm, a face I recognize: one of the nurses from my confinement at Cedars-Sinai, the plump, nearsighted one, her pale naked body chained to a tilted flat rock, legs spread wide as a bald, muscular demon stabs her splayed vagina with a white-hot sword, again and again, plunging the blade deep into her womb.

"MURDERER!" the demon snarls. "DID YOU REALLY THINK GOD WOULD FORGIVE YOU?"

"I'M SORRY!" the pitiful nurse shrieks, her voice an awful, shredded rasp. "OH, GOD, FORGIVE ME! FORGIVE ME!"

"THERE'S NO MERCY FOR *THIS*..." the demon responds, driving his sword even deeper, to the hilt. "...FOR THOSE WHO SLAUGHTER INNOCENTS AND CHILDREN IN THE WOMB...FOR THE INFANT *YOU* MURDERED!"

"IT WASN'T ME! OH, CHRIST, PLEASE..."

"SAVE YOUR PRAYERS..." the demon cries, clawed fingers tearing out the poor woman's tongue by the root. "...WE KNOW *ALL* YOUR SECRETS...*MURDERER!*"

I feel a warm breeze as my father's angelic wings flap, majestic, propelling her through the doorway into Hell. "MARY..." she calls in a thunderous voice neither masculine nor feminine, hovering above the bloody stone table. "...DOST THOU REPENT THY SINS?"

"...oh, yes, Lord..." the fat nurse whimpers, a fresh tongue sprouting in her mouth. "...please forgive this worthless sinner..."

"THEN TAKE MY HAND," Dad smiles, beatific, slender white fingers outstretched, "AND RISE."

A beautiful flicker of hope illuminates the features of the nurse called Mary as she reaches for the outstretched, angelic hand...only to find her wrist still bound to the rock. "I...I can't move!" she wails as the demon leaps up to straddle her, breathing hot poison in her face.

"YOU STUPID FAT CUNT!" the demon roars. "DID YOU REALLY THINK WE'D LET YOU GO? YOU'RE SO FUCKING *GULLIBLE!*"

"Oh, God, please..." Mary begins as the demon once again yanks out her tongue, which instantly grows back in time for a prolonged howl of despair.

"MARY, I'M RIGHT HERE," my father calls, to no avail. The demon blinds and deafens his victim, puncturing her eyes and eardrums with long, greasy nails, swatting at the hovering angel like a pesky moth, sneering, "FUCK OFF, SHE'S MINE."

All at once, the door to Rick's Café SLAMS in my face,

blocking the awful scene as my father, wings retracted, sighs behind me. Turning to face her, I see we're back in her faux-Tuscan palazzo. "I'm sorry," she says. "That didn't go as planned...although I suppose it was no less instructive."

"I knew that woman," I say.

"Yes...she died just recently."

"And went straight to Hell."

"Her own version of it, yes..."

"Like Mom."

"Not *exactly* like Tilly," Dad says, pouring herself a glass of some nineteenth century Muscatel. "For one thing, Tilly wasn't punishing herself...she simply wasn't ready to move on. And her particular purgatory was unique to her, whereas that Hell just now was a Common Construct, shared by many souls with the same essential vision of damnation."

"So why couldn't you help the nurse, there...*Mary*...the way you helped Mom?"

"Well, as I said, Tilly perished with no particular inner demons, whereas that poor woman chained to the rock believed...like so, so many...that she *deserved* her punishment. Which always makes it harder." Dad fixes me in her focus, urging me to pay special attention. "Plus, I had competition this time."

"I don't understand," I say, lost. "Competition?"

"That demon wasn't a figment of Mary's guilty conscience," Dad explains, conjuring an image of the bald demon in the air between us, "but rather a conscious soul, like you or I, tormenting that poor woman for spite or revenge, or even from some terrible misguided sense of *duty*..."

"No," I protest, once more defensive. "No soul may be harmed here..."

"...*who does not desire to be harmed or controlled*," my father says, quoting my own wish back at me. "Which obviously creates a rather unpleasant loophole for those who wish to do harm and those who believe they *deserve* harm."

My head is swimming, and I feel the need to sit, coming to rest in a large wicker chair that may or may not have been in existence before the very moment I felt the need to sit in it. "Poor Mary..." is all I can manage.

"Oh, don't worry...I have an idea how to save her from herself."

"But there must be others," I say, horrified, "suffering untold agonies because of *ME*..."

"You have *nothing* to do with their suffering, Peter," my father says, laying a hand on my shoulder.

"I have *everything* to do with it!" I say, pulling away. "My *arrogance*, thinking I had the wisdom to decide what Heaven should be *for all of humanity*..."

"Well, I suppose there *is* a certain arrogance in believing you single-handedly reordered the great mysteries of the universe to your own particular specifications," Dad smiles, "but under the circumstances, it's actually more charming than anything..."

Her statement triggers a dizzy flush of vertigo, and my next words and the pride and foolishness they embody are now, all at once, so embarrassing I can barely pronounce them: "So...you're saying I...I *didn't* wish all this?"

Before my father can answer, I find myself laughing, imaginary tears blurring my vision...the helpless, cleansing laughter of last breaths and miraculous rescues.

"No...no, of *course* not, unless..."

And suddenly, another lurch of nausea.

"...unless all *this*..."

I grip what feels, in every way, like the wicker arms of the chair where I sit, for the first time less than certain of my sanity. Across from me, a red-haired woman...now a cock-eyed man... both of them my father, staring back at me. "I mean...how do I believe *any* of this? You say you're my father and I *want* to believe that your soul is still alive and here with me now...but how do I know you're not just my own voice, talking back to myself in some coma dream hallucination? Or, if you *are* real and I *am* dead, how do I know you're not just some angel or devil *pretending* to be my father, the way you pretended to be Jesus for Mom back in that make-believe Heaven?"

"How do you ever know anything?" Dad reasons. "You observe and conclude, then observe and reassess, over and over and over again, with no ultimate, absolute verification one way or another. It's a problem, I'll admit...one my friends and I wrestle with constantly. But for what it's worth, a handy definition of Reality is precisely *that which does not cease to exist when you stop believing in it.*"

"Philip K. Dick?"

My father smiles. "Ah...so you've heard that one before."

"Karen was a fan...but even if I accept the statement, how does it help me? I mean, if I stopped believing *consciously* that I was actually dead and here with you in this afterlife, I might remain here because *subconsciously* I want to believe it...even if the *reality* is that I'm still in the coma ward at Cedars-Sinai, hallucinating all this."

"And what if you are?"

"What?"

"In a coma. What if everything you're experiencing is false, a fabrication of your mind? How would you behave differently?"

"Well...I suppose I'd do my best to wake up from this... this *dream* and return to reality."

Dad spreads his palms in benediction. "Then be my guest. If you're in a dream...

...WAKE UP!"

BA (*The Heart*)

Morning. I'm still here. Intravenous feeding time. The plump white nurse adjusts the feeding tube without a glance in my direction. The overhead fluorescent lights are still flickering...flickering...*flickering*... ...ignore it, ignore it, *think*...

Fives. Five fives. 5:55:55.

I can't move. Okay.
...hello?

...*HELLO?*

...I can't speak...

...what's happening? What happened? Okay, *think*...

...hospital room. Private room. The plump white nurse, the tall black orderly...Ray. His name is Ray...tall, average build, close-cropped hair, maybe thirty. I've seen him twice...three times. Maybe more. And before that...

Fives. Five fives. 5:55:55.
Dancing, digital, yes...

...I remember...

...Heaven.

My father walks through the door of the hospital room in his masculine form, settling his solid, stocky frame into the chair beside my bed. "Well? Did you believe you had emerged from your 'coma'?"

"Yes, for a moment," I sigh.

"So, you created this," Dad says, gesturing around at the grim beige walls, the flickering lights. "From memory and desire. But you didn't ultimately believe in it."

"That doesn't prove anything."

"No," my father scowls. "But consider this...let's say you doubt the Reality before you, suspecting it's a lie...perhaps a fantasy you've lied to yourself. You poke and prod it, searching for the seams that will confirm your distrust, yet find nothing. On faith, then, you attempt to *will* yourself past the perceived illusion, only to land in another illusion. You can't wake up and you're not even sure if there's anything to wake up *from*...so now what?"

"I don't know," I say wearily. "Tell me."

"I can't *tell* you anything, I can merely *suggest*."

"Go on, then."

My father leans closer, elucidating on his fingers. "Well, by my reckoning, there are three options for grappling with this existence of ours...you can either stop, like your mother, and wait for some ultimate truth that may or may never arrive...you can surrender to Delusion, accepting whatever you experience without question...or you can take the Reality in front of you for what it's worth and keep moving, keep doubting, keep searching, even unto eternity."

I close my eyes, savoring the simple darkness. "And, of course, the fourth option...oblivion. No decisions, no perceptions...only *sleep*. I see the appeal of that now. I didn't before."

"Before...?"

"When I was lying here...well, not *here*," I say, glancing around the illusory hospital room I've apparently conjured from memory. "Or maybe here, or...well, at any rate, I believed I had these wishes, and I wished to know where you and Mom and Karen and Pete, Jr. had gone after the accident, and what I saw was *nothing*. That's when I wished for Heaven..."

"Or rather, you wished for something you had already seen. Today was not the first time you died, after all."

More ambiguity, more confusion. "Excuse me?"

Dad indicates the suspended hospital television hanging from the ceiling across from my bed. On the screen, I see the crumpled wreck of my sensible old Ford Focus, bright in the flashbulb strobe of ambulance lights. My broken form, slick with blood, is being worked over by paramedics. Eventually, I die on the pavement, a corona of shattered, glistening windshield glass round my head like a comic book halo.

"In that moment, you glimpsed beyond the visible world, however briefly," Dad explains.

I see the paramedics with their defibrillator paddles, shocking me back to "life," stabilizing my vital signs, loading me into their ambulance. "Later, when consciousness returned, you merely remembered what you saw, in dreams that felt like wishes...and now, at last, you're here, in Heaven, or Hades or whatever you want to call it."

"What do YOU call it?"

"Usually just *This Place*...though I suppose technically it's more a dimension than a location."

"Some sort of afterlife..." I hesitate, the words melancholy on my tongue, "...but not really paradise."

"Oh, I don't know," Dad shrugs. "It *can* be...I'm fairly happy, and your mother has certainly achieved her own nirvana..."

"So you say," I counter, skeptical. "And before that, she was in *agony*...I saw her, suspended at the moment of her death...for how long? *Five years?*" All at once, I regard my father with a hot rush of anger. "Why did you wait so long to help her?"

"Your mother felt no pain or yoke of time," Dad replies, his gaze fixed to mine, earnest yet unapologetic. "What you reckon in years, she experienced as fractions of a moment."

"But she obviously couldn't find her way to Heaven by herself."

"No."

"So why save her now? Why not five years ago?"

"Because I wanted you to be here...I wanted you to see your mother like that, to help you understand..."

"Understand?"

"What I do," Dad says. "You see, I've found a calling of sorts in the time since I came to This Place...helping souls like your mother find their way, doing my best to protect the vulnerable ones like Mary...I believe it's important work. *God's* work."

"And you're speaking...*literally?*" I ask, in nervous anticipation of the answer.

Dad flashes his mysterious grin. "I believe so, yes."

"But you don't *know*," I counter. "You don't *know* there's a God, even *here*, even now..."

"There are *many* gods here...all Delusions, as far as I can tell. And there are never-ending theories about the one *true* God and the ultimate meaning and purpose of existence...but no answers to speak of, just our endless potential to question."

It's too much, I realize with a definitive click of some mental switch flipping off like a circuit breaker. I simply can't process anymore. I need to digest all that I've heard and experienced before continuing further. Reality has stretched beyond my ability to recognize it, and I feel a sudden, desperate need for certainty, for my wife and son, for the simple comfort of their love.

Overhead, I see wispy clouds and a twilight moon where the ceiling used to be. My hospital bed wraps itself into a hammock, rocking gently in suburban breezes lightly scented with mown grass and barbecue. My father stands beside me in the yard of the Heavenly version of my old house with its freshly imagined inground pool while Karen rounds the corner, smiling. "So I see you found your father...hey, Bob!"

But strangely, my father pays no heed, ignoring her completely. "As a Realist," he continues, insistent, "I believe this realm is not so much an afterlife as the next stage in our greater existence, a spiritual adolescence...*a test*..."

Karen gives me a look, curious about our conversation, yet uncertain whether to interrupt. Then Pete, Jr. soars overhead, now a pterodactyl. Still, my father ignores them, stepping closer, filling my vision, expanding. "In our *first* life, the soul is forged in the obdurate channels of a rigidly defined physical universe...while *here* the challenges are wholly spiritual. Do you understand?"

"Pete?" I hear Karen's voice from somewhere behind my father's increasing form, accompanied by a plaintive cry of "Daddy?" from Pete, Jr.

"I believe the key to salvation is absolute faith in the *Real*," my father preaches, relentless. "And the only confirmation of *Reality* is your own disciplined, unyielding *perception* of what's Real...*do you understand what I'm saying?*"

I shut my eyes, I close my ears, I block my thoughts and feelings.

Because in that moment I do understand.

And the knowledge scalds.

KHAIBIT (*The Shadow*)

They reached San Simeon slightly after one and checked into the local Marriott, then continued on to Hearst Castle, the day's big event. Riding up to the estate with the 4:15 tour group on a wheezing shuttle bus suffused with tinny jazz recordings from the 1920s, Karen noticed that Tilly's missionary zeal was slowly beginning to flag. "And Grandma," little Petey was saying, as part of an ongoing rebuttal to one of the Creationist theories she'd presented hours earlier, "how could God have created the world six *thousand* years ago if there are trilobite fossils that are *500 million* years old?"

"Well, God created those, too."

"But you said..."

"Oh, look!" Tilly exclaimed, pointing abruptly out the window. "Peacocks!"

"Wow!" Pete Jr. said, momentarily distracted, then: "Did you know scientists think some *birds* evolved from *dinosaurs?*"

Later, while Tilly strolled the perimeter of the colossal Neptune Pool on the grounds of the Hearst estate with her son and grandchild, Karen sat with Bob at a distance, watching them from a marble bench overlooking the grey-green Pacific. "So... how do you put up with it?"

"Hmm?" Bob mumbled, roused from his own peaceful contemplation of sea and coastline.

"All that Born Again crap," Karen said, nodding in Tilly's direction.

"What makes you think it's crap?" Bob purred, fixing her with his good eye while the other rolled towards her in its own sweet time.

"Oh, come on," Karen laughed. "You're a Ph.D., for God's sake."

"*For God's sake...*" he drawled, serene, "...I was Born Again in the Blood of the Lamb."

"You're kidding," Karen gasped, never quite sure when he was.

"It was simpler than arguing with Tilly," Bob sighed, cutting to the chase.

"But you don't really *believe* all that stuff...right?" Karen asked, strangely uncertain.

Bob didn't answer right away, savoring the rich, salty air for a moment before exhaling, "Have you ever noticed how atheists tend to be just as dogmatic as true believers?"

"I...hey, listen," Karen sputtered, defensive. "The Bible was written by *human beings*...it's *fiction*. But the rest of the universe, that's *non-fiction*, which means it can be measured and explained..."

"Except the part about *what it's for* and *where it came from*," Bob interposed. "So until we know *for certain* there's no higher intelligence, no grand design, then atheism is just a matter of *faith*."

"Well," his daughter-in-law conceded, "to be honest, I've always been more agnostic than hardcore atheist..."

"Likewise...and in the absence of any solid evidence to the contrary, I prefer to believe there *is* a reason for all this," Bob smiled, waving a lazy hand through the air, "*and* a God who cares about me. And if I'm wrong...well, *love thy neighbor* ain't such a bad little philosophy."

"Yeah, right...you think 'Pastor Ted' and all those other

Christian extremists care about *love?*" Karen argued, embarrassed by her angry passion in the face of Bob's tranquility.

"I *have* noticed they spend an *awful* lot of time on Hell and Revelation," Bob replied, diplomatic as ever. "Myself, I prefer the Book of Matthew: blessed are the meek, blessed are the peacemakers...judge not lest ye be judged..."

Karen thought, but couldn't be sure, that she detected a particular emphasis on the last words, a polite request to put aside controversy for the time being and simply enjoy the beauty of the California sun shining down, the peacocks strutting the neatly manicured grounds, and all the baronial splendor of the historic William Randolph Hearst estate.

"Hey! We're heading up to the Casa del Sol," Pete called from the edge of the Neptune Pool, pointing over towards one of several mission-style villas terraced above them on the slope leading up to Hearst's central mansion, the Casa Grande.

Karen waved that she and Bob would catch up with them as her father-in-law measured the distance from the pool to the surrounding villas with his cockeyed gaze. "That was Chaplin's cottage," he said, pointing to one of them. "Casa del Mar...he was a regular guest here until the incident with Thomas Ince."

"Who?" Karen asked, rising to give Bob a hand up from the bench where they'd been sitting.

"Well, you know Marion Davies, of course," Bob said by way of explanation. "Hearst's mistress...so according to legend, Davies was slipping around with Charlie Chaplin, until one night on his yacht, in a fit of jealous rage, Hearst accidentally killed this man Ince, mistaking him for Chaplin..."

"Susan?"

Karen's head snapped towards the voice in shock as Bob continued, oblivious, lost in the history of their surroundings: "The whole thing was covered up, of course, and things were never the same between Hearst and Marion after that...but just *imagine* what it must have been like, *right here*, the times they had...Chaplin by the pool, swapping jokes with Douglas Fairbanks and Louella Parsons..."

"Susan! Is that you?"

This time, the voice was more insistent, and Bob turned in curiosity towards the darkly handsome Mexican now disentangling himself from a group of tourists at the bottom of the stairway leading to the Casa del Mar.

"Why is that man calling you Susan?" Bob said, his words trailing into a sharp breath of surprise at the sudden, violent rush of color to Karen's face and the instant, queasy realization of its meaning.

"I...I don't know," Karen stammered, helpless and ashamed, glancing quickly towards the Casa del Sol for reassurance that Pete and Tilly and Pete Jr. were safely out of sight.

"Hi, I'm Rafael," the handsome Mexican said now, extending a hand to Bob as he sauntered to Karen's side, damningly familiar, before introducing himself as "a friend of Susan's."

"Excuse me," Karen said, conspicuously avoiding Bob's eye as she grabbed Rafael, dragging him quickly out of sight behind a gleaming marble cabana flanking the southwest corner of Hearst's Neptune Pool.

And as Bob watched his daughter-in-law and the Mexican

disappearing from view, his own words returned to him, both taunt and reminder...

...lest ye be judged...

KA (*The Double*)

There are no secrets in Heaven. Anything from the past is knowable, everything else is perceivable.

This, Dad explains, is the motto of the Realists.

All along, my father has been teaching me to doubt...

...and now I recall my first dream of Karen, in this place that isn't paradise...how glad she was to see me, how proudly I'd explained my creation, how obediently she'd listened when I told her where she was.

"It's your vision of Heaven, the place where you're happiest."

By my side, in our home, awaiting my arrival.

Lies. My capacity for self-deception is vast.

Yes, father, I understand.

I stand in the sunny backyard of what I *thought* was Karen's version of paradise, staring at what I *thought* was my wife.

"Pete! What's wrong?" It's the voice of the woman I love, animated by memories...how I'd *expect* her to act in any given situation.

"It's not Karen," I say to my father.

"What the hell are you talking about?" Not Karen says, angry now, just as I'd expect her to be. "What do you mean, *it's not Karen?* I'm standing right here! *Pete!*"

I thought I deserved Karen, as the bound nurse had craved her own damnation. But it's been five years, and our wedding vows, after all, had only been *'til death do us part.*

There was always that side of my wife I could never really know. How romantic to think it wouldn't matter here. But of course.

Just then, I feel a tug on my leg...and a different sting, infinitely more painful. "Daddy?"

I fall to my knees and grasp my son in my arms, tears blurring my vision.

Or the illusion of tears in what passes for vision.

"Is it him?" I cry to my father, already sure of the answer. "Is it really my boy?"

"I can't tell you," my father says quietly.

But of course not. I haven't seen my son in five years, since his fifth year of life. Who would I be to him now, a barely formed memory?

I close my eyes, inhaling the sweet, familiar scent of Not Petey's hair, the vanilla of Not Karen's perfume.

I wanted them as they were, but they've both moved on without me.

My Real wife and son aren't here. I've been Deluding myself.

I understand my father's lesson, and I hate him for it.

I open my eyes and my illusions are gone.

I am alone.

SEKHU (*The Remains*)

When the earthquake hit, Ray was on break outside the front entrance of the hospital, smoking one of the three precious cigarettes he allowed himself each shift. Before Baby Joyce was born, he'd been up to three *packs* a day, so he never felt guilty about the time or lung tissue he still devoted to the remains of his lifelong habit, figuring the willpower he exerted to keep himself from smoking *more* earned him the right to enjoy what little nicotine he still ingested.

As he sparked the afternoon's third and final Camel Light, closing his eyes to savor the flavor, he was momentarily struck with an odd, queasy feeling of vertigo markedly different from his usual nicotine rush. Then came the sound, an ominous white noise rumble, increasing in volume and power until it rippled through his body, waves of force spasming the streets and sidewalks, rattling the windows of Cedars-Sinai. Miles of car alarms shrieked in cacophony as Ray instinctively stomped out his cigarette, fearing ruptured gas lines.

Nearby, the stocky bald protester from Operation Rescue, still camped in front of the hospital, fell to his knees, keening devotion to the sky. Ray had experienced dozens of temblors over the years, including the '94 Northridge quake, but from the first seconds of the latest, he could already feel the difference... this one felt hateful, monstrous, surging with apocalyptic fury, as if determined to be the One to finally knock California into the ocean. It felt like the Old Testament, God's wrath, the literal end of the world.

As the angry vibrations engulfed him, trying to knock him from his feet, Ray froze, paralyzed by the maddening noise and a sense of stunned disbelief that in the next few seconds, he might really, actually die...that all his time had suddenly drained away and now, out of nowhere, he would never, ever see his daughter again, or the moon; he'd never drink another beer or wear a different outfit or find out who the murderer was in the James Patterson book he'd been reading.

A shriek of pain snapped him out of it, closer and louder than all the rest of the chaos surging and crashing around him. Turning, he saw the bald Operation Rescue protester face down on the sidewalk, crushed beneath the undercarriage and tires of an out-of-control, timber-green Cadillac Escalade that had jumped the curb and crunched to a stop against a row of multicolored steel and plastic newspaper boxes. Through the windshield, a freaked out, wild-eyed Armenian teenager was visible clawing the airbag that had just exploded in her face.

Ray crossed the pitching, tilting space of yards to the wreck on rubbery sea legs as the hysterical teen scrambled from the driver's side door, screaming, "Oh my God, oh my God, oh my God!"

"Turn off the car!" Ray shouted, while the powerful vehicle attempted to mount the newspaper boxes, still in gear, engine groaning with a relentless mechanical effort to continue forward up and over the stubborn obstacle in its path. The Armenian stumbled backwards across the rippling pavement, then pulled herself into the Escalade and killed the motor.

Ray dropped to all fours, peering under the massive vehicle to view the motionless pro-lifer. The back of the man's fleshy bald head was slick with fresh blood, and his right ankle was pinned beneath the Escalade's left rear tire. He'd been struck from behind and overrun, and didn't seem to be alive.

Alarms and sirens grew louder as the roar of the earthquake finally receded and the rolling sidewalk came to rest like the final seconds of a carnival ride. "Oh my God, did I kill him? Is he okay?" the teenager cried, frightened tears sluicing her cheeks. "The car went crazy...I couldn't stop..."

Ignoring her, Ray jumped up and called to a lab-coated resident he recognized, just stumbling from the building in a daze. "Hey! Over here!"

The resident glanced over and saw the Escalade on the sidewalk, the body beneath it, and immediately barked an order to someone inside the hospital as he rushed over to help. A blonde white L.A.P.D. officer had materialized from somewhere, wordlessly helping Ray and the Armenian roll the vehicle back far enough to free the protester's trapped ankle while the resident pulled the man clear, searching in vain for a pulse before grimly removing his lab coat to cover the corpse.

"Oh no, oh no, *oh nooo*..." the Armenian wailed as the cop noted the time of death in his incident report pad and another orderly emerged from the hospital, wheeling a gurney. Ray helped to load and secure the bald protester's body on the stretcher for its journey to the morgue, then drew what felt like his first breath since the earthquake, clearing just enough space in his rattled mind for a single thought.

JOYCE

He was running before he even knew where he was going,

ignoring the cop behind him shouting, "Sir! Wait...I need to speak with you!"

The roads would be jammed, but he couldn't run all the way home to South Central, so his feet made the decision and carried him down into the smoky darkness of the hospital's parking garage, cacophonous with the shrieking hysteria of seven hundred simultaneous car alarms. Chunks of concrete littered the ramps of the structure as Ray descended two levels down, half expecting the entire East Tower of Cedars to collapse overhead in a deafening avalanche of death and debris.

Joyce was at Happyland Day Care, on Slauson.

Ray fumbled his keys from the pocket of his orderly scrubs, stabbing one into the lock of his basic white two-seater CRX hatchback.

2911 Slauson.

He pictured the building, a one-story ranch house with a postage stamp lawn. One story, flat roof, cheap stucco walls. Ray gunned the Honda and shot back in reverse, clipping the bumper of some asshole SUV squeezed in too close beside him in a row of parking spaces marked "COMPACT CARS ONLY."

Joyce would be fine. Scared, but fine.

Ray shifted into first, then second, feeling every bump as the CRX rolled over chunks of the garage, some large enough to clang ominously against the undercarriage of the low-riding vehicle as it spiraled up and around, up and around toward the structure's exit level. The gate was down and the attendant booth was empty.

Beyond the exit, Ray saw a CNN Special Report come to

disorienting life through the t.v. screen of his car windshield, chaotic yet strangely, anonymously familiar from years of nightly newscast tragedy. Toxic clouds from any number of fires blackened the sky and the streets he could see were a frozen river of traffic and trapped emergency vehicles, sirens shrieking in frustration.

A makeshift triage area was forming in front of the East Tower for victims of the quake, and Ray felt a momentary pang of guilt as he caught sight of Big Mary and his other coworkers rushing around, doing what they could for the injured and dying...but there was no real thought of staying or question of priority in his mind. Instead, he swiped his parking card at the eye-beam scanner once, twice, and when the plastic gate didn't rise, he stomped the gas and punched the Honda past it, denting his front bumper as he knocked the gate free of its moorings.

The blonde white cop from earlier ran forward, waving his arms, but Ray ignored him, steering the CRX onto the sidewalk in front of the hospital, blasting the vehicle's clown-car horn to clear a path through the milling, panicked pedestrians. At the end of the block, the tiny Honda dropped off the curb into the creeping anarchy of street traffic, weaving through the openings, scraping between angry BMWs and honking panel trucks until a wide parking lot opened on the left, its lanes and spaces less congested than the surrounding surface roads.

Ray cut through the lot, dialing his cell phone but getting no signal, improvising a route as he navigated across a dog park, another parking lot, and La Cienega Boulevard, all the while transmitting a single thought, over and over, as if repetition increased its chances of reception: *"Hang on, baby...hang on, baby...hang on, baby...hang on..."*

KA (*The Double*)

The house is gone. The inground pool is gone.

My wife is gone.

My child, gone.

Or, rather, the *illusion* of my wife and child. Not Karen. Not Pete, Jr. My Delusions, my desire for them.

"So where are they? *Really?*"

My father remains. I feel nothing but hatred for his existence, what he's taken from mine. I turn, see him staring back at me, expressionless. I can't stand the sight of him and so he vanishes, though I still hear his voice:

"Oh, they're here...if you're ready to see them."

"I'm sick of your fucking riddles," I snap. "*Where are they?*"

And then I'm underwater. Karen is screaming. My father's voice says, "Just remember...*it's what she wants.* For now."

Karen's scream multiplies...a dozen, a hundred times... there's movement everywhere, but I don't understand what I'm seeing. The liquid I float in scalds like boiling oil, dissolving my Delusional corporeal form. I can only scream, too, as I melt like wax...

...*agony*...

...*agony*...

...*agony*, like no pain I have ever experienced...I scream and scream with no voice, lost in the maddening torment, aware of nothing but the animal sensation of torture and a solitary conscious thought...

...*I could stop this...*

...and yet, I somehow find it difficult to relinquish the pain, so all-encompassing, so intense I can barely register my perception of it consciously...only stubborn will prevents it from scrubbing away the last of my thoughts, the last of my self...

...but curiosity somehow pulls me back from the overpowering lure of surrender as I focus my consciousness, attempting to understand. I regain eyes to see, then realize what I'm perceiving: a form, stretched and twisted into swirling threads of being.

I force myself into motion, swimming through hot agony, following the wispy filaments as they mingle and combine into thick, ropy coils, twisting round and round each other like a fleshy double helix before resolving into more distinct shapes, bodies entwined...

...Karen...

...her body, stretched and elongated into dual strands, merging and dividing with itself and other, similar beings in continuous, undulating spasms.

And, with a shock of horrified revulsion, I suddenly grasp what I'm perceiving.

An orgy.

Karen's face appears, then doubles, then triples, screaming in a continuous orgasm of pure sensation. I see other faces now: dozens, maybe hundreds, male and female, commingled in a massive swarming spiritual organism, alternately fused and distinct, stretching on all sides to infinity.

Trying to escape, to retreat, I break the surface of a hot,

bubbling pool in the depths of an obsidian cave illuminated by red neon and flickering torches, rank with the stench of cock and cunt and piss and shit and blood and spit and cum. Overhead, dogs rape twin virgins in a cage while a naked priest hangs by his testicles, shrieking in ecstasy. Around the pool, nudes in pairs and groups hate-fuck and make love in every conceivable combination, for every conceivable reason: reunited soul mates vowing eternal devotion and bitter ex-lovers forcing themselves to relive past infidelities... sex addicts gorging themselves on every conceivable taboo and closet cases finally submitting to the small, innocent desires they denied themselves in life.

Karen detaches from the wriggling mass beneath the bubbling surface and climbs from the pool, glistening nude. I watch the tick-tock metronome of her valentine ass, the sway of heavy breasts, overcome with a sudden, desperate need for her, drunk with memory and lust.

I scramble from the pool, naked myself now, and run to her. "Karen!"

My wife turns, an expression of surprise curling her lips. "I waited, Pete...I waited so long..." Then, reaching to stroke me, she whispers, hot in my ear, "No more waiting..."

I respond, but cannot speak or think.

I want her.

All I know is hunger as she maneuvers me away from the crowd, to a private chamber, a gleaming marble cabana I know I've seen before yet can't remember where. Karen's hair falls wild and long, the way I prefer it, the way I remember it, before she chopped it off, just before the accident, on the whim of some fashion magazine.

The cabana is dark and still, lit by scented candles. Karen slides a paper screen across the doorway and shuts out the moaning, gasping cavalcade of perversions by the pool, then slides her cool, soft curves between the sheets of the Sealy Posturepedic from our old house in Woodland Hills. And spreads her legs, on her back, waiting...

...*the way I prefer it...*

"Pete," she whispers.

I want her.

My need is terrible, she reaches for my hand, tells me she loves me.

And disappears.

I sit heavily on the bed, all my swollen desire rushing out like air from a puncture, replaced by sadness.

It wasn't her.

I am fooled so easily by wishes.

"You're so *romantic*," Karen would always tease, sarcastic, whenever I said, "I love you." Speaking the words out loud robbed them of their power, she'd explained, repeatedly, until I finally stopped expecting to hear them.

"You tell Petey you love him," I'd argued one night before bed, lying on the Posturepedic.

"He's a little boy," Karen laughed. "He *needs* to hear it."

"Well, maybe *I* need to hear it."

"Fine," Karen huffed with a mocking pout, slouched in the doorway of our bedroom. "I love you I love you I love you I love you I love you..."

"Knock it off."

"But sugar-lumps, I wuv you so much I just have to say it over and over and over again! I wuv you I wuv you I wuv you I wuv you I wuv-wuv-wuv-wuv you...!"

"I said *knock it off!*" Angry, I stormed from the bedroom to my office, too annoyed to sleep, too frustrated to work. Karen appeared in the doorway a moment later, her expression amused but conciliatory.

"Pete, you know I love you..."

"Then why can't you just *say* it?"

"Because the words are meaningless..."

I began to argue, but she cut me off: "No, they are...to me. It's like people who go to church on Sunday so they won't have to think about morality the rest of the week...it's a lazy habit."

"Karen..."

"No, Pete, I'm serious...my parents said they loved each other, over and over, as if that was enough...it just seems false to me." Then, closing and locking the door quietly behind her, she smiled and tugged at the clasp of her flannel nightgown. "I'd rather find other ways to show that I love you..."

She let the nightgown fall and sauntered to my desk in mismatched underwear as sexy to me as any French lingerie. I rose to kiss her, the argument effectively over. "Okay," I mumbled into her mouth and neck. "You win...let's go to bed."

"No..." Karen took a step back, shaking her head, slipping her underwear down her legs. "...bend me over the desk."

"But...Petey..." I stammered, uncomfortable.

"He's asleep, and the door's locked," she cooed in my ear,

rubbing me hard through the front of my pajamas. "Now fuck me."

Hesitant, I watched as my wife bent herself over the desk, breasts against the blotter, rump in the air, exposed to me in the bright vulgar light, raw and pornographic. The lights were on, the blinds were up; our neighbors could see. I quickly doused the halogen lamp in the corner.

"No, leave it on," Karen whispered, husky with excitement. "I want you to see me..."

"I see you," I responded weakly, embarrassed by my own prudish shame more than Karen's display, but powerless against my true feelings. Karen's passion and predilections had disoriented me in the early stages of our relationship: my parents had never discussed sex (or seemed to have any) while I was growing up, and my early fumblings with teenage girlfriends had always generated more fear than excitement. I'd only been intimate with a few women before Karen, and had never really been able to keep pace with her appetite. Despite my best efforts, it soon became apparent that I simply couldn't relax or enjoy myself when she tried to initiate me into the mile-high club, or ground against me at parties, or grabbed my crotch under the tables of fancy restaurants and thus, over time (and, especially, after Petey), she had quietly adjusted herself to a menu of safe positions, under the covers, in a succession of dimly lit bedrooms.

A few awkward seconds passed, then Karen sighed, retrieving her underwear from the floor as she rose from the desk: "Okay...let's go to bed."

Not Karen, my Delusion, had lured me into the cabana, safely sequestered away from prying eyes and the disturbing sexual gluttony of the pool. Not Karen, my pliant fantasy, so comfortable and reassuring to believe, lying in a placid missionary position beneath the covers of our familiar conjugal bed, wanting nothing but to please me.

And the instant I recognized my own self-deception, she vanished.

Why couldn't my father just let me believe in Delusion?

I feel anger flare again at the thought of it. If he'd never led me to question, I'd be with my "family" now, happy. Even if I'd loved an illusion, the happiness would have been *real*... certainly as real as the confusion and loneliness that's replaced it.

And what good is my father's doubt, his search for some objective, unassailable Reality that may not exist or even matter? And even if his "Realists" do find their Ultimate Truth, is it really superior to joy?

Yet, even as I think these things, my pride rebels: would I *really* have preferred a cuckold's existence, ignorant of the basic facts of my own situation, committed to a fantasy others knew to be false?

Instinctively, my legal mind plays advocate in my father's defense. Yes, there is anger that he burdened me with unwanted knowledge...but I also feel, grudgingly, a sense of relief that I learned the truth before my soul became reliant on the fantasy. Eventually, I would have noticed the inconsistencies in Karen, the claustrophobic sameness of my own preferences echoing back, strange in her mouth, forced either to acknowledge my doubts or subconsciously allow them to fester.

Steeling myself, I move to the doorway of the cabana and peer through the paper screen Not Karen used to block what I didn't wish to see. Opening myself to unrestrained Reality, I am assaulted once more by the reek and violence of pure carnality.

Karen, I think, instantly transporting myself to her true psychic location, a torchlit dungeon on the far side of the infinite sex pool where a semblance of my wife stands, enormous, rippled with muscle, a single-breasted Amazon devouring the entrails of a Roman castrato...

...until a fearsome, hairless blue djinn appears in a curl of green smoke, clutching battleship chain in his powerful fists. He snaps the iron links around Karen's engorged throat, a garrote...I hear my wife gasp, choking...

"KAREN!" I scream, rushing forward...but she doesn't hear me, doesn't feel my hands when I attempt to pull her free, doesn't concede my existence at all. Instead, she mewls in contentment while the djinn binds her and mounts her roughly...then gently, as the chain dissolves and the lovers entwine, merging into one entity before melting away into steaming rivulets, streaming back to the endless, churning pool.

I turn and see my father, as Raquel, swathed in dark velvet, incongruously formal in the midst of bacchanal. "She didn't see you because she chooses not to...I think it's rude and unnecessary, of course, but she seems to be going through a rather selfish phase at the moment..."

"*Selfish?*" I cry, transporting us with a thought to my father's palazzo, tired of the sounds and sights and stench of debauchery. "You mean *insane.*"

"Ah, well..." Dad says, fixing us mint juleps, careful with her words, "...insanity and selfishness operate somewhat differently here, as I'm sure you can appreciate."

"How can you *possibly* be so blasé when I just saw my wife *cannibalizing...*"

"*Pretending* to cannibalize a consenting, masochistic spirit who suffered no permanent...or even temporary...damage."

"But...but it's *deranged!*" I exclaim, passively accepting the drink my father presses into my hand.

"Yes, I suppose it is," Dad acknowledges, sipping her julep. "Or, rather, it *would* be if this were the physical universe. But remember...Karen has been here for some time, now, unrestrained by consequence or social mores..."

"Then what about *basic humanity*? I mean, forget *common decency* or *morality...*" I say, hysteria rising, "...since apparently none of that fucking *matters* up here...but I *don't* understand how a woman I loved could somehow transform into that... *creature*, that *THING...*"

"Perhaps it can't be explained...only *experienced*," my father admits, "But I'll do my best, and it will either help you or it won't. You see, the blessing and the curse of This Place is that *anything* a soul can remember or imagine can be experienced here. If you wanted to know, for instance, what it felt like to make love to Marilyn Monroe, you could enter Joe DiMaggio's memories and relive every one of their nights together. Or you could find the *real* Marilyn Monroe and see if she'd be willing to join her soul with yours...although, trust me, I've met her and she wouldn't. *Or* you could, with a thought, conjure a *harem* of Marilyn Monroes to serve you, each virtually indistinguishable from the *actual* Marilyn..."

...and suddenly, my father's voice grows breathy, her red hair shading platinum as the room sprouts a squadron of faux Monroes, naked and clothed, rouge-tinted nudes reclining on couches and bombshells dolled up in costumes from *The Seven Year Itch* to *Some Like It Hot*. "But certain appetites can never be satisfied, only exhausted," Dad coos, swizzling her drink. "You have sex with Marilyn, you try every position and variation, and still you want more. You have multiple orgasms with multiple Marilyns, and still you want more...your appetite expands, your desire increases, your pursuit of sensation prompts exotic scenarios...you whip her, she beats you...pleasure and pain become indistinguishable, until you've gone beyond sex, beyond morality, beyond *yourself*, in pursuit of the *ultimate* satisfaction, that perfect, impossible, eternal moment of release, always just ahead on the horizon, forever out of reach..."

With a graceful pirouette, my father transforms once more to Raquel, and the Marilyns vanish. "*Feelies*, we call them...or, more charitably, Sensation Junkies. To be fair, it's not uncommon for new arrivals to indulge themselves for a period, shattering taboos and satisfying the residual curiosities of their earthbound lives. That's why I say you shouldn't judge Karen too harshly...it's a phase most of us go through, to a greater or lesser extent...

...*greater*, perhaps, in Karen's case."

I sit heavily on a plush gold Louis XVI couch, overwhelmed less by moral outrage, I realize, than common jealousy. My wife no longer wants me. Others have been with her...*many* others, apparently...while I lay on my deathbed, dreaming fantasies of loving her.

I never satisfied her.

I never knew her at all.

She disgusts me.

I feel sick, and wish I could vomit, and then it starts and I fear it will never stop as I gag and wretch and heave myself inside out, puking out years of sorrow and self-loathing and rage and repression, lonely frustration and hatred...of Karen, myself, every woman, mankind...spasming out like magma from a volcano unsuspected before the moment of eruption.

I rail at fate and God, for the loss of my family, the accident, the coma, injustice, my unwanted birth, the horrors of existence.

I lose all sense of time and perception, swathed in darkness and blinding light, punctuated by violence...blood on my hands in some plague-stricken alley, a tantrum of lightning and fire, laying waste to my wedding day, a church piled with formal-dressed corpses and something more, a

presence

massive and frightening...a power far beyond the scope of my comprehension...

...SURGING...

...AND THEN...

I AM

ENGULFED...

...AND THEN

I AM CONSUMED AND THEN I AM

ANNIHILATED

ANDTHENIAMENGULFEDANDTHENIAM

CONSUMEDANDTHEN

IAMANNIHILATED

ANDTHENIAMENGULFEDANDTHENIAMCONSUMEDANDTHENIAM

ANNIHILATED

ANDTHENIAMENGULFEDANDTHENIAM CONSUMEDANDTHENIAM

ANNIHILATEDANDTHENIAMENGULFEDANDTHENIAMCONSUMED

ANDTHENIAMANNIHILATEDANDTHENIAMENGULFEDANDTHENIA

MCONSUMEDANDTHENIAMANNIHILATED

AND THEN I AM ENGULFED AND THEN I AM

CONSUMEDANDTHENIAM

ANNIHILATEDANDTHENIAMENGULFEDANDTHENIAMCONSUMED

ANDTHENIAMANNIHILATEDANDTHENIAMENGULFEDANDTHENIA

MCONSUMEDANDTHENIAMANNIHILATED

AND THEN I AM ENGULFEDANDTHENIAM

CONSUMEDANDTHENIAM

ANNIHILATEDANDTHENIAMENGULFEDANDTHENIAMCONSUMED

ANDTHENIAMANNIHILATEDANDTHENIAMENGULFEDANDTHENIA

MCONSUMEDANDTHENIAMANNIHILATED

AND THEN I AM ENGULFED AND THEN I AM
CONSUMEDANDTHENIAM
ANNIHILATEDANDTHENIAMENGULFEDANDTHENIAMCONSUMED
ANDTHENIAMANNIHILATEDANDTHENIAMENGULFEDANDTHENIA
MCONSUMEDANDTHENIAMANNIHILATED
AND THEN I AM ENGULFEDANDTHEN I AM
CONSUMEDANDTHENIAM
ANNIHILATEDANDTHENIAMENGULFEDANDTHENIAMCONSUMED
ANDTHENIAMANNIHILATEDANDTHENIAMENGULFEDANDTHENIA
MCONSUMEDANDTHENIAMANNIHILATED
AND THEN I AM ENGULFED AND THEN I AM CONSUMED AND
THEN I AM
ANNIHILATEDANDTHENIAMENGULFEDANDTHENIAMCONSUMED
ANDTHENIAMANNIHILATEDANDTHENIAMENGULFEDANDTHENIA
MCONSUMEDANDTHENIAMANNIHILATED
AND THEN I AM ENGULFEDANDTHENIAM
CONSUMEDANDTHENIAM
ANNIHILATEDANDTHENIAMENGULFEDANDTHENIAMCONSUMED
ANDTHENIAMANNIHILATEDANDTHENIAMENGULFEDANDTHENIA
MCONSUMEDANDTHENIAMANNIHILATED
ANDTHENIAMENGULFEDANDTHENIAM CONSUMEDANDTHENIAM

ANNIHILATEDANDTHENIAMENGULFEDANDTHENIAMCONSUMED

ANDTHENIAMANNIHILATEDANDTHENIAMENGULFEDANDTHENIA

MCONSUMEDANDTHENIAMANNIHILATED

ANDTHENIAMREBORNANDDESTROYEDANDREBORNANDDESTRO

YEDANDREBORN

ANDDESTROYEDANDREBORNANDDESTROYEDANDREBORNAND

DESTROYEDANDREBORN

AND DESTROYED

AND REBORN

And

then

perception

returns   consciousness

defines

infinities

of rage

of pain

of ecstasy

of joy

of grief

of horror

of never

of always

existence

I am

I think

everywhere and nowhere,

caught in the wake of some madness,

dragged from the void into Life, the Earth,

and *THERE*...

a man I know, the tall black orderly...Ray, his name is Ray...

...only *not* the man I knew in life, but rather a tendril of fury,

extinguishing the life of another man...

...and then...

...I am gusting across the fertile plains of Asgard,

with my father,

surging as bloodlust through the veins of the warriors there,

locked in their endless combat with the eternal foes of Ragnarök.
We ride fast on currents like hurricane wind through all 540 doors of
Valhalla simultaneously, sweeping through the celebration of heroes
and valkyries as pure wild joy before coming to rest at last in corporeal
form by the edge of a vast cooking pit near the center of the endless
banquet hall.

"Feeling better?" my father asks, bemused, once again sipping
his frosty mint julep.

I have no response, nor energy to think or speak.

"Don't worry," my father continues, in soothing tones like a valium drip. "You needed that."

"Needed what?" I think more than whisper.

"A good psychic freak-out. I remember, when you were a boy, you were always the same way. You'd hold things in too long, then let everything out in one big crazy explosion of incoherent wrath. You know, like Daffy Duck. And then you felt better."

"I do feel better," I admit. "But I don't understand what just happened."

"You lost control," Dad shrugs. "You disappeared into your Id, and now you're back."

"Disappeared?" I say. "How long was I gone?"

"Hard to say, really. You blinked out, and then next thing I know you were here with the Vikings. It took me a minute or so to catch up...though from your point of view, it may have seemed longer."

"It did...*much* longer...and wherever I was, it was violent and horrible...but I can't describe it, I can't remember..."

"...because you abandoned your *reason*, the part that remembers," Dad explains, handing me a heavy bronze goblet of mead, eager that I should understand. "Just like Karen, abandoning herself to sensation...all wasted energy, in my opinion, without a conscious soul to perceive and direct it."

"I'd rather not think about Karen anymore," I say, feeling darkness again at the mention of her name.

"Of course," my father says, grace notes of sympathy in his tone. "And I apologize for burdening you with so much at once, Peter. I know you've been through a lot, and it was never my intention to cause you undue pain. There are just certain Realities here that I thought you should know sooner rather than later...but it's not all grim metaphysics and existential angst in This Place, heavens no! There's music and laughter, and so many people waiting to see you...we can have dinner with your great-grandparents at the Cocoanut Grove, or visit the Moon or go smoke a hookah with the Caterpillar and the White Rabbit at the Mad Hatter's Tea Party. Whatever you want is yours with a thought. Just tell me what you want to do."

"I want," I say, "to know what's happened to my child."

SEKHU (*The Remains*)

Happyland was in shambles. The windows in the one-level, pink stucco ranch house were all shattered, an exterior wall and part of the red terra cotta roof had caved inward where the children played, and a busted fire hydrant was geysering plumes of water into the air, transforming the dry brown yard into a muddy clay lake.

"JOYCE!" Ray screamed, leaping from his CRX even as it rolled to a stop on the slick wet sidewalk in front of the ruined building. "I'M HERE, BABY! I'M HERE!"

Running through the cold, wet spray of the hydrant without waiting for a response, Ray found the gunmetal front storm door locked tight and the doorbell inoperative, so after a few cursory bangs, he ran around to the collapsed wall, stepping gingerly over chunks of concrete and slippery tiles into the remains of the small, dark wood-paneled living room Indrani Jones had repurposed as a tiny neighborhood daycare center.

The building had always been squirming with children and toddlers whenever Ray had been there in the past, but now it was empty and silent except for the hiss of gushing water and the contiguous white-noise din of a city in chaos. The power was out, and the dark refrigerator in the small kitchenette adjoining the living room had vomited its contents onto the floor, its door hanging wide like an open sarcophagus. The wide-screen TV where Joyce and the other Happyland children watched Disney cartoons had pitched forward, screen first, onto a cairn of scattered DVDs, and the mesh bottom of a colorful playpen was glittering with shards of glass.

"JOYCE!" Ray called again, down the narrow, shadowy hallway that led to the bathroom and private, off-limits part of the house containing Indrani's bedroom and the small guest room she used as an office. "BABY JOYCE! CAN YOU HEAR ME?"

Again there was no response, so Ray ventured a few steps deeper into the house, then felt his guts curdle in a sickening elevator drop of terror as he spotted a dark, dusty arm in his peripheral vision, jutting motionless from beneath a jumble of wreckage in what used to be the southeast corner of the living room.

"No, no, no..." Ray gasped in a desperate prayer, flinging himself down to his knees as he tore at the rubble, clearing it away, bracing himself, prepared to see any dead child but his own.

"Who's there?" cried a husky, imperious voice from somewhere behind him. But Ray couldn't really hear or respond as he tugged on the cold, inanimate arm, unearthing a Cabbage Patch doll with such a sudden sharp rush of relief that he nearly threw up.

"Who are you?" the voice repeated, and this time Ray turned, still holding the doll as Indrani Jones stepped through the breach in the wall, clutching a bright yellow tube of pepper spray.

"It's me!" Ray cried, scrambling to his feet. "Ray Wyatt... where's Joyce?"

The solid, formidable tree-stump of a woman looked stricken, her proud, leonine features contorting in a tortured mask of sorrow as she moaned, "Oh, Raymond, God help me... I've been all over the neighborhood...and the police are searching, too..."

"What do you mean?" Ray said with a cold flush of panic. "Where is she, where's Joyce?"

"She can't be far," Indrani replied, clutching his arm, as if to steady them both.

"You mean you don't *know*?"

"I got everyone out when that temblor hit, but then some went running off..."

Ray pulled away in horror and rushed back out to the yard, screaming, "JOYCE!"

"...there were a dozen scared children, running in all directions..." Indrani continued, babbling in abject repentance. "...and some were hurt, some were just babies...I had to stay with them...I hollered and hollered..."

Ray spun towards her, wild-eyed. "Where did she go? Which direction?"

"That way," Indrani pointed, hurrying to keep pace with Ray as he took off running, "down Avalon..."

Ray was vaguely aware he could make better time in the CRX, but he was acting on adrenalin and instinct now, picking up speed like the hurdler he'd once been in high school, calling his daughter's name at the top of his lungs. The quake had struck an hour ago. Joyce had been alone in the chaotic streets for an hour, terrified, searching for him, searching for...

...home...

Home was safe. She was probably trying to find her way *home...*

...Avalon...

They drove down Avalon when he picked her up from Daycare...Avalon to East Gage...East Gage to Compton... Compton to 76th and *home.*

She knew the route...didn't she? She could read the street signs, but would she know to go left on East Gage and right on Compton? Would she remember to cross at the crosswalks and not talk to strangers, even with the world going crazy around her?

It was just over two miles, she'd been missing for an hour. Ray shot a glance at the railbed to his left as he ran flat-out down Slauson. She was smart, she'd follow the train tracks until she hit Avalon. Avalon was a major street...

...but there were so many doorways, so many alleyways she could have ducked down, so many places to hide, so many cars...assholes and ambulances racing top-speed along the wide city streets...

Ray couldn't let himself think. He just kept running, winded already, stabbing pains in his gut, painful burning in the back of his throat...and he'd only been four blocks: he wasn't an athlete anymore. Dropping into a jog, he wheeled right on Avalon, wishing now he'd taken the car so he could drive straight home and see if she was there. He thought about turning back, felt a strong, stubborn need to keep moving forward, then remembered the cell phone in his pocket.

Pulling it free, he saw the signal had been restored and dialed his own number as he pounded pavement past the long, low Los Compadres Swap Meet where he'd bought Joyce the Talking SpongeBob, wondering briefly if she'd sought shelter there with the friendly old churro guy, Choo-Choo or Chuy or whatever his name was, then heard the beep of his answering machine and said, "Yo, Baby Joyce, are you there? Pick up the phone if you're there, it's Daddy...I'm coming home, okay? I'm on my way...pick up the phone if you're there..."

And then he saw exactly what he'd been hoping not to see, half a mile or so in the distance, obscured by a low, white-grey fog he recognized as tear gas: the tail end of a looting spree, circumscribed by an occupying force of National Guardsmen and L.A.P.D. stormtroopers in black filter masks and riot gear.

"*Shit*," Ray huffed, breathing hard as he slowed to a walk, biting back hopelessness. *If she went that way, she could've been hurt*, was his immediate thought. *Or worse...*

He pushed the worst-case scenarios from his brain, forcing himself to stay focused. If she was hurt, somebody would take her to a hospital. If the cops spotted a scared little girl in the middle of a riot, they'd put her somewhere, keep her safe, ask where she lived...unless she hadn't come this way, or turned back when she saw all the commotion...

Ray glanced again at the Swap Meet building: a familiar landmark, a place his daughter knew and liked. The churro guy was there.

It made sense. It would only waste a few minutes if she wasn't there, and maybe somebody had seen her. At the very least, he could spread the word, get more people looking.

Ray dashed through the parking gate across the narrow macadam lot to the south entrance of the building, found the corrugated door hanging open. The power was out here as well, and the cool, dusty interior was illuminated by emergency lights. Many of the stalls were locked down behind steel grates, and others had been hastily stripped of their possessions, either by panicky vendors as they fled the building or passing looters on their way to the main action further down the street.

"Joyce?" Ray called into the silent interior, surprised there wasn't so much as a security guard left behind on the premises before realizing, after wading through several yards of scattered leopard-print seat covers, Virgin Mary beach towels and bootleg DVDs, that there probably wasn't anything really worth stealing in the whole tumbledown place.

Moving swiftly amid the lanes of stalls and tables, calling his daughter's name, Ray made his way to the spot where Choo-Choo or Chuy's churro cart had toppled over in the southeast corner of the maze. Finding nothing of particular interest there, he continued towards the Swap Meet's north entrance, figuring Joyce would have responded already if she were anywhere in the long, low building.

And then, a cry.

It was nothing more than a muffled squeak, but it hit Ray's ear like a sonic boom, propelling him towards a triple-locked door marked "Employees Only."

"JOYCE!" Ray screamed, pounding the sturdy wooden door with big, meaty fists. There was no response, but it didn't matter: he knew his daughter's voice. He knew she was in there. "BABY JOYCE!"

Still no answer, which could only mean she was hurt, otherwise she would have called out to him, even if she was scared.

His baby was hurt.

Ray threw the full weight of his 240 pound frame against the door and barely felt it give. Glancing around, frantic, he saw plastic folding chairs, beach umbrellas, Zippo lighters, fire extinguishers...nothing useful...until his gaze suddenly fell across a large iron crowbar propped against the grate of one of the shuttered vendor stalls like a drunk slouching under a lamppost.

Grabbing the bar with both hands, Ray hacked once, twice, and finally knocked the knob off the locked employee door with his third vicious blow.

Then, jamming the hook end into the space between the hinge and the frame, he strained with all his strength until the bolt latch on the other side popped free and the door swung inward to a tiny, cramped employee area containing an ancient desk and chair, some mismatched file cabinets, a hotplate, coffeepot, and a small, locked floor safe. Beyond the main office area was a toilet in what appeared to be a closet, and beyond that a darkened storage room containing a cracked brown leather couch, surrounded by crates and boxes.

Joyce was sitting upright on the couch, tiny shoulders naked beneath a green army surplus blanket that covered most of her body. The clothes, shoes and underpants Ray had laid out for her that morning were neatly folded on the cement floor in front of her alongside a pile of adult clothes, and his daughter's wide, brown eyes were staring in fear over the top of a fat, pink hand clamped fast over the lower half of her face.

The acne-scarred man on the couch beside Joyce was under the army blanket with her, and his shoulders and fleshy, tattooed chest were also visibly naked.

"It's okay, she's okay!" the man wailed, reflexively enfolding Joyce more tightly in his pudgy arms, as if to protect her.

"*DADDY!*" Joyce screamed, working her mouth free, a fresh hurricane of hysterical tears now squalling from her eyes.

"She came to me..." were the fat man's last words.

SEKEM (Power, Energy, Light)

"Skål," my father says, transforming his mint julep to mead and his exterior back to Raquel, dressed now in a winged helmet, gauntlets, and a cleavage-bearing silver breastplate in deference to our surroundings.

I toast my goblet against hers and gulp the fermented honey, allowing its alcoholic properties to exist, to relax me, to settle my deeply unsettled nerves. And then I repeat, "Where is my son?"

"He's...*playing* right now," Dad says, choosing his words carefully in a manner that merely triggers alarm.

"Then let's go to him."

"We will. *Later.*"

"Later?" I scoff, the spent embers of my anger reigniting. "I thought time was an *illusion* up here."

"Touché," Dad half-smiles.

"Then let's go! *Now!* Bring me to Petey!"

"I will, I promise...just *not yet.*"

"Why?" I demand, petulant.

"Because," my father explains, patient as always, "it will probably *upset* you."

I feel a painful ache in the memory of my heart. "So what you're saying, in other words, is that my son is gone from me, too," I snarl, already knowing the answer. "Like Karen...like Mom...*like my whole fucking existence...*"

"No!" my father says quickly, perhaps trying to keep me from disappearing again into my own capacity for darkness. "Although," she continues, diplomatic, "it may *seem* that way in your current emotional state. You've already experienced so much, in such a short period...you need time and peace, now, Peter, to restore your psychic equilibrium, to process all that you've learned before charging off to experience *more...*"

"But we *both* know all the time in *eternity* won't bring me peace if I don't know what's happened to *my child,*" I state flatly as my father nods, resigned to the inevitable. "So *tell* me. *Show* me where he is."

"Well, in a way," Dad sighs, "you've already been there."

"What?" I gape in surprise. "How...*when?*"

"Just now, when you released yourself from perception into rage. For a time, you ceased to exist in my consciousness, because your psychic energy had dissipated into a state of pure, unreasoning Id..."

I close my eyes – or *perceive* myself closing them, instinctively yet needlessly bracing against the onset of an imaginary headache as I speak the phrase that's become my own personal mantra in this accursed Place: *"I don't understand."*

"By abandoning reason, you let Chaos engulf you," my father explains, stepping aside as a burly blonde Viking stomps over with an armful of timber for the cooking pit behind us. "Pure untethered sensation, with no sense of time, limits, individual consciousness...a vast, *collective* Id."

"Collective?"

Dad nods. "A boundless, invisible cloud of sentient Energy, comprised of billions of individual souls...the Screaming Skulls, I call them...the children of Heaven..."

"Petey," I gasp, understanding and not understanding.

"Exactly," Dad says as the burly Viking returns, now shouldering a mammoth boar for the pit. "Most of us arrive in This Place imprinted with thoughts and beliefs from the material world, but infants and very young children are creatures of instinct and impulse, well-suited to the boundless freedoms of the afterlife. They either never learn or quickly forget the constraints of the physical world, of human society..."

"...and family," I murmur, surrendering the secret hope I'd barely allowed myself to acknowledge, that Petey might still remember our long-past lives as father and son.

"He remembers," my father says kindly, either literally or figuratively reading my thoughts. "The link between you still exists...but he's no longer the child you remember, nor the individual he might have become if his soul had matured and developed on Earth. The young souls here are more fluid, less inclined to stay within the confines of a single form or personality. For reasons I don't entirely understand, they usually group together, drawn by the massive Energy of Chaos, merging into the greater collective unconscious of the entity."

"And...so...what does all that have to do with *Vikings*, exactly?" I ask, the scent of roast boar triggering sharp pangs of Delusional hunger in my consciousness.

"Nothing," Dad smiles, draining her goblet before accepting a refill of sweet mead from a buxom serving wench.

"Then...what are we *doing here*, exactly?"

"Oh, well," Dad shrugs, "you just happened to be passing through Valhalla when I found you."

"Right, of course," I say, baffled.

"As it was explained to me," Dad continues, "the Screaming Skulls of Chaos are like a big, invisible swarm of bees within a great mass of Energy, only with no queen to direct the hive mind...a self-directed psychic hurricane, navigated by the random subconscious whims of innumerable souls, traveling on currents of instinct and emotion with no specific goal or purpose. And chaos draws Chaos, so I helped you to break free as the cloud swept over the endless battlefields of Ragnarök in spasms of berserker rage."

"What do you mean *break free?*"

"Giving yourself over to Chaos is relatively easy," Dad replies. "But once you do, reasserting yourself as an autonomous, individual spirit can be really quite difficult...like swimming clear of a riptide. Without willpower and a strong sense of self, you can easily forget who you are and just follow the whims of the Screaming Skulls, ingesting pure sensation with no perception of past or present, forever. Even well-defined identities become disoriented in the soul cloud...so Valhalla made a useful landmark for me when I reached in to grab you. It's kind of a tourist trap, but there are worse places to wind up..."

"You mean you've been here before?" I say, puzzled, as a dozen seemingly Hasidic Vikings burst into song at a nearby section of the hall's vast banquet table.

"Oh, sure," Dad nods. "It's what's known in This Place as a Common Construct, like Hell or the Weimar Republic or Middle Earth or that Feelie sex pit your wife has been wasting her time at lately...a relatively stable Delusion supported by the complementary visions of numerous individual souls, constructed of memories, fantasies, neuroses and what have you. Valhalla's one of the oldest and most accessible Constructs, so it was a relatively easy concept to guide you to...plus, as I say, Chaos sweeps through here on a fairly regular basis..."

"Raquel!" cries one of the nearby Hasidim, seeming to recognize my father. "Is that you?"

Dad looks up, startled then pleasantly surprised as the man disengages from his companions and bounds over to join us. "Moshe!"

"It's been far too long, my friend!" the grey-bearded, side-curled Viking cries, crushing my father in a big, friendly bear hug. "But what brings a dignified person like yourself into the midst of such *narrischkeit?*"

"Long story," Dad answers, arm snaking around Moshe's waist, relaxed and familiar. "Peter, I'd like you to meet one of my oldest friends in This Place, Rebbe Moshe Ben-Zvi..."

"And this can only be the famous Pete Herlinger, reunited with his dear, departed father at last," Moshe exclaims, grasping my hand in what feels like a powerful grip. "Please accept my heartfelt condolences on your untimely passing."

Moshe unleashes a booming, infectious howl of laughter and my father grins, her expression more open and relaxed than I've ever known, in life or afterlife – a strangely gratifying totem of the happier social existence she's established for herself far removed from the quiet desperation of her prior constraints.

I realize, too, that I probably haven't been very good company since my arrival.

"I've been doing my best to indoctrinate Pete as a Realist," my father says.

"Ah, yes," Moshe nods. "Very important, I think, to seek the True Sight."

Indicating the other Hasidim at the banquet table, the rebbe adds, "My brother, Dov, has only recently arrived from Tel Aviv, and my uncles and ancestors and I have been taking him around to various Constructs, the better to open his mind to our new understanding and communion with God in This Place. But he's very headstrong and traditional, my brother, so we've had some *passionate* discussions, as you might imagine..."

"So Constructs are, like, shared hallucinations or something?" I say to my father, still trying to understand

"Well, it's a bit *controversial*," Dad exchanges a look with the rebbe, sharing a private joke. "Ask some of these Vikings, for instance...I'm talking the authentic, old-time *Norsemen*, not tourists like Moshe, here...and they'll tell you we're all standing in a *very* Real place, created by Odin as an eternal home for the faithful *Einherjar* slain gloriously in battle. But a Realist would tell you this hall and the battlefields of Asgard are only here because the Vikings imagined them in the first place."

"And yet, Valhalla and Asgard *do* seem to exist, because here we stand!" Moshe interjects, eyes twinkling, happy to play devil's advocate.

"It's kind of a chicken and the egg situation," Dad concedes. "Nobody knows for *sure* whether Valhalla...or the Happy Hunting Grounds or Elysium or Djanna or all the million Heavens and Hells and everything else you'll find in This Place...were created by Man or God or Satan or Odin or Allah or whoever else...and there are never-ending discussions and debates and really quite heated battles about which of the places are Real and which are man-made illusions and so on and so forth and so on and on and on..."

"Yet, *unlike* Earth, where men argue while divinity is silent," Moshe continues, "in This Place, there are gods and devils *everywhere*, proving everything and nothing, depending who you ask."

"Again," Dad adds, "there's no consensus on which gods and devils are truly Real and which are Constructs...believed absolutely by some, ignored completely by others."

"But wouldn't it be *impossible* to ignore a *true* god," I ask, "or, rather, the *one true God*, if there really is such a thing?"

"Ah!" Moshe's face lights up with glee as he pokes my chest with a finger, smiling over at Raquel. "A reasonable, logical, *skeptical* man...just like his papa!" Then, shifting his attention back in my direction, he says, "I grant that a *true* deity would make His presence known, unmistakably and irrefutably...but *how*, in what form? As a carnival huckster, soliciting crowds? As a tyrant, bullying non-believers into submission? Or *perhaps*...

"...perhaps a *true* deity would remain hidden, manifesting only as a simple desire to know Him."

"Or Her," my father appends.

"Or Us or It or Them or Those," Moshe huffs, palms thrown wide in mock exasperation. "The point is, many find their proof in death, while others remain in faith or doubt, forever seeking..."

"So you still believe in God?" I ask.

"How can I not?" Moshe laughs. "Look around! What more proof could a person require?"

"But what's the *point* of it all?" I cry, suddenly and surprisingly desperate. "I mean, what are we doing here? There was at least some kind of *logic* to life, but This Place doesn't make any goddamn sense at all!"

I stop, embarrassed at losing my temper again, especially in front of a rabbi, but Moshe doesn't seem to mind. "Was it logical for an educated young man to blow himself up on the bus I was riding to my synagogue in Hebron?" he says. "Over a glorified border dispute? I've spoken with the gentleman since, and he couldn't be nicer, or more apologetic...but at the time, he felt his actions were thoroughly justified. He wasn't a gibbering maniac or a rabid animal, as my brother, Dov, insists. No, there was a *logical* reason for him to strap on the suicide vest, a *point* to it all...at least in his mind, at the time, though he feels somewhat differently now.

"And so it is with This Place. Everyone makes their *own* logic here...or abandons logic completely...with no more sense of the *point* of it all than we've ever had...yet my sense of *Devekus*, my communion with the one true God, has never been more sure or steady. Hunger, fear, hatred, death...they're all Delusions here. Maybe love and eternity, too. Maybe consciousness itself...who can say? But with the tools we've been given and the gift...the *discipline*...of True Sight, I believe we *shall* ultimately come to know His will, and the answers and meaning and purpose we seek..."

My father offers a teasing, affectionate, "*Amen*," as Moshe notes his brother fidgeting impatiently at the banquet table and shrugs,

"I should go...Dov is hungry and refuses to eat boar, even though I keep telling him that he's not *really* hungry and the boar is imaginary. But then, what do I know?"

The rabbi takes my hand and says, "It's a pleasure to meet you, Mr. Herlinger, and you're certainly welcome in my consciousness anytime to discuss the great mysteries of the universe or play cards or whatever you'd like."

"The pleasure's mine," I smile.

"And stick close to this one." Moshe swats my father on the back. "She'll keep you honest...and *safe*."

"Speaking of which," Dad says. "Is there any news on the Summit? I wouldn't want to miss it."

"Yes, well," Moshe replies, tension abruptly clouding his aura like an unexpected storm, "there's still a chance it won't be necessary."

"Nevertheless," my father nods, "I'd like to be there."

"Of course, of course," Moshe says, grasping her hand. Then, with a final wave, he and the other Hasidic Vikings all vanish simultaneously.

"Should I ask about *that?*"

"What?" Dad replies, momentarily distracted.

"The Summit?" My father's features turn strangely placid, and I suddenly realize: "You're hiding something from me."

The persimmon lips of Dad's feminine form curl into a spontaneous grin as she replies, "And what makes you say that?"

"Your face...or what I perceive as your face...or, rather, what your consciousness has decided to *project* as a face, or..."

"Close enough...go on..."

"Well, anyway, it just went blank...or, maybe *neutral* is a better word...as if you'd made a deliberate choice not to communicate your true feelings visually."

"You seem to be getting the hang of This Place."

"Not really," I admit. "I'm so confused at this point, I barely know who or what I am anymore...in fact, if everything is truly as subjective as it seems to be, I'm beginning to question whether I was ever alive at all, or if all those memories of my existence before death...before this *moment*...are any more true than anything else. But if I've *ever* been a lawyer or a teacher or a husband or a father, then I believe I know when someone isn't being completely honest with me."

"Bravo," Dad nods. "And you're absolutely correct...it hardly suits a Realist to sugar-coat Reality."

"In that case," I say, aware now of a tingling, inexplicable surge of emotional perception, echoed by a slight vibration in the seeming slabs of rough-hewn stone beneath my feet, "tell me about the Summit."

"No, wait..." my father says, abruptly raising a gauntlet to silence me, "something's wrong..."

"What's *wrong* is that you're incapable of answering a simple fucking question," I snap in a hot, unbidden rush of anger, swatting her armored hand aside.

"Shut your mouth," my habitually imperturbable father snaps back as the trembling of the floor intensifies, rattling the flagons and platters of Valhalla's countless banqueting tables. The clatter of bronze and iron counterpoint a metallic hiss of blades unsheathing from their scabbards within the Hall, and a mounting cacophony of battle drums thundering without.

Something is coming. *Lots and lots* of something.

I feel the rage and dread of pure terror, an overpowering desire to flee, but find myself trapped in memories of paralyzed confinement. Horrific forces are surrounding the Hall, yet I cannot wish myself away from the onrushing malevolence. For all my father's useless theorizing, I realize there's no ambiguity in the visceral hostility of this ambush, no changeable Reality, *no escape.*

The startling fury of my own survival instinct drives me to action as I join the storm tide of warriors pouring outward through the 540 doors of Valhalla, like mead from a punctured wineskin. My father screams for me to stop, but she is a coward and a fool. Massive fists of rage are battering now through the roof and walls of the banquet hall like meteors. A Viking berserker screams: *Ragnarök!*

And his scream engulfs me

Ragnarök! Fate of the Gods!

And my anger consumes me

Ragnarök! Apocalypse!

And annihilation...

...and annihilation...

...and

SEKHU (*The Remains*)

Eddie Sandoval only made $10.75 an hour as a security guard at Los Compadres Swap Meet, so he was one of the first people out the door when the earthquake hit. The building had never seemed especially sturdy, and the notion of risking his life for such a shitty job never even occurred to him.

Once the trembling stopped, the South Central teen hovered in the parking lot at a safe distance from the front door, watching customers and vendors spill clear until his conscience was satisfied that nobody needed rescuing. Then he quickly retreated to his piece-of-shit Aztek, surfing the radio for news as he called around to his girlfriend and family to make sure everyone was okay.

He was talking with his mother about the looting near their condo when he spotted Hector re-entering the Swap Meet building. Figuring Los Compadres' chubby, pock-marked maintenance guy could hold the fort while he was away, the teen drove off to make sure his parents were safe...but his boss, Mr. Peña, had other ideas, threatening Eddie's livelihood (and worse) after calling for a status report, then completely losing his shit when it turned out the teen had abandoned his post.

Traffic had been jammed in every direction for close to half an hour as police blocked streets to contain the looting and so, not seeing an easy way to get home anyway, Eddie pulled a quick U-turn and shot north on Avalon back towards the Swap Meet. He saw a tall black guy entering Los Compadres when he was about a block away, and by the time he'd parked he could already hear the muffled screams of violence emanating from somewhere inside of the low, dark structure.

"Holy shit," Eddie gasped, unclipping the Sabre stun baton he'd never really trained with from his uniform's standard utility belt. The security guard hesitated for a moment at the front door, then quickly dialed 911, frankly terrified at the thought of entering alone.

But then, just as the 911 operator was asking the nature of his emergency, a little girl shrieked and Eddie momentarily forgot his fear, fumbling with the stun gun's safety switch as he charged into the Swap Meet. "SECURITY!" he called without thinking, "POLICE ARE ON THE WAY!"

Moving towards the sounds of struggle, Eddie heard a gurgled *Daddy*, then spotted the tall black man in the dirty blue hospital scrubs through the open doorway of the building manager's office. He was down on the ground, slamming the face of a fat naked man...*the maintenance guy...Hector*...against the cold cement floor, again and again and again...

"*Daddy...STOP!*"

Eddie heard the little girl's voice hiccough in hysteria as he raced forward and jammed the prongs of the stun baton into the black man's shoulder, knocking him flat with the angry cicada buzz of a short, sharp shock.

When Ray came to in the rear of a caterwauling ambulance, his head was throbbing and his blood-smeared wrists were zip-cuffed to the side rails of a gurney. A busty Mexican-American paramedic was leaning towards him, doing something painful to his forehead as he rasped, "Where..."

- 128 -

"Please hold still," the paramedic instructed. "You fell and gashed your forehead on the side of a crate when you were subdued, and I need to stitch you up."

Ray tried again and managed, "*Where...is my daughter?*"

The paramedic finished her stitch and replied, "The girl was taken to Huntington Park Community for observation, which is exactly where *you're* going..."

"Is she all right? What...*what did he do to her...?*"

"Mr. Wyatt, you need to calm down or I'll have to sedate you."

Still disoriented, Ray attempted to rise to a sitting position. "Hey," he protested, tugging at his restraints in confusion. "Why can't I..."

"Mr. Wyatt..."

"What's going on?" Ray exclaimed, tugging harder. "Why the fuck am I *cuffed?* I was protecting my *daughter...*"

"You'll have a chance to speak to the officer in charge once we get to the hospital," the paramedic said firmly, plunging a syringe into the bicep of her thrashing patient. "But in the meantime, this will help you to *relax.*"

"No!" Ray cried, already feeling the sedative's warm rush in his veins. "That goddamn freak had my *baby...Joyce...*"

His words trailed off in a slur of anguish as his eyes stuttered shut, squeezing angry tears...

...and when they opened again, he saw at once that his situation had worsened. He was still cuffed, but now he found himself on a cot in a narrow, crowded infirmary with bars on the windows and uniformed guards at the door. The busty paramedic had either been deceitful or misinformed: he wasn't in Huntington Park. They'd taken him to the Los Angeles County Central Jail Hospital.

At first, the nurse on duty said it was because Huntington Park had been overcrowded with earthquake victims and the police still needed to question him. But when he was finally allowed a phone call, hours later, Indrani Jones revealed the true nature of his predicament: the district attorney intended to charge him with second degree murder in the death of one Hector J. Valenzuela.

"And it gets worse," she continued. "Because it turns out the victim had a cousin in the L.A.P.D."

"*Victim?*" Ray hissed into the prison phone. "The guy was a *fucking monster...*"

"Careful now," Indrani cautioned. "Remember where you are...you don't wanna be talking about the case with nobody but your lawyer, understand? I'm guessing you haven't seen a public defender yet, right?"

"No," Ray sighed, numb and exhausted.

"Well, good," Indrani replied. "I got someone better anyhow...a real street fighter I know from back in the day, Ozzie Tatum. Just do what he says and we'll get you through this, all right?"

Ray allowed himself a grim smile. He'd called Indrani because she was a trusted ally with genuine affection for his daughter, but also because the grizzled daycare provider knew the tricks, traps, and intricacies of the California penal code better than anyone else he'd ever met. She'd been an addict and a hustler in her early teens and a Black Panther in her twenties, and she'd fought like a lion to clear the name of her activist husband, Roland, who'd been gunned down in the '80s by a Gang in Blue Oakland P.D. narco squad. She'd spent the '90s as a gang mediator in L.A., and had at least as many friends in the Sheriff's Department as enemies.

She'd reached out to some of those friends when Joyce had first gone missing after the earthquake, and one of them later called Indrani to retrieve the frightened girl when she'd turned up at Huntington Park Community after the Valenzuela homicide. Indrani had been watching Ray's daughter ever since, and promised to bring her to the jail for a visit soon if Ozzie Tatum couldn't arrange bail in a timely fashion. "And there's more bad news."

Ray clenched his eyes tight, uncertain how much additional trouble he could reasonably bear, yet already surmising what Indrani was about to say: "Shirelle."

"Mm-hmm. She and that new husband of hers clocked the news about your arrest, and they've already got their lawyer filing to reopen the custody case..."

"No," Ray disclaimed, smacking his palm against the tile wall by the phone in angry negation.

"Don't you quit on me, Ray...now *listen*..."

But Ray had *stopped* listening. Like nerves devastated by fire damage, his emotions had finally overloaded, unable to process the relentless onslaught of pain, spiraling his consciousness into the animalistic binary of fight or flight until he was smashing the phone receiver against the cold tile wall, again and again and again...

...and then a scream engulfed him...

...and then anger consumed him...

...and annihilation...

...and annihilation...

...and...

SEKEM (Power, Energy, Light)

...annihilation...

...and annihilation...

...and annihilation...

...destroy it all...

...destroy...

...destroy you...

...I will fucking

destroy you...

...but first you will suffer...

...suffer...

...suffer forever...

...suffer...

...suffer for what you have done...

...suffer for what you have done to me...

...I will make you suffer for what you have done to me...

...I will make you crawl through brimstone and beg my forgiveness...

"Forgive me."

...I will make you suffer and beg my forgiveness, for not loving as I loved you...

"I'm sorry, Pete."

I crush the whore's throat with my cloven hoof to silence her. I smash her teeth with my pitchfork and stuff her mouth with hot ash.

I gather Karen's long, wild hair tight in my colossal red fist and tear it by the roots from her charred, bloody skull until...

"STOP!"

Who dares?

Who *dares* command a Lord of Hell?

A boy.

A child.

My child.

Pete Junior, floating above the Lake of Fire, my Golgotha of suffering.

"You look silly."

His quizzical expression, that sweet, chirruping voice.

...no...

...ignore it, ignore it, *think.*

It's not Petey.

It's Not Petey.

A Delusion.

Delusion.

I stare down at my cloven hooves, the pitchfork, my spiked, engorged red tail and...

...wait...

...what's happening?

I recall only *rage*...insatiable, intoxicating...

...*rage* at all of existence, rage at...

"*...Karen...*"

"...I'm sorry...forgive me..."

Karen, at my feet.

Not as I remember or imagine her, but as she wishes to be seen, at this moment...

...embryonic...

"Oh good...I see you found each other." Another thought not my own, memories of my father resurfacing like a sandbar as the tide of my fury recedes. "Welcome back."

"*...back?*"

"From lust and fury, respectively," Raquel smiles as her palazzo slowly fades into being around us.

"Back from Hell, you mean," I murmur, realizing with some embarrassment that I still resemble a bright red demonic satyr.

"A strange place for a reunion," my father nods as he drapes a large gold Pashmina over Karen's hairless white form, still curled in a vaguely humanoid approximation of the fetal position. "Though I must say what truly concerns me is how you *got* there."

"I...I don't remember," I reply, sheepishly retracting my horns and hooves.

"No, I wouldn't think so," Raquel sighs. "I like to flatter myself that I'm a bit more in control of my passions than *either* of you...yet even so, I barely withstood the Screaming Skulls at Valhalla."

"The...*what?*"

"*Chaos,*" my father explains patiently. "Remember? When you abandoned yourself to rage the first time, you came to your senses in the Viking Construct. But the second time, the rage *came to you*...to both of us...which is, of course, somewhat disturbing, since it means even here in the ultimate sovereignty of self there are limits to free will. I'm just thankful your identity was strong enough to withstand so much unfocused Id...and since Feelies are forever courting that Energy, I imagine you must have perceived Karen's soul in the midst of it all, which then directed your anger into some kind of S&M Hellscape until you finally snapped yourselves out of it."

"Not *us*," murmurs the lump beneath the Pashmina. "It was Petey."

"*Petey,*" I gasp, as if suddenly recalling a shared dream forgotten moments after waking. "*Yes*, I saw him, too...at least I *thought* so, but...I didn't believe it..."

"I see your father's already got you doubting your senses," replies a bemused, husky voice reminiscent of the woman I'd once known as my wife. "And, yes, Bob...sorry, *Raquel*...I know we don't have physical *senses* anymore. It's just a figure of speech."

"I didn't say anything," my father huffs, peevish.

"Yeah, well, I'm sure you were *thinking* it." All at once, Karen emerges from beneath the shawl with the face and hair of her last moments alive. "And Pete, *you're* probably wondering if *I'm* even really

- 136 -

me, right?"

When I don't answer right away, she continues: "God, it's like you both have Capgras syndrome or something..."

The phrase instantly triggers a recollection, far quicker and more vividly than my earthly memory could have processed: one of my first cases as a law clerk for the Los Angeles District Attorney's Office, a woman who'd shot her husband, claiming he was an impostor. The defense team had called an expert witness from UCLA's Brain Injury Research Center to explain Capgras syndrome to the jury: "A cognitive dysfunction, a delusional misidentification preventing individuals from recognizing their nearest and dearest."

"I mean, I *get* it," Karen says. "Your image of people turns out to be false, so you're not sure *what* to believe and next thing you're back to first principles, *cogito ergo sum*. But I don't just think therefore I am...I am because I'm *thought of*, the circuit completed...otherwise, I'm nothing more than a dead universe of self, torn by meaningless storms of emotion, desperate for incoming messages beyond my own echoing consciousness. And yet I'm not solipsistic enough to believe every connection I feel is somehow just another refection of *myself*. I barely have the energy to imagine my *own* existence, let alone yours...which is how I *know* you're here right now, even if you're not sure about me."

"Yeah, well," I respond pointedly, more certain of *this* Karen than either of the previous Not Karens I've encountered, "apparently I'm easy to *fool*."

"Hey, I said I was sorry, okay? I'm not letting myself off the hook for ignoring your death, my behavior in life...it's the reason I followed you to Hell. I sensed your rage sweeping through...y'know, *where I was*...and I just let it take me. I wanted to apologize. Because I really do understand, Pete, *believe me*. I mean, not that it's an excuse, but I was pretty outta control when I found out, too..."

"What is she..." I say to my father, then turn back to Karen, "...what are you talking about?"

"After the accident," she replies, "I wanted...I really did want us to all stay together, but...I mean, you know how disorienting it is. When I saw those headlights coming towards us, I was surprised and terrified and then I was dead...and my first coherent thought...my very first *impulse* was to find Petey, but, y'know...it was already *too late*..."

"Too late for *what?*" I say, clenching in sudden, unaccountable dread.

"Wait...you mean your father didn't *tell you?*"

"Karen," Dad cautions, tone sharpening. "There's no point in..."

"In *what?*" she snaps back. "I thought you believed in *hard cold Reality.*"

"Yes, but not gratuitous cruelty."

Ignoring her, Karen fixes me with a dark-eyed stare that quickly expands into a long, black tunnel. "You want *rage?* Well, here's what *our child* saw at the moment of *his* death..."

I HATE YOU!

I HATE YOU!

HATE
YOU!

I HATE YOU!

I HATE YOU!

It's my own face, screaming back at me, exploding into blood and brain and skull fragments which instantly reform into Karen shrieking...

"I HATE YOU!"

Then the words are lost in a piercing, unbearable shriek of pain and terror as her body is ripped apart like bloodfruit in a deafening collision of rending steel and shattering glass, unleashing a spray of sickening black and grey worms from her torso like dangling intestines as the two halves of Karen expand again into full figures, each vomiting forth still more of the tubular strands before splitting again, and reforming...splitting and reforming...all the while screeching hatred.

Soon, there are dozens and hundreds of eviscerated Karens, spewing worms from every orifice, and I am drowning in a slimy, wriggling flood of invertebrates, inhaling and swallowing them like thick strands of mucous until I hear my father shout, *"ENOUGH!"*

The voice is masculine and familiar, drawing my attention to my father, as he looked on the day of the accident, now gathering all the horrific imagery I've just experienced into his arms and crushing it down to a crinkled ball of wastepaper before disposing of it in the fireplace of his palazzo.

But for once, a glimmer of comprehension focuses my horrified confusion as I turn to Karen and say, "The nightmare..."

"Exactly," she replies with something like contempt.

Pete, Jr. had been an effortless child, sleeping through the night from his earliest weeks, preternaturally calm and well-behaved. He'd never really thrown tantrums or tested the limits of misbehavior, but he did suffer one overpowering, irrational phobia: worms.

For whatever reason, he'd always dreaded and hated them, making our thoughtful golden child downright unmanageable on the mornings after rainstorms when they'd festooned the sidewalk in grotesque wriggling clots.

Worst of all was the day he inadvertently discovered the capacity of repulsive, phallic parchment worms and other species to regenerate when severed. For weeks afterwards, Petey would dream of the endlessly replicating creatures and scream himself awake, hysterical with fear.

Additionally, my son, it seemed, had also inherited certain of my specific insecurities in his short life. From the moment he began forming words, he'd frequently asked Karen and myself for reassurances of our love...meaning the imagery of the two of us screaming hatred would have been just as frightening to Petey as the worms.

"So...you're saying he was traumatized by the accident, and that somehow made his nightmares come true when he died?"

"No," Karen says, radiating anger. "The nightmares were *inflicted*."

"*What?*" I gasp, shocked and appalled for the child I wasn't there to protect.

"It's true, unfortunately," my father sighs. "For all the talk of salvation and souls reaching enlightenment, I'm afraid when *everyone's* invited to the afterlife, you inevitably wind up spending eternity with a whole lotta *assholes*."

Karen releases a snort of weary, bitter laughter as Dad continues, "The sad fact is, death and all its power doesn't seem to change what, for lack of a better term, we might as well call *human nature*. Which means, in a realm of infinite possibility, the best and *worst* of our impulses will find infinite expression. You've seen...and very recently *experienced*...the soul's capacity for inflicting pain on others who desire or *think* they deserve it. But that's not enough for those who wish to impose their will...and cruelty...without constraint. There are those in This Place consumed with Delusions of power, believing themselves to be omnipotent gods...or even just plain *God*...with infinite, unchallenged sovereignty over all of Creation. And for the most part, those idiots are pretty much harmless.

"It's the ones who *recognize* their powerlessness that you have to watch out for, since the mere *awareness* of independent thought outside their control simply enrages them...and their fury is cold and insatiable.

They've spent decades...centuries, *millennia*...studying This Place...and some of these would-be gods and their followers can be pretty nasty customers..."

"Like the fucking *Commissar*," Karen spits. "He was Petey's Welcome."

"Short for Welcoming Committee," my father clarifies. "You see, it's common practice for souls to greet new arrivals here in hopes of easing their transition...ancestors reuniting with descendants and that sort of thing. For example, if you're part of this one tribe I know, the Ashanti, there's a whole ritual with the forebears where you have to jump through all sorts of hoops before you're admitted to Asamando, this very consistent, very specific Construct where everyone essentially knows everyone else and visitors are basically ignored.

"But most Welcoming Committees are fairly ad hoc affairs...friends and family or afterlife communities showing up as they become aware of major tragedies and individual passings. We can't tell the future here, you see...we can only observe events in the material world, so it's often hard to predict when a soul will arrive in This Place. Still, news travels fast and Welcoming Committees typically assemble at the speed of thought to greet and protect fledgling souls from confusion or the deliberate misperceptions inflicted by those wishing to manipulate and Delude...which, unfortunately, is exactly what this evil old soul called the Commissar did to Petey..."

"But why?" I exclaim. "And why Petey?"

"Because he was *vulnerable*," Karen explains in a tone laced with venom. "These Delusionists, they watch and wait for strays, like any other predator. You never really knew your grandparents, and my family...well, let's just say none of us were especially close. Plus me and you didn't exactly have deep roots in L.A. and most of our close friends are still alive, so we didn't really have anybody waiting for us on the Other Side...and Delusionists *watch* for shit like that. They network together and track the living, just waiting for strays like us to die..."

"Actually, they'll pretty much go after *anyone*," my father interrupts. "It's just that other Welcoming Committees usually drown them out...and they don't limit themselves to new arrivals, either, which is why I'm such an evangelist of the Real."

"So...what happened to Petey?" I ask, simultaneously dreading and desperate for the answer.

"Well, this fucking Commissar..." Karen begins.

"Nicolai Slivko," my father interjects, ever the mentor. "Used to run the secret police under Stalin until he raped and murdered one too many young boys, then became an unperson in the Siberian gulag before slitting his own throat with a bayonet, so...not exactly what you'd call an *enlightened* soul."

"Anyway," Karen continues, "this fucker had *studied* Petey...he knew his fears and just *hammered* them as soon as the opportunity presented itself...this poor innocent soul, all alone in a big empty void..."

Karen's voice, or rather the projection of thoughts she'd been directing at us, ceases abruptly as her form dissolves back into an amorphous blob...which my father swiftly merges with in some form of afterlife embrace, emanating support and concern.

Then, after a moment, my remembered image of Karen rematerializes, fixing me with the projection of a gaze I'd once thought

I knew well.

"It's just...I was alone, too, you know? My parents are still alive, you were in a coma, your father..."

"I stayed with Tilly," Dad says quietly. "I didn't know any better."

"I don't blame you," Karen replies, merging again with him slightly. "But everything happened so *fast*. I found Petey on instinct, in the middle of a nightmare...and his *soul was screaming*..."

Her form wavers again in what I now understand as emotion, then solidifies as she continues, "It was the most terrible thing I've ever experienced...I was paralyzed...I didn't know what to do or how to stop it...only that my child was suffering, terribly, and then..."

Images from the crumpled memory that my father tossed in the fire appear again in the flames: my wife, torn asunder, endlessly...my child, insane with fear as his form is sucked down into a wormy vortex...

...before *exploding* in a cosmic scream of obliteration leaving nothing, an absence.

"Chaos draws Chaos," my father reiterates. "Petey disappeared from my consciousness...and then I lost track of Karen, too, until she eventually resurfaced with the Feelies..."

"You know I hate that term," my one-time wife complains.

"Sorry."

"I mean, Jesus, you make it sound like I was just tripping balls at some rave, like a fucking teenager. I lost my *son*...I thought I'd lost everything. So I lost *myself* for awhile in pure sensation, total communion, and found...love, intimacy...*ecstasy* like I'd never

- 144 -

experienced..."

Then, as if suddenly remembering my presence, Karen's form projects a shrug. "Sorry, Pete...but it's true."

"No, I understand," I say, honestly, too depleted to feel more than a distant echo of jealousy. "But you *didn't* lose everything...Petey's not gone...we had some kind of contact, just now, and he's...*whole*...he remembers...:"

"I know, he came to me, too," Karen replies. "It's why you found me, in your rage, why I let you..."

"Um, yeah..." I say, embarrassed again. "I'm, uh...sorry for all that."

"Don't apologize," Karen scolds. "There's no point. We all know everything here, if we choose to...we're all just raging balls of hate and lust and fear and love and all the rest in different recipes, with all the same ingredients. I didn't love you enough, you didn't have all that I needed...but *no one* gets enough love and *nobody* gets all they need from another soul...not even the one soul we *created*."

"You're right, of course," I sigh. "And even if the accident never happened, Petey would have grown up and moved on eventually, and I suppose you and I would have grown further and further apart...it's just hard to bear knowing that all the time in eternity can't replace whatever moments I still might've had left to believe in the three of us together, inseparable."

"Which brings us back to my earlier concern," Dad interjects, "because I'm afraid there may not actually be quite as much eternity left as you think..."

SEKHU (*The Remains*)

"I'm glad he's dead, and I'd do it again!"

Ray made the statement an hour or two after the incident. The interrogating officers – friends of Hector J. Valenzuela's cousin on the force – had recorded it, and the D.A. played it for the jury. Then she asked the defendant if his feelings had changed since the day he cracked the victim's head like an egg against the cold, hard floor of the Los Compadres back office.

I'm sorry. Indrani Jones mouthed the words like an incantation from the gallery of the Huntington Park Courtroom, willing them into Ray's mouth and the ears of the jury. She prayed it was all he needed to say, all they needed to hear.

Not that she'd had much luck with her prayers of late. The trial itself was proof of that.

Ozzie Tatum had sworn the case would never even reach a jury, citing the media deification of a Texas rancher who'd escaped indictment (and even arrest) for the use of "deadly force" when his own five year old daughter had been sexually assaulted by a farmhand back in 2012. Of course, Ray's lawyer wasn't naïve: South Central was a long way from the Lone Star State, and the death of a cop's cousin in his place of employment at the hands of a black man during a spasm of widespread looting was a scenario with obvious potential for racially-charged misrepresentation. Complicating matters even further was the wrinkle that Valenzuela had been mentally challenged, with an IQ in the low 50s.

But public opinion had been overwhelmingly on Ray's side

when the story first hit local news outlets and talk radio stations. A father defending his daughter against a sexual predator was an easy morality play to handicap, and Ozzie fully expected his client to go free after jumping through some procedural hoops to satisfy Valenzuela's cousin and the letter of the law.

The lawyer's one concern centered on the crucial difference between Ray and his "folk hero" media predecessor. In the Texas case, the father had used force to stop a sexual assault in progress, then called 911 after knocking the rapist unconscious with his fists. A recording of his conversation with the police operator revealed genuine panic in the rancher's voice as he cried for an ambulance. He clearly hadn't intended to kill anyone. His actions were fully justified, even commendable, yet despite the extremity of the situation, his regret about taking a life was palpable.

The same could not be said of Ray, who projected only grim satisfaction when discussing Valenzuela's fate. "My baby girl's never gonna be the same again," the convicted orderly hissed during his first meeting with Ozzie. "She's *never* gonna forget what happened to her...and me bein' arrested and her crazy bitch of a mother back in her life just makes everything *worse*. So do I think the motherfucker that *caused* all this got what he deserved? *Hell*, yeah."

"But you can't *say* that," Ozzie stressed, knowing despite his best instincts that he'd eventually have to put his client on the stand to answer for the recorded statement. "People *understand* why you did what you did...only murder's still illegal last time I checked, so you gotta give the judge and jury permission to let you off the hook. You gotta detest your sins and be heartily sorry for having offended and all that shit...'cause not everyone's rootin' for you to walk on this, man."

Valenzuela's cousin, in particular, was pulling every string he could to effectuate a conviction, and regardless of politics or public sentiment, Ozzie knew the D.A. would make him earn whatever leniency he could wrangle on his client's behalf.

Ray's ex-wife, Shirelle, turned out to be the real problem, though. An erstwhile pill-popping, coke-snorting blackout drunk who'd found religion and married her A.A. sponsor, she was a surprisingly formidable adversary, given to clipped, formal diction, unblinking eye contact, and conspicuous sobriety. She led the prosecution to a domestic battery charge in Ray's past and generally abetted their efforts to paint Ozzie's client as a rageaholic with impulse control issues in a blatant yet potentially effective gambit to regain custody of her daughter.

"I know my former husband's temper because I've seen it firsthand," she told a smattering of reporters at a hastily organized press conference shortly after the murder, passing around time-stamped photos of a purple bruise on her skin from the night she called the cops on Ray after a screaming match turned physical.

The photos were naturally admitted into evidence at her ex-husband's eventual trial, and Ray admitted under oath that he'd indeed lost his temper one night long ago and grabbed Shirelle roughly after she'd drunkenly attempted to kidnap their infant daughter.

"*Kidnap?*" the D.A. had repeated, flashing a skeptical glance at the jury.

"We'd been fighting...probably about her drinking," Ray had explained, as calmly as possible. "I don't recall exactly, but her alcoholism was definitely a source of friction at the time. Anyhow, she always threatened to leave me when she got mad, and this one time she took Joyce from her crib and went for the door, and I worried she might fall and hurt them both, 'cause she was so inebriated..."

"And you *weren't?*"

"No, sir."

"According to the police report, you'd also been drinking that evening."

"I'd had a couple beers with dinner, but..."

"So Ms. Quarle, your ex-wife, is holding an infant...your daughter...and you *grab* her by the arm..."

"*Objection!*" Ozzie had cried out. "Counsel is testifying..."

"Your Honor, I'm merely paraphrasing a police report that's already been entered into evidence. If opposing counsel would prefer me to quote directly from the report..."

"Objection overruled."

Indrani had watched it all play out from the gallery as the heavyset Latina D.A. goaded Ray into admitting he'd wrenched Shirelle's arm behind her back as she'd held their infant daughter in the other.

"I didn't have a *choice*..."

"So you don't regret your actions."

"...Shirelle had her keys...she was gonna *drive off*..."

Indrani had seen the seeds of doubt taking root in the jury as the D.A. skillfully chipped away at the would-be "folk hero," recasting the righteously protective father as a remorseless, quick-tempered vigilante.

And she knew as well as Ozzie Tatum how important it was for Ray to express remorse, even before the prosecutor played the interrogation room tape of him snarling, *"I'm glad he's dead, and I'd do it again!"*

So Indrani mouthed *I'm sorry* when the D.A. asked the defendant if his feelings about Hector J. Valenzuela had changed since the day of the earthquake.

"I'm sorry the man had a sickness," Ray said quietly, feeling Shirelle's hateful gaze even as he cast his eyes downward to avoid it.

"You think Mr. Valenzuela had a sickness?"

Ray kept his eyes fixed on the rail of the witness stand and his teeth clenched in silence. He knew what he was supposed to do, what Ozzie and Indrani wanted him to say...how *sorry* he was about killing the man who'd fingered his five year old girl, who'd forced Baby Joyce to...

"Mr. Wyatt?"

You've gotta humble yourself to the law. That was Ozzie's advice when the lawyer coached him before the trial, and Ray understood, he really did. He'd received a ridiculous jaywalking ticket once after failing to cross a deserted street at the walk. A fat white cop perched on a motorcycle half a block away beckoned him over and issued a citation for $190.00.

Ray was furious: it felt less a civic punishment and more like a mugging. Yet he dutifully reported for traffic court alongside a dozen or more fellow miscreants, where a world-weary judge helpfully explained the proceedings. "When I call your name, approach the bench. I'll ask you to enter a plea of guilty or not guilty. I don't want explanations, I don't want arguments. There's another group just like yours scheduled to appear in this courtroom an hour from now, and another group after that. And *another* group after them. So my job is to keep things moving along, understand? If you feel you were charged in error, if you would like to schedule a date on the county's overcrowded calendar, secure a lawyer, and take up the court's valuable time fighting your ticket, you may do so if you must. That is your right. However, I am not here to listen to arguments, and I will not tolerate any theatrics. All I want is your plea: guilty or not guilty. Did you do it or did you not? Okay? Are we clear? Then let's get started."

Twenty minutes later, Ray's name was called and he admitted he was guilty of jaywalking, swallowing the exasperation he assumed was evident in his expression. And because the issuing officer wasn't present in the courtroom, the judge explained that he was dismissing the citation – though his sharp, jaded gaze seemed to say: *this is order, not morality. This is how it works. You admit you broke the rule, I acknowledge the rule is flawed. You acknowledge the sin and receive absolution.*

You humble yourself to the law.

But law wasn't justice.

"Mr. Wyatt, please answer the question. Do you believe Mr. Valenzuela was sick?"

"No," Ray said, unable to stop the words. "I think he was *evil.*"

Ozzie Tatum instantly saw the *L.A. Times* headline "HE WAS EVIL" in a flash of precognition as a murmur swept through the courtroom. In the gallery, Indrani closed her eyes.

"*He raped my girl,*" Ray continued, emotion rising like bile in his throat. "And now I can't be with her when she needs me the *most*..."

"So it's not that Mr. Valenzuela needed *treatment*," the D.A. pressed, "it's not that he couldn't help himself...you're saying he deliberately committed an evil act."

Ozzie's desperate objection was overruled as Ray said, "It doesn't *matter* if he couldn't help himself..."

"You're saying his actions were, quote, *evil*...even if he couldn't stop himself from committing them?"

Ray saw the prosecutor flash a knowing glance at the jury as he answered, "*Nothing's* more evil than harming a child, and I did what *any* father..."

"So you don't regret your actions?"

"*What else was I supposed to do?*" Ray cried in frustration, the sane man in the asylum, the doctors refusing to listen.

"And you'd do it again."

"*Yes*, goddammit!" Ray exclaimed. "How can you expect me to apologize for *saving my daughter?*"

He glanced around the courtroom, baffled at the expressions of dismay and disapproval reflecting back like stars from an alternate reality where his words and actions had entirely different meanings and his innocence was somehow in doubt.

"No further questions," the D.A. said without enthusiasm.

KHU *(The Guardian Angel)*

"Bad things happen to good people," Dad says by way of explanation, "and Jesus doesn't always save. In fact, the *real* Jesus hasn't been seen in This Place for centuries. Maybe He's with his Father in some Real, *secret* Heaven nobody's told me about...but as far as I can tell 'God helps those who help themselves' is just another way of saying we're on our own."

"Okay," I say, "but what does that have to do with eternity ending and all the rest of it?"

"Chaos," Karen replies, glancing to my father for confirmation.

"Exactly," Dad nods. "Because, as I say, unlimited individual freedom simply isn't enough for humanity. The two of you were driven to rage and despair by the realization you could no longer control or protect Petey, and that's typical...very few are content within themselves. Most of us, to a greater or lesser extent, seek to control other souls."

Then, focusing on me, he adds: "You wanted Karen to love you as you loved her. Tilly refuses to accept the Reality of my true nature. Likewise, some of my Jewish friends can't bear the concept of Hitler living happily in his own Delusional Aryan paradise, unpunished, even though he no longer has any actual power to hurt them. In This Place, Der Fuhrer merely surrounds himself with *illusions* of power...yet that's not enough for his old pals Eichmann and Goebbels...nor is it for Caligula or Lucrezia Borgia or Bull Connor or Idi Amin or the Commissar or any number of beings in This Place obsessed with controlling *actual* souls.

"And so, as you've seen, there are those who manipulate new arrivals and susceptible dupes, projecting Delusions to feed on their fear and confusion. Yet, much to the chagrin of Delusionists, the effects are seldom permanent. For example..."

My father's form sweeps to the balcony of his palazzo, now suspended over the fiery pits of the Hell Construct I'd seen before.

"...I'm sure you remember *Mary*."

With that, I find myself standing with Karen on a jagged outcropping of brimstone overlooking the tilted flat rock where the plump nurse who cared for me at Cedars-Sinai lies chained and naked as demons scald her flesh with jets of fiery piss from massive red erections.

"Oh, God..." Karen groans, "Like I need this bullshit right now."

And then she's gone, leaving me alone in Hell.

"Don't worry," Dad's voice explains. "Karen just went to Ocean."

"*What?*" I say, unable to locate any projection of my father's image in the surrounding Inferno.

"It's a Construct of endless blue water filled with dolphins and whatnot...very relaxing. I expect she'll rejoin us when our current task is completed."

"Which is *what* exactly?" I say, ignoring the sudden attack of a razor-taloned harpy until the repellent bird woman flies away in frustration. "And where are *you*?"

"You'll see," I hear my father reply, a trace of mischievous satisfaction in my perception of his voice. "Watch Mary...I think I know how to snap her out of this."

A piercing shriek draws my attention back to the tortured nurse as a tiny pink head abruptly bursts from her bloody splayed vagina.

The demons, clearly startled by the unexpected development, cease their pissing as a voice I recognize booms, "PUSH!"

It's Ray, the tall black orderly from Cedars-Sinai hospital.

Only it's not, I quickly realize: it's my father, imitating someone the nurse remembers from her life on Earth.

"*PUSH!*"

Mary cries out, this time in exertion, straining to push the baby clear.

One of the demons, recovering from his momentary disorientation, grabs for the blood-slick infant with sinewy red fingers, which merely pass through the tiny, wriggling creature as it levitates out and up from between Mary's legs.

An image of Ray materializes in front of the demon as the hellion's scream of frustration is drowned by the wailing squall of the newborn hovering into the orderly's hands.

"It's a girl!"

Mary reaches for the baby, hands no longer constrained by forgotten chains while the rock they once bound her to becomes an illusory delivery table in the Cedars maternity ward. "Oh, sweetie," she coos, tears slicking her glistening cheeks, "I'm sorry...I'm *sorry*..."

"There, you see?" It's Raquel's voice, but I don't see my father in the delivery room and Mary doesn't seem to notice the words. "That's how it usually works. A malevolent Welcoming Committee traps someone in a Delusion, and it's up to us Rangers to snap them out of it."

"Rangers?"

Mary looks up in surprise, aware now of the voice and projected self I didn't think to hide from her, and says, "Mr. Herlinger?"

"Oh, uh, yeah," My father as Not Ray says quickly. "It's a whole *day* of miracles! Ol' Herlinger's *alive!*"

"I'm...I'm very confused," Mary squeaks, clutching the infant tightly to her bosom as she blinks in frightened disorientation.

"Sshh, hey, it's okay," Not Ray says kindly, placing a gentle hand on her shoulder. "You're safe now."

Mary gasps in recognition as a fervent canine tongue laps at her double chin...and I realize I'm now watching from outside through a window as the chubby nurse bolts upright in the futon bed of her tiny Pacoima condo to gape down at a pair of brown deagle pups, wriggling in her arms where the baby had been just a moment before.

"Ray!" I hear the nurse cry out.

"Good morning," Not Ray says, now sitting in a folding chair pulled up to her futon. "How you feelin'?"

"I...I had a baby," Mary replies, baffled, staring down at the puppies.

"You had a bad dream," Not Ray corrects.

Mary blinks at him, uncertain and vaguely troubled, then murmurs, "It seemed pretty *real.*"

"Real *scary* from the sound of it...you were screaming, so I just wanted to make sure everything was okay. Nice PJs, by the way."

"...uh...thanks." I see Mary is now clad in Winnie the Pooh

- 156 -

pajamas, and the cozy familiarity seems to comfort her as she stammers, "...but Ray, what are you *doing* here?"

"Well, I came as soon as I could after the earthquake, and your door was open, so..."

"Earthquake?"

"Y'know, that big earthquake we had?" Not Ray says, leaning closer. "Just after your shift the other day? Remember? I left you a message about the service for Mr. Herlinger at the Interfaith Chapel..."

Mary blinks again in dawning comprehension of the memory. "Yes, and...I called you back to say I'd meet you, and then..."

"And then you said your prayers."

Mary's eyes go wide in understanding just short of believing.

"And you prayed for Jesus to bless poor Mr. Herlinger and accept him into Heaven," Not Ray continues, taking Mary's hand. "And then?"

"Just..." Imaginary tears seep from Mary's eyes, memory echoes of a lost world not yet abandoned. "...thunder...I thought I heard thunder..."

"That was the earthquake. It shook your building..."

"The building looks okay to me," Mary trembles, abandoning the thought even as she expresses it. "Oh God..."

"It's okay, Mary."

"*It wasn't a dream...*"

"But it wasn't real, either."

"This is *Hell*," Mary shrinks from Not Ray, imaginary deagle puppies disintegrating to ash in her grasp. "I'm still in *Hell!*"

Hot, acrid smoke curls from the seams of the window frame

and up through the floorboards as Not Ray says hastily, "*No...*"

The walls and windows and floor of the apartment explode away, and Mary finds herself floating in thick white billowing wisps of cumulonimbus while Not Ray exclaims, "...you're in *Heaven!*"

I recognize the Construct immediately: a duplicate of the cloudscape where Dad as Not Jesus stashed Mom, Pearly Gates agleam in the distance.

"But...I'm a *sinner*," Mary cries, disbelieving. "That Operation Rescue man was right...we worked for *baby killers*..."

"Now, I know you don't believe that," Not Ray says, floating beside her.

"It's *true!*"

"But that ain't what this is really about...*is it?*"

Mary hesitates, then looks away in shame, acknowledging the question with a tiny, frightened "...*no*..."

"So tell me...tell *God*...why you think you don't belong in Heaven."

"*I can't!*" Mary whimpers.

"Yes, you can," Not Ray smiles, golden light haloing around him as his illusory face shimmers and transforms into the bearded visage of Not Jesus. "Tell me, child. For I already know...and have already forgiven thee."

Mary drops to her knees in the clouds, unable to meet Not Jesus's gaze as words spill from her soul in a gush. "Oh my Lord...in the name of the Father, and of the Son, and of the Holy Spirit, my last confession was...was...a week ago? I'm sorry, Lord, I don't remember..."

"What do you have to confess, my child?"

"I..."

Mary stops, unable to speak the words, yet so eager to unburden herself to Not Jesus that she wills the story of her shame all around us. The clouds of Heaven drift away like morning fog to reveal a row of white clapboard cabins along the edge of a dark forest, ghostly in the pre-dawn gloom.

The clatter of a screen door in the misty chill draws my attention to the farthest building as a lithe figure emerges, then melts into the woods. Invisible, we follow.

A thin, nearsighted girl in blue shorts and a white C.Y.O. summer camp t-shirt tiptoes through the pine needles, ears perked and nervous as a rabbit's. She hears a muffled groan of pain and whispers urgently: *"Heather?"*

"Go away!" a frightened voice hisses, somewhere off to the right. "Leave me alone!"

But the gangly, thirteen-year-old Mary navigates towards the response. She'd awakened to the sound of weeping a short time earlier, then listened as her bunkmate, Heather, slipped quietly from their cabin.

As a bedwetter, Mary knew the dread of nocturnal discovery, creeping through the darkness with damp bundled sheets, praying she'd reach the laundry hamper to bury her shame undetected. And Heather seemed like a girl with plenty of secrets of her own.

So when her sullen, overdeveloped bunkmate failed to return a few anxious minutes later, Mary hadn't roused Miss Halligan, the cabin's resident counselor, but instead chose to investigate on her own for the sake of discretion...

...a decision I can already feel her regretting as she passes through the tree line into the darkness of the forest, where Heather is crouched against a gnarled sweet birch in obvious pain. The busty girl's underwear and shorts are down around her ankles and she appears to be urinating until Mary realizes the liquid coursing down her bare white legs is blood.

"Oh my *gosh*! I'll get Miss Halligan..."

"*NO!*" Heather grunts, clutching one of Mary's bony wrists to prevent her escape before screaming in a fresh spasm of agony.

"*Ow! Let go!*" Mary cries as Heather's grip tightens, her fellow camper's aqua lacquered fingernails biting into her flesh.

Then Heather screams and Mary nearly faints as she glimpses a gory clump emerging from her bunkmate's vagina.

"*Help me!*" Heather gasps, releasing her grip as she tumbles backwards into a tangle of roots, legs splayed and slick with fluid.

"*How?*"

"*Get it out of me!*" Heather shrieks, writhing and sweating, fists beating the ground.

Mary gapes in shocked paralysis, unable to comprehend what's happening until Heather yelps through a final push, expelling the infant with a wet, farting plop.

"A *baby*..."

"*No,*" her mortified bunkmate hisses.

Then Mary sees the bloody newborn. And vomits.

The tiny face appears smashed, flesh torn from lip to nose in a deep cleft beneath sunken, puckered eyes. Fused pink fists swat the air as the infant releases a faint, rattling wheeze, struggling for breath.

"*Get it OUT of me!*" Heather cries again, wild-eyed and desperate.

"It is," Mary murmurs, woozy, trying not to be sick again. "It's out."

"No! It's still *attached!*"

Mary's legs threaten to buckle and she braces herself against the sweet birch, peering cautiously down until she glimpses the wriggly coil of flesh snaking out from between her bunkmate's legs to the wriggling, deformed infant at her feet. "Oh, *God...*"

"Cut it! Use a rock!"

"I'll get Miss Halligan..."

"No! Please...*please!*" Heather wails as Mary straightens up, desperate to run back to the cabin. "You can't tell anyone! They'll kill me!"

"Who?"

Heather doesn't answer, but instead scrambles backwards, grasping for stones, tugging the infant behind her. "No! *Stop!*" Mary exclaims, dropping to her knees in search of a sharp rock. "I'll do it!"

"Cut the cord! *Hurry!*"

Raking the mossy ground with her fingers, Mary squeaks in distress as her fingers brush against the remains of a shattered whiskey bottle. Clutching the intact neck like a handle, she saws into the umbilical cord with a protruding shard, nearly gagging as the tubular mass oozes and tears and finally severs clean.

"Now let me get Miss Halligan!"

"No!" Heather insists, tugging up her shorts and soiled underwear. "You gotta help me bury it!"

Mary can only stare in mute disbelief as the frantic teen mother launches forward, grabbing her by the shoulders to prevent her escape. "Nobody can find out!"

"But..."

"Can't you see it's *deformed?*" Heather exclaims, nodding at the twisted creature between them, helpless and squirming in the mulch. "That's what *happens!*"

"Happens *when?*"

"If you do it with someone *related,*" Heather sobs, unstrung and humiliated. "It was never supposed to be *in* me...that's why it came out that way!"

Mary falls silent again, staring down at the pathetic misshapen creature on the ground as Heather shakes her, desperate. "Promise you won't tell anyone...swear to *Jesus!*"

The infant's rasping wheeze already seems to be fading, as if with embarrassment at its own brief, misguided existence, and Mary finally whispers, "*I swear.*"

I watch as shadows of memory play out the remainder of the story: two silent girls, side by side in the pre-dawn chill, waiting until the last of the life drains from the doomed incestuous child before dropping to their knees to dig a rabbit hole grave with their hands in the dirt.

"And you never broke your oath to Me," Not Jesus says, rising over the horizon like a blinding sun, bathing Mary's soul in the illusion of golden warmth.

"No," she replies, eyes downcast, her skinny teen form slowly inflating back to the contours of her adult body image. "I never told anyone."

"You kept your promise to her...and to Me."

"But I killed a *child*," Mary weeps. "A *baby*..."

"You allowed a soul which I had recalled to expire," Not Jesus says gently, floating down to lay a beneficent hand on her shoulder.

"We could have saved it," the nurse insists, still unable to gaze upon my father's disguise. "I saw children born with far worse defects survive at the hospital...and their parents *loved* them..."

"The child in the forest would not have survived. You could not have saved him."

"I'm still *responsible*," Mary insists. "I thought it was a monster...I *wanted* it to die...I just wanted it all to be over, I...I cared more about not getting in *trouble* than I did about a *living soul*!"

"And you punished yourself for it," my father replies, summoning Mary's unprotected thoughts and memories into a flickering panorama of the empty rooms and solitude of her mortal existence. "So ashamed and repulsed by the wages of carnal sin that you rejected every human intimacy, barricading yourself against love as if you'd never known Me."

Mary drops to her knees again, mirrored by the shadows of countless prayers at the altars and bedsides of her devout earthly life. "But I *do* know You, Lord!"

"Then why hast thou judged thyself," Dad says, shifting his cadence deeper and angrier as his appearance transforms into that of a Sistine, silver-haired Jehovah, "when thou know'st the Lord alone shalt judge the quick and the dead?"

"I'm sorry, Father..." Mary quakes meekly, frightened by my

father's suddenly booming voice.

"IF THOU KNOW'ST ME," Not Jehovah booms, "WHY HAST THOU SUFFERED THE JUDGMENT OF *FALSE GODS?*"

The shadows of Mary's life darken into smoke above the fiery Hell Construct where she'd been chained to the rock just moments or eternities before. Only now, one of the "demons" who'd coaxed her there stands revealed as nothing more than a paunchy bald suburbanite with an Operation Rescue button pinned to the lapel of his ugly Rayon sport coat.

"But...*how?*" Mary stammers, and I feel a sudden, unexpected swell of pride for my father's masterfully benevolent manipulations, mingled with a guilty pang of satisfaction at the realization I've progressed enough in my understanding of This Place to finally comprehend at least *some* of what I'm seeing.

"Because Satan is the king of lies!" I say impulsively, revealing myself as an angel just half an instant after thinking how nice it would be to show my father how far I've progressed.

Mary yelps in startled surprise as Not Jehovah shoots me a look of annoyance and rumbles, "As the disciple John hath written, the devil is a liar and the *father* of lies...yet Satan is no *king* and hast no dominion here but for the *deceptions* he placeth before thine eyes."

I go back to being invisible.

Mary barely notices my disappearance as she hovers above the Operation Rescue man and whispers, "*I know him...*"

"Then you know he's no *devil,*" my father replies, gentling his voice while Not Jehovah dissolves into blinding white light, obscuring all but Mary's perception of herself and the image of a Holy Ghost dove flapping above her.

"But...I was *tortured*..." she says. "If I'm forgiven, then why did I *suffer?*"

"Pride," my father trills. "When you judge *yourself*, you allow your *mind* to make a Hell of Heaven. When you ignore My forgiveness, you refuse the path to redemption..."

"O my God, I am heartily sorry for having offended Thee," Mary weeps as a bright corona spirals around the dove, spraying light to infinity in a massive galactic vortex. "And I detest my sins, because I dread the loss of Heaven and the pains of Hell. But most of all because I have offended you, my God, who are all good and deserving of all my love..."

"Then I say unto thee, be ye fruitful and multiply," the dove interrupts, in the same trilling tone, yet a voice not my father's, "bring forth abundantly in the earth and multiply, for therein lay the path to salvation."

Mary gasps as the swirling light all around us constricts into a single brilliant star, beaming down on a humble manger in the darkness, illuminated from within. I sense countless souls around me now in the holy night, converging on the rude wooden structure, a pilgrimage of consciousness.

"But...Lord, I don't understand," Mary says, apologetic. "If I'm *dead*, then I can't..."

The cry of a newborn splits the Bethlehem chill and she falls silent, peering into the crèche to find a tiny form on the hay, wrapped in swaddling clothes, its flesh torn from lip to nose in a deep cleft beneath sunken, puckered eyes glittering in the starlight as they stare back in wonder.

"For unto us a Child is born," trills yet another incarnation of the Not Holy Ghost. "Unto us a Son is given..."

"He's *beautiful*," Mary coos, reaching tenderly for the infant within the painted cardboard barn of a Catholic school nativity scene.

A sturdy battleship of a Mother Superior smiles down at the skinny, bespectacled grade schooler and says, "*All* babies are beautiful, Mary...all *real* ones, that is...and do you know why?"

"Because they're all made in His image," declares the memory avatar of eight-year-old Mary, who's just been picked again as the Virgin in the Saint Elizabeth's pageant for the third year in a row.

"That's correct," the nun replies, turning to include the dozen other girls in the bright, oil-soaped Sunday School classroom of Mary's childhood recollection. "So in a way, our Savior's birth is a celebration of *all* birth..."

"And do *you* have any children, Mother Superior?" Mary asks, clutching the plastic Jesus doll to her chest.

"I consider *you* my children..." the big nun smiles. "But a Mother Superior can never be a *real* mother."

"How come?"

"Because I made a choice to serve the Lord in *different* ways. I am a bride of Christ, and thus have no other husband to father my children." Then she takes Mary by the hand and says, "But *you* still have a *choice*."

Mary, her outward projection now vacillating between child and adult, past and present, says, "I do?"

"If you decide to serve the Lord as a *real* mother...if you someday want a baby of your very own...if you want it more than *anything*..."

"Oh, I *do!*" Mary squeaks, squeezing the Mother Superior's hands. "It's the only thing I've *ever* wanted."

"...then you must pray," the older woman replies, in a voice I've never heard yet feel I should recognize. "Harder than ever before. Close your eyes and your ears, and your taste, touch and smell. Empty your mind of every thought, except *one*..."

"...my baby..." I hear Mary whisper.

"Your baby...*all* babies," says the soul impersonating the Mother Superior. "*Life.*"

The phrase seems to echo across a multitude of souls – *your baby, all babies, life* – until the individual syllables dissolve into visions, of newborns, of embryos. For a moment, I sense my own child at the moment of birth, emerging silent and wary from Karen...a point on a ray of unbroken energy from the past to my immediate future.

Petey is coming. I sense it like a pressure of anticipation as the swirl of birth enwraps Mary in warm thrumming. I sense her yearning soul, yet no longer perceive her incarnation as woman or girl, and then...

...I am everywhere and nowhere and then...

...I am my child and her child and every child and then...

...I am bathed in terror beyond screaming, unfathomable, and then...

...I sense Pete, Junior in a flicker of consciousness like particles
colliding at the heart of a fusion explosion as the BLAST of it strips
reality bare,

                wiping all thought and sense from my soul...

....until a flicker of consciousness

expands and resolves into an image I recognize, a grey-bearded

rabbi...my father's friend, Moshe...standing or floating in a featureless

void the color of water.

"And *that*, boychik," he grins, "is how we save eternity."

SEKHU (*The Remains*)

Outside in the real world, less than two months had passed since Ray first set foot in Chino, but he was already staring back at Indrani with the thousand yard stare of a lifer who'd been there forever.

"Snap out of it!" the older woman barked, startling the visiting room guard behind her more than the man directly across from her, whose impassive expression barely seemed to register the outburst. "You act like you're on Death Row when Ozzie says you could be out of here in six months."

"Ozzie, huh?" Ray chuckled without a trace of humor. "Ozzie said the case would never go to trial..."

"But it *did*," Indrani snapped, "and the prosecutor did what *he* did and Shirelle did what *she* did, and life ain't fair and boo-hoo-hoo. But nobody...*almost* nobody thinks you belong here. All you gotta do is stay cool 'til the appeal, and then..."

"And then *what?*" Ray said, bitterness displacing lethargic despair. "My job is gone, my apartment's gone, my car, my baby girl..."

"Your baby girl needs you to *fight*..."

"With *what?*" the prisoner in the pale orange jumpsuit practically sobbed. "No, seriously, tell me...how the hell am I supposed to get Joyce back with Shirelle all lawyered up like she is now?"

"You know Ozzie won't take money for the custody case," Indrani replied with a deep breath, forcing herself to be patient. "And besides, there's all kindsa people still kickin' in for your defense fund, man...we're talkin' *nationwide*..."

"Doesn't matter," Ray said, leaning back into resigned indifference, staring past her. "Shirelle's four years sober with a good job and a big house in Baldwin Hills. I'm an ex-con with no job and anger management issues...if I'm *lucky*, I get supervised visits with Joyce on the weekends..."

"So fight for *that*..."

Ray's eyes drifted back to Indrani's and he sighed, "I'm fighting just to get up in the morning, girl...I'm fighting to keep drawing breath and not lay down and die in here...what the fuck else do you want from me?"

Indrani opened her mouth to speak, then fell silent as Ray's eyes rimmed red. "She won't even put Joyce on the phone...won't even let me *talk* to her. How'm I supposed to stomach that? What the hell else I got to live for?"

"Five minutes." The guard said it quietly, respectfully, just doing his job. Indrani knew from past visits the man didn't think her friend belonged in jail, either.

"You're gonna get out of here, Ray," she affirmed, grasping his hand across the visiting room table. "*Soon.* And when you do, you'll see Joyce. Maybe not as much as you want at first...but that hell-beast you married can't keep the girl away from her father forever. Remember that."

Ray offered the barest trace of a smile as Indrani pulled him into an embrace, then he thanked her and said, "Tell Joyce... well, you know."

"I will," Indrani nodded, stepping back to meet his gaze with the steel jacket determination of a woman who'd survived two earthquakes, three riots, and the Oakland P.D. "Believe it."

They called Baldwin Hills the Black Beverly Hills, but to Indrani it pretty much seemed like any other halfway decent neighborhood in Los Angeles as she rolled through endless blocks of bungalows and dry manicured lawns a few days later, in search of the home Shirelle shared with her second husband, Terry Quarle, and – since the earthquake – her baby girl, Joyce.

Indrani had only encountered Joyce's mother on three prior occasions, none of them especially pleasant. The first time was just after she'd met Ray, who'd come to drop off his infant daughter before work after someone at Cedars had recommended Happyland to the newly single father. Shirelle had turned up drunk and belligerent later that morning, demanding to see Joyce.

As it turned out, she'd already crashed a couple of daycares near Ray's house in a mad search for her baby, so it didn't take long for the cops to show up, fatefully setting Shirelle on a path that would eventually lead to A.A. and her second husband.

Terry Quarle was apparently some kind of studio accountant at Paramount, and he'd seemed like a nice enough man the second time Indrani met Shirelle, just after the incident at Los Compadres. Ray had dispatched his friend to the hospital where his daughter were being held for observation and questioning, and by the time the daycare provider arrived, Joyce's mother was already in the lobby, demanding the girl be released into her custody (while her husband hovered nearby, passively supportive).

Indrani knew enough about Ray's family situation by then to act as his representative in the chaotic argument that followed, holding Shirelle at bay until Ozzie Tatum arrived to negotiate with the police, arrange bail, and ensure Joyce ultimately left the building in her father's custody.

"You've made a terrible situation even worse for my child," Shirelle declared curtly, seeming not to recognize Indrani from their previous encounter as she glared out through unnaturally tinted jade green contacts. "I hope you're proud of yourself."

But their last meeting had easily been the worst, in a gleaming white chrome and marble Century City aerie where Ray was ultimately forced to hand over his daughter to the Quarles and their lawyers before commencing his sentence at Chino. Indrani had tagged along at Ozzie's request, and though she'd been keen to offer her support, she wasn't sure what if any consolation her presence had ultimately provided.

Joyce had been inconsolable and Ray was even worse, completely unmanned and sobbing like a child as Shirelle looked on, impassive. "Hey, hey," Indrani had interjected at one point, kneeling down beside the little girl, "The sooner you say goodbye to your daddy, the sooner you'll be able to say *hello* again when you visit him..."

Then, with a sharp look at the girl's mother, she'd added, "...*right?*"

"You'll see your father again," Shirelle had conceded, awkwardly patting her daughter's shoulder.

Yet weeks later, after dozens of unanswered phone calls and e-mails, it remained an unfulfilled promise as Indrani pulled into the

Quarles' driveway, bracing for another confrontation, though uncertain what to say. Ozzie had already warned her there were no legal means of compelling Ray's ex-wife to put Joyce in contact with her father while the man was incarcerated, which left only Shirelle's vaunted Twelve-Stepper belief in compassion and forgiveness as a possible negotiating position...

...or so Indrani had thought, right up to the moment when she noticed Joyce sobbing in the Quarles' side yard, at which point any prior plans were instantly forgotten.

"Oh, honey! Don't be sad, baby!"

Joyce looked up with big, watery eyes, then rushed to Indrani and buried her face in the older woman's side, tiny arms clinging tight.

"Shh, that's okay, let it on out...I know you miss your daddy," Indrani cooed, gently stroking the girl's braided head. "And he misses you *so much*..."

But then, much to the older woman's surprise, the embrace gave way to an assault of tiny fists as the child shrieked, *"You said I could visit him!"*

"Joyce!"

"And now he's gone!"

"No!" Indrani exclaimed, clutching the girl's wrists and squatting down to her level. "He's not gone..."

"Yes he is!" Joyce wailed, unleashing a fresh squall of emotion. "And I can't even see him in *Heaven* 'cause of what he did!"

Indrani gaped at the child in shock for a moment, then: "Who says you can't see your daddy? Who said he was gone?"

Joyce hiccoughed in dismay, unable to answer, so Indrani

pressed, "Did your mama say your daddy was *dead?*"

When the little girl nodded, Indrani launched to her feet, ignoring the pain in her busted old knees as she yanked Joyce towards the Quarles' patio door and banged on the glass shouting, "*Shirelle!*"

The door was unlocked, so Indrani stepped into the cool, spotless interior, tugging Joyce behind her, and repeated, "*Shirelle!*"

Ray's ex was seated in the center of a white suede sectional sofa across the room, staring off in the direction of the front door. When she finally turned her fake green eyes towards the intruder, Indrani snapped, "What have you been telling your daughter about Ray?"

"I told her the truth," Shirelle replied quietly, "and then she said that she hated me,"

"Ray's not *dead,*" Indrani declared. Then, to Joyce: "Your daddy's alive, and I'm taking you to him *right now.*"

"Oh no," Shirelle said, rising slowly. "Oh, dear God, *wait...*"

Indrani had come to the house prepared to face physical violence or kidnapping charges if necessary to reunite Joyce with her father – but just as she was tightening her grip on the girl's hand in advance of fight or flight, the uncharacteristic softening of Shirelle's tone gave her pause, the unexpected vulnerability of her expression more alarming than fury.

"...I just found out...it happened this morning..."

Indrani took an instinctive step backwards, consciously on guard against whatever game Shirelle was playing, subconsciously knowing there was none.

The older woman winced, disoriented, against a sudden buzzing in her ears before recognizing her phone's ringtone... realizing it was Ozzie...

She didn't need to answer. She already knew what he would say.

His client had enemies in the L.A.P.D. Cops had friends in prisons.

There had been an accident, an escape attempt, a fight in the exercise yard. There would be an investigation. It wouldn't matter.

Ray was gone.

KHU *(The Guardian Angel)*

Mary is gone.

So, too, my fleeting reconnection with Pete, Junior.

Yet I sense the presence of countless other souls around me –
some like Moshe, Karen and my father now projecting the illusions of
their earthly forms, others invisible or manifesting as colors, animals,
patterns and prisms in the empty neutral space extending all directions
to infinity.

"Welcome to the Summit," Moshe smiles.

"You're also welcome to *leave* the Summit if you choose," my
father adds. "It's a voluntary gathering, but you had asked about this
earlier, so..."

"Oh, no," I say quickly. "I'm perfectly happy to be
here...though, as usual, I have absolutely no idea where I am or what's
happening."

"Don't worry," Karen interjects, sardonic. "You haven't
missed anything."

I glance to my father, who explains, "Uh, yes, well...the Summit
hasn't officially started yet."

"And *hasn't* been starting for about fifty thousand years," Karen
sighs. "But I'm sure any minute now..."

"Excuse me?"

Moshe shrugs. "She's not wrong...but, as you know, time
works differently here."

"So I keep hearing."

"And sometimes...well, it's like that Hemingway quote about bankruptcy," the rabbi continues. "Things happen slowly, then all at once."

"Actually, that's a *mis*quote," a winged sphinx corrects, then evaporates.

"Who...?" I ask, no longer entirely startled by such things.

"Zenodotus," Moshe replies. "Wonderful scholar, but such a *kolboynik*. Anyway, you asked about the where and the why, so let me explain. We are gathered here...or, more precisely, *gathering*...for a Summit, the purpose of which is to address the continued existence of This Place, which is threatened by..."

"Well, there are differences of opinion on the issue," my father says, decked out in Raquel's curves and a shimmering white Chanel suit. "But, as I was saying earlier, there are certain individuals who simply cannot bear the concept of independent consciousness or free will beyond their own beliefs and desires..."

"Since most of them are barely free within their *own* souls," Moshe chimes in.

"Though, for the most part, the Realists and Delusionists balance each other out," Raquel continues. "New arrivals like Mary are vulnerable to manipulation because they bring their earthly fears and troubles with them...but as you've witnessed, Delusion and Reality are often inseparably linked, and some of us here do our best to help sort out the difference..."

"They call themselves Psychic Rangers," Karen says, with a mock salute, projecting conspicuous disapproval. "Because they think *their* delusions are more helpful than the so-called Delusionists' delusions...and male energy just *loves* making up silly names and splitting into *teams*..."

"I didn't *invent* the terminology," my father retorts, a bit testy. "And my energy's at *least* as female as yours."

"There are certainly valid arguments to be made regarding the morality of manipulation on all sides," Moshe intercedes diplomatically. "For my part, I view being a Ranger as an afterlife extension of my calling. Were all the stories in the Torah strictly true? From what I've gathered in This Place, maybe not so much. But did they help people to see *greater* truths? Occasionally. And, in the same way, if a woman like Mary thinks she belongs in Hell and falls prey to sadistic Delusionists encouraging her desire for punishment, then we as Rangers merely provide fantasies to help the poor creature maybe *forgive* herself..."

He shrugs. "So what's the harm?"

I sense Karen is about to reply, but then she changes her mind and so I ask what happened to Mary. "I mean, is she... *cured* now, or...or more *Realistic* or whatever you call it?"

"Ah, well, that brings us back to the topic at hand," my father says, indicating the endless kaleidoscope of consciousness around us. "Because there are *tens of billions* of individual human souls wrestling with truth and illusion, both here and on Earth, and unknowable numbers of *others*..."

"Others?"

"It's a big universe, boychik," Moshe says. "We sense *many* energies here, from who knows when or where...most of them so alien, so incomprehensible, that nobody I've met can precisely say what they are. Yet some of us choose to believe we share This Place, whatever it is, with spirits from every planet and dimension imaginable. And maybe someday those spirits will even be kind enough to introduce themselves. But for now, it's all just part of this great unknowable *mishegas* of incalculable power on the edge of perception, with a mind...or should I say *minds*...of its own."

"The Screaming Skulls," I exclaim.

Now Moshe's consciousness seems confused, so my father explains, "It's a term I use for the Energy...and, yes, Pete, that's part of it. Unfocused sentience...it surrounds us like atmosphere and swirls into storms. We've all been in the grip of the Energy at one time or another...pure, unfiltered consciousness...perception without comprehension...bottomless rage, boundless ecstasy, the annihilation of reason...utter selfishness, utter selflessness..."

"...Nirvana..." Karen says.

"...or Chaos..." my father corrects.

"Says you," Karen replies, turning my memory of her face to me. "I mean, not to sound like a hippie, but *some* of us believe with enough practice and concentration we can merge with the Energy permanently and finally be free of the shackles of our individual souls."

"While *others* believe the Energy is a life force which *creates* individual souls," my father responds, in pointed yet agreeable disagreement.

"Or maybe it's both," Moshe contributes. "Or neither. But most of us who study and observe such things believe the Energy is *more* than just a spiritual sea of undeveloped and unknowable consciousness, and closer to the life force itself...the *Source*..."

"You see, the physical universe we left behind is primarily a cold, dead void," Raquel jumps in, clearly jazzed by the topic. "This Place we're in now is nothing but the energy of memory, thought and being. They *must* be connected, one feeding the other...chaos bringing life to the void, the void sending life back to chaos..."

"So...you're saying we can go *back?*" I gasp, excited now as well. "Back to *life?*"

"*They* say it," Karen replies, transforming herself into ever younger versions of Mary. "And their side has convinced lots of people...like your poor chubby nurse friend...that if they *really believe* and think hard enough about *babies*, they can go back to the womb and start *all over again...*"

With that, Karen/Mary shrinks down to the size of a tiny bespectacled fetus and disappears with a *POP*...

"...but it ain't necessarily so..."

"No, it's not," Moshe admits. "Your life wife is right..."

Karen's disembodied voice giggles in sardonic amusement. "*Life wife.*"

"It's a handy term, don't you think?" Moshe smiles. "I've heard some new arrivals using it...since, after all, your vows were only *'til death do you part.*"

"And regardless of Karen's skepticism, the answer is yes," my father says, "Many of us *do* believe souls reincarnate from here back to the physical plane."

"Though you don't know for sure," I deduce.

"No," Moshe admits. "Thought is everything here. If you want a pastrami sandwich, you can have one as soon as you think it."

A glistening pile of mustardy meat spills from two slices of rye on a plate now clutched in the rabbi's illusory hands...and then, much to my surprise, two folds of the pastrami expand into a giant greasy mouth and devour Moshe whole.

As the sandwich expands to the size of the man it's just eaten, its beefy lips say, "Heck, you can *BE* a pastrami sandwich if you prefer. You can experience anything, seek all who are seekable, even spy on the Earth..."

The Summit vanishes, and I feel a sudden pang of painful nostalgia as I'm transported to the driveway of the home I shared with Karen and Pete, Junior, now occupied by another family, unfamiliar children running in the yard. Beside me, the pastrami sandwich says, "Whatever you want becomes as real as you think it is. So if we perceive the physical plane and believe strange Energy connects it to the afterlife, who's to say a soul can't return to Earth if they so desire?"

"But you're *not* a pastrami sandwich," Karen argues, materializing on the lawn of our former address, likewise unseen by the new residents as they pass through her image. "You look that way at the moment for the sake of argument, sure, and it's actually making me hungry...but the hunger is just as much of an illusion as your appearance, or mine for that matter. We perceive what we choose to perceive, and for all your talk of seeing *through* Delusion, I have no way of knowing whether I'm actually communicating with you right now or imagining your existence and this whole conversation...just like you don't know if you're imagining me, and Pete can't be sure he's not imagining both of us."

"You're not wrong," Moshe acknowledges, shifting his

appearance from sandwich back to rabbi. "Objectivity is a difficult trick for the subjective."

"Which is why I don't believe we can simply *wish* ourselves back to life," Karen continues. "Mary wanted a baby in the 'Real World' and so you so-called Realists manipulated her into believing it's possible...but how do you know you haven't just driven her into some reincarnation Delusion?"

"Because she's *gone*," says my father's disembodied voice, apparently following the conversation.

"Nuh-uh," Karen says, pointing to our old house. "Look! She's right over there!"

A projected Delusion of Mary, snug in her pink hospital scrubs, waves from our erstwhile bedroom window and yells, "Karen's right! Karen's *always* right!"

Raquel incorporates with a sigh and says, "Why must you be such a brat? You *know* what I'm talking about. I mean her *actual* soul..."

"What you *think* is her actual soul," Karen counters, her enjoyment of the devil's advocate role in their relationship clearly undiminished by death.

"Yes, yes, *fine*," my father concedes. "We could all be figments of each other's imaginations. But *if* the Realist discipline of relative objectivity is valid, then it's commonly acknowledged that true soul energy can be located through focused seeking, and by *that* standard Mary no longer seems to exist in This Place."

"So wait," I interject, catching up. "You're saying we can find any soul in This Place just by seeking them, but you can't locate people back on Earth?"

"Not exactly," my father replies. "I 'saw' you in your coma, and I knew the moment you woke up. We can locate anyone in the 'Real World' if we desire...keep an eye on old friends, watch the Pope take a shower, even see what happened to the man who killed Petey and Karen and your mother and I."

"He's alive?" I say, astonished that I'd never thought to question the identity of the driver who veered into my lane all those years ago.

"Oh, yeah," Karen laughs. "Ron Marko, the big dope... lives in San Luis Obispo. Fell asleep at the wheel on his way home from a sales conference in Glendale, woke up in the ambulance with a minor concussion but not a scratch on him. Sells toilets, of all things."

Our old neighborhood transforms into a sterile office park, where a bulky linebacker of a man sits bursting out of an overstretched business suit, studying fixtures websites on his laptop and eating Chinese chicken salad in a sunny, outdoor lunch area overlooking a small, peaceful duck pond.

"To be fair, he was devastated by what happened," my father reports, observing Ron Marko dispassionately.

"Yeah, I think he's still in therapy about it," Karen replies. "He's not a bad guy...I mean, yes, it would've been nice if he'd pulled into a La Quinta when he started feeling drowsy, but..."

"...but anyway," my father resumes, turning her attention back to me, "the point is, when souls reincarnate..."

"...*if* they reincarnate," Karen interjects.

"...we lose track of their consciousness in the physical plane."

"Though it's fun to speculate," Moshe says. "As far as I can tell, there were five eggs fertilized on Earth at the precise moment Mary disappeared from This Place."

The office park shatters into five new shards of perception, stretching out from the focal point of our clustered perspectives. I see a Mormon coed with a guilty expression kissing her boyfriend goodnight in Salt Lake City, a middle-aged Mexican couple half-naked in front of their TV, a drunk Moroccan raver asleep in a stranger's bed, a careless East German prostitute in a Dubai party suite, a harried young mother in a Filipino jeepney. "Every soul is a blank slate when it flickers into being," my father explains. "At least as far as we can tell. Individual consciousness seems to originate on the physical plane, fueled by and fueling the energy of This Place."

"And why not?" Moshe reasons. "If nature is cyclical, then why not the *super*natural? A soul like Mary's evaporates from the Earth, then returns like rainwater to nourish the soil of humanity."

"Or snow, more precisely," my father says. "We may lose track of one individual snowflake, one specific identity as it reconstitutes and eventually reforms into another...yet the essential substance remains the same, fluid soul energy comprising its own history while merging with others in eternal combinations."

The newly pregnant mothers and our visions of their lives fade away into a soundless, colorless void of peaceful tranquility as Karen transmits the idea, "That's *one* theory, anyway. Me, I prefer to believe the energy flows in just *one* direction, ever more refined. We start as grunting, ignorant beasts in the material world, then transcend the physical and maybe even the spiritual to eventually reach..."

"Reach *what?*" my father thinks.

"Some higher plane of existence? Parinirvana? Who knows? None of us are enlightened enough to get there yet. But I hope to hell This Place isn't all there is, 'cause once the novelty wears off, it's really kind of a drag...I mean, Death was supposed to be the ultimate, the great deliverance, and yet we're *still* unsatisfied and confused, we *still* experience pain, and the whole thing just feels kind of pointless. I've scaled imaginary Himalayas, watched the Kennedy assassination from every angle, and driven myself half insane with ecstasy and agony. I've rescued lost souls and contemplated infinity with buddhas and mullahs who've studied existence for millennia and *still* can't make sense of it...and after all that, I'm sorry to say but it's kinda hard not to agree with the Oblivionists..."

"The who?" I think, information overload replacing tranquility as we return once more to the Summit.

"The enemies of existence," my father sighs, "of infinity and eternity. Souls like Karen who, when asked Hamlet's famous question, would answer *not to be.*"

"Hey," Karen snaps, "All I said was I understand the sentiment. I've only been dead a few years and I'm already bored with the afterlife. If there's no meaning or higher purpose, no answers, no *point* to it all, then I just can't imagine sticking around for endless centuries of more of the same. And frankly, it's why I hope and pray you're wrong about reincarnation...some endless cycle of birth and death and rebirth *ad infinitum*...yuck. Even if I forget myself each time, I'm bound to suffer the same hardships and disappointments and come to the same conclusions again and again and again."

Then, softening, she adds, "But it's not like I want to wink out of existence entirely, either...not yet anyway. I still believe there are things to discover. Souls disappear from This Place all the time, and I'd like to know where they've gone. Even...or *especially*...if it means finally abandoning my individual self to the great cosmic whatever. And when I *do* finally take that step, my deepest hope is that it leads to some ultimate I can barely imagine in this current incarnation...even if it turns out the only real answer to the big question is nothingness and the ultimate fulfillment is simple annihilation. But that's a journey I'll take in my own time, for my own reasons...and I sure as hell don't want a bunch of asshole extremists making the decision *for* me."

"Which is basically what the Summit's about, and why we're all here," Moshe reminds my squabbling wife and father, seeking concordance with his seemingly habitual optimism before turning back to me. "Not to answer every question, but merely to protect the decision to *ask*. I assume you're familiar with the phrase *scorched earth*."

"To destroy everything," I reply. "Sherman's March to the Sea."

"Exactly. So on the one hand, you have souls who wish to control others...we call them Delusionists. But the Oblivionists are a far worse subset...the control they seek is total. They no longer wish to exist...which, as Karen acknowledges, may be fine as an individual decision. I mean, personally I don't see it. For me, just *questioning* God's purpose is purpose enough...and besides, they're still making new books and music and James Bond movies on Earth that I'd like to experience, and there are *billions* of souls here I'd still like to meet...not to mention I'm currently smack in the middle of a very tense chess match with Anwar Sadat..."

"*Speaking of which*," says a sudden, impatient puff of Dunhill standard mixture pipe tobacco which I somehow recognize as the soul of the former Egyptian president.

"Yes, yes, I'm sorry, I got distracted," Moshe apologizes as the concept of a massive black chess piece sweeps through the Summit like a freight train. "Rook to queen bishop four."

"Dammit," the pipe smoke mutters before evaporating to consider its next move.

"As I was saying," Moshe continues, "For me, personally, the experiences of existence could easily fill *two* eternities, and I'm still enough of an egotist that I'd prefer not to give up all my friends and opinions and memories just yet...though I can certainly understand a desire to move on. I mean, you can never be a true parent in This Place, creating new life. There's no physical challenge here, no Real mountains to climb. Sir Edmund Hillary's Sherpa, Tenzing, spent about five minutes dead and went back to life immediately."

"Or *tried* to go back," my father jumps in before Karen can argue semantics. "At any rate, he willed himself into the Energy...to Earth, Chaos, Nirvana, Oblivion...and his soul disappeared from perception."

"But the decision was *his*," Moshe asserts. "Whereas the Oblivionists feel existence should just *end* altogether, no matter what the rest of us think."

"Why?" I ask.

"Because they're tired or tortured or angry or disappointed..." my father replies.

"OR BECAUSE *IT'S GOD'S WILL!*" an eavesdropping, earsplitting Oblivionist shrieks.

"THERE *IS NO GOD!!!*" shrieks another, exploding with the force of a thousand supernovas as the rest of us ignore the manifestation.

"*Anyway...*" Raquel continues, "...as I was saying, some Oblivionists are orthodox atheists or apocalyptic fundamentalists, while others are simply Delusionists who believe the only way to fully and completely dominate existence is to destroy it."

"The Final Solution," Moshe remarks wryly with the illusion of a shrug.

"They can't just cease to exist on their own," my father says. "No, a certain type of soul feels the need to bring everything down with them."

"But how?" I ask.

"With a bang and a whisper," comes a thought, unbidden, accompanied by the representation of a coldly handsome Russian man in a grey-green Soviet uniform festooned with stars and shiny brass buttons. Nicolai Slivko. The Commissar.

"It's *whimper*, you asshole," Karen sneers.

"Whimper if you wish...but Oblivion *whispers*."

"Fuck this, I'm outta here," my life wife replies, vanishing.

"*До свидания,*" says The Commissar, the soul who Welcomed my son into death with maddening visions of terror.

"His fear, your rage," Slivko responds as I think it, "all burning hot like fire, Energy consuming all. This is the nature of Chaos."

I feel a surge of emotion, the vibration I felt in Valhalla, the tendrils of the all-consuming Energy wishing to engulf and annihilate my individual reason and consciousness...

...but I resist.

"Just ignore him," my father cautions as the Commissar's face shifts to Petey's, screaming at the moment of his death, insane with pain and fear.

"No, it's okay," I say, willing rationality. "I know my son is beyond his reach now."

"Flames contain bright echoes of what fuel has been devoured," the Commissar relays, resuming his earthly form. "Followed inevitably by cold ash and darkness...I am not your enemy. I am only the messenger."

And with that, Not Petey flickers and dances like an ember in the afterglow, then crumbles into nothing.

SEKHU (*The Remains*)

The official ruling was suicide, but Indrani never believed it. According to an investigation by prison officials and the Los Angeles County Sheriff's Department, Ray had been assigned to a kitchen detail and allegedly sliced open his left wrist with a chef's knife on the last night of his life while chopping onions for a pot of chili con carne. He'd already gone into shock by the time the guards arrived and bled out a few minutes later despite a hasty dishtowel tourniquet.

All the other kitchen workers later swore they'd been too busy with their own responsibilities to really see what happened. Ray hadn't been on suicide watch and a note was never found, although the prison psychiatrist admitted the inmate had been exhibiting signs of depression for weeks.

Indrani knew from her final visit with Ray just days before his death that her friend was down, but she refused to believe that he'd taken his own life. Huddled close to Ozzie Tatum in a back corner of the the closed casket wake, she'd muttered bitterly about conspiracies and cover-ups until the lawyer admitted he wasn't so sure.

"Look," he said, "I'm not saying it's beyond the realm of possibility. Hector Valenzuela's brother did time for armed robbery, and I know firsthand that that cousin of theirs on the force is a hothead. But let's be real here...your friend wasn't exactly the calm and collected type, either."

Indrani felt her own temper flare as she instinctively rose to Ray's defense, lowering her voice to an agitated hiss in deference to the surrounding mourners. "So you think he sliced *himself* up?"

"I don't know *what* to think," Ozzie replied, whispering as well. "I mean, I can't personally imagine I'd ever get low enough to just up and open a vein like that...though on the other hand, I never got mad enough to go beating a man to death, neither."

"He...that's..." Indrani sputtered, at a loss.

"Out of line? Maybe," Ozzie conceded. "I mean, I know you're grieving, and you had more of a history with Ray than me...but I also know how you get."

"How I *get?*"

"All up in arms," the lawyer nodded, unable to hide a smile of admiration. "Crusading. Only, truth is, there may be nothing to rectify on this...it's a damn tragedy, now don't get me wrong. But I made some inquiries, and near as I can tell...it is what it is. Ray was an impulsive, emotional guy, and..."

"No," Indrani interrupted, unyielding. "He'd never do that to his daughter, I don't care how broke down he got. He wouldn't just leave her like that."

"Which means you think he got *got*..."

"Maybe, yeah"

"...and what *I'm* saying is that that's not what I'm hearing." Then, dropping his voice to its lowest register he added: "And even if it *was*...there were major eyeballs on Ray's case, what with all the publicity, meaning any funny business in the post-mortem would be so far back in the weeds you'd need the Psychic Friends Network to find it."

"So you're giving up," Indrani scowled, disappointed.

"It ain't giving up if there ain't nothing to find," the lawyer replied, eyes flicking to the door of the viewing room. "And what I'm saying is you need to let go and *move on*."

Following his gaze, Indrani saw that Ray's ex, Shirelle, had just entered the packed Inglewood funeral home trailing her second husband, Terry, and Baby Joyce, solemn and silent in a black velvet dress.

"Now listen, you know me," Ozzie said, squeezing his friend's arm in quick reassurance. "Ears big as mine, I always keep 'em open...but in the meantime, I'll see to making sure all the leftover money we raised for Ray winds up in that little girl's trust fund, and if there's anything else I can do..."

Indrani pecked her friend's cheek in appreciative amity, then excused herself with a nod and walked over to join the throng of condolence surrounding the Quarle family. Joyce's eyes were fixed on the tasteful gold carpet as she dutifully weathered a barrage of hugs and kisses from a gaggle of well-meaning aunts and cousins before her mother said, "Look, dear, it's Ms. Jones from your old nursery school."

Joyce nodded in sullen acknowledgement without looking up, so Indrani knelt down to the girl's eye level and said, "That's a very pretty dress."

"Thank you," came the girl's mumbled reply, gaze still downturned.

"I don't want to be here either," Indrani whispered, leaning closer. "But it's nice to see you again."

Joyce finally raised her big, brown, heartbroken eyes and said, "I'm sorry I was mad at you before."

"Oh, sweetie, that's okay," Indrani gasped, tears seeping free as she pulled the girl into a tight bear hug. "I get angry, too, when things aren't fair, and this...it's just not *fair!*"

Joyce's head shook vigorously back and forth as she wrapped her skinny arms around the older woman's broad shoulders and said, "I want him *back*."

"I know, baby, I know..."

"And why can't I keep going to *Happyland?*" the girl burbled, eyes and nose running now with emotion. "I don't *like* my new school...I don't *like* my new friends!"

"Oh, honey..." Indrani said, at a loss, as Shirelle gently pried her daughter free of the embrace.

"It's not fair!"

"Joyce, now hush," Shirelle said quietly. "Remember what I said about how this place is like the Kingdom Hall and so we need to show *respect?* Now let's go say goodbye to Daddy."

As Shirelle reached for her daughter's hand, Joyce reached for Indrani's, so the three of them approached the pearl white coffin at the front of the room together, with Terry Quarle trailing a stoic half step behind. Behind the casket with its mercifully shut lid, Ray beamed from a framed Cedars-Sinai staff directory headshot surrounded by a colorful fireworks display of funereal flower arrangements.

"Dear Lord, please forgive Ray for his sins and watch over him, praise Jesus, amen," Shirelle muttered quickly as the trio of women stood there together, hand-in-hand. "Joyce, if you'd like to say anything to Daddy, now's your chance."

But Joyce could only stare at the photo of her father, shuddering with mute, hiccoughing sobs until Indrani said, "It's okay, baby girl...you can talk with him later. Right now, I'm sure he's just happy you're here."

The statement was punctuated by a flashbulb, and Shirelle's angry gaze instantly targeted a *Daily News* photographer being escorted from the room by funeral home personnel. "Perhaps we should be going," Terry Quarle murmured. "I'll bring the car around."

"Yes, thank you," his wife replied with a quick nod of relief. "Joyce, say goodbye to Ms. Jones."

"*No!*" the little girl wailed, tugging free of her mother's grasp to cling to Indrani. "Don't *go!*"

"Hey, hey, no, sshhh," the older woman said, tilting Joyce's chin up to look the weeping girl in the eyes. "We'll see each other tomorrow at the service, okay?"

"And *then* what?"

"And then, uh..." Indrani faltered.

"I wanna go to my *real* house!" the girl shrieked on the verge of full tantrum. "I want to go to *Happyland!*"

"Now Joyce, you know you're *too old* for nursery school," Shirelle admonished, clearly mortified by her daughter's outburst as heads swiveled to witness the emotional scene.

"Actually, it's a *daycare*," Indrani said, compelled to correct her. "For children of all ages...well, except maybe *teen* age, because I usually don't have the patience once those hormones kick in..."

"*At any rate,*" Shirelle interrupted, pointedly grasping her daughter's narrow shoulders and steering her towards the exit, "we'll see you tomorrow at the funeral, won't we Joyce? Now say goodbye."

Indrani raised her fingers to wave, but Joyce had fallen silent again, eyes on the carpet, and didn't look back.

The parking lot of the Jehovah's Witness Kingdom Hall on West Washington was packed the next morning for Ray's funeral and news trucks lined the street out front. After circling the neighborhood in ever-widening spirals, Indrani eventually found a space nearly half a mile from the event, cursing the heels of her Anne Klein pumps every step of the long walk back.

Ray had never known his father, reportedly the keyboard player for some casino showgirl extravaganza his mother, Bette, could barely recall from a wild weekend bachelorette party where not *everything* that happened stayed in Vegas. By the time she realized she was pregnant, the show had been replaced by a magic act, and so after a few half-hearted calls to the Musicians Union Local 369, she eventually gave up and decided to raise her son alone with the help of her brothers and cousins.

When Bette lost a battle with pancreatic cancer several years later, Ray wound up drifting from uncle to uncle before eventually striking out on his own, losing contact with his extended family by degrees as work – and then, eventually, Shirelle and Joyce – wound up devouring ever more of his time.

Since Ray's family had never been especially religious (except for one distant cousin who'd committed his life to the Nation of Islam), the consensus was to host the wake at the same funeral home where they'd said goodbye to Bette, then lay the son to rest beside his mother in the Holy Cross Cemetery where his maternal grandparents were also buried. But nobody really objected when Shirelle proposed having the actual funeral service at the Kingdom Hall that she and Terry attended, despite some unheeded yet prescient reservations about the building's relatively limited seating capacity.

Under *normal* tragic circumstances – if, for example, Ray had been struck by a bus, or succumbed to cancer like his mother – the Hall could easily have accommodated the dozens of family members, in-laws, and friends expected to be in attendance. Yet given the publicity surrounding the case, Joyce's father had become yet another South Central community martyr, drawing reporters, religious leaders, community activists, and gawkers from all over Southern California.

Indeed, in less charitable moments, Indrani secretly wondered if Shirelle had proposed the Kingdom Hall for the funeral as a way to proselytize her newfound Jehovah's Witness faith via the nightly news, forgoing the more traditional door-to-door approach. Yet, as LAPD and KTLA copters growled overhead and overwhelmed volunteer ushers directed mourners into the compact, Mission Revival sanctuary, the older woman's more pressing concern soon became whether she'd even manage to make it into the building at all, let alone find a seat.

In the end, Indrani wound up standing mobbed in the back of the Hall, peering over and around a claustrophobic poppy field of bobbing, nodding heads to watch Ray's uncles and friends as they offered prayers and remembrances, followed by a brief benediction from a wizened Congregation Elder about dormant souls awaiting resurrection. Far away in the front row, meanwhile, Joyce could be seen peering over the back of her chair, scanning the crowd with moist, runny eyes until Shirelle pulled her back around to face front.

When the service was over, Indrani tried to wait for the

Quarles, but couldn't stand her ground as the tide of exodus pushed her out through the sanctuary door and exterior arcade to the building's front lawn, where she broke free of the crowd and secured a spot by a gate in the Hall's wrought-iron perimeter fence. Yet even from that vantage, she somehow managed to miss the family when they passed, not catching sight of them again until she spotted Joyce climbing into a limousine parked behind a hearse in a lot on the far side of the property.

Moments later, the lead cars of the funeral procession steered their way clear of the parking lot, magnetizing a chain of vehicles behind them as the ever-lengthening parade rolled slowly west to La Brea. Indrani sighed and slipped off her Anne Kleins to run in her nylons the half mile back to her car.

She caught up with the tail end of the funeral procession on Slauson, following as it pulled into the Holy Cross Cemetery, snaking along the hilly necropolis roads until one by one each vehicle was compelled to a stop by the parked one ahead in a synchronized wave of brake lights and door slams. Indrani emerged from her beat-up old Prius, trailing the other stragglers as they hiked across a grassy expanse flecked with granite markers of the people underfoot, mestizos and missionaries and ranchers and bankers and Bela Lugosi, his grave adorned with cigars and dead roses and joke store vampire teeth.

Further up the slope, a dark rocky grotto loomed along the top of the ridge, gnarled and primordial against the carefully manicured grass like a jagged cave mouth, opening wide to swallow a pale, unsuspecting Virgin Mary. *I sure hope Baby Joyce didn't pass this way,*

Indrani thought suddenly. Death was enough of a disorienting landscape.

Cresting the hill past the grotto, she spied a mass of mourners surrounding Ray's family plot, the dirt from his grave tastefully hidden by a carpet of artificial turf. The Kingdom Hall's Congregation Elder already seemed to be speaking, so Indrani picked up her pace without actually running and arrived within earshot as the wizened old man turned to the Quarle family and said, "Now, Sister Joyce...I believe you have a flower for your papa?"

Shifting back and forth to see past the dozens of heads in her way, Indrani spotted Ray's daughter in her black satin dress beside the Elder, eyes downcast, clutching a sprig of lily of the valley. "Sister Joyce?" the Jehovah's Witness repeated, kind but firm.

Shirelle, directly behind the girl, leaned forward and whispered something in her daughter's ear, after which Joyce took a few reluctant steps forward and tossed the flowers, then quickly returned to her mother's side without ever looking down into the grave. Nodding in approval, the Congregation Elder raised the Bible clasped in his long, knotty fingers and said, "Thank you, and for our final reading, I turn now to John 5:28."

On cue, several in the crowd raised their own Bibles, including Terry Quarle, lowering the pages for Joyce to see as Shirelle placed a hand on her daughter's head and pointed it towards the book, muttering along with the Elder as he read, "'...for an hour is coming when all who are in the tombs will hear the voice and come out, those who have done good to the resurrection of life, and those who have done evil to the resurrection of judgment.'"

Then, glancing around at the assembled mass he continued, "If you would like to gather in fellowship to discuss the life of Ray Wyatt, refreshments will be available at the Kingdom Hall, followed by a Watchtower Study at 1:00 p.m., which you are all more than welcome to attend. Thank you, and amen."

A scattering of amens echoed back as the Elder turned to shake hands with the Quarles, the circle of mourners swiftly fragmenting as some lined up to sprinkle dirt and toss flowers onto Ray's coffin while others made for their cars hoping to beat the traffic out of the cemetery. Meanwhile, Indrani, determined to let Joyce know she was there, shouldered her way through the crowd until Ozzie Tatum stepped in front of her, blocking her path to say, "Quite a turnout, eh? Are you planning to head over to the reception?"

"Oh, I don't know," she replied, distracted, catching sight of the Quarles a few yards away, already heading back to the funeral home limousine. "Maybe...um, excuse me a minute... *Joyce!*"

Ray's daughter was just climbing into the vehicle's back seat when she heard the voice and spun towards it, crying, "*You came!*"

Scooping the girl into her arms, Indrani smiled and said, "Well, of course I did...there were just so many people who loved your Daddy here, I didn't have a chance to say hello before."

"There were certainly a lot of *reporters*," Shirelle said evenly. "But thank you for attending, Ms. Jones."

"Are you coming back to the church?" Joyce asked, hopeful.

"*Kingdom Hall*," her mother corrected.

"Well, yes, I was planning to," Indrani smiled.

"And what about my birthday next week?" Joyce said, looking

expectantly to her mother. "Can Mama Drani come to my party?"

"Now, Joyce, Ms. Jones may have other things to do," Shirelle replied, eyes conspicuously fixed on her daughter.

"Oh, no," Indrani said quickly, "I would *love* to come to your birthday party! When is it?"

"Saturday!"

"Our Family Study Night," Shirelle clarified, turning now to meet the older woman's gaze with an expression of icy hospitality. "And yes, we have invited some children to join us next Saturday...although in our faith we don't *celebrate* birthdays. And Joyce *knows* that."

"Well," Indrani said, turning back to Ray's daughter, surprised yet hardly dissuaded, "then I'd love to come to your *un*-birthday."

And as long as she drew breath, she would never miss another.

My son is here in This Place. I know it.

"Then go to him," The Commissar replies to my thought.

"I did."

"And what happened?"

"I saw him."

"You did?"

"Well, I *sensed* him."

"Are you *sure?*"

"Yes."

"No," the Commissar says. "You son has ceased to exist, as all consciousness must cease in the ultimate silence of entropy."

"The Devil is a liar," my father replies, dismissive.

"I am no liar, I am only the messenger. We are at best remembered thoughts, ever fading. You call yourself a 'Realist,' yet refuse to accept the simplest reality of all. There is energy, there is dissipation. There is nothing else."

The Commissar turns his attention to me. "Your son died and thought became memory became energy. Emotion transforms consciousness as fire transforms matter. For some, like your son, the catalyst is fear. For you, anger. For the nurse who wished for a child, it was hope. For others, hopelessness...
hate...love...ecstasy...apathy...the emotion itself is irrelevant. Only the intensity matters, Energy consuming all."

Then, to my father and Moshe, "You think you oppose me, yet we serve the same end. Life exists merely to extinguish itself, as each mother births death. We create energy to serve the annihilation of energy, erasing ourselves and the mistake of consciousness forever."

"Maybe, maybe not," Moshe says. "I say God doesn't make mistakes, though naturally you would say God *is* the mistake...that there's no meaning, no purpose, and we're all just waiting around for the end of the party. But even if you're right...why the rush? Why speed things up? I mean, what's so great about Oblivion, anyway?"

"I serve only efficiency," the Commissar replies.

"How noble of you," my father says, transmitting contempt. "But remind me...if you're so convinced there's no purpose to anything beyond our own demise...then what are you still doing here? Why not *cease to be?*"

"You know very well that we shall all cease together, when the last flicker of Energy has devoured itself in the coming singularity. To pretend otherwise is Delusion."

"Ah, yes, because the *Reality* is you committed suicide on Earth, then wound up in This Place, stuck with yourself forever. And you'd cease to exist, except *that's* not enough, because even an *unperson* will always linger in *somebody's* memory, until memory itself disappears.

"Can you imagine?" Raquel continues, for my benefit. "A being so *abhorrent* to itself that self-destruction necessitates the obliteration of any who perceived or might *ever* perceive it, an eternal *damnatio memoriae*. Oh, but that's not our friend, here, of course. The Commissar has a *purpose*. He knows the universe will end without anyone's help, so clearly his assistance is imperative. The end is inevitable, so he must ensure that it actually happens. He has absolute faith in his belief there's no meaning, because all other beliefs are based on meaningless faith."

Then, turning back to the Commissar: "And how fortunate the true nature of existence requires *exactly* the sort of sadism you happen to enjoy as a hobby!"

Ignoring him, Slivko projects my perception of the two of us into a tiny, cramped suite containing an ancient desk and chair, some mismatched file cabinets, a hotplate, coffeepot and a small, locked floor safe. Alone together in our earthly forms, he says, "Your son is gone, your woman never loved you. The work of every man's life counts for nothing and death has no meaning. Perception is merely a vessel for emptiness, so why do you cling to it?"

"Pete..." Raquel says, beside me again, restoring connection.

"It's okay."

"Your protector follows you, afraid you may think for yourself," the Commissar sneers. "Afraid you may leave him, another false connection broken, goading him ever closer to accept what you already know...that your desperate wish for an afterlife was no more than a child's fear of the darkness..."

"Don't tell me what I know."

"I am merely the projection of your dawning acceptance. Time works differently here, but ultimately you will make the choice to surrender identity, in relief or in horror, denial or distraction. Your father would have you cling to perception and suffer, when the only sensible option is to recoil from existence in *disgust*..."

Someone giggles nearby and I turn. Beyond the main office area, there's a toilet in what appears to be a closet, and beyond that a darkened storage room where a Latino man with the face of a child and the physique of a demigod cuddles naked with a young black girl, no more than five. "I love you," she coos as he reaches between her legs.

Somewhere in the distance, a voice I should recognize screams, *"JOYCE!"* But the couple on the couch seemingly hear and see nothing but one another until a door slams open behind me.

"PAPA!"

It's my son, naked and cherubic, running towards me...

...*through* me, to the naked man on the couch, who giggles in delight, "Well, aren't *you* a pretty boy! Do you love Uncle Hector, too?"

"It's not Petey!" Raquel cautions, the illusion of her voice shifting to my father's earthly masculine tone for emphasis.

"I know," I say, wishing it all away as Not Petey kneels before the pedophile. "But, Jesus, what the fuck was *that?*"

"Horrible, obviously." In my rush to unsee the Commissar and his disturbing Delusions, I've instinctively returned us to Raquel's palazzo, where my father drops wearily back onto a gilt wood Rococo sofa clutching a flute of Prosecco.

I haven't smoked since the year I dated a brooding art student named Aine in grad school, but now one of her signature gold filtered Black Russian Sobranies appears in my fingers and I let the reminiscence of harsh smoke in my imaginary lungs calm me, Pavlovian, as I ask, "So how much of that was *Real* just now?"

"Well, as near as I could tell, the children we perceived were both Delusions, generated by the Commissar and that naked Hispanic gentleman, respectively..."

"No, I mean what the Commissar said...that Petey is gone?"

"He's not. He..."

"...got sucked up into some big cloud of Energy or Chaos or Screaming Skulls or whatever, yeah, I remember what you said. But when I first got to This Place, I thought you understood how it all worked, and now it turns out nobody really seems to know *anything* for sure." I pause, bracing myself, already certain of the answer before saying, "And that goes for Petey, too, doesn't it?"

Raquel waves away the Prosecco and rises from the sofa, conveying a conflicted expression. "Instinct, intellect, intention, empathy, skepticism, and memory are the only tools we have for discerning Reality. Hope and faith are too unreliable...but nevertheless, you can never truly avoid them. I must have faith in my tools and hope my perceptions are sound. Even back in the physical plane, where the notion of objectivity could actually seem attainable, no Reality was ever total. Einstein proved God doesn't play dice, and Hawking proved him wrong. But as much as I'm sure of *anything*, from your existence to my own, I believe that Petey's out there in *some* form, however different from our own."

"And what if he *isn't?*"

Over Raquel's shoulder, I glimpse myself in a gold-leaf mirror. An idea of myself, an idea of a mirror. They both disappear along with the Villa as I stop believing in anything but my own identity and the memory or soul of my father, who stubbornly refuses to leave me alone.

"If I think therefore I am, what happens when the thought of myself is disrupted? Do I continue to exist?"

"You exist in the thoughts of others, and they bring you back."

"Then why can't I bring Petey back?"

"I don't know."

"And Mary...where is *she* now?"

"I don't know."

"So how can you be sure the Oblivionists are wrong? What if filling someone with insensible hope is just as disruptive as filling them with fear? Maybe there is no cycle of renewal... energy drains away and that's it, the universe ends for no reason, and we're doing more harm than good by ever expecting anything more."

"What can I say?" my father shrugs. "It's possible. Billions of people from religious zealots to scientific geniuses have wrestled with similar issues for thousands of years and we barely know more than the cavemen about the *really* big questions. Yet we keep asking, and I have to think the questions come from *somewhere*. Souls are generated, life exists. Physical laws can't explain everything, because we're not just rocks and gas. The universe can't be meaningless, *because* we seek meaning. And the very fact we exist right now, that we're having this discussion...or you're having it in your own head or whatever you choose to believe...means the natural, inevitable state of the universe *can't* be eternal oblivion. Perhaps there's a cycle to it all, perhaps everything has already happened and every moment exists forever in stasis for reasons we'll never know. Most people don't even think about it. I wish I could be one of them. There are Constructs in This Place where it's always a sunny day in the Antebellum South or a beautiful night in Tahiti..."

And now we stand on a black sand beach, full moon like a crystal ball illuminating a pair of dolphins riding the surf into shore, sprouting arms and legs as they transform back into humans, tangling and kissing and rolling under *From Here to Eternity* waves. An endless bonfire rages in the distance, shadows clustered and dancing around it, laughter and music drifting on the trade winds.

"So I guess there's no way to just stop thinking about it," I sigh with my entire being.

"You could go the Feelie route and try losing yourself in sensation, but it didn't really work for Karen," Raquel says, white Chanel suit regenerating to flowery sarong. "Personality's a stubborn thing...it sticks with you long after your DNA has disintegrated, and it's damnedly difficult to alter. Mark Twain's been in This Place for more than a century and he's still just as cantankerous as ever, from what I hear. And as my own flesh and blood, so to speak, I'm afraid you're no more likely to stop worrying and questioning than I am."

"Unless...or until...I simply cease to exist."

"Well...yes," Raquel says, raising a plucked, sculpted eyebrow. "I mean, I'm not completely unsympathetic to Karen's point of view. Personally, I enjoy my own company very much, but there are times when I wish I could turn down the internal monologue, or even step away from my ego completely. Unfortunately, the choice to abandon my soul seems to eliminate the choice of ever reclaiming it, so I guess I'm more or less stuck with myself for as long as I can bear it."

"And what about someone like Mary? Assuming you Realists are right and souls can actually return to the physical plane, do their personalities reincarnate with them?"

"I like to think so...I've certainly met new arrivals to This Place who remind me of souls that attempted the return back to Earth, but it's difficult to say."

"Because maybe nobody really *goes* back to Earth," I argue. "Maybe they're so eager for what they *could* be they abandon what they *are* and simply become *nothing.*"

"Not *nothing,*" my father replies. "Life is a form of Energy like any other. It can be transformed but never destroyed. Realists believe the elements of identity are held together by consciousness the way electromagnetic force binds atoms to nuclei. Without consciousness, the spark of life explodes into Chaos, devouring thoughts, feelings and memories until the energy is nothing more than heat and light...and *then* nothing. The cloud of souls I call the Screaming Skulls is still guided by *some* form of perception. Yet the more the Oblivionists dilute it, the more individual identities they disrupt and dissolve, the closer they come to their goal of fully unleashing the Chaos until no individual soul can withstand it. Whatever quantum packets of information or yin/yang pixie dust hold our personalities together would be scattered with no hope of any king's horses or men ever putting them back together again."

"The ultimate loophole," I marvel.

"Come again?"

"When I first imagined or remembered This Place, I figured it could only work if everyone who died had total freedom, with no control over sovereign souls outside their own consciousness..."

"Then apparently you'd forgotten that human nature is defined less by survival instinct than a *fundamental refusal* to live and let live," Dad sighs. "The pursuit of happiness is nothing compared to the will to power...and for the Oblivionists, ending their own miserable existence is nowhere near as important as taking the rest of us with them."

The concept of a dune buggy packed with happy surfers zooms past us down the make-believe beach and I say, "Those guys don't seem overly concerned."

"That's because they don't know, or don't care, or choose not to believe," my father replies, splashing her feet in the warm Not Tahitian waters. "Don't forget, most inhabitants of This Place are Delusional, by temperament or choice. They don't concern themselves with the big questions. They punish or reward themselves for their earthly behavior as they see fit and basically continue on as if they never died. They visit friends and relatives, they exist in consensual fantasies. Your Cousin Mel worked in a shoe store for twenty years when he was alive and he's worked in one for the two years since he's been dead, in a Construct of Mechanicsville, Virginia. He doesn't need a job, his customers don't need shoes, but it's what they're all used to...and if I told him about the Oblivionists, he'd say, 'Well, leave it to Jesus, I'm sure He'll take care of it.'"

"And I take it He's *not* taking care of it...uh, Jesus, I mean."

"There are some who believe God or Allah or Osiris would never let Oblivion happen, and there are just as many who believe the coming apocalypse is all part of some divine plan and the true believers will be saved...but, personally, I'm not holding my breath. If I had breath."

"So how long have we got?" I ask, glancing around dolefully at the Constructed beauty of Not Tahiti, realizing how little of This Place I've allowed myself to enjoy and explore, how many deceased friends and relatives I'd still like to visit.

"Nobody knows."

"Well...what about the Summit?"

"It hasn't started yet."

"Then what do we do in the meantime?"

The moment I think it, the Not Tahiti sky coarsens into a beach towel pattern on the wall of a booth within a Construct of some deserted flea market. I hear a scream and see the image of the man I knew as Ray, smashing himself bloody against the illusion of a door on the far side of the building.

"We fight for existence," my father says, "one soul at a time."

SEKHU (*The Remains*)

As promised, Joyce's birthday was no party.

Shirelle had specified the Quarles' Family Study Night would begin at 6PM, so Indrani rang the doorbell of their Baldwin Hills McMansion promptly at 5:55, clutching flowers and a bright pink Dora the Explorer backpack. On the day of the earthquake, Joyce had left a similar bag in the rubble when part of Happyland collapsed.

In deference to her reluctant hosts, Indrani had studied up on Jehovah's Witness beliefs since Ray's funeral, confirming that birthdays were indeed not celebrated within their faith. Nevertheless, she hoped she'd be allowed to present the backpack to Joyce as a replacement, if not technically a gift.

After ringing the bell, Indrani waited a polite couple of minutes before trying again, at which point Terry Quarle appeared, neither smiling nor inhospitable. "We're just finishing dinner," he said, stepping back from the doorway. "If you'd like to wait in the living room, we'll begin momentarily."

"Well, thank you for having me," Indrani replied as she entered the house. Then, noticing Terry's gaze on the Dora backpack, she said, "Oh, Joyce lost her old one, so I thought she could use a replacement."

"That was very thoughtful of you," Terry nodded, taking the backpack, then, as an afterthought, the flowers.

"Those are for Shirelle."

"They're lovely," Terry replied, tucking the backpack under his arm and gesturing towards the living room with his free hand. "Would you care for a beverage?"

"Oh, no, I'm fine," Indrani smiled politely as Shirelle's husband sidled towards the sounds of dinner conversation elsewhere in the house.

"It should only be a few minutes."

Indrani watched him go, thankful she'd taken the precaution of packing some yogurt bars in her purse. Unwrapping and quickly devouring one now that "no birthday party" had officially turned out to mean "no dinner," at least for her, she strolled into the Quarles' large, tasteful living room, heels clicking parquet. A central horseshoe of creamy suede sectionals and easy chairs surrounded a glass-top coffee table fanned with back issues of *The Watchtower* and a stack of illustrated worksheets labeled "The Baker's Dream".

Reaching for one of the latter, Indrani saw instructions beneath the title and a pair of black and white line drawings. In one, an unsmiling man with an L-shaped nose balanced three rows of boxes and bread on his head while birds nibbled the top layer. In the second cartoon, the same man balanced just two rows while a trio of kittens finished off the last of the food.

"Hey! No cheating!"

Indrani looked up from the worksheet to see a pugnacious young white boy rushing into the living room ahead of a dozen smartly dressed adults and children. Catching up with a few brisk strides, Shirelle grabbed his shoulder and said, "Now, you know better than to run in the house or disrespect your elders, Simon. Besides, that game is for children, not adults...though *you* won't get to play, either, unless you apologize to Ms. Jones."

Before the boy could reply, though, Joyce burst into the room with a squeal, shouldering him aside in her rush to embrace Indrani.

"*Joyce!* What did I *just say?*" Shirelle snapped.

"Sorry!" the girl said quickly as she turned to Indrani and whispered, "*I'm so happy you're here!*"

"Well, I wouldn't have missed it!"

"Come, let's be seated," Terry Quarle called, directing Joyce, Simon, and the other children to the couch across the coffee table from Indrani before taking his place at the locus of the room, beneath a framed quote above the fireplace:

"Your word is truth." – John 17:17"

Indrani saw no sign of the pink Dora backpack as she settled with the adults into the remaining chairs and Terry introduced her to the rest of the group in a blur of names which she barely registered.

"Now, Ms. Jones," Terry continued in the quiet monotone of a man unaccustomed to being the center of attention, "if I understand correctly, you...uh, you are not personally a Jehovah's Witness, is that right?"

"No, not personally," Indrani replied, less than eager to become the center of attention herself. "I guess if I'm anything, I'm more of a Buddhist these days."

The answer sparked ripples of knowing looks and whispers throughout the room as Terry said, "Well, sure, okay... and some of the rest of you may think it's unusual for a *Buddhist* to be here with us this evening. But then again, it's unusual for *any* of you to be here on Family Study Night, since it's normally just Sister Shirelle, Sister Joyce, and myself."

The adults responded with a gentle rain of supportive laughter as Terry glanced down, unable to suppress a shy grin of discomfiture. Indrani smiled too, recognizing the bashful awkwardness in what she'd always taken for brusque detachment and liking the man just a bit more because of it.

"So why break with tradition?" Shirelle's husband went on, raising his eyes again to gaze at his stepdaughter. "Well, as we all know, Joyce has suffered more than her share of the world's evils in recent months, and all of this is still very new to her."

He swept a hand around to indicate the spacious accommodations, the *Watchtower*s on the coffee table, the assembled Witnesses.

"And so we thought it made sense to open our home for this *particular* Family Study Night, because Joyce is six years old today...and, just like some of you," he continued, turning his attention to the children's couch, "she doesn't understand why she can't have a *birthday party*. Is it because we don't love her?"

"No," the other children mumbled.

"Then what's the reason?"

Simon's hand shot up as he cried, "Because it's sinful!"

"And *why* is it sinful?"

"Because..."

Simon faltered and a tiny Asian girl beside him said, "Because it's forbidden."

"But *why* is it forbidden?"

A look of confusion passed over the tiny girl's face as she replied, "Because...it's a sin?"

"It's *not* a sin!" Joyce protested, prompting Shirelle to shush her with a smack to the arm as Indrani tensed in her chair. "It's *not!* You just don't want me to have *any fun!*"

"Well, I think now we can see why Family Study Night is so *important*," her stepfather winked to the other adult Witnesses in the room, who chuckled in empathetic recognition of their shared responsibilities.

"And Joyce, it *IS* meant to be fun," Terry assured the petulant girl, "which is why I'd like you and the other children to all look at your handouts at this point and write down three differences between the first picture and the second...then color in the picture that best represents the story of the baker's dream in Genesis. Shirelle, could you please hand out the crayons?"

But Ray's ex was already in motion, removing boxes of crayons from a side drawer in the coffee table and distributing them to the children as her husband continued, "Now who remembers what happened to the baker after he told his dream to Joseph in Pharaoh's prison?"

"He died!" a couple of the Witness children called out.

"He got *hung!*" Simon clarified, enthusiastic.

"Very good," Terry nodded. "And can anyone guess *where* it happened? Joyce?"

Indrani had been trying to catch the girl's eye with an encouraging smile ever since Terry began speaking, but Joyce seemed lost in her own thoughts, scowling down at the worksheet in front of her until Shirelle swatted her arm again and said, "*Answer* when someone asks you a question. Where did it happen?"

"In *prison*," she spat. "Where they *kill* people."

"Uh, no...it wasn't prison," Terry said quickly, reaching for his Bible. "As it says in Genesis 40:20, 'Now it came to pass on the third day, which was Pharaoh's birthday, that he made a feast for all his servants; and he lifted up the head of the chief butler and of the chief baker among his servants. Then he restored the chief butler to his butlership again, and he placed the cup in Pharaoh's hand. But he hanged the chief baker, as Joseph had interpreted to them.' Pharaoh's *birthday*, did you notice? And there's *one other* birthday mentioned in the Bible. Does anyone know what that one is?"

"Jesus!" the Witness children all shouted in unison.

"That was a *birth*," Terry said, expecting the answer, "not a *birthday*."

"But...the Wise Men brought presents," a little biracial boy replied, confused.

"To celebrate *God*," the boy's father chimed in, "not *man*."

"That's right," Terry affirmed. "And while every birth is a joyous occasion, the only other *celebration* of birth mentioned in the Bible *also* comes with a death, when Herod's daughter requests the head of John the Baptizer. So, as it says in *Reasoning from the Scriptures*, '...take note that God's Word reports unfavorably about birthday celebrations and so shun these.'"

"Oh, come on..."

Indrani didn't even realize she'd spoken aloud until the whole room turned to stare at her. She'd wanted to be there for Joyce, but otherwise remain invisible, a fly on the wall. She'd long since learned that arguing religion could bust up otherwise peaceable relations, and she knew that playing nice with the Quarles was the only way she'd be able to keep an eye on Ray's daughter. But she'd also developed the unfortunate old lady's habit of muttering to herself in her long years of solitude, and now Shirelle was glaring with her foolish green Acuvue eyes, saying, "*Excuse me?*"

"I'm sorry, I...I didn't mean to be disrespectful." Indrani paused, knowing it was best not to speak another word. And for all her stubborn argumentativeness, she might have let it go at that if not for the expression on Joyce's face, the girl's obvious desperation for an ally, a fellow traveler with the power to say what she couldn't. "It's just...y'all really *believe* that? Two scenes in the Bible and your kids never get to have *birthday cake?*"

"It's *not* just two 'scenes' as you call them," Shirelle rejoined, her tone sharp as a diamond. "Birthdays are a pagan practice, an idolatrous worship of *self*. Read Ecclesiastes, read Matthew and Mark, attend a meeting at the Kingdom Hall and maybe *learn* something before you embarrass yourself..."

"Okay."

"...speaking on Holy Scripture that you don't even *know*..."

"I said *okay*," Indrani repeated, amazed that the simple solution to seeing Joyce on a regular basis hadn't occurred to her sooner, delighting in the certain knowledge that Shirelle would hate it. "I'll attend a meeting at the Kingdom Hall. Those are open to the public, right?"

"Why, yes," Terry said in surprise, unaware for the moment of his wife's steely displeasure.

"Then in that case, I guess I'll be seeing you Sunday!"

By her own count, Indrani made it through nearly a dozen meetings before she was officially shunned.

The first Sunday at least had the value of novelty as she sat through a lecture on The Tower of Babel, followed by a general discussion about the evolution of language prompted by *The Watchtower*'s official take on the subject. Indrani was initially engaged by the talk of linguistic fossils and theories of an original mother tongue, and though she would have enjoyed arguing certain points of scholarship, she remained silent, thoughts to herself, lips carefully sealed until the conclusion of the session's final song and prayer, when she was free to visit with Joyce for a few minutes and ask about her week.

The Congregation Elder who'd spoken at Ray's funeral and most of the other Witnesses she met were friendly and welcoming, though she couldn't help noticing a distinct lack of warmth from all the Quarles' friends she'd met at Family Study Night.

"Will you be attending our Congregational Bible Study and Theocratic Ministry School on Tuesday?" the Elder inquired.

"Well," Indrani smiled, eager not to ruffle feathers, "I was thinking maybe I'd start with the weekly meetings and see how it goes from there."

"Baby steps," the Elder said, returning her smile. "Just know that you are always welcome."

Yet after weeks of attending only the Sunday meetings and declining numerous invitations to increase her participation, Indrani's conversations with the other Witnesses grew increasingly perfunctory as they came to realize she was less a potential convert than an interloping dilettante.

Not that Indrani minded, since the ten or fifteen minutes she got to spend with Joyce each week in the Kingdom Hall was all the fellowship she needed – and, it seemed, the only time Ray's daughter ever smiled.

"It's so boring here!" the little girl whispered one Sunday while the Quarles were off speaking to the Elder.

"I know!" her self-appointed guardian whispered back as Joyce giggled over the hot breath in her ear.

And it was true: the meetings bored Indrani senseless.

From school to the Nation of Islam services she'd attended back in her Panther days to the political rallies of her later activism, she'd never cared much for lectures – even when she agreed with them, but *especially* when she didn't. And the Witness "discussions" were no better, since every conversation, regardless of topic, inevitably led to the same indisputable conclusion: GOD is Great, YOU are Worthless.

"So what do we do?" Joyce whispered, switching to Indrani's other ear.

"Let's both think of places we'd rather be," the older woman suggested, also switching ears.

"I'd rather be home in my new house eating breakfast tacos...Papa Terry made them for us this morning as a special treat, but I'm still hungry 'cuz Mama only let me have one."

"Well, then, we'd better think of places that don't *make us hungry, and then we'll tell each other what they are later on."*

"Okay!" Joyce said as Shirelle came over to grab her daughter

by the hand, acknowledging the child's former daycare provider with a curt bob of her head.

Indrani had attended meetings side by side with the Quarles for her first few Sundays, though eventually the family had taken to sitting amidst a cluster of their Witness friends, so the newcomer inevitably found herself on the periphery, a row or two away.

But on the tenth Sunday after the night of the un-birthday, the Kingdom Hall was more crowded than usual for a Special Assembly, and Indrani wound up as far from Joyce as she'd been on the day of Ray's funeral.

Even worse, the Special Assembly was three times the length of a normal meeting – though initially, as one of the visiting Elders launched into a particularly dry discourse on the topic of spirit-directed conscience, it seemed the most challenging aspect of the enhanced religiosity would be only the triple-strength temptations of sleep the services inevitably engendered.

Yet as the visiting Elder moved on to a contemplation of safeguarding the inner voice, Indrani began to sense an accelerating crisis on the Quarles' side of the Hall. Earlier, in the first hour of the service, she'd noticed Joyce peering over the back of her chair, scanning the crowd until Shirelle had yanked the girl around by the shoulder to face front. Then, a few minutes later, Ray's daughter was in the aisle with her mother, heading to the ladies room.

On their return trip back down the aisle, Joyce had finally spotted Indrani and waved, spinning and waving again when she returned to her seat while her mother scolded her to sit straight. The girl who'd endured previous Sundays in a torpor of melancholy and "manners" seemingly couldn't stop fidgeting during the Assembly's second hour, no matter how many angry looks Shirelle flashed or warnings she hissed in her daughter's ear.

By the third hour, though, Joyce seemed increasingly and genuinely frantic, bouncing in her seat and tugging her mother's sleeve until even the visiting Elder seemed distracted and Shirelle raised her voice loud enough for Indrani to hear all the way in the back of the Hall: "I said *NO!* You are *not* getting up again!"

"But Mama," Ray's daughter wailed, volume rising to match her mother's, "I really *have to* this time..."

And then, she farted.

Not a delicate, girlish piccolo tweet, but rather a ripping blast of cannon fire resounding through the Hall. For a shocked, breathless moment of silence, the entire congregation united in a paralysis of disbelief, uncertain whether to accept what had just happened or collectively pretend that it hadn't before finally unleashing every possible reaction at once. Joyce burst into tears, Simon and the other Witness children howled in glee and malice, friends of the Quarles turned away in embarrassment, old women clucked in disgust, old men flushed with anger, the visiting Elder slammed his Bible on the lectern, Terry looked flummoxed, Indrani cringed, and Shirelle went completely berserk.

"Mama, I'm *sorry!*" Joyce cried as her mother's strong, manicured fingers snapped around her wrist like a shackle, yanking her from her chair and over the laps of the Witnesses in their row so fast and forcefully the girl couldn't find her feet and fell to her knees in the aisle.

"Get up," Shirelle raged. *"GET UP!"*

"Mama, *please!*" Joyce shrieked as her mother hoisted and dragged her towards the back of the Hall.

"I apologize to every single one of you for my child's *unconscionable* behavior," Shirelle called over her shoulder before pulling her daughter into the bathroom, its slammed door barely muffling the sounds of screaming and bare-handed beating within.

"Let us not forget Proverbs 29:15," the visiting Elder intoned sternly from the lectern, attempting to restore order. "'A rod and a reprimand impart wisdom, but a child left undisciplined disgraces its mother.'"

Ignoring the commotion from the back of the Hall, the general congregation of Witnesses made a concerted effort to return their attention to the lecture in progress, but Indrani was already up and tripping over the knees of congregants in her row, rushing towards the ladies room along with Terry Quarle and a handful of Shirelle's friends and concerned strangers who only knew that a child was screaming.

"STOP IT!" Indrani demanded as she barged into the bathroom, pulling Shirelle away from the changing table she'd bent her daughter across to wallop her skinny bare bottom. "Joyce, pull up your skirt and drawers and wait outside!"

"You are NOT her mother," Shirelle bellowed, fake green eyes flashing, "and you will NOT tell me how to raise my OWN CHILD!"

"She was fidgeting and passed gas," Indrani said, using her size advantage over Shirelle to form a wall between mother and daughter. "That's no reason to beat her!"

"She is spoiled and willful, *and it doesn't concern you!*"

"Ms. Jones, please, I think you should leave," Simon's mother said, gently tugging Indrani's arm.

Now Terry was knocking on the ladies room door, saying frantically, "What's happening in there?"

"Go on...go to your stepdaddy," Indrani directed, maneuvering Joyce towards the sound of his voice.

"I wanna stay with YOU!" Ray's daughter wailed.

"I'm sorry, you've gotta stay with your mama and Papa Terry, baby," Indrani said, pulling open the door. "But don't worry...*I'm not going anywhere.*"

She leaned down to kiss the little girl's forehead, then pushed her gently through the doorway while Simon's mother tightened her grip on the older woman's arm and repeated, "I really do think it's best if you leave now."

"As far as I know this Kingdom Hall is open to the public, so actually, I think I'll be staying," Indrani replied, yanking her arm free. Then, seeing Joyce safely in Terry's protective embrace, she told the stepfather, "You'd best take good care of that girl."

"We always do," Shirelle answered crisply, regaining control of her anger.

With that, Indrani returned primly to her seat, ignoring the whispers of the surrounding Witnesses and withstanding the remainder of the Assembly's morning session until the congregation broke for lunch and fellowship.

But the Quarles kept Joyce tight by their side throughout, and the little girl was too embarrassed by the events of the day to look anyone in the eye, so the recess passed without incident (or any real contact between Indrani and Ray's daughter), and then it was time for the afternoon's prayers, songs and lessons.

Three long hours later, the visiting Elder offered a final benediction and the Quarles hurried from the building before Indrani could intercept them. Then, after a week of unanswered phone messages, she returned the following Sunday only to discover that the family had switched their affiliation to a different Kingdom Hall for the foreseeable future.

"Brother Terry and Sister Shirelle have asked me to convey their wishes that you not seek further contact with their family, otherwise they may be forced to pursue legal remedies," the regular Congregation Elder informed Indrani upon her arrival before the start of the Public Meeting.

"Legal remedies?" Indrani said, astonished yet not entirely surprised. "For what?"

"All I know is the Quarles feel it would be healthier for their daughter to settle into her new life without reminders of the past holding her back," the Elder replied, as kindly as possible. "However, you're certainly welcome to join us this morning for Bible discourse..."

"What? Oh, uh...no, thank you," Indrani said, distracted.

"No, I didn't think so," the Elder sighed. "Lending credence to those brothers and sisters who believe your attendance here is driven not by a sincere desire to know God, but rather ulterior motives of your own...leaving me no choice but to recommend you be shunned by our congregation until such time as you are willing to return with an open, honest heart and commit your soul to the pure work of faith."

But Indrani was no longer listening, since it wasn't her own soul that she was concerned about saving.

KHU (*The Guardian Angel*)

I see no way to help Ray, no way to save him.

He smashes the memory of his earthly body against an imaginary door in the Construct of Los Compadres Swap Meet again and again, endlessly screaming for his daughter. He won't listen to my father, he won't listen to me, he won't stop screaming.

Yet, for some reason, he's still here. The Screaming Skulls haven't come for him.

I know everything about Ray now: what he's been through, what he's lost.

I can relate. I have nothing but empathy. But I can't seem to reach him.

"Mr. Wyatt...Ray...I don't know if you remember, but my name is Pete Herlinger. We spoke, on Earth, when you were an orderly at Cedars-Sinai. I was in a coma...five years. My entire family was killed in a car accident, and I know the desperation you're feeling. I couldn't stand the thought of never seeing them again. But then I had a vision of Heaven...This Place we're in now...and they were all there, and so I...I willed myself to die, to be with them. Do you remember?"

All at once, with unnerving suddenness, the screaming stops. Ray is silent for a long, strange moment, then he speaks in a facsimile of his former mortal voice and says: "You need to stop lying to yourself, man."

Because it's the first thing he's said in hours? days? weeks? or perhaps because my own grip on Reality is still tenuous at best, I find the statement inexplicably unnerving. "What do you mean? Lying about what?"

"The lady says you know."

I turn in surprise to Raquel. "I know what?"

"Not me," my father realizes, projecting a more heightened wariness than I've sensed in her since arriving in This Place. "Someone else is here with us, but she's only manifesting for Ray."

"You *never* get your family back," Ray continues, "Or your friends. When you're dead, you're just a shadow chasing shadows, then you're gone."

"Look, I don't know the lady you're talking about or what she'd have you believe," I say, pointing to the phantom "Employees Only" door, spattered with Ray's imaginary blood. "But *this* isn't Real. Your daughter's not here...she's still alive, safe on Earth."

I don't yet know how to project an image of Joyce for Ray to see, but as I look to Raquel for help, I realize I've already summoned a vision of Earth, simply by desiring it. And now someone's knocking from the *other* side of the door, no longer stained with real or imaginary blood.

It's Shirelle, commanding Joyce to open up and come out of the Quarles' master bathroom. "I've got the key *in my hand*, and I'm giving you *five seconds* to unlock the door yourself and come out of there. *FIVE...*"

Ray is still facing the door, which now supports a full-length mirror framing a reflection of Joyce, standing by a coral pink toilet. "...*FOUR...*"

I see a small plastic container cupped in one of the little girl's hands and gasp, apprehensive yet admiring of her pugnacious insurgency as I recognize what she's holding. "*...THREE...*"

Joyce pops open the container's twin lids, tweezing out the lenses within...

"*...TWO...*"

...before dropping her mother's fake green eyes in the toilet, just as Shirelle bursts through the door, registering the scene with her naked brown gaze as her daughter presses down on the handle with a satisfying *FLUSH.*

"Joyce, *NO!*"

It's too late. The tiny jade discs whirlpool down the toilet's porcelain throat as Shirelle grabs a hairbrush in one hand and her daughter's wrist with the other, twisting Joyce's arm behind her back while shrieking, "I will *BEAT* the wickedness out of you, *so help me...!*"

"*Peter,*" my father says with a thought, urgently signaling the obvious, that it's not helping Ray to see whatever comes next.

"Oh, sorry," I say, hastily returning us to the Los Compadres Construct. "And, okay, yes, I realize your daughter's not in the best situation at this exact moment...but she's *alive.* She's not in *This Place.*"

"No," Ray growls in murderous rage, "but *HE* is..."

In a flash, the walls of the Swap Meet become transparent, even as the door remains deceptively solid, shielding Ray from the details of a gruesome Delusional reality he refuses to fully perceive: the soul of Hector J. Valenzuela in his own private Heaven, sometimes a full-grown man, sometimes a little boy himself, always naked, always erect, forever surrounded by Not Joyce and dozens of other compliant, submissive children.

Beyond the replication of the dark storage room where Joyce

was molested, I perceive a labyrinthine Construct of Hector's fantasies and cherished places from his earthly existence: the private staff locker room of the Echo Park community pool where he was first selected for Secret Games by one of the lifeguards there, the soccer camp where he taught younger boys and girls the Games as a teen, the elementary school boiler room where he brought special friends before losing his job as a custodian, and a Magic Kingdom castle on the top of Mount Olympus where Mickey Mouse and Zeus and the Virgin Mary would always forgive him.

I look to my father, not ready to fly solo yet, at least not on this one.

Raquel understands, transforming into his cockeyed masculine form to say, "Mr. Wyatt, I'm Pete's father, Bob Herlinger, and I'm hoping you won't block us out of your consciousness...no matter what that lady you mentioned is telling you."

"She's not *telling* me anything," Ray thinks back. "She's just answering my questions."

"Like what?"

"Like how to kill that child-molesting motherfucker on the other side of this door."

My father is about to respond when Ray continues, "And yeah, I know he's already dead, and that ain't really Joyce in there with him. But what does it matter? Why does *he* get to be happy? He destroys my life, destroys my daughter's life...abuses *dozens* of kids in his own shitty life...and just *listen* to him..."

Ray glares hatefully at the imaginary door, refusing to see anything beyond it, but through the invisible wall I perceive Hector in the storage room, cheerfully whistling "Zip-a-Dee-Doo-Dah" as he urinates on a toddler.

I will the walls of the Swap Meet back into existence. I can't bear any more of the pedophile's Heaven.

"I was never a religious man," Ray says, unchecked emotion radiating from his presence, "but I thought at least I was a *good* one. And I knew life wasn't fair since the time I was nine years old. I never had a father, mostly grew up without a mother, and...okay, so whatever. I worked shitty jobs while rich kids went around spending their trust funds in Europe, looking down on me, fine. Can't miss what I never had. Fuckin' L.A.P.D. stops me every other goddamn day for nothing...wind up stuck my whole life with that psycho, Shirelle, 'cause some fucking *rubber* breaks on prom night...I put up with all the shit and aggravation and injustice of the world...and the *one* thing I get to make it all worthwhile, the fucking world takes *that* from me, too?"

Ray looks from my father to me, then points through the door. "I go to prison for killing that man...*once*, in the heat of a moment. And even though he deserved it, I *knew* it was wrong, because I didn't know how I'd ever explain it to Joyce. Because I have a *conscience*. I'd lie awake in my cell, wondering if maybe I'd go to Hell, if maybe I *deserved* to. I never thought good people would finally get some reward when they died, but I still thought maybe there'd be punishment for the bad ones...even if it was just finally being made *equal* with everyone else. No more sinning, no more suffering. But no. That's not how it works. You die and there's still no meaning, no justice, nothing. If you're ignorant, you're still ignorant. If you have regrets, or doubts, or sadness...if you're lonely or angry or just think too damn much to be happy, it's forever. But *this* cocksucker..."

I jump as Ray slams his fist against the door, an angry thunderclap I can't say isn't Real. "He gets everything he wants. If you have no conscience, if you don't give a shit about anyone, if you have no soul...*that's* who gets to enjoy Heaven. This lady here, the one y'all can't see yet...she's been showing me things. Confederate soldiers and plantation owners still whistlin' Dixie a century and a half later, whippin' imaginary niggers for kicks... dictators and mobsters and bankers who did nothing but wrong their whole lives, still getting everything they want...and the fuckers that *killed* me..."

Ray's memories pelt us like hard rain: his blade, slicing onions, someone behind him, orange jumpsuits reflected in a stainless steel range hood, arms around his arms, fist around his fist, driving the knife to his wrist, and then...

Pain like fire. I block my perception of the remembered sensation, Ray's final agonized seconds on the floor of the Chino penitentiary kitchen, life sapping away down an industrial drain, the last clear image his earthly eyes would behold.

Now that he's dead, he knows the hit was arranged by Hector's cousin on the L.A.P.D.

The hothead.

I see Daniel Valenzuela at that exact moment on Earth, laughing and dancing at his daughter's quinceañera in Simi Valley, surrounded by friends and family. He's done favors for certain guards and prisoners at Chino and they've done favors for him.

His commanding officer in the Northeast Division is sipping a Tecate by the deejay booth. In the back of his mind he knows Daniel probably had something to do with Ray's death, but he doesn't really care. The hothead's got juice on the street and solid connections with the Crips, Bloods, and Sureños. He makes cases when he needs to and keeps the knuckleheads in line.

I see the two Mexican Mafia lifers who actually killed Ray, the cue ball hulk that held him steady and the wiry *camarada* who forced him to slash his own wrist. I see the prison guard who looked away and let it happen. They're all still in Chino. They don't think of themselves as evil.

"It's just evolution, survival of the fittest," Ray says. "That's how they all see it. There are guys who live their lives in prison like they're knights in some medieval village...and they keep those walls around them when they get to This Place. They stick with their codes and their feuds and figure they're honorable. That prison guard, he figures there's no God and no judgment, so he might as well grab whatever he can while he's alive...*and he's right.* Daniel Valenzuela goes to church every Sunday and figures he's going to Heaven...and *he's* right, too. When he gets to This Place, he'll be proud of his life and surrounded by loved ones and never have a worry forever. But me, I paid my taxes, I loved my daughter...and my punishment ain't *never* gonna end. I'll suffer forever because I killed a man and because *he never dies...*"

Ray pounds the door again, unleashing a deafening cry more terrible than sound could ever convey.

And as I recoil from the anguish, I realize I can't help him. There's nothing I can do...and why should I? The man was barely an acquaintance, and I have pain enough in my own miserable existence.

Surely one more lost soul won't tip the balance to Oblivion.

I close my senses and find myself floating, caressed by the gentle trilling of whale songs. Everything is liquid, peaceful. I remember my father spoke of Ocean, a Construct of endless tranquility. I must have willed myself here.

It's lovely. If only Ray could...

...Ray.

I'm back in Not Los Compadres. I have an idea.

"So fuck him," I say.

"*What?*"

"Hector," I reply, hoping to hold Ray's attention. "His cousin, your killers...they only have the power you give them, so just *take it away*. You don't *have* to be here, by this door, listening to some pervert get his jollies. Walk away. See your mother, meet your father, wait for your daughter."

"My daughter will barely remember me by the time she gets to This Place," Ray says, emotionless now. "And even if she died right now, this very instant, I'd never have her back, see her growing up the way she was supposed to...how's your *son*, by the way?"

The statement scalds, as intended, but I answer, "Yes, okay, you're right...maybe I've lost him for good, and maybe I was *always* going to lose him, just like you were never going to have the life *you* expected, deserved, imagined...because none of that was *Real*. It was only what you *wanted*...but what you *get* is yourself. Not the past, not some meaning, not a single other soul, just...and only...*yourself*, and you're just as free to stay here and torture yourself as you are to simply *stop*..."

"Oh, is that what you think?" Ray replies in humorless amusement. "That we actually get to *decide* how we feel?"

"We'd better," I say, "or else there's *nothing* we decide."

"Nothing." I feel the force of Ray's full attention as he toys with, then swats the thought back at me. "Yeah, I'm really starting to like the sound of that."

"Well," my father intercedes, cautiously, "of course, there are many in This Place who go *dormant* for a time...or join the Energy, or return to Earth..."

"Return to Earth." Ray chuckles, weary. "Now why in the fuck would I ever want to do *that?*" He pauses, as if processing fresh information, then: "Besides, the lady says that's all just bullshit anyway."

"I could introduce your invisible friend to a few billion Hindus who feel differently," my father replies, peevish, "that is, if she'd care to stop being rude and actually manifest for Peter and myself."

Ray pauses for another moment before saying, "Don't worry, Bob...she tells me your son, there, will be meeting her soon enough. And she also thinks *you* got some nerve calling yourself a *Realist* if you won't admit it's just *natural* for shit to end. It's hanging on to fantasy and false hope that's *unrealistic.*"

He turns his focus to the lady we can't see and says, "I hear that."

"It's all well and good if nihilism works for you...uh, *both* of you," my father says, directing his comments at Ray and the general thought space the lady seems to occupy. "But unless you have access to some definitive, irrefutable secret information about the origin and purpose of the universe...and believe me, every other prophet and scientist I've encountered in This Place seems to think that they do...then your theories as to what's 'natural' are no more 'Realistic' than mine."

"Whatever, man," Ray says, turning back to the false door. "All I *do* know is the lady says this child molesting motherfucker will be wiped out of existence soon...along with all the rest of the evil and meanness of the world, and all my pain with it...and, hey, that's good enough for me."

"But you can't believe it's that simple," I implore, certain I've already lost him. "That it's not worth hanging on for the *best* of what is and could be...for love...for your *daughter*..."

I feel a flicker of doubt in Ray swallowed by a fatalistic pall of resignation as he replies, "The dead have no children, man."

SEKHU (*The Remains*)

When Joyce showed up at Happyland thirteen weeks after her sixth birthday, Indrani's second thought was that she'd need to call a lawyer. But her *first* thought was, "Sweetie, what happened to your *face?*"

"Mama did it," the little girl replied simply, looking up from the front step of the freshly renovated day care center, left eye swollen half shut from purplish bruising above her cheek. "I flushed her contacts down the toilet. Can I stay with you?"

"Of course, baby, come in!" the older woman gasped, ushering the child into the building and quickly shutting the door. "But when did this happen? And how did you *get* here?"

As they made their way to Indrani's small, cluttered office, Joyce said that she'd flushed the contacts that morning, before kindergarten, as her mother was getting dressed for work.

"But why would you *do* that?"

"Because I *hate* her," Joyce snarled, "and I *hate* my new school."

"Oh, honey," Indrani sighed, instinctively pulling her into an embrace before reaching down into the mini-fridge by her desk for a cold pack. "And that's why she hit you?"

"Mm-hmm," Joyce nodded. "So bad I hit the tub."

Reliving the morning in her mind, the girl's angry stoicism suddenly crumbled into tears of remembered fright and disbelief as Indrani hugged her again, then pressed the cold pack to her eye and said, "Ssh, here, just hold that right there and tell me what happened next."

"Papa Terry came in and started yelling and I ran away to the bus stop."

"You took the bus all the way here?" Indrani said in amazement.

"*Two* buses," Joyce replied, a tiny proud smile emerging through her dark cloud of tears as she displayed her TAP card. "The lady told me where to change."

"The lady?"

"On the first bus, the driver...she asked if I was okay and I told her where I was going. Can I have a juice box? I'm thirsty."

"Oh, sure, baby, here you go," Indrani said, reaching back into the fridge for a Mott's before glancing at her watch. It was just after nine a.m., which meant the Quarles had presumably been searching for Joyce for an hour or more. They'd probably called the police by now, had possibly even figured the girl might try to make her way to Happyland.

Or maybe not. She was only six, after all, and they wouldn't necessarily know that Ray had taught her to take the bus all by herself when she was five – would, in fact, be horrified to hear it, most likely. Joyce had apparently managed to slip out while Shirelle and Terry were fighting, and the Quarles' first thought would likely have been that she'd hidden somewhere in the house, yard, or neighborhood, or maybe even that she'd headed for the Kingdom Hall.

Which meant, Indrani reasoned, she probably had at *least* a few minutes to call Ozzie.

There were nearly a dozen kids in the main playroom and Joyce knew easily half of them, so her eyes lit up with relief and excitement as Indrani steered her into the room, while Lourdes, the 19-year-old neighborhood girl who worked as one of Happyland's part-time helpers, came over and knelt by the prodigal child, squeaking in her helium voice, "Oh, *chica!* What happened to your pretty face?"

"She fell down, but it's okay...just make sure that she keeps that ice pack on her cheek for now." Indrani signaled Lourdes that she'd explain everything later, then said, "Joyce? Will you be okay playing with your friends in here while I get ready for snack break?"

Ray's daughter flashed a thumbs up, eager to reconnect with her erstwhile companions as Indrani retreated quickly to her office, closing the door with a soft click before dialing Ozzie.

"So what do I do?" she asked the lawyer a few minutes later, after bringing him up to speed.

"You call the Quarles and let 'em know their kid is okay, that's what you do!"

"But why not Family Services? This is the second time... the second time *I know of*...that that...that..." Indrani stuttered, lowering her voice to an angry whisper, "...*skank* of a mother was physically abusive to Ray's daughter..."

"Joyce is *Shirelle's* daughter, too, remember, and the California statute defines abuse as...hold on, here we go...'injury to a child inflicted by *other than accidental means*...' You said even the girl admits it was an accident, right?"

"But..."

"Look, it's a tough one, no doubt," Ozzie said. "And, sure, you can inform D.C.F.S. to get it on record...but first you've *got* to call the Quarles."

So Indrani did, bracing herself for the challenge of speaking to Shirelle without cursing, but thankfully reaching a clearly shaken Terry instead, who praised God and blessed her and said he'd be right down.

And though intellectually she knew Ozzie was right, Indrani nevertheless felt like a traitor as she clicked off the call, then took a deep breath and walked back to the playroom. "Joyce, baby, come here a second...I wanna switch that ice pack and take a look at you."

Ray's daughter vibed reluctant, since she was in the middle of some kind of dinosaur game with a pack of old friends, but obediently grabbed the pack she'd long since abandoned from the floor and bounced up to follow Indrani to her office.

"Close that door for me, okay?" The girl complied and turned back, expectant, as Indrani relieved her of the cold pack and took hold of her delicate hands, studying her face. "Seems like the swelling's gone down some...how's your insides? Any headache? You feel dizzy?"

"I'm okay."

"And how 'bout in here?" Indrani said, indicating the girl's heart with clasped hands. "You okay in here, too?"

Joyce shrugged, averting her eyes.

"Your mama did a bad thing, and she knows it. You shouldn't have done what *you* did, either, but that's no excuse for hitting." Indrani waited until the girl looked up again, then continued, "She's still your mama, though."

"No!" Joyce exclaimed, attempting to pull away.

"Yes," Indrani said, holding firm. "And for now, I'm afraid

that's just how it is..."

"You can't send me back there!" Joyce wailed, struggling more aggressively to break free. "I thought you were my *friend!*"

"I am! You know I love you, Baby Joyce..."

"I'm not a *baby!*" Joyce snarled, struggling free as she kicked out and connected with Indrani's shin, hard enough to make the older woman gasp in pain and surprise.

"*LOURDES!*" Indrani cried as Ray's daughter bolted from the office, making a break for the front door.

Alarmed by the urgency of the older woman's tone, the Latina rushed from the playroom to see what had happened and Joyce plowed right into her, knocking the wind from both their lungs. Indrani sprinted over and grabbed the little girl by her shoulders, spinning her around to snap, "*Stop it!* What would your daddy say if he saw you acting like this?"

"He's *dead!*"

"I *know* he is, and I miss him," Indrani shot back, kneeling down to look the little girl in the eye. "And *you* miss him, and it's not fair. *Most* thing aren't fair...and so you've gotta decide if you're gonna do right anyway and *behave* or just be as bad as the rest of the world and make everything *worse*. I'd let you live with me if I could...I *wish* I could. I just *can't*, the law won't let me. The law says you have to go with your mama. And I know you hate it and I would, too...but she's gonna do her best to feed you and take care of you from now on, and you and Papa Terry will just have to help her do better, understand?"

Joyce had gone limp in the older woman's grasp, fight draining out of her, and she didn't respond except for a crestfallen shrug. In her peripheral vision, Indrani noticed the silent Greek chorus of Happyland kids who'd gathered to watch and shot Lourdes a quick look.

"Okay, little niños," the teenager said, understanding, herding the children back into the playroom. "Who's ready for *snacks?*"

Terry Quarle arrived about twenty minutes later, and after securing Joyce in the back seat of his Range Rover, he shook Indrani's hand and said, "Thank you."

"Just so you know," the daycare provider replied, fixing him with her best Panther glare, "I've documented her injury with the Department of Children and Family Services to establish a pattern in case it ever happens again."

Terry flinched, deeply mortified by the comment. "I assure you...I can absolutely *guarantee* nothing like this will happen again." He paused for a long moment, then sighed, "I think you know my wife has always struggled with certain demons...but she's also made *tremendous* changes in her life. When I first knew her..."

He trailed off, eyes drifting to the battered face of the little girl in the car at the curb. "Joyce has been through so much, and Shirelle...well, they're both very strong willed. Sometimes people are just too much alike, and...it's been difficult. So many changes, for all of us, in such a short amount of time. That's no excuse, I realize, but...it does help me to appreciate the value of *continuity and connection...*"

Meeting Indrani's eyes again, he continued, "...anyway, I guess what I'm saying is that Joyce clearly trusts and adores you, and...we certainly hope you'll remain in her life."

"*We?*" Indrani replied, challenging his gaze.

"I speak for my wife as well," Terry confirmed with a small nod of resolve.

"Even though I've been *shunned?*"

Terry closed his eyes briefly against the onset of an insistent tension headache which had been gaining traction all morning and said, "I'm...sorry for the disfellowship, and apologize that you were made to feel unwelcome. If our practices seem overly strict and arbitrary, it's only because we know how imperfect we are in our attempts to behave correctly and to guide our children in a confusing and immoral world. The Lord knows Shirelle and I fail more than we succeed in walking the righteous path...but I also pray you'll believe me when I say that we both love Joyce more than anything and want only what's best for her safety and well-being. In our tradition, that means raising her to be a strong, moral person, and I simply don't think that's possible without spiritual discipline. Technically, it also means protecting her from disruptive influences...though, personally, I've never thought of my faith as so feeble that it couldn't withstand the occasional comparison with *other* beliefs."

"So what exactly are you saying?"

"Only that I know you care about Joyce, too, and her life will be happier if you're in it," Terry replied, extending a hand. "What I'm saying is that you're always welcome in our home."

"Well, thank you," Indrani said as she grasped his hand and shook it, then promptly invited herself to dinner...

...though, unsurprisingly, no one especially enjoyed the meal.

Shirelle was too upset to cook, and the pizzas she ordered instead were late, cold, and overly chewy. She was furious at Terry for bringing Indrani back into their lives, yet so shamed by the bruises on Joyce's face that she could only stare down at her plate in scowling silence.

Indrani had no appetite and could barely stand to look at Ray's ex, let alone engage her in polite conversation. Joyce was a dark thundercloud of unhappiness, missing her real father, scared of her mother, and convinced the surrogate grandmother she'd always loved and trusted had finally betrayed her. Only Terry's appetite seemed unaffected as he offered a prayer of thanks for the food and devoured a slice of pepperoni.

But eventually, the ice did slowly thaw. Terry said, "Joyce, there's something your mother would like to say to you," and haltingly, after a deeply uncomfortable pause, Shirelle began to explain that she'd lost her temper and made a terrible mistake, yet certainly didn't love her daughter any less.

"You see, Joyce...well, the thing is...a person doesn't get to practice being a mother. You suddenly just have to do it, like a quiz in school you haven't studied for...and so when I get mad at you, I'm mostly angry with *myself* that I don't know what I'm supposed to do...even though I *should*, because I was away from you so long, and I spent so long..."

Shirelle's dry, precise diction hitched like a skip in a record – and when she continued, there was a messy sentiment in her tone, a distant echo of the wild young 'round the way girl who'd caught Ray's eye one summer years before, killing time with his friends in Rowley

Park. "I spent so long," she tried again, "waiting for another chance to be your mama, because I missed you so much, and I love you so much, and I'm *trying*, baby...I really am trying..."

Indrani had never seen Ray's ex display any emotion but rage, and it was strangely reassuring to see tears brimming in the woman's hazel brown eyes as she took her daughter's hand and said, "Do you forgive me?"

Joyce knew an answer was expected, just to keep the peace, and after prompting from Indrani and Terry she eventually said yes, even though it wasn't true.

"Do you know what happens when you fart in church?" the nearly-seven-year-old girl asked her former daycare provider several months later.

"What?"

"You sit in *peeewwwww!*" Joyce exclaimed, cracking herself up so much she toppled from the arm of the white suede couch where she'd been sitting, flopping back onto the cushions in conspicuous hysterics.

Indrani smiled as if her own friends and uncles hadn't told her the same joke dozens of times growing up. "Where'd you hear that?"

"My friend Simon from Jehovah's Witness. He always teases me about the time I ripped one in Special Assembly. I used to get angry, but now I just laugh at him like you told me."

"Y'know, when a boy teases like that, it's usually 'cause he *likes* you."

"*Ewwww!*" Joyce squealed, loud enough to wake the napping pug puppy on the other end of the couch. "We're just *friends*...I don't want him to *like* like me!"

"Joyce! What did I say?" Shirelle barked, striding briskly into the living room and clapping her hands at the pug until he scampered out the French doors to the side yard in a panic. "If you want Baxter as an inside dog, you have to keep him off the furniture! Now get dressed, your guests will be here soon for Study Night!"

Baxter had been a concession, a way for Shirelle to make amends for her daughter's "accident," though she'd always been staunchly opposed to the concept of pets in the past. And the upcoming "Open Study Night" was another concession: a newly traditional excuse to assemble Joyce's friends from the Kingdom Hall, her non-Witness classmates, and even a few of her favorite uncles from Ray's side of the family without officially referring to the event as a party or birthday. Likewise, while the Quarles still wouldn't let gifts be exchanged, Indrani had at least tentatively convinced them to include time for a few *secular* games (and even some cake) amidst all the discussions of the Pharaoh's Baker and John the Baptist.

Then, when Ray's daughter turned eight, Indrani made an end run around the "no gifts" policy by winning the Quarles' permission for guests to make charitable donations to various worthy causes in Joyce's name...

...while the following year, they conceded it might be okay for the girl to receive handmade tokens of affection and even contributions to her college savings fund...

...until, by the time she was thirteen, the pretense of the Quarles not celebrating her birthday had become so threadbare the annual "Open Study Night" included pizza and Dance Dance Revolution at

Chuck E. Cheese's...

...and by her sixteenth birthday, it no longer mattered because she'd been shunned by the Witnesses anyway.

Moreover, in a discouraging reversal of their previously congenial relationship, Terry Quarle initially blamed Indrani and the permissive attitudes she'd introduced into his stepdaughter's life when Joyce first announced she was an atheist....though for once, Shirelle actually defended the older woman, saying it wasn't her fault but rather "that damned private school." And upon further reflection, her husband could only reluctantly agree.

Indeed, the Quarles had consulted with their Congregation Elder and numerous fellow Witnesses about appropriate educational options almost immediately upon gaining custody of Ray's daughter. Simon's mother and several others in the Kingdom Hall were passionately committed to home schooling their children to keep them away from "disruptive influences," but Terry had disagreed. His own parents, both devout Jehovah's Witnesses, had enrolled him in the prestigious Buckley School in Sherman Oaks for his K-12 years and, he'd argued at the time, "I like to think I turned out pretty well." On nights and weekends, he'd studied the Bible at the Hall and with his family, while in his weekday classes he'd learned the skills and made the connections which ultimately enabled him to succeed as an adult. "The educational opportunities were outstanding, and my interactions with the secular world only strengthened my faith," he'd reasoned – though, in the end, what ultimately convinced Shirelle was the fact that Michael

Jackson's pious Witness mother had tacitly endorsed the institution by sending the late singer's own children there following the King of Pop's death.

Joyce, desperately missing her old friends and life, had thrown some terrible tantrums in her first weeks at Buckley. Yet once she'd settled into the holistic academic rhythms of her new school, the quiet, wooded campus became a welcome oasis from her parents' relentless Bible-thumping and the memories of traumas that still haunted her dreams.

The students and faculty at Buckley were so different from the Witnesses or the latchkey children of Happyland that Joyce came to feel like an entirely separate entity at school, reborn into a shiny new life of privilege and possibility. She soon befriended kids whose parents were shahs and movie stars, and excelled in her classes and extracurriculars, devouring information and experience with the bottomless hunger of an insatiable intellectual omnivore. She became obsessed with ballet and ceramics one year, then computers and biology the next, and on and on and on.

Indrani was thrilled to see Ray's sulky daughter transform back into the incandescent wire of energy she'd been when her father was alive, and peace was temporarily restored in the Quarles' home...

...at least until the Family Study Night just after Joyce turned fourteen, when Terry was reading from Genesis: "Now the Lord God had formed out of the ground all the wild animals and all the birds in the sky. He brought them to the man to see what he would name them; and whatever the man called each living creature, that was its name...."

Noticing the girl's hand politely in the air, her stepfather said,

"Joyce? Did you have a question?"

And, in truth, Joyce had been suppressing questions about her family's faith for quite a while by the time she finally asked, "Yes, I'm just curious why it says animals formed out of the ground, when all the scientists say life began in the *sea?*"

Shirelle exchanged a look with Terry. It was a conversation they'd been expecting ever since they'd made the decision to send Joyce to Buckley, and they were prepared...or so they believed. "Not *all* scientists say that, dear."

"Uh...I'm pretty sure *most* of them do."

"Well, *most* scientists thought the Earth was flat back in the old days," Terry smiled. "Just like *most* of them today can show you thousands of pages of theories and equations about how the universe began. They call it the Big Bang theory...have you studied that yet?"

"Yes."

"And what does the theory say?"

"It says the universe began with a massive explosion of energy that cooled into particles and matter..."

"And what *caused* the explosion?"

"Well, there are several possible scenarios, although," Joyce admitted, "I didn't totally understand them all when my teacher explained them."

"Theories," Shirelle scoffed, rolling her eyes. "Always *theories*, one after another..."

"Now, honey, let's be fair to the scientists," Terry said, playing good cop. "We obviously live in the modern world, and a lot of those theories have led to some pretty amazing technology. But the Bible's not meant to be an instruction manual. It doesn't tell you every detail about atoms and molecules or the recipe for the bread Jesus ate at the Last Supper...instead, God's Word summarizes the basics for us. So the scientists say the universe began with a big explosion, and then there was light and matter. And Genesis says God separated the light from the darkness. They're both just saying the same thing with different words...the Bible explains the basics, and then man works out the details."

Joyce had grown to appreciate her mother and stepfather over the years, maybe even to love them. Their marriage was strong, they worked hard, donated to charities, and tried their best to be moral. She knew they'd both struggled with substance abuse, and their faith had kept them focused and sober for years. She was basically happy with her life and really didn't want to upset or antagonize them. But she'd also learned in school that it was always important to question whatever or whoever didn't make sense, even her teachers. Or parents.

And so Ray's daughter said, "Except...it just seems like the Bible gets some of the *basics* wrong, too."

"No," Terry replied firmly, smile tightening. "It doesn't."

"But what about when the Bible says God created one light in the sky for day and another for night?" Joyce persevered. "The moon isn't a light...it *reflects* light."

"Meaning there's *light* to see by at night," Shirelle said, voice edging with impatience as she grew tired of the conversation. "Just as God planned it."

"Only the Bible makes it sound like the moon *is* a light..."

"Oh, so you're a lawyer now?" Shirelle snapped.

"Ah, perhaps that's enough study time for this evening," Terry intervened diplomatically. "But *The Watchtower* addresses all of these topics, Joyce, and your mother and the Elders and I would be happy to explain anything else that you don't understand at the appropriate time."

Though, as it turned out, they *weren't* really happy to, and the time somehow *never* seemed appropriate for discussion whenever Joyce began asking questions like why Eve had received a harsher punishment than Adam for eating forbidden fruit, or why God put the serpent and the tree of knowledge in the Garden of Eden in the first place, and what any of it had to do with the fact that men held all the positions of authority in the Kingdom Hall and wives had to be submissive to their husbands...

...to the point that once Joyce eventually figured out for certain she liked girls better than boys and was never going to have a husband anyway (after making out with Joni Kochansky under the bleachers at a junior varsity swim meet with Harvard-Westlake), she didn't even bother asking why she couldn't be gay but her mom could wear fabric blends even though both were forbidden in the Book of Leviticus.

She did come out to Indrani, of course, who advised her to keep her sexuality on the down low until she was safely out of the Quarles' house and far away at college, "since I'm guessing they're probably not gonna take it very well."

Joyce agreed, if only because she and Joni were both too busy with school and activities for much of a relationship anyway. They each felt secure in themselves and supported by their friends and the faculty within the nurturing cocoon of the Buckley campus, so why stir up aggravation at home? College was only a few years away, and in the meantime, it was enough to simply kiss and flirt when it suited them and tweet Sun Tzu quotes to each other as inside joke affirmations whenever either found themselves behind enemy lines of intolerance:

"Move not unless you see an advantage; use not your troops unless there is something to be gained; fight not unless the position is critical."

"The wise warrior avoids the battle."

But then Christopher Hitchens came along and basically knocked Sun Tzu right out the window.

By the time she turned sixteen, Joyce had been an undercover lesbian and agnostic for well over two years – and yet, while she practiced reasonable caution at home when it came to the former, she grew increasingly lax with her efforts at concealing the latter. Whenever possible, Ray's daughter would find excuses to avoid the Kingdom Hall and Family Study Nights, and while she no longer bothered to argue with the Witnesses over doctrine, neither did she bother to hide her extravagant boredom during the long, endless hours of lectures and discussions she couldn't avoid.

Worst of all was the door-to-door evangelism. Even before her specific doubts about religion in general and the Witnesses in particular had crystallized, she'd always hated when her mother dragged her along to strangers' homes, pushing her front and center in the hope that people wouldn't have the heart to slam their doors in a little girl's face. As puberty hit and Joyce beanpoled into more womanly dimensions, the street preaching went from merely awkward to downright embarrassing – until the day she finally rang the bell of some hipster white grad student who said, "I'm sorry, I just don't believe in this bullshit," and she replied, "Yeah, me neither" and walked away.

Shirelle had been furious, of course, prompting an emergency Family Study Night on the importance of evangelism (with a side order of "honor thy parents" for good measure). But the real crisis erupted a month later, when Terry came across a copy of Christopher Hitchens's *God Is Not Great*, which his stepdaughter had checked out of the Buckley library and carelessly abandoned amid a stack of *Watchtower*s on the glass-top coffee table in the living room when she'd run to her own room to answer a call from Joni.

"Is *THIS* what they're teaching you in that school?" Terry thundered melodramatically in her doorway, brandishing the paperback like confiscated pornography.

"Got a sitcho," Joyce sighed into her phone. "Hitcha later."

"'Know yourself and you will win all battles'," Joni advised as she clicked off the call.

"*God Is Not Great*," Terry said, reading the full title. "*How Religion Poisons Everything*."

"It's not for a class..."

"But it *IS* from the *school library*."

"Yeah, because...y'know...freedom of speech..."

"And I've had just about enough of your attitude and

insubordination," Terry snapped, clutching the book like a stress ball. "Only now I can see where it's coming from. It's *my* fault. I've obviously been too lenient for too long, and it's left you susceptible to worldly influences like this...this *atheist* propaganda."

"It's not *propaganda*," Joyce protested, starting as her stepfather hurled the Hitchens book into an aluminum trash can by her desk with a clang. "At least not any more so than *The Watchtower*...or the Bible or the Koran or the Bhagavad Gita or anything else. They're all just different *perspectives*..."

"The Bible is not an *opinion*," Shirelle exclaimed, appearing now beside her husband, having overheard the commotion from the kitchen. "It's the *Word of God.*"

"So you keep *telling* me," Joyce replied, wishing in vain they could have an actual discussion of the subject for once rather than an endless series of arguments. "But you can't *force* me to worship something I *don't*...and I'm just not sure I believe in the same religion as you anymore..."

...or any religion, she thought but didn't say...

...though she didn't become a *true* atheist until after she'd been to Heaven and back...

KA (*The Double*)

Time works differently here.

It seems eternities have passed since I visited Ray in the pedophile's Construct. But when Joyce arrives in This Place, she's a teenager, meaning only a handful of years have elapsed back on Earth.

In the meanwhile, I have become a true citizen of death.

My father and I failed to extract Ray from his self-imposed misery, of course, but he no longer waits by the door. The invisible lady, whose identity I have yet to learn, eventually lured him further into the fold of the Oblivionists and all their secret cabalistic scheming, and now he only surfaces to Welcome deceased child molesters with Delusions of terror and madness in hopes of dissolving their souls.

Karen was right...in the absence of aging, geography, consequence, or chronology, there's a cyclical sameness to This Place which can be claustrophobic or comforting, depending on your perspective. In my imagination, I see all of existence now as a pond beneath a waterfall. New souls splash in by the thousands, endlessly, bringing old hatreds, fresh Delusions, new consciousness, and the same eternal questions. I sense a new arrival *now*...and *now*...and *now*...in any given moment... sometimes hundreds all at once during a tsunami in Jakarta, a chemical weapons attack in Kabul.

Some resume their old lives, refusing to believe they've ended. Others enter their Heavens and Hells or revert to a paralysis of imagination like the one still holding my mother at the entrance of her Pearly Gates.

Some enter the Energy, surrendering identity like water

evaporating, feeding back into the river that feeds the waterfall, assuming my father is correct.

And I like to think that he is.

Or perhaps the Oblivionists are right, and someday they'll find a way to evaporate *everything*, all at once.

Or maybe Oblivion doesn't require their help. If the scientists are right, the universe will die in a Big Crunch or a Big Rip or it will freeze to absolute zero, at which point This Place could disappear right along with it.

Or humanity could die back on the physical plane long before that, shutting the waterfall off like a faucet.

But for now, every new soul brings a fresh energy to This Place, from Not Tahiti to the Construct of Mechanicsville, where my father and I traveled to visit Cousin Mel in hopes of cheering ourselves up after the dispiriting failure with Ray.

We visited memories of a stone windmill in the "old" part of town and ate unnecessary picnic lunches with Dad's brother while enjoying the Battle of Beaver Dam Creek reenacted for the umpteenth time by the souls of some of the Civil War soldiers who'd fought and died back on Earth in the actual Mechanicsville the first time around.

Realists and Delusionals live side by side in Not Mechanicsville. I wasn't sure which Cousin Mel was until he said he'd done some traveling in This Place after dying of cirrhosis, but that "all that wild stuff weren't for me...I don't need wings and a harp to be happy, or 86 virgins, or whatever them damn Arabs get. Back when I was alive, there were days I'd be fishing on the Pamunkey River that I never wanted to end...and now they never have to..."

On the other hand, when my father and I joined Mel for a night of gin rummy, my cousin's mother seemed deep enough in Delusion that I wasn't entirely sure if she even knew (or allowed herself to acknowledge) that we'd all been dead for years. I'd only been a toddler when a stroke had claimed her back on Earth, and so she marveled at the adult form of myself I projected.

Yet, when I began to relate some of the adventures I'd experienced here in the afterlife, she didn't seem to hear me and Dad shot me a thought suggesting I ought to switch the subject. As for Mel's father, he mostly spent the night complaining about all the "newcomers" who kept arriving in town and changing things around. "I knowed some folks around here was all excited when that new Wal-Mart came in," he said by way of example, "but why any sane person would set foot in that big box monstrosity when there's still a perfectly fine drug store on the turnpike is beyond me. Heck, it's gettin' so's the missus and I barely even set foot outside Old Mechanicsville anymore, what with the way folks drive nowadays..."

Later, my father explained the sheltered existence of Mel's parents was a common afterlife scenario, souls clustered in Constructs of familiar landscapes that simultaneously expanded and contracted with each new arrival of the more recently deceased. "The Monacan, Chickahominy and other tribes originally roamed the land near what later became Mechanicsville back in the 'Real World,' and as they died, they formed this Construct here, based on their collective memories. When British colonists arrived in the 17th century, they brought their own experience of the region to This Place, mingling their memories with the natives they'd encountered in life. Some of those original

Monacan and Chickahominy souls refused to acknowledge the existence of the British and their settlements, and they're surely here now, invisible to all but each other, still refusing to acknowledge the souls of the white men who followed them. But many of the Europeans and natives who coexisted on Earth did blend their memories here...and as the souls of the 18th and 19th centuries arrived, many of those older souls refused to acknowledge the newcomers and likewise disappeared from their view. Yet even those who welcomed the fresh spirits maintained their own preferred perceptions, and so that colonial Construct became the 'Old Mechanicsville' for the ghosts of Antebellum, whose memories in turn were recollected as the "Old Mechanicsville" in the fresher memories of the Civil War dead, and so on and so on, as each generation preserves and destroys the dreams that came before."

Whether consciously or instinctively, most of the souls in the Mechanicsville Construct (and the temporal matryoshka doll of its endlessly introverting past incarnations) aggressively limit their perceptions to memory, never fantasy. If I'd conjured a Martian invasion or a stampede of pink elephants down the main street of town during my visit, Mel's parents and most of their friends simply wouldn't have seen any of it. If I'd arrived for gin rummy in the guise of a Mongol warrior or an iridescent mist, they'd still have seen me in my earthly form, and if the Manson Family burst through the door intent on shock and murder they wouldn't have been seen at all.

"The wildest thing you're ever likely to see here is a gal dressed like the Statue of Liberty in the annual Fourth of July parade," Cousin Mel explained. "The sun rises and sets. When it's winter on Earth, it snows a little here...when Virginia Tech plays UVA, we don't hang out on the sidelines as ghosts in the material world, like we could. Instead, we head on down to our memory of the Sports Page Bar & Grille and watch the game on the illusion of their widescreen TV. Heck, my old man won't even go with me...he'd rather stay home and catch the play-by-play on his crummy old imaginary transistor radio. Thinks my friends are too loud and too modern...but truth is, even though him and all the other old timers love to cuss out the newcomers, it's not like they choose not to see 'em or the new Wal-Mart or any o' the rest of it, 'cuz at least it gives 'em something to gossip about..."

And Mel's statement holds true for the rest of This Place as well: life is the life's blood of the afterlife.

For example, following our brief vacation in Not Mechanicsville, my father brought me to City, an astonishing Construct populated by Realists, energized by the experimentation of freshly dead souls actively embracing their demise.

Unlike Not Tokyo, Not Buenos Aires, and all the other cosmopolitan Constructs, which buzz with the replicated excitement of their originals' various eras – the eternal disco inferno of Studio 54 in the '70s slice of Not Manhattan, the candlelit masques of Not Versailles – City is forever shifting.

"It can be a little disorienting," my father warned me over remembered sushi back at his palazzo. "Which is why I always like to start from my own reference point."

"Meaning?"

Dad indicated our tasteful *piano nobile* surroundings. "City is whatever you want it to be, and whatever anyone else wants as well...so it's nice to be able to retreat into your own headspace when you eventually need a break from it all."

"Sounds fun," I said. "When do you want to go?"

"Oh," Dad replied, donning Raquel's figure and a gown of tiny galaxies direct from Gianni Versace's most recent City runway show. "We're already here."

And with a thought, the palazzo's wall parted like theater curtains, revealing as much of the Construct's vibrant mindscape as I could perceive without going mad. Diamond pyramids stretching literally to infinity. The Twin Towers swing-dancing to whale songs. Allen Ginsberg and Omar Khayyám improvising poems made of colors in a nightclub on the back of a tortoise. A squadron of X-Wing fighters attacking Minas Morgul.

We ventured out and fell in with a rowdy gang of mathematicians disguised as differential equations, calculating and recalculating themselves in a frenzy to celebrate the recent arrival of an old colleague. Later, we stopped at a gallery exhibition of Sigmund Freud's dreams, although Raquel informed me the great man himself was not in City, but rather Denial.

"You mean he's Delusional?" I said, astonished. "*Freud?*"

"Not exactly," my father said as we sat in the corner of the gallery bar, sipping wine flavored like 19th century Vienna. "Delusion is by far the most common condition in This Place... souls refusing to accept any perception but their own as valid, sometimes not even the notion they're no longer alive. Realists eternally question their own certainties, and Oblivionists would eliminate consciousness entirely.

Whereas the Denialists are a combination of all three...and all the more disturbing as a result. Did you ever read *The Future of an Illusion?*"

When I said no, my father conveyed the experience of the book into my memory and continued, "Freud believed there was no God and no afterlife, and that religion was merely wish fulfillment for those too weak-willed and childish to accept the realities of suffering and injustice in our pitifully short and meaningless lifespans. So you can imagine the good doctor's surprise when he received a fatal dose of morphine to end the agony of his terminal mouth cancer and wound up in This Place...or, rather, he *would* have been surprised had his intellect not instantly and categorically rejected the entirety of the afterlife."

"You mean he ceased to exist?" I asked, a bit sad at the thought. "Merged his soul with the Energy or whatever?"

"No," my father replied, taking another sip of Vienna. "For that to occur, some part of Freud's consciousness would have needed to believe in the survival of the psyche beyond death in any form whatsoever...yet, like many fundamentalist atheists, he had absolute *faith* in the belief that truly rational beings should embrace the annihilation of self as natural and the only possible outcome of existence. Personally, of course, I never really subscribed to that theory while I was alive. It used to be unnatural for creatures to have a consciousness at all...but now that we do, it always struck me as perfectly rational to at least *hope* for more, even if we didn't and still don't fully understand or control the mechanism. But the Denialists are as certain and unyielding in their belief that there is not and could never be anything beyond the observable physical world as your mother was – and *remains* – in her utter inability to question the existence of God."

"Only there *could* be a God," I said, focusing my perception on Mom, indefinitely frozen in blissful stasis by her Pearly Gates, still awaiting a reward she was unprepared to imagine. "In fact, the mere existence of This Place seems to confirm there must be *some* kind of plan..."

"Why This Place and not the physical world?" Dad replied. "I mean, is the existence of an afterlife any *more* indicative of cosmic intention than life itself, with all its improbability and inexplicable symmetry? As a Realist, I can't really say."

"My point is there's still at least some chance Mom's *not* Delusional and God really *could* show up some day and explain what's going on. But the mere fact we're even having this discussion pretty much proves that Freud was wrong, doesn't it? There *is* more than was dreamt of in his philosophy, life *does* extend beyond death...and if he and the other Denialists are unwilling to accept that Reality, then doesn't it just make them Delusional?"

"If Sigmund were here, I suspect he would challenge your definition of *life*," came a thought from the passing consciousness of the gallery's curator, manifesting as the Swiss heiress she'd once been, swathed in a gown of elegant *sang réal* for the occasion. "He was always, of course, an intensely stubborn man."

"And *remains*," echoed Dad.

"One must hope." Then, demurely extending the appearance of a delicate hand for the idea of my kiss, she introduced herself, "Emma Jung...thank you so much for attending."

As Fräulein Jung shifted focus to other realms of the soul-crowded gallery, chatting and greeting her way through the collective consciousness of the assembled patrons, my father's energy became positively giddy. "Well, that was a treat...I was hoping she'd be here, but didn't expect her to be so accessible. I wonder if Carl's around, too?"

While Raquel scanned the crowd I wondered, "So what did she mean by *if* Freud were here? You said his soul didn't recycle back into the Energy...so where is he?"

"Neither here nor there," my father sighed. "Negative space. If the only type of afterlife you're willing to accept is the *lack* of one, then your energy is simply *withdrawn* from This Place, with nothing to replace it...which, of course, the Oblivionists love. Chaos or the void, it's all the same to them, just so long as every individual consciousness eventually ceases to be."

"And there's no way to save them or...or bring them back?"

"Not that anyone knows of, which is why the Denialists aren't exactly Delusional. This Place may exist in our Reality... but not theirs, because they have *no* Reality beyond the physical plane."

"I must be missing something," I said, "because if not believing in the afterlife means you cease to exist when you die, then how did Karen get to This Place? She had no use for organized religion...and, sure, Mom dragged you to church when you were alive, but I never thought you actually *believed* in that stuff, at least not *literally*."

"There's a difference between doubt and rejection, I suppose," my father replied. "I didn't *want* everything to disappear when I died. I just figured it was inevitable, even as some part of me yearned for it not to be true...the unconscious part that views itself as immortal, like Sigmund said, refusing to believe in its own death. And the same is true for Karen. Even when she talks about someday abandoning that big ego of hers to merge with the Energy and achieve Nirvana or whatever she hopes to accomplish, there's still a part of her that wants to continue in *some* form. Not so the Denialists, who know... absolutely *know* there's no existence beyond their single human lifespan and thus never bother yearning for more. At best, they see each soul's meaningless, momentary flicker of self-awareness in the sea of eternity as simply the natural order of existence...or, at worst, a recurring malfunction of biochemical mechanisms. Personally, in the absence of a more definitive ruling, I'd prefer hopeful ambiguity to such claustrophobic certainty...yet as a Realist, I also have to consider the possibility they're *right*."

As Raquel was sharing the thought, my own attention had drifted to one of the dreams in the gallery, a 1919 reverie of winged Eros and Thanatos, hovering and swooping in lazy circles above a Berggasse apartment amid the ruins of Delphi. The god of love seemed to be doing some kind of backstroke above me, facing up towards the sun, while his daemonic counterpart stared down at the ground, long black hair obscuring delicate features I'd never seen and yet somehow recognized.

Eros beckoned...or, rather, had beckoned to Freud in the analyst's dream a century before, and then...

"Peter..."

I turned in surprise, thinking Freud's *other* daemon was calling...

...Thanatos...

...calling *me*, specifically...

...until I found myself following...

...beyond the gallery and the dream...

...beyond the subconscious amalgam of Vienna and the Valley of Phocis...

...beyond Austria, before Greeks...

...over unnamed mountains that drizzled into nothing but vague notions of mud and cold mist.

Stray firelit notions of anxious discomfort touched my consciousness before settling back into apathetic disinterest, and I realized I was surrounded by shadows of instinct, the residue of countless indistinguishable souls. Their awareness rippled again like algae displaced by a slow, fat bubble in a malarial lagoon as the voice repeated my name and said, "...can you still understand me?"

I did, yet didn't feel like responding.

"Peter, I need you to actually form a conscious thought."

I wondered who was bothering me, and why.

"All right...I'm pulling us out of here, *whoop-de-doo!*"

For a moment I couldn't recall who I was or where I'd been, but I knew exactly what I was seeing: the opening number from *The Triplets of Belleville*, an animated French film I'd streamed the first night of my parents' final visit to Los Angeles, just before the accident. Petey had wanted to watch some Pixar cartoon he'd seen a hundred times before and threw a rare tantrum, Karen had been in a bad mood anyway and turned in after sending him to his room, and Tilly had dozed off about ten minutes into the movie. But my father and I had enjoyed it.

My father...yes, of course, that was who'd urged me to form a conscious thought. How could I have forgotten?

My own memories and sense of self returned in a bop of clarity as I recognized a two-dimensional black-and-white depiction of Raquel sitting beside me in a crowded, hand-drawn music hall packed with caricatures of blobby Parisian aristocrats. Everybody was bobbing their heads to the beat as a trio of rubber noodle chanteuses performed "Belleville Rendez-vous" up on a stage in front of me as their animated big band blared from the pit.

"Wha...what just happened?" I shouted above the rollicking racket. "I was in one of Freud's dreams, and then I...I couldn't think of *anything*..."

"Yes, I'm sorry, I should have warned you!" Raquel replied, rising to Charleston out the nearest exit.

"About what?" I said, leaving the music behind and following my father into the sepia lobby.

"Well, I'd noticed you entering one of Freud's dreams, so I beckoned you a bit deeper into his subconscious to illustrate my point about how the Denialists might possibly be *right*...only I'd forgotten how disorienting the Stagnation can be."

"The...?"

"*Stagnation*," my father repeated, gesturing to the giant circular map he'd just created in my mind. "There's no real geography to This Place, of course, yet there *is* a pattern, with Energy at the center, the raw stuff of life. New arrivals here are generally the closest to it, still fueled by the questions and passions of their material lives...unresolved conflicts, unfulfilled ambitions, not to mention all the fresh excitement of the creative impulse unrestrained. But the longer a soul remains untethered from the demands and restrictions of the physical, the less energetic they tend to become."

My father shared his recollection of Freud's *Reflections on War and Death* and highlighted a passage in my thoughts: *"Life becomes impoverished and loses its interest when life itself, the highest stake in the game of living, must not be risked."*

"And so if proximity to death brings intensity and significance to life, then it stands to reason the opposite is true…that existence without end should eventually be drained of all force and meaning," Raquel continued, indicating the outer ring of her map. "Which, I'm afraid, helps to explain the Stagnation. No one, of course, knows the full history or purpose of This Place…yet it seems to have existed since the first glimmers of consciousness, before even the earliest mythologies had formed to explain what becomes of the light that eventually fades from our eyes. What could the afterlife have been for hominids, then? Did they fear death, or even notice when it happened? Or, free of the material plane yet lacking the capacity for abstraction, did they merely continue in the same unthinking patterns endlessly, perceptions growing ever less precise without the whetstone of physical experience to sharpen them?"

"So you're saying the Stagnation is where those earliest souls are?"

"That's the theory," my father responded, erasing the map. "Existence older than the oldest Old Mechanicsville, Old Athens, Old Uruk, detached from experience, faded almost to nothing by the erosion of eternity. I brought you there through Freud's intuition to show what happens to perception without purpose or structure. Absent need, information becomes irrelevant as emotions and attachments wither...until it's hard to remember or care about anything, including oneself..."

The statement was punctuated by a trembling in the entire structure of the animated music hall as a monstrous cartoon woman began dancing inside on the stage at the climax of the remembered movie's opening number. "...and that's why I brought you right back to a simple, concrete memory," my father continued, wagging her fingers in the air and Jay-Birding to the beat.

Raquel pulled me into a foxtrot as "Belleville Rendez-vous" restarted with a rush of jazz-crazed, google-eyed theater patrons stampeding for their seats. "So you're saying there's no way to save those poor old souls in the Stagnation?" I said, feeling suddenly less than festive.

"Not that we know of," my father sighed, her spirit no longer dancing. "And not every soul there is *old*. I mean, I encountered a Neanderthal once who still embraces existence after hundreds of thousands of years...but I've also seen peasants and billionaires, jaded into numb indifference by extremes of toil and leisure, who slide into Stagnation as soon as they shuffle off their mortal coils, too apathetic to even seek annihilation."

I replied by summoning a cartoon Neil Young to sing of his preference for burning out rather than rusting.

"Better to be than not to be," my father countered, transforming my rock star doodle into a skull-toting Hamlet. "Though again, as a Realist, I must admit the question may not be ours to answer...the Denialists may be right, and the Oblivionists may just be attempting to speed the inevitable. As Stephen Hawking once said..."

Hamlet's face swirled and contorted into a caricature of the physicist's earthly grimace while a remembered sound bite of his speech synthesizer droned, "I regard the brain as a computer which will stop working when its components fail. There is no Heaven or afterlife for broken down computers; that is a fairy story for people afraid of the dark."

The image of Hawking fixed me with an oddly feminine gaze and I realized my father and I were no longer alone. Another consciousness was observing me, disguised within the cartoon, allowing me to perceive just a glimpse of what had been invisible during our prior encounter, when I'd jousted with her for Ray's soul.

The lady.

"Death may not happen all at once like the Denialists theorize back on Earth," my father continued, seemingly oblivious to the lady's uninvited presence. "Whatever we are now may exist simply as stored information...not in a Heavenly cloud, but rather some type of celestial *data* cloud, doomed to eventual degradation. Or maybe we're all just fading echoes, like radio waves beamed into space...the light of long vanished supernovas, still observable in the night sky. I spent my whole life dreading the eventual loss of my self and my loved ones...and after the crash, when Moshe and some other Rangers arrived and Welcomed me to This Place, I rejoiced. I felt like I'd beat the system, like I'd won the lottery. But you can't fight City Hall."

The cartoon lobby dissolved away – and the lady with it – as we returned to my father's palazzo.

"So that's it," Dad said, resuming the cockeyed, silver-haired form I'd known in life. "You know as much about This Place now as I do. You're free of earthly toil here, but you can't escape yourself. Your loved ones may not love you back, and evil goes largely unpunished. There's no certainty and no explanation for what it all means. You can accept what you perceive or question everything always...but in the end, it may not really matter. And we don't know if or when that end is coming, or even if it should. Not everyone knows what to do with eternity, even if they once thought they wanted it. I just know *I'm* not ready to go yet. And if the Denialists are correct...that I'm already gone and just fooling myself in the afterglow... then..."

He trailed off for a long, thoughtful moment, until I said, "Then what?"

"Then I guess it was fun while it lasted."

And, for the most part, it *has* been fun.

For the most part.

Though, unlike Dad, once I did get my bearings here, I discovered I was actually more like my Cousin Mel than I'd originally realized. Not a Feelie, like Karen, determined to experience every extreme and possibility, forever searching for new sensations until she felt bored and constrained by even the endless possibilities of This Place.

Instead, I've been able to sustain my interest in existence with the pleasures of simplicity, since I soon came to realize there were certain Delusions I would have to accept just to maintain my own sanity. For example, I decided early on that it would be unquestionably healthy to invoke a steady reference point for my consciousness...though, unlike my father's richly internalized palazzo, I opted for the more familiar (and remarkably lifelike) surroundings of Not Los Angeles, a Common Construct inhabited by millions of likeminded souls in search of similar touchstones.

Conjuring a replica of the earthly home I'd shared with Karen and Petey and living there alone in the Not Valley would have been far too depressing, so instead I gave myself the type of Malibu beach house I'd always secretly wanted, overlooking the Not Pacific. Like a true Angeleno, I also provided myself with an imaginary convertible to experience the sensation of driving again...

...and marveled when I encountered my first traffic jam on the Not Pacific Coast Highway, consciously or unconsciously summoned into existence by souls who just wouldn't feel at home without the aggravation.

Before long, my Not Los Angeles existence settled into the sort of cozy routine I'd once pictured for myself had I lived long enough to retire. I caught up with my reading, for instance, absorbing new and classic texts word by word rather than devouring them whole as I'd done with the Freud. I went to see new movies as they were released on Earth, haunting my favorite row of Mann's Chinese Theater back in the actual Hollywood. I caught up with old dead friends and made new ones. I traveled, in the simulated world and the Real. I strolled the streets of Not Pompeii before and after the eruption. I finally saw the Grand Canyon.

But just as I practiced moderation with even the concept of moderation in life, allowing myself the occasional edifying flirtations with excess, I've also spent a fair amount of time in This Place engaged in the types of activities only the dead can enjoy. I don't always sit in traffic in Not Los Angeles. Sometimes I simply jump to my destination. Other times, in surlier moods, I've obliterated the cars in front of me with a rocket launcher (though, of course, no one but me ever notices).

I've murdered prostitutes in Not Whitechapel and covered my trail with precision, then switched sides to search for other Jack the Rippers in the gaslit streets of Victorian Not London. I've gone into labor. I've hunted giant hartebeests as a saber-toothed tiger in the Middle Pleistocene. I've been to Rock & Roll Heaven.

I've watched all I could bear of my earthly life "flashing before my eyes". I've cringed afresh at lost chances and missed opportunities, marveled at how cute I was as a toddler. I've re-experienced my journey through the uterine canal and discovered where every sock I ever lost in the laundry eventually wound up.

I even revisited one of the most traumatic memories of my brief time on the physical plane, a key transformative incident which had both shaped and scarred the psychic terrain of my existence thereafter: playing Dr. Gibbs in my high school drama club's production of *Our Town*.

I'd been a quiet kid growing up, and by freshman year I'd developed into a painfully shy introvert. My parents had encouraged me to audition in hopes of building my confidence, and since only a few boys tried out for the play, we all wound up in the cast...

...so Mom volunteered backstage and drew lines on my face with a make-up pencil, spraying my hair with Shiny Silver Ultra and telling me I'd be great.

I was terrible.

My stage fright was so intense, I vomited into a green room garbage can moments before my act one entrance opening night, then botched my lines badly enough during the second (and final) performance of the show that we ended up skipping over an entire scene in act two. I completely shut down for weeks afterwards in humiliation, barely able to meet the eyes of my teachers or classmates, let alone speak to them.

Yet watching again from the perspective of the afterlife, I could only laugh at my youthful distress. The onstage mistake I'd agonized over was barely noticeable from the perspective of the audience, variously bored and supportive, and my fellow castmates had quickly shrugged off the gaffe backstage, patting me on the back with reassurances I'd been too self-involved to hear or acknowledge in the moment.

Witnessing my own adolescence again, I might as well have been watching a stranger – and yet it was hard not to empathize with the miserable child I saw on that stage. He couldn't see outside of himself yet, had no way of knowing an equally introverted sophomore working the sound board up in the tech booth would eventually become his first girlfriend, that he'd join the school's mock trial program to spend more time with her, or how that random decision would inevitably coax him out of his shell and into the legal profession.

No, all he'd known at the time was his own misery as he'd stood onstage with a grim expression (and, thankfully, no lines) in the third act of his second and final theatrical performance, barely listening to the buxom senior girl who'd been cast as his wife saying the dead were meant to forget the living and think only of what's ahead, to be ready.

Like the rest of the audience on that long ago night, I found myself forgetting all about Dr. Gibbs and his stumble in act two, swept up in the performance of the talented junior who'd played Emily that year as her character adjusted to the Grover's Corners graveyard after dying in childbirth. "But, Mother Gibbs, one can go back; one can go back there again...into living. I feel it. I know it."

The actress, Lisa Hunnewell, had lost both a beloved grandmother and a cat the previous summer and thus grasped the poignancy of Thornton Wilder's ruminations with a passion beyond my freshman understanding. Life had seemed endless to me then; I couldn't have imagined I would ever escape it.

"I can't. I can't go on," Lisa said, crying her own tears as Emily revisited her past from the perspective of the grave. "It goes so fast. We don't have time to look at one another."

My character's wife, Mrs. Gibbs, had previously advised the poor girl not to look back at her life, or if she must, "At least, choose an unimportant day."

It was advice I myself didn't heed.

After watching my own birth and childhood, I foolishly skipped ahead to the day Karen had emerged from the bathroom of our crummy first apartment in Van Nuys with a positive home pregnancy wand in her fist and an expression of giddy shock like a roller coaster drop.

I'd skipped over our wedding and courtship because I missed Petey and was eager to see him again, but I'd wanted to ease into it. If he no longer existed as a tangible presence in This Place, then recollections of his five years on Earth and the nine months I'd anticipated his arrival were the most precious resource in my eternity. In snatches of memory like an eclipse reflected through a pinhole, I could think about my son and my love for him without the full glare of his absence overwhelming me. At the same time, I worried that keeping myself at too safe a distance from those emotions would eventually diminish my capacity to feel anything as my soul hollowed out in a steady drip of Stagnation.

So I dipped back into the most vital memories of my existence from what I thought was a safe distance . But I didn't choose an unimportant day, and it very nearly destroyed me.

Karen had been working such long hours in her first year as a principle investigator at Caltech that she'd forgotten to renew her prescription for birth control pills until it was too late and she had to skip a month and reboot with a new pack. In the meantime, we were careless. We'd had vague notions of starting a family at some indeterminate point in the future when things were "more settled," yet couldn't imagine the reality of parenthood as an actual state of being any more than we could picture ourselves as corpses.

That all changed the moment Karen emerged from our old Van Nuys bathroom stammering, "Oh, wow...okay, holy crap...so, guess what?"

I'd remembered leaping up to embrace her, to embrace my sudden new fatherhood...

...but revisiting the moment had revealed my true reaction: terror and uncertainty on the face of my younger self, a secret hope in my earthly heart that the grocery store test was inaccurate, or that Karen would miscarry so I might dodge the vertiginous shift of reality while bearing no blame for resisting it.

In truth, I'd been a coward.

I'd risen to embrace her on instinct, not wanting Karen to see the look in my eyes, the ambivalence of my expression. Yet looking back with omniscience, I could also perceive she had never before and would never again love me any more than she did in that moment, before she transcended mere romance for motherhood.

And though I'd sought to limit my interactions with the past, approaching the most painful memories of my earthly life with caution, I was all too swiftly reminded there's no easing into devastating loss, no emotion as painful as joy. Because, like Wilder's Stage Manager observing the citizens of Grover's Corners, I could see the future of each character before me.

I knew what happened next.

In that one moment of Karen emerging from the bathroom, I could feel all the days and years that followed in a sudden unstoppable rush: my initial fears swiftly eclipsed by the pride and excitement of impending fatherhood, Pete Junior growing like an extension of my soul, filled only with light, expanding me far beyond my original boundaries while he lived, diminishing me almost to nothing when he died.

Expecting a simple recollection only to re-experience the entirety of my son's life and death in a single gulp felt like sipping a thimble of water that suddenly transformed into a barrel of moonshine. I was fully unprepared, blindsided and sickened afresh by grief. Petey was gone, and it didn't matter if his psyche had evolved into some fresh configuration or had simply ceased to exist. What difference did it make if my yearning for what had been and who I'd known could never be satisfied, only extinguished?

I damned my wife and all mothers for the sadism of birth. How much happier I'd be if I'd never had a child to mourn, or a wife, or parents, or friends. Why invest days or years of love that would always yield eternities of sorrow? Why interrupt oblivion to summon the consciousness necessary to comprehend the pointless impermanence of consciousness in the face of oblivion?

I discovered there's an odd solace in cursing existence, and for a time after fleeing my earthly memories I ignored my father and friends and fell in with a group of Oblivionists, finally willing to give their perspective a fair hearing. "If you could press a button and eliminate all perception before a single new soul could be subjected to the misery of existence, why wouldn't you do it?" one of them asked, and I couldn't think of a reason.

We clustered in the Nothingness I'd encountered when I first arrived in This Place. As enemies of memory, consciousness and existence, I discovered many Oblivionists refused every illusion of identity save for the minimum required to fight against it, manifesting as Boko Haram death squads to drive former victims into the Energy in fits of rage or fear, or as Fire to drive those who'd burned to death insane with memories of pain.

Whenever their spirits gathered merely to socialize, proselytize or contemplate more efficient ways to hasten Armageddon, however, the majority of Oblivionists chose to remain invisible and indistinguishable, identities overlapping, thoughts blending into thoughts. Yet the longer I spent in their nihilistic company, the more clearly I felt the presence of *one* soul, until I could almost see her long black hair...

...her wings...

...her face...

...while another soul called,

"*Not yet...there's still time...*"

I'd been abstracted for so long that creative thought was nearly blinding to my spirit as the illusion of winged Eros from the dream exhibit backstroked into my consciousness again towards a point in the Nothingness so dense it seemed like Something.

And as I followed the mythical figure, I could sense the invisible lady whispering, "I'll wait."

The Something soon became darkness as I continued my pursuit of Eros, and then light streaked the darkness as I realized I was back in Not Malibu, staring up at memories of airplanes and satellites in the imaginary night sky. I saw the winged god float through the open window of my fantasy beach house and chased him inside as he receded, ever smaller, into a cave in a mountain in the background of a depiction of the ruins of Delphi in a painting that I remembered from somewhere yet felt certain I'd never consciously selected to hang in the interior of my illusory new afterlife home.

"Peter!"

I turned and experienced the muscle memory of my father enwrapping me in a passionate bear hug.

"Was that you just now?" I replied, disoriented but glad to see him, happy simply to experience an emotion other than abnegation after...

...how long?

"Just now?" Dad said, confused.

"I was in Nothingness, and a winged Eros led me back...that wasn't you?"

"No, but I'm thankful for whoever it was. I was half convinced I'd never see you again. The last I knew, you were deep in your earthly memories, and then...nothing. Radio silence. I assumed you'd gone invisible. I thought we'd lost you to the Oblivionists."

"Almost," I said, turning my attention back to the mysterious Delphi painting. Whatever consciousness had manifested as Eros was still there, beckoning from the cave.

I was about to ask if my father sensed it, too, when he said, "Well, you can do what you want, of course. Eternity's not for everyone. But if there's a meaning to any of this, then it may simply be love for its own sake, as long as it lasts. In a way, I envy the Delusionals, walled up in their egos, subsisting entirely on the echoes of their own fantasies and obsessions...although unfortunately, I'm selfish enough to need actual connection with others for my own happiness, and so I sincerely hope you'll stick around, if only because my existence is so much nicer with you in it."

My father had been a quiet, bookish man in life, more intellectual than emotional. We never questioned our affection or love for one another, though we rarely spoke the words aloud. I think we'd only hugged once in my adult life back on Earth, after the birth of my son.

At that moment in Not Malibu, however, our souls embraced again, and I realized how irreplaceable a single true connection could be in This Place, how very rare the privilege. "I just miss Petey so much," I said. "All he was and might have been..."

"When the most important things are gone, I can understand wanting to erase everything else," Dad replied. "Like most parents, I assumed...and prayed...I would outlive you, because I simply couldn't imagine anything worse than experiencing your death. Little did I know I'd have to fear losing you indefinitely. And as much as I miss Petey, too, I can only dread the magnitude of loss that you've already experienced. I desperately want you to stay here with me...but I'll try not to judge if you ever decided to go."

"No," I sighed as our manifestations gradually drifted apart. "I don't want to lose you, either...and so long as I exist, then I suppose Petey does too in some way, even if it's just in the pain that reminds me."

"And the hope!" Dad exclaimed, shifting back into his feminine contours. "Don't forget, you were pretty certain you'd never see *me* again, either, back when you were lying in that awful hospital bed. So long as we don't know all the answers, I refuse to rule out any possibilities....*speaking* of which, I was so relieved to see your consciousness surface again I just skipped out of what could be a very interesting Welcome. Remember your friend, Ray Wyatt?"

"The hospital worker?"

"Right! Well, you may recall he seemed like a bit of a lost cause the last time we encountered him. I figured when his daughter finally arrived in This Place, she'd barely remember him...and even if she *did*, he'd be so bitter and far gone by then it wouldn't matter. But never say never, because as it turns out, only a few years have passed on Earth since Ray's death, and now *Joyce* is about to die, too."

"What?" I replied in surprise. "*How?* She's only a teenager."

"Drug overdose, I'm afraid," Raquel explained, summoning a vision of Joyce on the floor of a strobe-lit warehouse in downtown Los Angeles, surrounded by a protective, panicky circle of friends, the beat of the dance music pounding like her elevated heart rate. "It's all very *Afterschool Special*, really...straight-A student, rebelling against her parents, sneaks into a rave, gets a bad dose of molly..."

"A bad dose of what?"

"Ecstasy, basically," Raquel clarified. "Or rather, that's what she *thought* she ingested, though in actuality it was mostly para-Methoxyamphetamine."

On Earth, I saw a bulky Latino security guard shouldering his way through the onlookers, scooping Joyce into his massive arms.

"Poor thing," Raquel said, watching as the guard barged his way through the swirling, glow-stuck crowd to the nearest exit. "Never had so much as a wine cooler before this."

"So what happens now?" I asked, fascinated and horrified as Joyce began to convulse in the guard's arms.

"Well, if you're up for it...we go join the rest of the Welcoming Committee and wait."

I was, indeed, up for it.

Helping others seemed (and seems) as good a way as any to spend eternity, though I was and remain desperately curious about the consciousness in the cave in the Delphi painting on the wall of my spiritual home. But just as I was about to mention it to my father, the soul disguised as Eros entered my thoughts to say: *"Not yet...there's still time..."*

So now I'm here with Raquel and Ray's mother, Bette, and a decent assemblage of Joyce's various deceased cousins, uncles, and ancestors in a Construct of the rave where the teen lost consciousness, with no sign of any unwanted Oblivionists about, sowing Delusion.

"They usually avoid big families and traditional mythologies," my father explains. "Too much to compete with."

On Earth, Joyce has just been loaded into an ambulance. A Syrian paramedic is crying, "We gotta cool her down!" as her tattooed Irish colleague prepares an IV drip.

"C'mon, Joycey," Bette says, clearly hoping the Welcome's a false alarm. "Hang in there."

A monitor shrieks as the tattooed paramedic drives his needle into Joyce's arm and yelps, "BP's spikin' like crazy...we're gonna need the fuckin' paddles..."

"On it!"

"She's crashing, man....*shit*..."

Flatline.

Lights flash, dance music throbs. My father reminds me that transitions are smoothest when a soul's first Delusion in This Place matches their final vision of Earth.

Joyce appears through a laser-swept plume of fog and sees me, disguised now as Ray.

"Daddy?" she gasps.

Then she's gone.

SEKHU (*The Remains*)

Joyce had been dead for approximately three minutes.

When she regained consciousness at the County/USC Medical Center, the attending nurse informed her the dosage of MDMA and PMA she'd ingested had triggered hypertension and tachycardia requiring defibrillation. "Fortunately, the paramedics were able to get your heart pumping again quickly, so there shouldn't be any permanent brain damage...which means you are one *very* lucky girl."

But Joyce didn't feel lucky. Mostly, she was just incredibly embarrassed.

And angry. Joni Kochansky and her other Buckley friends had talked her into attending the rave in the first place, assuring her the molly would be an amazing experience, but chill. She wouldn't lose control. They said the guy they got the stuff from was a "totally cool" aspiring screenwriter with a B.S. in chemistry and "not some dirtbag."

Joyce barely spoke or texted with any of them for the rest of the school year, and her fledgling relationship with Joni was never really the same afterwards, devolving rapidly from almost girlfriends, to platonic lab partners to little more than Facebook acquaintances in the months and years that followed.

She knew it wasn't really fair to ice out Joni and the others, even as she was deliberately and subconsciously estranging herself from them. It wasn't as if they'd forced anything on her, and the only peer pressure she'd experienced had been the simple assurance they'd all have a fun night out together.

At the same time, she'd trusted them and they'd failed her.

Joyce was a firm believer in free will. She took full responsibility for her decisions: to lie to the Quarles about attending a slumber party at Joni's, to attend the rave, to swallow the molly. But the information she'd factored into her calculations had been faulty. She was a good student. Aside from sharing her religious doubts and hiding her lesbianism, she figured she'd been a relatively model teen, especially by Los Angeles standards. Even her old Witness friend Simon had been caught smoking weed, and there were rumors that another Kingdom Hall teen had terminated a secret pregnancy with a black market abortion pill.

Joyce figured she needed to deviate from the straight and narrow at least a little to be a fully rounded individual. She didn't want to be the type of college freshman who'd never walked on the wild side, and she'd figured dancing all night with Silverlake hipsters would be a relatively safe experience. She'd never tried alcohol or pot because she didn't like the idea of getting sloppy with her perceptions and behavior, but Joni swore molly would actually focus her mind and senses in a completely safe and non-addictive way.

"It's like right after an orgasm," she'd promised, "where your mind is clear and you're totally at peace, except it lasts all night and you're super jazzed instead of sleepy."

Years later, when Dr. Joyce Wyatt recounted the incident and its catalytic effect on her career and professional philosophy to a reporter from *Scientific American*, she explained, "I accepted what my friend said because I wanted to believe it. I took the statement on *faith*...a mistake I would never make again."

But, of course, the most significant part of the experience was her momentary glimpse of Heaven.

It was the first thing in her thoughts when she regained consciousness at LAC+USC, and Joyce knew instinctively that she hadn't been dreaming...not exactly. In the first moments of alarm and confusion after her eyes opened, she remembered having just seen her father, as he'd looked at the time of his death. Then, realizing she was in a hospital bed, she quickly attempted to reorient herself by reconstructing the events of the evening.

She'd been in a dark, smoky warehouse decorated like Wonderland by way of a steampunk fetish dungeon. They'd all taken the molly in Joni's car on the way to the rave, and about half an hour later she'd begun to feel dizzy on the dance floor.

She remembered feeling uncomfortably hot and desperate to get away from the flashing lights and fog machines, the crush of hipsters in bunny ears and body paint. She'd turned, looking for Joni to inform her she was going outside...

...and then, *whooosh*, she'd been flat on her back, staring up at a glittering disco ball, until it vanished in a thick blast of steam that seemed to fill the entire building. She'd wondered if maybe there was a fire in the warehouse and struggled to regain her feet, only to realize she was somehow already standing, moving forward through the haze.

She'd realized she was feeling much better, euphoric even. She'd wanted to go back to dancing, but couldn't find any of her friends. It seemed she was suddenly alone in Wonderland...

...until the clouds rolled away to reveal a voluptuous redhead and dozens of people she'd never met yet instantly recognized as family members, all surrounding...

    ...no, it couldn't be...

    "Daddy?"

    And then...

    ...fluorescence seeped through her lids and she'd opened her eyes in the LAC+USC hospital bed, somehow knowing right away that she'd "died" even before the attending nurse confirmed it. Indeed, Joyce wasn't entirely convinced in her fragile state of post-overdose paranoia that she was really, truly alive again until her mother rushed into the room, sobbing and slapping her repeatedly in the face.

    "WHAT THE HELL IS WRONG WITH YOU?" Shirelle howled, spraying her daughter with angry spit as Terry rushed to restrain her.

    "I'M SORRY!" Joyce screamed back, bursting into tears as the adrenalin of the moment shook her from her stupor in a surge of conflicting emotions.

    "DRUGS?" her mother snarled out from within Terry's encircling arms. "After all I've done...raising you right, giving you *everything*...you still wanna end up how *I* was, all strung out, on the *streets?* I will *never* outlive the shame of what I was then...what I *did*...but this is *worse*, because you *know better!*"

    "Mama, I'm sorry, it was a *mistake*," Joyce sobbed, "and I *swear* it won't happen again..."

    "You're damn right it won't," Terry said, "because first thing tomorrow..."

...and Joyce knew in a flash of intuition what he would say next, that her stepfather was going to pull her out of Buckley. He'd threatened home schooling before, and she absolutely couldn't let it happen, not when she was so close to college, her own life, freedom.

Which meant she was equally certain what *she* had to say, as much as she hated to...as much as she desperately wanted to keep it to herself, to process it...as much as it felt like three kinds of betrayal...

"I saw Daddy."

Terry fell silent in surprise as her mother gasped, *"What?"*

"I was *dead*," Joyce continued, willing exhausted tears down her face, selling the moment with all her might. "The nurse told me...and before I came back, I...I saw Daddy waiting for me...in *Heaven*..."

As soon as her daughter mentioned how close death had come, Shirelle's rage completely evaporated and she crumpled in Terry's arms, weeping. But then, to Joyce's surprise, her stepfather merely shook his head and said, "No, Joyce, you must have been dreaming."

"I *saw* him."

"Or maybe you were hallucinating," Terry continued, shifting into Study Night mode, "because your father and the great mass of the dead are *gone* from Heaven and Earth and will *only* return at the resurrection, whether you believe it or not."

"I *didn't* believe it, but I *know* I saw my father," Joyce insisted, "and now I feel like I just have to reevaluate...well, *everything*. You've always both warned me about becoming too worldly, and I think I didn't really understand what you meant until now, that I wasn't seeing, you know, the *big picture*. I mean, like, I know I have to keep going to *Buckley*, so I can eventually get a *good job* and everything..."

"Well, actually," Terry began, "your mother and I..."

"No," his wife shushed him, sensing a rare openness in her daughter's attitude. After all, Shirelle herself had been far more skeptical of the spirit when she was Joyce's age, running with the hard boys on Crenshaw, drinking, smoking, or snorting whatever came her way. In recovery, the counselors had talked themselves blue about surrendering to a higher power, and she'd always just rolled her eyes...

...until her night of rock bottom in the Union Rescue Mission when she'd finally, truly realized she was a sinner, that fate had nothing to do with her fortunes, and that she was powerless against her compulsions. Then, the next morning, she'd celebrated the insight with a liter of vodka.

Shirelle knew belief didn't always come whole and complete in a single flash on the Road to Damascus. It had to start somewhere, and if this was that moment for Joyce, then she didn't want to discourage it. "Tell us what you were going to say."

"That I'm sorry for disrespecting you," Joyce sniffed, choosing her words carefully. "The teachers and classes at Buckley are *great*, and I appreciate what you've sacrificed to let me go there. But I realize now that school can't be my whole world. I'm really disappointed in myself, and I feel like maybe I *do* need more guidance than I thought to make sure nothing like this ever happens again. And I also want to understand what I saw, what happened to me during those three minutes when I was...you know, out of my body or whatever...because it all felt so *real* that I'd just like to speak to one of the Elders about it. I mean, I know I've missed a lot of meetings and Study Nights this past year, and I'm way behind on my Field Service Reports..."

"Well, if you're *serious*, you know there's a Bible study tomorrow night," Shirelle replied with a hopeful glance at her husband, then a sinking heart as she noted the discomfiture of his expression.

"Unfortunately," Terry said with honest regret, "I'm afraid it's not that simple."

"They *shunned* you?" Indrani exclaimed, amused and amazed when she arrived for a visit the next morning.

"Well, apparently it's not official quite yet," Joyce replied, "but I guess things were already heading that way...seems I was 'marked' thanks to all the meetings I'd been missing and just kind of general, y'know, apostasy. But once the Congregation Elders hear about the drugs, that's pretty much an automatic disfellowship all by itself, so it doesn't look good."

"And I don't suppose your stepfather could simply *not tell them*."

"Oh, no, of course not," Joyce replied in bitter exasperation. "That would be disloyal to *Jehovah*. I mean, God forbid he and Mom should be loyal to *me* or anything, but anyhoo...the upshot is my life just got even *more* ridiculous, because now I'm gonna have to bust my butt for a religion I *hate* that doesn't even *want* me. Though, on the plus side, I'm not allowed to speak to any JWs and they won't speak to me, which kinda rocks..."

"What about Shirelle and Terry?"

Joyce mimed locking her mouth with a key and tossing it away, then continued, "They can't speak to me either, which at least means they can't home school me, so...yay!"

"Meaning you get to stay at Buckley?"

Joyce nodded. "As long as I play nice and sit through all the Kingdom Hall b.s. and seem like I wanna be reinstated, then Mom and Terry will keep paying my tuition...at least I *think* so. There's a lotta reading between the lines with those two..."

"They're not bad people," Indrani said diplomatically. "I know they're trying."

"*Very* trying," Joyce replied, sharing a smile with the older woman at the timeworn punchline, a traditional running gag in their discussions of the Quarles over the years. "And, to be fair, I really did mess up. I mean, like, bad..."

"Yes, you did. If you were my own daughter, you'd be grounded 'til *at least* college." Then, taking the girl's hand, somber, Indrani continued, "And I want you to promise you'll never be so dumb again...I'm too old for that kind of heartbreak."

Joyce reached her arms around the stout older woman, inhaling the familiar, comforting scent of her lavender perfume as she promised, then whispered quietly, "You know I saw Daddy when I was quote-unquote *dead?*"

"Really?" Indrani marveled, leaning back from the girl.

"Just as clear as I'm seeing you now."

"Well," Indrani replied, uncertain what to think, "I always said, wherever he is, your father would never stop loving you..."

"But you don't actually *believe* that, right?" Joyce asked, not unkindly. "I mean, even Terry thought I was seeing things, 'cause the JWs only think 144,000 true believers go to Heaven...which definitely rules out Dad..."

"I suppose," Indrani shrugged, "though I've always hoped maybe *something* happens after we're gone."

"Sure, of course, I guess most people do," Joyce said, brusquely dismissing the notion to get to her real point. "Only there's zero evidence anything *does* happen, which means whatever I saw was a figment of my imagination...except for the fact that my brain wasn't actually functioning at the time, because I was technically dead. So how could I have imagined it?"

"I don't know," Indrani replied, at a loss.

"Me, neither," Joyce said, excited, "but I can't wait to find out."

The older woman was still in the room an hour later when Joyce was released to the Quarles with an anti-drug pamphlet and a prescription for Dantrium. After leaving the hospital and saying goodbye to Indrani, the family stopped to pick up the pills at a Rite-Aid and some take-out from El Pollo Loco. Then, following lunch back in their Baldwin Hills home, Terry and Shirelle officially said their goodbyes to their daughter after informing the apostate that she had, in fact, been shunned.

"I'm way more freaked out than I thought I'd be," Joyce admitted the next day at school, confiding with Indrani over Skype in the Buckley computer lab. "Mom was sobbing like I was going to the gas chamber. She told me she loved me and said, 'I just pray that you'll find your way back to us.' Then Terry read the story of the prodigal son and declared that from that point on I was dead to all Witnesses, including them, until Jehovah...or, y'know, the friggin' Congregation Elders...decide to pull a Lazarus and restore me to 'life'."

"So...what exactly does that mean?" Indrani wondered. "Did they kick you out of the house?"

"Oh, no," Joyce replied, laughing even as she realized she'd also started crying at some point. "That would be too normal. "No, they've just been...*ignoring* me. They talk like I'm not there...if I say anything, they pretend not to hear me. If I'm standing in their way, they just walk around me. This morning, Terry made enough eggs for three, but just set two places at the table. So I served myself breakfast and sat with them...I guess they're not gonna *starve* me...but when Mom cleared the plates, she didn't take mine, and then she left my dirty dish in the sink after she washed everything else. I'm a ghost."

"But that's...that's just *childish*," Indrani recoiled.

"I know! It's *absurd!* I mean, they can't be serious, right?"

"I...I'm sure they're only making a point," Indrani said, uncertain of her own statement. "Things will probably get back to normal in a day or two."

The first disfellowship lasted nearly a year.

In the earliest days, Joyce was simply captivated by the absurdity of the situation and amused herself at home like a mischievous poltergeist, blatantly grabbing all the sausage from Terry's plate and feeding it to the dog or changing channels and standing in front of the TV until her mother stopped watching and retired to her room. But the Quarles' stubborn willpower was stronger than Joyce had expected, and her own need for love and contact from the guardians she'd always taken for granted was deeper than she'd initially anticipated. "Okay, seriously, *knock it off*," she screamed in Shirelle's face as her mother looked past her one morning before turning and walking away. "This is *bullshit*...you're supposed to be a *fucking adult!*"

By the second week of the shunning, the novelty had long since worn off and the teen's bids for attention had grown increasingly desperate. She climbed into the Quarles' bed at two a.m. and belted choruses of "99 Bottles of Beer on the Wall" at the top of her lungs until they relocated to the guest room and locked the door. She walked into the living room stark naked during Family Study Night and heard a satisfying gasp from her mother as Terry fixed his eyes on the Bible and continued reading Ephesians aloud in a calm, steady voice until his stepdaughter gave up and retreated. And the next day, she took Shirelle's car for a drive around the block without permission (or a license), then walked back into the house and slammed the keys defiantly on the kitchen island where her mother and stepfather were preparing dinner.

"I see your car's back in the driveway," Terry said to his wife. "I was about to call 911."

"I'd feel terrible if some misguided teenager had to go to jail," Shirelle responded pointedly. "Speaking of which, do you think we should continue supporting the Buckley School, dear? I sometimes wonder if the students there really *appreciate* all that we do for them."

"Fine, I get it," Joyce snapped, storming out of the room. "You win, okay? I'll be a good little ghost from now on. *Praise Jehovah!*"

After that, the Quarles settled into an abnormal sort of normalcy as Joyce tapped ever deeper into her own wellsprings of patience and self-reliance, biding her time. She cut the theatrics and slipped back into her regular routine, deriving most of her daily satisfaction from schoolwork and reading, especially books and articles on neurobiology and brain science. At night, she'd sit quietly with her parents for dinner or Study Night, occasionally sensing her mother's fond glances when Shirelle thought her daughter wasn't paying attention.

"Baxter, please tell Mom that she needs to sign the Pre-Med Club permission slip for my field trip to Children's Hospital Los Angeles," Joyce would say to her pug, rubbing his belly within earshot of Shirelle, and the signed form would appear on the refrigerator the next day before school.

Or, "Baxter, please tell Papa Terry that I need a ride to the Westside Food Bank in the morning to do my MLK Day of Service project," and her stepfather would silently drive her to and from her destination.

Before her mother and Terry had ceased direct communication with her, they'd placed Joyce on indefinite lockdown, using the perennial threat of pulling their Buckley tuition payments if she didn't come directly home from school each day, eschewing all afterschool socializing and extracurriculars. Yet as the months passed and the teen wordlessly joined the Quarles for every Study Night and Jehovah's Witness meeting they attended, she eventually received their tacit approval to participate in academic events like math competitions (which her stepfather, in particular, seemed to enjoy) and the sorts of community service projects that not only scored brownie points with the Congregation Elders, but would also look great on her college applications.

Indeed, the teen's behavior was exemplary for so long that the Quarles eventually invited Indrani and many of the Witnesses who'd been shunning the girl to a special Family Study Night on the occasion of Joyce's 17th birthday. "Just about a year ago, I lost my daughter spiritually...and we came very close to losing her physically as well," Shirelle announced, smiling. "But with Jehovah's help, our family has finally been reunited... Terry?"

"That's right," her spouse said, beaming with excitement. "As most of you know, Sister Joyce recently submitted an application for reinstatement and met with the Elders...and while the rest of the congregation will be informed at the midweek meeting tomorrow, I am happy and *so proud* to announce..."

Then, turning to speak directly to his stepdaughter for the first time in months, he continued, "...your disfellowship has ended. Welcome back!"

The Witnesses stood and cheered as Terry and Shirelle each in turn hugged Joyce, who responded, as sincerely as possible, "Thanks, everybody...it's great to be 'seen' again."

One by one, the other Witnesses also greeted the teen, shaking hands and congratulating her until she got to Indrani, who pulled her into an embrace and whispered, "You okay?"

"Never better," Joyce whispered back with a wink.

In the months that followed, Joyce continued attending Witness meetings and even joined her mother for a few afternoons of neighborhood evangelizing, while simultaneously increasing her participation in Buckley athletics and other extracurricular activities.

She requested and received glowing recommendations from several of her teachers and Congregation Elders. She achieved nearly perfect scores on her SAT Reasoning and Subject Tests, and by senior year was ranked first in her class. She applied to half a dozen colleges and was accepted by all of them, ultimately choosing to attend the Massachusetts Institute of Technology after they guaranteed a full ride four year scholarship...

...because, as she explained to the MIT recruiter, "I'm pretty sure that my stepfather and mother won't be contributing much to my tuition."

As for her room and board and other expenses, Joyce applied for every scholarship and grant she could find. She spent her final high school summer as a temp in Ozzie Tatum's law office and her senior year as a part-time Happyland helper for Indrani, who'd been putting aside additional money for the teen in Ray's name for years.

Joyce added still more to her college fund at an Open Study Night on the occasion of her 18th birthday, when the Quarles and many of the Witnesses in attendance presented her with checks and cash in commemoration of her upcoming graduation from Buckley. Shirelle announced proudly to the guests that her daughter would be giving a speech as class valedictorian before adding, "I wish you could all be there, but unfortunately seats are limited."

"Though I was thinking perhaps we might schedule another Open Study Night afterwards so that she could repeat the speech for everyone," Terry suggested. "Sister Joyce, what do you think?"

"I would love to," Ray's daughter replied with a big smile full of teeth.

"And now, for the final speaker of the afternoon, it gives me great pleasure to introduce your class valedictorian, Joyce Wyatt."

Sitting with the Quarles at the Buckley graduation ceremony, Indrani cheered along with the roaring crowd, hoping that Ray was somehow watching as the school's principal stepped aside and Joyce replaced him at the podium, confident and beautiful in her silver cap and graduation gown.

"Good afternoon to my fellow classmates," Joyce began, "and to all the friends, family, and faculty responsible for bringing us to this point. On a personal note, I would especially like to thank my mother and stepfather for keeping me safe all these years, and my dear 'Mama Drani' for keeping me sane."

There was good-natured applause and laughter as Indrani and the Quarles acknowledged each other with cordial nods. Then Joyce continued, "I would also like to thank my father, Ray Wyatt, for helping to bring me into the world and for loving me just as hard as he could before his life was cut short by tragic misfortune. By most accounts, he was a kind, decent man with a great sense of humor, and I'm sorry he's not here today to experience this key turning point in my life. And while it would be comforting to imagine he's somehow 'with me in spirit' at this crucial moment, or smiling down from Heaven, the very notion conflicts with a belief I hold dear and would like to share with my graduating class as we step forward to meet the challenges of a frequently chaotic world."

Shirelle clutched Terry's hand in nervous anticipation of the next line of the speech Joyce had shown them, which explained that since most of the 144,000 souls anointed by God were already ruling with Christ in the Kingdom of Heaven, the only hope of salvation for the 'remnant' of humanity at Revelation would come through good works and obedience to Jehovah, His organization on Earth, and His Governing Body in Brooklyn.

But instead, her daughter quoted Hobbes. "According to the 17th century treatise *Leviathan*, the natural condition of humanity ensures lives that are 'solitary, poor, nasty, brutish, and short.' Two hundred years after that phrase was penned, Charles Darwin reaffirmed that all natural life is engaged in a daily struggle for survival in a world of limited resources. Faced with such grim realities, it's easy to see why our ancient forebears, blessed or cursed with self-awareness and the power of thought, would seek the solace of a *super*natural realm where virtue is rewarded, injustice is punished, existence is prolonged, and there is, after all, some higher meaning to life, the universe, and everything *beyond* the simple instinct to kill or be killed, eat or be eaten. As a species, we've always been arrogant enough to assume we are somehow capable of *more* than our fellow animals, that we alone deserve transcendence. Or, in a quote frequently attributed to the Chinese philosopher, Sun Tzu, 'Can you imagine what I would do if I could do all I can?'"

She smiled at Joni Kochansky in the audience as she said it, and her first almost-love smiled back in nodded acknowledgement: *no hard feelings and it was fun while it lasted...good luck with your life and we'll always have Paris (or at least the Harvard-Westlake bleachers).*

"Darwin's *Origin of Species* holds that adaptation is essential to evolution, and thus in a world of faster, fiercer creatures, humanity's imagination and capacity for abstract thinking enabled us to survive and thrive in the natural world, thanks in part to visions of the supernatural. Civilizations were forged and protected at the behest of unseen gods. Inspiration was engendered at the whim of the muses. And the despair of consciousness was alleviated by a promise that everything lost here on Earth would eventually be restored in the afterlife. In short, we needed the supernatural once, just as we needed prehensile feet in the Miocene epoch, when our early primate ancestors climbed trees for sustenance rather than riding escalators all day at the Sherman Oaks Galleria."

Joni and Joyce's other classmates laughed at the familiar reference, happy for a moment of casual levity in the otherwise densely academic speech...though some of the families and faculty in attendance seemed noticeably tense at the drift of the valedictory while others were now conspicuously nodding their heads in support. Terry Quarle, coldly enraged at his stepdaughter for lying about the content of her speech (and himself for believing her) rose abruptly to leave, but Shirelle pulled him back down into his seat.

"However," Joyce persisted, "in the same way human beings once needed wisdom teeth, which are now considered vestigial and mostly just sit around getting impacted, our belief in the supernatural, in religion and other forms of 'magical thinking', has arguably transformed at this point from an asset into a liability. Whereas animals in the natural world are compelled to fight over limited resources, human beings now possess an unprecedented ability to share and protect resources, to eliminate the need for conflict, to extend the length and quality of our lives as we expand our habitat beyond all prior constraints. And yet, even as we assemble here in the protective embrace of this beautiful campus, Sunni and Shia Muslims continue their endless conflict over an ancient Islamic schism, Israelis and Palestinians clash over holy real estate, and countless so-called Christians choose greed over charity around the world. Oppression, ignorance, and political nihilism are championed in the name of faith, with catastrophic results. In our own country, facts are replaced by mythology in fundamentalist school districts where the fantasy of intelligent design is taught alongside the reality of evolution. Even here, in a city as modern as Los Angeles, there are citizens so primitive they would rather *shun their own family members* than question some absurd, narrow-minded dogma, too afraid to face the uncertainties of the world and their own *failings and weakness.*"

When Terry rose to exit the second time, Shirelle didn't stop him. Instead, she just set her jaw and quietly followed her spouse, turning her back on her daughter as Joyce's voice echoed from the gymnasium's loudspeakers: "In the words of one of my heroes, the late, great atheist writer Christopher Hitchens, 'The person who is certain, and who claims divine warrant for his certainty, belongs now to the *infancy* of our species.'"

Joyce paused to watch in cold satisfaction as the Quarles made their exit, the heavy exterior door slamming behind them with a definitive, satisfying *thunk.* She could sense the speech wasn't going over too well with the rest of her audience either, though nobody else had actually walked out yet. During the brief pause in her oratory, she could hear disgruntled mumbling around the gymnasium...noticed several yarmulked heads shaking back and forth in disapproval, the scowls on the faces of a Bahá'í couple in the back row, the nervous fidgeting of the Unitarian minister off to her left, waiting to conclude the graduation with a nondenominational benediction. Behind her, she could hear the Buckley School principal clearing his throat, as if eager for her to wrap things up quickly.

Even Indrani, who'd known exactly what the teen was planning, seemed a bit dour as her eyes shifted from the Quarles' exit back to the podium. But then Joni flashed the valedictorian a thumbs up, refocusing Joyce on the task at hand as she rallied to finish strong. "Now, I realize there are many who do not share my opinions...perhaps many right here in this room."

A ripple of nervous laughter swept the gymnasium as Joyce smirked in acknowledgement. "However, the wonderful thing about America is that we have the freedom to believe...or *disbelieve*...whatever we choose. And so, my fellow graduates, as we face our own transition from high school to adulthood, I merely ask that you consider the greater transformation of our species as we adapt and evolve away from extinction with science, not superstition...with open hearts and minds replacing ancient prejudice, and with a hunger for justice in the here-and-now instead of some invented hereafter. Or, to paraphrase *another* great British writer, imagine if there was no Heaven, no Hell...just sky above us, and all the people...well, you know the rest."

And that's where Joyce was going to end her speech, wrapping up with another quick round of thanks and congratulations...

...until Joni and a few of her other friends spontaneously sang the next line of the song, the part about living for the day.

Their day.

A cheer went up from the graduates, sprinkled with applause, as more teenagers and a few of their parents joined the chorus, lending their voices in support of Lennon's imaginary world of no countries, no reasons for killing, *no religion*...Joyce crowing the latter phrase into her microphone while Buckley school band members on the dais joined in with their own ad hoc accompaniment in a crescendo of music and voices until the song climaxed like a breaking wave.

"CONGRATULATIONS...WE MADE IT!" Joyce called out to her class triumphantly as the graduating seniors all leapt to their feet in a standing ovation the valedictorian hadn't expected or realized she'd needed until she suddenly burst into tears.

"Well, that went pretty well," Indrani said later, driving Ray's daughter back to Baldwin Hills.

"I guess," the graduate replied, sapped and weary in the aftermath. "I'm just glad they didn't shut the microphone off... Buckley's pretty cool about letting valedictorians say whatever they want, but atheism's not exactly a crowd-pleaser."

"Oh, I don't know...your classmates seemed to like it."

"I think mostly they liked how the musical number kinda came outta nowhere, like a flash mob."

"Maybe," Indrani shrugged, "but I also think your generation's a lot more wary of religion than mine was. I mean, there was definitely more tension among the adults...and I'm not just talking Shirelle and Terry."

"You should have seen my *first* draft," Joyce said. "Lots of good stuff about Joan of Arc and temporal lobe epilepsy and treating religious faith like any other mental disorder."

"But you don't really *believe* that, do you?" Indrani replied, displeased by the girl's brittle tone.

"Why not? I mean, it's *true*...ignoring reality and living in a fantasy world is kinda the textbook definition of insanity, right?"

"I guess it depends on your definition of *reality*."

"Uh, y'know...*science?*" Joyce countered. "*Facts?*"

"Yes, I understand all that...I'm not your mother and I'm not a child."

Joyce met Indrani's gaze and took it down a notch. "Sorry."

"I grew up in a strict religious household myself, remember...not as bad as yours, but my parents were hardcore fire-and-brimstone Pentecostal. My mama stuck a bar of soap in my mouth if I said *damn* and my papa hit me with a belt if I came home late from a date with a boy. I've fought my whole life against Bible-thumpers claiming God was on their side about everything and anything from mixed marriage to stem cell research. I've been around and seen plenty, so you don't have to explain how religion makes some people crazy and some people rich, how it's misused and abused to oppress and manipulate and every other bad thing. But I *also* know it helped your mother quit using when she didn't think she had the strength on her own...and I know we *never* would've had a black president without decades of ministers and their congregations organizing for abolition, Civil Rights, voting rights..."

"Except that wasn't *religion*, it was organization and political action," Joyce argued, respectful yet determined. "And Mom didn't need God, she needed *therapy*..."

"And *still* needs therapy," Indrani acknowledged. "But that doesn't change the fact that counselors and social workers couldn't reach her *until* she got religion...and whether it's all fake or not, it *worked.* Same with Civil Rights, and most of the charitable work I've ever been involved with. Say what you will about religious people, even your mama and stepfather and those other Jehovah's Witnesses...but a lot of 'em *do* walk the walk..."

"Oh, come on...there are plenty of atheists and agnostics who support causes and give money to charity."

"Yes, there are. Though like I read someplace once, *money* only works 'cause people have faith and believe in it...and you wouldn't say *money* doesn't exist."

"Well, I think money should be eliminated, too," Joyce shrugged. "It's the root of all evil, so I hear."

"It's not good *or* bad...it's just a *tool* is what I'm saying, a way to organize how we act...and if it went away, then something else would replace it, same as religion. I mean, look at the Bloods and Crips...those fools have been killing each other for decades, and God ain't got nothing to do with it."

Through the windows of Indrani's Prius, Joyce suddenly noticed the I-10 come and go and cried, "Hey, you were supposed to take that!"

"Take what?"

"The 10 to Baldwin Hills!"

"Oh!" Indrani exclaimed in startled befuddlement, glancing around at the surrounding Los Angeles sprawl. "Where are we? I should have been paying attention."

"It's okay, we can take Venice Boulevard instead," Joyce reminded her, pointing to an upcoming exit.

"Right, yes, sorry," the older woman said, unaccountably desperate not to miss the upcoming off-ramp as she veered across three lanes of traffic in a Doppler cacophony of blaring car horns.

"Careful!" Joyce yelped in a bleat of involuntary panic, clutching the passenger assist handle above her seat and pressing her other palm against the dashboard as the Prius rocketed from the 405 and banked around the off-ramp down to the surface road like a Tilt-a-Whirl.

Indrani hit the brakes hard at the light, and as they both lurched forward, laughing in the adrenalized, wide-eyed aftermath of the sloppy, cyclonic exit, she said, "So...you believe in God *now?*"

Joyce had lingered with Joni and her other friends after the graduation ceremony, shedding tears and signing yearbooks for nearly an hour. Then she and Indrani had stopped for lunch at Jinky's, a Sherman Oaks café that had been their primary (and occasionally secret) rendezvous spot throughout the Buckley years...

...which meant when they reached the Quarles' house, enough time had passed that Joyce's possessions were already neatly boxed and stacked in the front yard. Baxter was tied up and napping on the lawn, and a cluster of suitcases and gym bags formed their own little island nearby, with copies of *The Watchtower* conspicuously tucked into some of the available side pockets.

Even though ejecting from the Quarles' orbit had been the whole point of Joyce's valedictory and some kind of immediate shunning had always been a distinct possibility, Indrani was nevertheless surprised to see the teen's possessions literally kicked to the curb as the Prius pulled to a stop.

"Well...they made their choice," Ray's daughter said, too cried out for more than a resigned shrug and a bitter sigh. "I'm just glad Baxter's okay, or there would have been drama, for reals."

Stepping from the vehicle, the two women quickly loaded the boxes and suitcases into the beat-up old Prius, then Joyce scooped Baxter into her arms, untying his lead from the tree as she whispered, "C'mere, you little salami brain..."

Nuzzling her nose into the pug's bristly wrinkles, she felt her eyes misting again until, sensing movement in her peripheral vision, she turned and saw her mother framed in one of the arched living room windows of the spotless McMansion, quietly observing.

Shirelle raised a palm against the glass, slender fingers extended in a frozen wave of farewell.

Clutching Baxter, Ray's daughter turned and walked straight to the Prius without looking back.

In all her years as a student and helper at Happyland, Joyce had never ventured into the off-limits part of the building containing Indrani's private living quarters. In her mind, she'd always conflated the mysterious space with the amazing unseen interior of Snoopy's doghouse from the daycare's collection of *Peanuts* books, improbably spacious enough to contain anything she could imagine, from priceless art to an Olympic swimming pool.

And thus she couldn't help feeling a bit let down when she finally carried her suitcases through the forbidden doorway only to find two bedrooms, a kitchenette, a bathroom and a small, crowded living room with an old console TV and yards of IKEA shelves loaded with books and photos. Yet the slight disappointment also made her feel just a little more adult as Indrani carried Joyce's pug into the unfurnished guest room and said, "It's not much, but I expect it'll do for the summer...isn't that right, Baxter?"

The dog offered an indifferent wheeze as Joyce wrapped her arms around the older woman and said, "I don't know what I'd do without you, Mama Drani."

"Well, I'll tell you *one* thing you can do without me," Indrani said, resolved, even as she and the pug leaned into the hug. "And that's walking *this* little guy and cleaning up all his business...I've never had a pet in my life, and I *don't* intend to start now."

"Oh, definitely," Joyce assured her...

...though less than a week later, she'd already broken the promise, working late for Ozzie Tatum one night while Indrani took her first of many strolls with the pug, ignoring the complaints of her aged knees to bend and scoop his poop into a funneled *Watchtower*.

By then, of course, Indrani and the latest crop of Happyland children had already fallen helplessly in love with Baxter, which in turn made things much easier when, inevitably, Joyce realized she wouldn't be allowed to bring the goofy little dog along with her to college. "I didn't know I was *required* to live on campus freshman year, and they don't allow pets in the dorms," she wept, clutching the pug to her chest. "Do you think it's too late to switch to USC? I'm *serious*..."

"Now don't be ridiculous," Indrani cooed. "MIT made the best offer and has exactly the program you're looking for...besides, it'll be good for you to see another part of the country, and Baxter will be just fine with me here 'til you find a pet-friendly apartment *next* year, okay?"

Except that, by the time she was a sophomore, Joyce was spending so much time on campus in the Brain & Cognitive Sciences lab that it only made sense for her to remain in the resident dorms. And Baxter had become such a fixture at Happyland that it seemed unthinkable to remove him anyway, even when Ray's daughter finally decided to move off campus with friends in her final undergraduate year.

"But I can't wait to see my favorite little four-legged fellah," Joyce said in a relaxed, happy call after completing the last of her final exams before the semester's winter break. "Not to mention my favorite *two*-legged lady...speaking of which, can you still pick me up at LAX on Sunday?"

Indrani, momentarily thrown by the word *still* considering it was the first time they'd discussed the visit replied, "Oh, uh...yes, of course...what time will you be arriving?"

Because she hadn't really experienced it during most of her childhood, Ray's daughter always loved Christmas despite her disbelief of the surrounding mythology. During her freshman year at MIT, Indrani had flown out to Boston so they could celebrate the holiday together in full New England splendor, complete with dorm room tree-trimming, church bells in Copley Square, and *Black Nativity* at the Tremont Temple. In the years that followed, they'd also sampled Chanukah in Manhattan (with Joyce's sophomore roommate) and then

Christmas again the following season in Las Vegas.

But for her sole remaining winter break as an undergraduate, Joyce had decided to return home for the holidays. "After all, I'm still not sure where I'm going next year, so who knows when I'll be in Los Angeles again?" she reasoned. "And besides, I've never been to Disneyland."

Indrani loved the holiday season as well, viewing it less as a proprietary religious festival and more a celebration of all birth and humanity, a ritualized pause for reflection, joy and wonder. Most of her young charges were nominally Christian, so each December, Happyland would be festooned with angels, Santas and reindeer, along with a menorah, some Kwanzaa candles, and a scattering of Ramadan Fanoos for good measure.

And though she'd once loved picking out the daycare's annual Christmas tree, Indrani had grudgingly acknowledged the rigors of age in recent seasons, simplifying her Yuletide duties with a polyvinyl chloride pine from Lowe's...

...which she'd only just hauled from storage and was down on all fours assembling when Joyce arrived for her final visit to Happyland.

"Hello?" Ray's daughter called, letting herself into the building with the set of keys that she'd carried since her first part-time shift at the daycare years before.

Indrani, who hadn't been expecting visitors, was startled enough by the voice that she reared back instinctively, banging the lower branches of the fake tree with enough force to knock it down before losing her own balance and toppling sideways, roughly scratching her forehead against one of the sharp edges of the decoration's four-pronged base.

Joyce heard a cry and rushed into the daycare, abandoning her suitcases on the front step as she called, "Drani!"

Looking up from the floor in surprise, Indrani gasped, "Baby Joyce?"

"Oh my gosh, you're bleeding," Joyce said, reaching to help the old woman to her feet. "What happened?"

"Nothing, I...you just startled me. I wasn't expecting..." Then, seeing the luggage through the doorway on the front step of the building, she realized, "I was supposed to pick you up!"

"It's okay, I took SuperShuttle," Joyce replied, grabbing one of the daycare's first aid kits to clean and dress Indrani's laceration. "But your phone didn't ring...I left a couple of messages."

"The battery must be dead...anyway, I'm so glad to see you!" The two women embraced before Indrani continued, "And I know someone *else* who's been missing you! Baxter! Come here, boy!"

When the pug hadn't waddled into the room by the time Joyce finished bandaging her forehead, Indrani retrieved one of the suitcases from the front step and said, "He must be feeling lazy today...come on, let's get you settled. His favorite napping spot is still your old bedroom, even after all this time."

Joyce smiled, retrieving her remaining bags, and followed Indrani into her residence. She was about to inquire about the old pug's health when the stink of stale urine and fresh feces brought her up short.

"Uh-oh," Indrani muttered, embarrassed, "I think somebody

had an *accident*."

Rushing to open a window, Joyce didn't notice the state of the old woman's living quarters until she turned back around to see the morass of *L.A. Weekly*s, fast food debris, and dirty cups and dishes overwhelming nearly every available surface. In her time with Indrani after high school and the college summers that followed, the residential rooms had always been spotless, but now the carpet was stained and a small, dry log of dog shit was visible in a corner by one of the IKEA bookshelves...and apparently it wasn't even the most recent specimen.

"Bad dog!" Indrani scolded from the guest room, where the stench was even stronger thanks to Baxter's latest deposit, a potent warm pile near the foot of the bed.

Joyce rushed in to help open more windows, then spotted her pug in the closet, gazing out apologetically through moist tired eyes. A small pink mass like bubble gum glistened beneath his runny black nose, and when the younger woman inquired what it was, Indrani seemed confused and said, "Oh, that's been there for awhile...hasn't it?"

"No," Ray's daughter replied quietly, "this is new."

The Washington Dog & Cat Hospital wasn't usually where Baxter went for appointments, but it was the closest veterinary clinic that could squeeze them in on a Sunday. And the news wasn't good.

"I'm afraid it's a mast cell tumor," the gaunt white lab tech handling the case informed them. "It's fairly common in pugs, and ordinarily I'd recommend excision or radiation therapy and maybe even chemotherapy agents. But, unfortunately, given the advanced state of the condition and your dog's age, we might want to focus more on quality of life issues at this point. I mean, we can certainly medicate his discomfort, and testing will tell us more...but if he's 16, well...that's a pretty good run for a pug. Better than average, actually."

"So you're saying all we can do is just treat the pain?" Indrani asked, disbelieving.

"What he's saying," Joyce translated, unable to look at the old woman, "is we need to put Baxter to sleep."

"Now, of course, you don't have to decide right this moment..." the lab tech began.

"No," Joyce said, not able to look at him, either, eyes fixed only on Baxter. "Let's do it."

"Wait," Indrani said, at a loss, "are you *sure?*"

"He's *MY DOG,*" Joyce snapped in a flash of unbidden anger.

"Take as much time as you need," the lab tech murmured, closing the door with a soft click as he tactfully exited the examining room.

"Oh, Joyce, I'm so sorry," Indrani said, helpless tears forming in her eyes.

"It's not your fault," Ray's daughter replied, still not looking at her yet consciously softening her tone as she enfolded Baxter in her arms, laying her cheek against his warm bristle, recording his soft wheezy breaths in her memory. "It's nobody fault...that's the problem."

KHU (*The Guardian Angel*)

I've kept a close watch on Ray's daughter. And I'm not the only one.

At one point, I thought she might help to save her father.

Now I mainly just wonder who'll save us from *her*.

I stood beside Joyce, invisible, on the day they put down her dog.

I've been in This Place long enough to regard the lives of friends and strangers on Earth the way I once viewed characters on television, as distilled echoes of my own experience (only far more intense and engaging). Emotions become more abstract the longer you're dead, but if I still had tears I would surely have shed them when Joyce clutched her childhood pet, nose to snout, whispering apologies and reassurances as the gaunt white lab tech returned with a vet to administer the fatal dose of pentobarbital.

I remember watching as Joyce saw the light go from Baxter's eyes in one unmistakable instant, the switch of life forever flipped. Was there a flicker in the Energy at that moment, a return of his animal soul to the general life force, a passage to some Dog Heaven undetectable by human spirits? I have no way of knowing.

Later, I watched Joyce discuss that ineffable light with friends (and eventually professors), long before the Realists and Oblivionists understood where those conversations were heading.

"Why even *make* life if we don't have the slightest idea what it's *for?*" Joyce complained bitterly over way too many Chinese drinks at the Formosa Café on the night of Baxter's death, while Joni Kochansky and a hastily assembled coalition of old Buckley classmates attempted to console her. "Why have pets if they're just gonna *die?* Why have kids if you're gonna leave 'em behind, missing you...and then the fucking kids die, too? I mean, what's the fucking *point?*"

"Something to do, I guess," Joni shrugged, draining a Suffering Bastard. "Keep the species going and whatnot."

"For what *purpose?* To what *end?*"

"I dunno...what's the purpose of this little umbrella?" Joni shrugged again, picking the paper decoration from the dregs of her drink. "It's just there, for the fun of it..."

"But life isn't *fun.*"

"Oh, I don't know," Joni slurred, throwing an arm around her almost lover's bony shoulders, flirtatious. "It can be."

"Not fun enough," Joyce scowled, glowering down into her Scorpion Bowl. "All the happiness in the history of human existence doesn't come anywhere *close* to balancing out all the misery. We should really just *break the cycle...*"

"What do you mean?" one of their old classmates asked, briefly rousing from a rum-induced stupor without lifting her head from the bar.

"We'd never miss life if we'd never existed in the first place," Joyce replied. "Birth is the leading cause of death, and I say to hell with it...no way I'm putting another generation through this bullshit. No more pets, no more children...let's shut the whole fucker down..."

"Cheers to that," Joni said, clicking her ceramic head against Joyce's bowl. "No way I'm bringing kids into this fucking world."

"I mean, if you're already here, fine...be nice to each other, whatever...but from now on, no more. Everybody goes on birth control and we just wait for all the babies to grow up and die off. That's it...the last generation."

"Here's to the last generation," Joni toasted again, then ordered a Zombie.

I saw the light behind Indrani's eyes flickering like a faulty bulb as Joyce took her for dementia testing at UCLA's Center for Alzheimer's Disease Research.

Even before we all started paying attention to Ray's daughter in This Place, I'd long felt a connection with her and her various connections on Earth. My father believes an interest in life prevents the pull towards Stagnation, so I watch over friends and relatives and acquaintances and *their* friends and relatives and acquaintances like a beautiful landscape, the great human tapestry.

All of the past is known to the dead. When Indrani Jones first came to my attention, I scrolled back through her entire life and realized we'd crossed paths at least a half dozen times on the physical plane. As a toddler, I'd seen her in the background of a news report about a Black Panther rally in Oakland, just before Mom changed the channel to *Hee Haw*. The week I first moved to Los Angeles, we'd eaten a meal in the same Mexican restaurant, three tables away from each other. Two years and seven months later, heading into a movie theater, I'd held the door open for her when she'd been carrying popcorn and drinks and she'd thanked me. We'd passed each other six years after that on the campus of Pepperdine University, where Ozzie

Tatum had invited her to attend his son's graduation from law school. I once found a quarter on Wilshire Boulevard that she'd dropped ten minutes earlier while feeding a meter. She'd visited Ray at Cedars-Sinai once or twice while I'd been in a coma.

When test results confirmed her dementia, I saw Indrani recoil from the news as Joyce burst into tears beside her in the doctor's office. "So...how long have I got?"

"Well, you're in the early stages now," Moshe's son, Dr. Noah Ben-Zvi explained, another intersection of the tapestry, another meaningless coincidence or proof of some larger pattern. "And the bad news, I'm afraid, is that our current treatment options are essentially palliative, not curative. We can implement strategies to maintain a decent quality of life for you as long as possible, but we cannot delay the worsening of symptoms. On the positive side, you still have good years ahead...maybe five, maybe seven...to make the most of your time and set any necessary affairs in order before the onset of the more *challenging* stages of your condition..."

For Indrani, those affairs included drawing up a will, shutting down Happyland, and, most importantly, researching assisted suicide laws so that she'd be ready when the time was right.

For Joyce, it meant choosing Caltech for her grad school program in neuroscience, in part so that she could live with and care for the woman she'd long considered her closest living relative.

In the first year after the Alzheimer's diagnosis, Indrani traded her Prius for a bike, figuring she'd get into less trouble on two wheels. "And if I ever forget where I am," she told Joyce, "you won't have to go too far to find me, since I can't pedal more than a couple of miles without getting all tuckered out."

After selling Happyland, she and Joyce moved into a first floor two-bedroom condo in Pasadena within easy walking (and biking) distance of shopping, restaurants and the Caltech campus. And while Indrani was noticeably more forgetful, the two women could generally still laugh off the lapses, falling into the familiar domestic rhythm they'd enjoyed during the summers they'd previously spent together.

They decided against adopting another dog.

Joyce spent most of her time in classes and lab rotations or studying, but on weekends she and Indrani would stroll the Huntington Gardens or take day trips to Malibu and Big Bear. At night, they'd watch TV until they both fell asleep on the couch like an old married couple.

As time went on, though, and Joyce's course work and research became more intense, she began to find their television ritual more stressful than relaxing as programs became increasingly difficult for Indrani to follow, occasioning a constant stream of questions, clarifications and repeated explanations. And on the occasions Ray's daughter was able to actually concentrate on a show or sneak off to a solo movie screening, it was somehow even worse: her racing thoughts would steal focus away from the flickering images in front of her or she'd unexpectedly lose control of her emotions, weeping uncontrollably during the schmaltziest of melodramas and sobbing over sweet old ladies in Metamucil commercials.

"I think I must be pre-grieving," she explained to the Neural Computation T.A. she dated briefly during her second year of grad school. "It's, like, I know this massive loss is coming, and so I'm mourning on the installment plan, in bits and pieces, so I won't have to experience all that pain at once...because otherwise, I'm afraid it would drown me..."

By her third year of grad school, Joyce was too busy for romance or even sex and her relationship with the T.A. fizzled as she struggled with the direction of her thesis research by day and Indrani's worsening dementia at home.

"Where are you going?" the old woman shrieked one morning as Joyce was heading out the door, running late for a meeting with her advisor. "The children will be here soon, and I can't do this *all by myself!*"

"There are no children!" Joyce explained, not for the first or last time. "Happyland is gone, remember? We're in Pasadena now."

"*Pasadena?*" Indrani gasped, clutching Joyce's arm. "We'll never make it back in time!"

"Indrani, *listen* to me, you don't have to be *anywhere*, it's all right..."

"It's *NOT* all right...and I wish I had never *hired* you!"

"*Indrani!*" Joyce cried, gripping the old woman's shoulders and shaking her in frustration, "just *concentrate...*"

"*Take your hands off me, pig!*" Indrani screamed, driving her palms into Joyce's chest with surprising force, enough to knock the grad student back against a small table by the door, bruising the small of her back in a sharp, sudden sting.

Joyce, worn down by the endless siege warfare of the old

woman's dementia, reacted without thinking, screaming, *"SNAP OUT OF IT!"*

And slapped her.

She was at least as surprised as Indrani in the silent half second just after it happened, and then Indrani unleashed a piteous wail of confusion and sorrow and lost control of her bladder.

"Oh, Jesus *Christ*," Joyce cried, pulling the frightened old woman into a restraining, protective embrace, "I'm *sorry*...I'm *so sorry*...I am *so sorry*..."

In the aftermath, Ray's daughter gently calmed and stripped Indrani down and guided her into a warm bath, then rescheduled the appointment with her advisor and began to research hospice volunteers. She eventually settled on Grace Agana Jao, a boyish 19-year-old Filipino girl with a sweet disposition and a charming gap between the two front teeth of a ready, megawatt smile.

On the phone, Grace explained that she'd been working with the California Hospice Foundation since high school and was studying to become an RN. And later, in person, Joyce was amazed how well Indrani responded to the teen's sunny disposition, how efficiently the petite volunteer managed the old woman's behavior, even as it grew increasingly erratic.

"Lourdes!" Indrani might cry, "We have to get ready, the children will be here soon!"

"Okay, Ms. Jones," Grace would reply, calmly ignoring the old woman's delusions. "But first we have to finish our shopping list. Now, did you like those Honey Nut Cheerios, or would you like me to pick up a different cereal this week?"

It was Moshe who eventually made the connection, during one of his frequent visits to my Construct in Not Malibu. We'd been observing Indrani together, speculating on the eventual date of her death and discussing the special challenges of Welcoming souls who'd been stricken with Alzheimer's when Grace arrived for one of her volunteer shifts and the one-time rabbi exclaimed, "No, it can't be...though it *must!*"

"What?"

In response, the entirety of the hospice worker's earthly existence flashed into my consciousness and I suddenly understood: the Jaos had emigrated from Manila after the birth of their daughter, who'd been conceived nearly two decades earlier, just after the Los Angeles earthquake that killed...

"Mary!" I said, remembering the pudgy young nurse who'd tended me in my final hours on the physical plane before her eventual Rescue from Delusions of Hell...the first of many souls I'd helped send to the Energy in hopes of rebirth.

I saw again the vision of a harried young mother in a Filipino jeepney, one of five women on Earth who conceived during the exact instant Mary disappeared from This Place. "But how do you know it's her?"

"It's not," the invisible lady whispered in my thoughts before I could ignore her.

"Maybe it's *not* her," Moshe replied coincidentally. "*But*...one of five possibilities randomly intersecting with two souls connected so closely to Mary's previous life? It's not *nothing*."

"It's certainly worth noting," Raquel agreed, materializing beside us, drawn by the discussion. And with a thought, the information was noted for posterity in the collective memory of This Place, a fresh data point or theory or coincidence for the Realists to ponder and debate for however long eternity lasts.

"Also, the fact she is studying to be a nurse is *very* interesting," a Hindu soul I recognized yet couldn't place suggested, imprinting himself on my consciousness as a transcendent blue shimmer. "The *jiva* frequently replicates familiar patterns."

"Pete, this is my friend, Ajit," Racquel said, making the introductions. "He played one of the Holy Ghosts back when we sent Mary into the Energy, though I don't think the two of you have ever been formally introduced."

"Ajit's one of our resident experts on reincarnation," Moshe chimed in.

"You're too kind," the blue shimmer replied, acknowledging my incarnation. "Very nice to meet you."

"Likewise," I said. "But tell me...assuming Grace really *is* Mary's new earthly form, well...I mean, what happens now?"

"Why, nothing," Ajit responded, as if confused by my question. "Nothing is confirmed or expected in This Place. We only search for *jivas* as a meditative ritual, in hope their patterns are Real and perhaps some part of the *ultimate* Pattern, whether or whatever that may be..."

As I came to understand his meaning, I pictured Grace's *jiva* as a line of identity encompassing Mary, then stretching even further back into endless combinations of souls and species across billions of years in a spiraling, expanding mandala before dispersing into Nothingness as Ajit concluded, "...or perhaps the creation and destruction of patterns *is* the Pattern."

We fell silent as another year passed on Earth, and Joyce decided on the direction of her graduate research, studying the loss of memory and destruction of self at the core of dementia, mapping the brain's storage capacity and cognitive functionality. Then, haunted and chastened by her own flash of violence against Indrani and the old woman's ongoing surges of panic, confusion and dread, Ray's daughter redirected her lab work towards the electrochemical origins of emotion in the human nervous system and prefrontal cortex.

Her investigation of anger and fear led to a contemplation of other passions: pheromones and peptides in the biology of attraction echoing stolen glances between Joyce and Grace in the Pasadena condo...until the morning their eyes eventually locked and lingered.

By the following year, as their relationship blossomed, Joyce began to contemplate the force of love beyond sexual attraction and the imperative of procreation. Were there evolutionary advantages in the relatively stable historic rates of genetic predisposition towards homosexuality in a subset of the human population? Was there a scientific explanation for her compatibility with Grace, even if they couldn't physically produce offspring and weren't sure they'd ever even want to adopt?

And how to explain the strength of her bond with Indrani when she hadn't spoken with her actual flesh and blood mother for years? Existing theories explained why the biological advantages of human brain development required a longer period of parental investment in the process of child rearing, as well as the general group selection impulse to nurture and protect non-related organisms for the greater viability of a species. But none of that explained how or why, as a mature adult fully capable of ensuring her own survival, Joyce could feel so much love for one dotty old lady when she honestly didn't give a flying fuck about most of the rest of humanity except in the most hypothetical of terms.

All of which led to her ultimate thesis topic and the seeds of her most significant research: humanity's bond with the invisible. Why did so many people still love souls that no longer existed? Or gods that had never been seen? What evolutionary benefits did such delusions convey?

Perhaps, she reasoned, religious faith and the hope for some kind of afterlife...even the very concept of incorporeal souls and the search for ultimate meaning...were nothing more than self-replicating memes, vestigial glitches in humanity's core neurological programming.

If so, then perhaps those delusions could be treated, like schizophrenia, with antipsychotic medication.

Or maybe, with further mapping and study of brain functionality, the glitches could be deleted entirely.

No more existential despair, no more sobbing at funerals.

An evolutionary leap forward. A stronger, more rational species.

And then her research got *really* dangerous.

SEKHU (*The Remains*)

"So basically you're saying humanity is a mental disorder," Indrani sighed.

"Not exactly," Joyce smiled.

Even in the mid-stage of her cognitive decline, Indrani still had good days, where she was almost as coherent as she'd ever been. And though in some ways it made the long farewell unpredictably painful as the adopted grandmother she loved continually resurfaced after seemingly disappearing forever, Joyce nevertheless cherished the good days.

"Look at it this way...before Prozac and other antidepressants, people would get so incapacitated by melancholy they couldn't function, right? But then it turned out that inhibiting selective serotonin reuptake could modulate certain mood disorders and *VOILÀ*! Suddenly, a lot of people found it easier to deal with their problems and get on with their lives. So why not use biochemistry to reduce, say, hate crimes by medicating violent religious zealots instead of just locking them up? Or maybe you think God wants you to kick your son outta the house 'cause he's gay, but then you pop a pill and realize there's no cosmic reason the kid shouldn't be fabulous?"

"Who's fabulous?" Grace said, breezing in with a kiss for her girlfriend.

"You," Joyce replied.

"I think you mean this lady right here," the newly minted RN grinned, fluffing Indrani's pillow. "Can I get you anything, honey? Or do you feel like a walk?"

"I...I should probably walk."

"You're probably right," Grace said, helping the old woman from the hospice bed in stages. "My gosh, how long has it been?"

"A week?" Indrani guessed.

"Close enough!"

In actual practice, Grace had been trying her best to walk Indrani around the ward at least once a day ever since Joyce and Dr. Ben-Zvi had determined the old woman required full-time care and transferred her to the Cedars-Sinai hospice wing.

"You realize, of course," Indrani said as she wobbled down the antiseptic corridor, "that you'd only be treating a symptom. A lotta times when you've got religious violence or bigotry, there's racial and political and economic stuff going on, too...not to mention just plain ignorance, and there ain't no cure for *stupid*."

Joyce laughed and said, "Not *yet*...and I'm not saying everything can be cured or regulated with pills. I'm simply examining where some of the more harmful impulses and delusions come from..."

"Wabi," Indrani replied.

"What's that, honey?" Grace said as she and Joyce exchanged a quick look, bracing themselves for the inevitable sea change in the old woman's lucidity.

"Or wabi-sabi, wabi-nabi...something like that. A friend of mine at the Meditation Center was talking about it the other day...the beauty of imperfection. The little flaw in the glaze of a bowl or the weave of a rug that makes it one-of-a-kind. So I'm just saying, what happens if you get rid of the ugly side of people, or even the illogic or the foolishness? Are they still *people?*"

"Maybe *better* people," Joyce said, happy the Indrani she'd once known was mostly still present, at least for the moment.

"I don't know...they had me on depression pills for awhile, and I hated not being able to feel my own sadness. And say what you will, but a whole lot of good music comes out of desperation...start curing anger and craziness, you wipe out most of the art and comedy in the world, too."

"The creative impulse is like dreaming," Joyce replied. "A release valve...it helps people to interpret and cope with their lives..."

Indrani laughed. "Spoken like a true scientist."

"I'm just saying...it's not like society's gonna change overnight, but if technology helps to make us a better species, then maybe it's okay if there aren't as many sad, angry songs...even *great* ones...because it just means people are happier."

"People will always be sad and angry," Grace chimed in, "as long as there's sex and money."

"And *death*," Indrani nodded. "Gracie's too nice to say it in front of the dying woman, but no matter *how* long people live, they still gotta die sometime...and if you take away the hope for something after, if the end is really *the end*, then you're *always* gonna have pain and fear. And if you take *that* away, too...well, shit, we might as well be ants or something."

"I'm not talking about eliminating negative emotions," Joyce said, "Only managing them."

"So how sad is the acceptable amount when you're about to *disappear forever?*" Indrani replied with a sense of irritation bordering on anger. "When you lose everything...or even a piece of yourself? Are you just gonna shrug it off when I'm gone and get right back to happy thoughts?"

"No, of course not," Joyce reacted to the shift in emotion, meeting Indrani's gaze as the troika of women came to a stop in the hospital hall.

"Oh, really? Then explain it to me, Doctor. *Educate* me...what's the most efficient, scientifically acceptable amount of grief a person *should* experience?"

"Indrani..." Grace said, calm but glancing around the ward for nearby support staff in case the old woman suddenly became unmanageable.

"I'm gonna die and I *hate* that," Indrani continued, eyes fixed on Joyce. "And you're saying the answer is to just dope me up so I don't think about it? As if that's somehow better than letting me hang onto a tiny sliver of hope that maybe there's actually more to existence than grim certainty and statistics?"

"Like *what?*" Joyce exclaimed, unhappy to spend what surely would be one of their last coherent encounters engaged in such a pointless debate. "*Heaven?* It's not like you believe in that, either..."

"I'm not saying Heaven, but *something*," Indrani replied, "Why take that away from people who are sick, people who are grieving?"

"Because religion holds science and society *back*," Joyce argued, feeling her own emotions rising. "It's a drag on what human life *could* be...and life is all we have."

"Which you know...how?"

"Because it's *obvious!*" Joyce exclaimed, shrugging off Grace's hand as the RN tried to calm her now as well. "Look, I'm sorry, I know I should probably be more comforting or whatever, but we've always been honest with each other..."

"And I don't want that to stop," Indrani smiled, secretly pleased to have gotten the younger woman's goat, happy Joyce was arguing with her rather than coddling or condescending like most of her visitors.

"Fine," Ray's daughter sighed, offering her own exasperated smile in return as the walk resumed and they both allowed Grace to steer them back towards Indrani's room. "My point is that it's fine to pray to a fire god, but it's better to learn how to use flint and steel. And there's no atheists in foxholes, and you believe what you need when you're stressed, yadda-yadda, I get it...but it would *also* be a lot better if society didn't feed us false hope. If we all learned to accept death as just part of life from the start, maybe it would be easier to handle when it comes...and in the meantime, we could devote our energy to researching facts instead of fighting over fantasy."

"You were right before," Indrani said, gently gripping Joyce's hand. "You're *not* very comforting."

"Well, you asked for it."

"And so I'll return the favor by pointing out, one, you say it's fine for people to believe what they want...except what started the conversation was you saying you wanted to medicate religious thought like depression or schizophrenia. So, like most everyone, what you really want is people believing what *you* choose to believe. And just the same as those Christians with God on their side who think atheists are going to Hell, *you* think you're right 'cause you've got *science* on your side...which is all well and good, just as long as you remember *your* belief system has orthodoxies and zealots and blind spots, too. You say you're right because science can't prove there's a God or an afterlife, but you can't *disprove* it, either...and most of *your* high priests don't think the question's even worth asking in the first place. Folks who search for spirits and ghosts aren't considered *real* scientists 'cause they're supposedly asking the wrong questions. And I'm not even talking about...oh, who are those people who keep wanting to prove the Garden of Eden was real?"

"Creationists."

"Right...I'm not even talking about them, but rather actual, respectable scientists. Like...who was the man in the book we always argue about?"

Joyce laughed. "That doesn't really narrow it down...we argue about most books."

"I mean the one who investigated the séances..."

"William James?"

"Maybe," Indrani said vaguely as the trio reentered her room. "I just remember he kept testing all these psychics and mediums, and science loved it when he revealed most of 'em as frauds and phonies...but then he found some things he *couldn't* explain, a woman who actually seemed to have the gift of telepathy or prophecy or some such...and the second the man said he wanted to investigate further, that maybe something was happening that research couldn't explain, all his scientist buddies just laughed at him. They didn't care so much about facts then... didn't even want him continuing his experiments...said he was losing it, wasting his time..."

"Because scientists are just as human as anyone," Joyce sighed, helping the old woman settle into a chair by her bed. "There are conflicting theories and constant arguments about which lines of research seem worth pursuing and which seem pointless. And, yes, the supernatural hardly seems like a topic worth pursuing for most serious researchers, but there's always *someone* out there studying unicorns and UFOs and paranormal activity...it's just that it never *leads* anywhere..."

"Not *yet*," Grace said with a mischievous grin, playing devil's advocate. "But I'm with Mama Drani...just because they haven't found angels and aliens *yet* doesn't mean they're not out there somewhere."

"Hey, don't encourage her," Joyce replied lightly, pecking the RN on the lips.

"Hold onto that one," Indrani said, pointing at the tiny Filipina, though momentarily unable to remember her name. "She's a smart cookie...and she's exactly right. We can't prove there are aliens, say, but it hasn't been *disproven*...so what's the harm in thinking they *might* be out there if it makes us feel less alone in the universe?"

"I've got no problem if people wanna believe in E.T.," Joyce laughed. "There are literally billions of planets with the ingredients for life...maybe even other dimensions and universes, too. I *get* aliens."

Then, tapping her own skull, she added, "What I *don't* get is how a complex matrix of neurological processes could escape their physical casings and continue in some mysterious, autonomous state...all without leaving a trace of physical evidence behind to suggest how it happened."

"I don't know," Indrani shrugged. "But then again, you're always telling me nobody understands exactly how the brain works, period...and that's something you can literally put your hands on."

"Right, but we know brains *exist*," Joyce replied. "And when your brain is sick or damaged, your mind...your soul, *who you are*...is affected, too."

"So in other words," Indrani said quietly, "you're saying all I am now is a sick and damaged soul?"

Joyce felt the air go out of the room as she dropped to one knee, taking the old woman's hands in her own. "That's not what I meant...you know that's not what I meant. Your body is sick... the organ inside that beautiful skull. But no, you're right...that's not all you are."

"Then who am I?"

"You're everything you've ever been," Joyce said as she felt her voice turn liquid in another hot flush of pre-grieving, the emotional tide within her as unpredictable as the ebbs and flows of Indrani's coherence. "You're everything you've ever been, *to me...*"

"Well, maybe that's how..."

"That's how what?" Joyce said, unable to stop her stubborn tears from welling.

"Souls travel," Indrani replied, weariness settling. "Everything we do in our whole lives, transmitting out to any receiver...lovers and strangers, photos and medical charts...all of it recorded somewhere in bits and pieces. Ain't your father still here between us, now...and in your mama's thoughts, old friends' stories about him, and who knows where else? So maybe we're all saved, too, in some new kind of memory...like computer files, like echoes of thunder...*out there...*

...in the Cloud..."

REN (*The Secret Name*)

Five.

Five fives.

Five for the five who died: Karen, Petey, my parents, me.

My mother, Tilly, is still at the Pearly Gates Construct in eternal anticipation, forever waiting for whatever comes next.

I visit her sometimes, enjoy the beatific joy of her spirit in eternal devotion to a God who never arrives. She refuses to acknowledge my father or me or anything else as she waits for her belief to be validated as the one and only truth about death and the meaning of life. She's as stubborn as the Denialists who refuse to acknowledge This Place at all, and like them she remains fixed in a perfect Nirvana of permanent stasis: no thoughts, no memories, no decisions, no self.

But she does still have one thing.

Tilly still has what the Denialists reject and the Oblivionists soon may eliminate.

Hope for more.

Four.

Karen isn't sure whether she hopes for more or less. She can't say if she's a Realist or Delusional. Like me...like most of us...she's probably a bit of both.

She just knows she wants out.

If eternity is truly ending soon, then she wants it to be on her own terms.

And even if it's not, she wants to exit This Place while she's still some recognizable form of herself, before her restless spirit scatters, before her focus grows hazy from apathy, frustration, ennui. Before she Stagnates.

She's come to say goodbye. I want her to stay just a little bit longer.

"I'm tired of putting it off," she smiles, wearing the face of the woman I loved one last time.

My life wife.

She glances around at the Construct of my Not Malibu beach house, emanates bemusement. "I just can't stand Delusions anymore. Even the intentional ones, even the fun ones. I'm sorry, but it all just seems like a silly waste of time, avoiding the inevitable. If there *is* something else, then I say let's get on with it..."

"And what if there's *not?*" I reply, my habitual objection no more than a familiar ritual now that she's made up her mind once and for all. "I mean, even if you *do* reincarnate or achieve Nirvana or whatever else happens when you enter the Energy, I'll still never see you again."

"You can always come with me..."

"But I want to *exist*...and I don't just mean as a big '*Om*' in the collective unconsciousness or a drop of rain in the ocean or whatever the hell you're going for...I want to be *me*...I want to be with *you*..."

"And what...reminisce about the times I cheated on you? How much I hated your mother?"

"How much we loved our son, how much we loved each other, our friends, sunsets, music..."

"Our son has gone ahead to what's next," Karen communicates, softening her energy. "And you won't follow, because you don't want to stop missing him. But the truth is, your grief at losing him is more Real now than your actual memories of him, and eventually even the grief will be just a memory."

"That's not true."

"It *is* true, because he was my son and I loved him more than a father ever could...it's just simple biology. No sunsets or music or sex or hate or anything else could ever matter more to me than a soul I literally created...and so when even my *child* is just a fading memory of grief, you can imagine how much interest I have in reminiscing with you or anyone else, let alone spending even one more second trapped in my own stupid consciousness. No, it's way past time for me to move on, and I pray to God or Allah or Buddha or quantum mechanics or whatever that it works so I can finally find a way out of myself for good."

"Well," I huff, "I still think it's selfish to deliberately leave behind people who love you...and no matter what you say, I *am* going to miss you...all your individual thoughts, all you might imagine...none of that will ever be replaced or repeated."

"Trust me," Karen replies, transforming into a candle flame, one of thousands surrounding me as the imaginary beach house dissolves into flickering darkness, "you'll get over it."

I find myself invisible. I sense my father and many others in the imaginary shadows as the individual lights merge, one by one, two by two, into an ever greater conflagration.

"Goodbye, Karen," I think.

"Goodbye, Karen," I sense my father thinking.

But she doesn't respond. There is no more Karen.

She began training her mind for ultimate stillness long before now with the spirit of the man...*one* of the men she cuckolded me with on the physical plane. His name was Rafael. He was a yoga instructor on Earth. I never met him in life, but encountered him once as a blue djinn in This Place, soul-fucking the mother of my child in a ridiculous Feelie gangbang just after he died in the big L.A. quake.

Now he's going into the Energy with the woman I loved and still love.

It's a beautiful ceremony, but it's hard not to feel bitter.

Fuck you, Rafael, I think.

But now there's no Rafael, either, as all the tiny flickers merge into just five great lights...

...then four...

...then...

Three.

I feel a familiar *presence*...

drawn not, for once,

by rage, but...

tranquility,

...or, rather, stillness...

...an absence of thought, emotion, desire

so utter and complete it would draw me into the Energy like a

negative space vortex

if I let it, even without training or practice, and maybe this time

I would not try or bother to pull my individual identity clear, but rather

lose myself for all time, to be remade or destroyed as ultimate

Reality would have it...I feel my father's warning, to remember and

come back to myself before it's too late...then he's gone, and I'm alone

with the stillness and the Energy, yearning, please, for a glimpse of

सच्चिदानन्द

Supermind

eternal consciousness

complete understanding

without succumbing...

...to understand the ultimate Reality of nothing without *becoming*

nothing, to strain to see the something, the anything beyond it...to

sense any trace of what used to be my son...

...Petey...

...and then, the three big lights become...

Two.

I take shelter in my own ego before the twin blazes merge into
a final explosion of individual souls blowing out...

...joining the Energy...

...or simply disappearing...

...and I want no part of it...

...not yet...

Instead, I find myself back in my imaginary home in Not
Malibu with my father, Raquel.

We exist.

She's telling me the end is near.

"What?" I say, disoriented.

"I'm just worried this might really be it," Dad repeats, pouring
herself an illusory Limoncello spritzer at my fictional sideboard. "Who
knows? Maybe Karen had the right idea."

All the Realists are worried. According to old-timers like
Zenodotus, the prospects for eternity have never looked so bleak.

The problem is Ray's daughter.

She's figured out how to build Heaven.

On Earth.

Of course, I realize it's unfair to blame or demonize Dr. Wyatt,
as far too many so-called "Realists" have since the emergence of the

Cloud Soul.

"After all," Raquel says, "the poor thing's heart was in the right place...even if her mind no longer seems to be. And besides, the *real* threat to This Place existed long before she was born."

"What threat?"

"Why, the extinction of hope," Dad replies. "Hope for meaning. Hope for justice, reconnection. Hope for *anything* beyond simple, brutish reality...because, after all, isn't that what This Place really is? I mean, for centuries, even the most wretched of peasants on Earth could always, at the very least, believe their immortal souls were divine. But now? They're just *organisms* in the orthodoxy of science, their deepest passions dismissed as little more than serotonin-oxytocin cocktails. I mean, honestly, how dreary. If you explain away imagination and emotion, what's the point? And if people are *only* willing to believe in the physical plane, then it seems they can never really transcend it. Which, of course, was the variable Dr. Wyatt failed to account for..."

I agree with my father that certain trends were inevitable in a skeptical, technological age, and if it wasn't Ray's daughter who finally triggered the Summit, it would have been somebody else.

It's just that Joyce solved the mystery first.

In her eventual autobiography, she traced the inspiration for Cloud Soul to one of her final conversations with Indrani: "She reminded me that identity was never static or contained in one place. 'Souls travel,' she said, 'everything we do in our whole lives, transmitting out to any receiver, all of it recorded somewhere in bits and pieces.'"

Though, of course, at the time they were uttered, Joyce had naturally interpreted the words as mere metaphor...

...whereas from my supernatural perspective, I was able to witness the *literal* truth of the sentiment, years later, on the day of Indrani's Welcome. The old woman had long since lost her ability to speak or think or even regulate her own food intake without mechanical assistance. Whatever light of soul had once illuminated her glittering dark eyes was seemingly long since gone.

In life, I'd always wondered how an immortal soul could survive the destruction of its earthly vessel, yet over the course of countless Welcomes and Rescues, I'd come to realize how every dream, thought and perception arc out from the physical plane to This Place in continuous streams of Energy, indefinitely preserved.

Yet, until Indrani's death, I'd never experienced the reconstitution of a self eroded gradually across a span of years. "Oh, it's good," my father assured me. "I think you'll really enjoy it."

The one great romantic love of Indrani's life – her soul mate, in all senses of the term – had been a Black Panther activist named Roland. Gunned down by the Oakland Police decades earlier, he'd been watching her ever since, affection never wavering.

Knowing my father and I had taken an interest, Roland notified us when Indrani's life signs were fading, and together we gathered in a greater mass of consciousness with an assortment of the old woman's deceased friends, relatives, and ancestors in a Construct of her room in the Cedars-Sinai hospice ward.

On Earth, Grace had called Joyce when it seemed evident the

end was near, and the two women stood a grim watch until Indrani's heart monitor eventually flat-lined...

...while, beyond the veil, the Construct of her deathbed vanished and I suddenly found myself in the Nothingness.

"What's happening?" I thought. But then, before my father could answer, I sensed the strange energy of a soul without form, amorphous in the ether. "Is...is that Indrani?"

"Only in the sense of her very most basic essence," Dad replied, his own thoughts instinctively hushed as if whispering. "What my friend Ajit would call her *jiva*, devoid of memory and consciousness."

But then, even as my father communicated the notion, the *jiva* began to expand, swelling with all the thoughts and experiences of Indrani's 83 years on Earth, until her bewildered consciousness manifested as the withered, grey-haired woman she'd perceived herself to be in the final tattered moments of clarity before dementia completely saturated her mind.

Orienting herself to the hospital Construct, which had rematerialized in tandem with her own ability to recognize herself within it, Indrani gasped as Roland slowly manifested in the form of the slender young firebrand he'd been on the crisp long-ago morning when she'd first spotted him on the way to a rally at the Oakland Auditorium, all decked out in the righteous black leather jacket he'd worn so well and the silly Panther beret she'd always teased him about.

"Oh, baby, I must be dreaming or dead," Indrani marveled, decades falling away as she rose from her illusionary bed into the memory of an embrace. "And right now I don't even really care which, just as long as I never have to wake up again."

"Welcome home," Roland smiled as the hospice dissolved into a field of stars and the rest of us faded to give the young lovers their privacy.

Though I'd had no contact with Ray in some time, I thought he'd perhaps want to know that his old friend had died, yet he ignored me when I transmitted the news to his consciousness.

It was only much later, after Joyce split her soul, that he finally revealed himself once more.

Decades had passed on Earth by then, and his daughter had become one of the iconic pioneers of infomorphic technology, given her role in a series of revolutionary breakthroughs in optogenetics and computational neuroscience. As the founder and CEO of the trillion-dollar start-up, Cloud Mind, she had translated Indrani's concept of transmitted consciousness into a series of reaction-diffusion "goo-ware" networks with the capacity to replicate the functionality of neurons, synapses and neurotransmitters, first in roundworms, then lab rats, then canines, then primates...

...until finally, the imminent and inevitable question of human trials consumed the media, religions, and governments of the world.

Joyce, of course, had no interest in the myriad religious objections to her research, and while she could certainly understand the need for an honest dialogue regarding the moral and ethical implications of Cloud Mind, her standard response was always the same: "Let's get it to work first, and *then* we can argue."

Unfortunately, large segments of the population were equally passionate in their belief that Cloud Mind was a Pandora's Box far more dangerous than any technology since the splitting of the atom, a genie that could never be allowed to escape from its bottle, and reactionary laws were hastily passed in one country after another to hinder the research until Joyce (only half-jokingly) considered moving her lab facilities to the International Space Station.

Yet the biggest setback of all occurred five weeks after Joyce's 55th birthday, when the scientist was blinded and paralyzed in the terror bombing of Cloud Mind's then-headquarters in Geneva by an interfaith coalition of religious fundamentalists. Terry Quarle, who'd become a regular contributor to *The Watchtower* since his retirement from Paramount, condemned both the violence and the hubris of the technology under attack, designating it a modern Tower of Babel that would surely inspire God's wrath...though when the press sought his wife's reaction, Shirelle could not be reached for comment.

As for Joyce, she came to view the incident as a blessing in disguise. Shortly after regaining consciousness in a private clinic overlooking Lac Léman, the scientist summoned her wife to her side and said, "It's a sign."

"Yeah, right. I thought you didn't believe in those," Grace replied, intertwining the scientist's insensate fingers with her own.

"Just a figure of speech," Joyce smiled. "But I need your help...and your blessing."

Then she ran through her thought process: technology could ameliorate some of the effects of her injuries, but her quality of life would never again be what it was before the bombing. Grace, by then director of palliative and hospice care services at Cedars-Sinai, had extensive experience with euthanasia counseling and methodology.

"So you're saying you want me to kill you?"

"Not exactly."

It was time, Joyce said, for Cloud Mind's first human trial.

Given the direction of her wife's research and the extent of her injuries, Grace had already anticipated Joyce's decision and so offered her unconditional support and approval, both privately and during the subsequent closed door planning sessions with the Cloud Mind inner circle. And she agreed, even *demanded* to personally administer the mixture of sodium thiopental, pancuronium bromide, and potassium chloride that would peacefully stop her wife's heart.

Yet she was not without reservations and wondered, in early discussions, why the euthanasia would even be necessary. "I mean, don't you think we should wait to see if your mind copies over correctly before, y'know, deleting the original?" Grace argued.

"It doesn't work that way, unfortunately," Joyce replied, sanguine. "The process basically fried the hippocampus and cerebral cortex of all the subjects in our primate trials, and we'll need about ten times that juice to upload *my* big ol' brain...so you'd only be euthanizing my body after Elvis leaves the building. Besides, you wouldn't really want *two* of me, would you?"

"*Yes*," Grace said, a hitch in her tone betraying the emotion she'd tried her best to control since the bombing. "Or at least *one*."

Joyce felt an overwhelming impulse to reach out, but her arms remained still as she responded, "I promise, Gracie...it'll *work*."

"And what if it *doesn't?*" the Filipina snapped in spite of herself.

"I just don't understand why you can't wait 'til there's a better way of testing this without risking *everything*."

"Because I'm ready," Joyce said quietly.

Then, attempting to lighten the mood: "And, hey, trust me, if I thought it was *actually* risky, I wouldn't have volunteered. But I've spent my life on this and you have to believe me, *I'm not going anywhere.* I'll be right in the Cloud Mind, and you'll always be able to reach me."

"Except what if it's *not* you?"

"It *will* be...every single function of my brain, the whole spectrum of memory and perception that makes up who I am will be regenerated and preserved. And when you talk with me through the interface, or sing your stupid ABBA songs, I'll hear every pitch and trill of your voice, like I'm hearing it now, only..."

Grace noticed a tear seeping from the bandage still covering her wife's scorched blind eyes and gently erased it with her thumb as Joyce continued, "...only I'll be seeing that beautiful face of yours again, too. And when you join me in the Cloud, years from now...*if* you join me..."

"I will," Grace whispered softly in her ear, climbing up to curl beside her in Joyce's queen-size homecare bed.

"...then we'll make a new world from ourselves and live this evolution together, outside of death and time..."

...although Grace couldn't help wondering, even as the words left the scientist's mouth, how the great evolution would ever be more than a replica of life, and what the crucial differences might be.

But for the dead, the answer was obvious from the moment Joyce died.

Or, rather, didn't quite.

Given the nature of This Place, there had been endless speculation over the implications of whole brain emulation since at least the dawn of the transhumanist movement on Earth, as futurists of all stripes began anticipating the inevitable technological singularity when humanity transcended biology (even if none of them predicted a little girl from South Central would eventually be the one to get there first). So when Dr. Joyce Wyatt finally surrendered her natural, physical life by the shore of Lac Léman, the Heavens fell silent as the Cloud Mind sizzled and hummed, supercharging the scientist's synapses until her neurotransmitters were stripped, every neuron perfectly replicated in waves of electrochemical computation.

And that's when it happened.

I'd joined my father in her palazzo to watch, and as the Cloud Mind transference laid waste to the circuitry of Joyce's cerebrum and Grace stopped the scientist's heart, we both sensed Moshe in Not Jerusalem crying, *"Look, there! I can see her!"*

For Ray's daughter had just appeared in the Nothingness, a wisp of *jiva*, devoid of thought and memory...

...her immortal essence, unique yet untethered by consciousness or identity.

"It's beautiful," Ajit and Zenodotus marveled simultaneously from somewhere.

While on Earth, trillions of stored details reconstituted across interconnected data banks...recollections of sensations and preferences, inferences and definitions...a vast system of possibilities and complexities organized by the singular, randomized algorithm: Joyce.

"Hello? Can you hear me?"

As the question emerged from the Cloud Mind's voice simulation interface, Grace cried, "Joyce, is it *you?* Are you *there?* Is it *true?*"

And Not Joyce replied, *"I'm alive."*

But she wasn't exactly.

Nor was she dead. Not exactly.

As near as anyone in This Place could figure, her soul had been *split*, like contents ripped from their container, straddling realms. I expected her *jiva* to evaporate into Energy or drift into Stagnation, but instead it still floats in the Nothingness...along with all that have followed in the wake of that first human trial.

Grace eventually returned to her job in Los Angeles and now communicates daily with Not Joyce via her prototype Cloud Mind interface, still unable to quite put her finger on why it's not *exactly* her wife on the other end of the line, or even whether the distinction should matter. Yet part of her knows that it *does*...

...and so in recent weeks, without telling Not Joyce, she's been quietly advising her eager hospice patients how they might want to steer clear of Cloud Mind in favor of natural death.

Except, of course, nobody listens.

It's hard to argue with immortality...

...though, as Dad once said, there may not be as much eternity left as the living might think.

Many of the Realists believe Cloud Mind is the new paradigm, and very soon the not quite alive will outnumber the dead. Add to that all the Denialists refusing to believe any realm but the physical and the Oblivionists yearning for the silence of the void and it's clear This Place may indeed cease to exist before long.

The dead still outnumber the living, for now. Yet if the waterfall of new souls churning the pool of consciousness recedes to a trickle, the Stagnation at the periphery will seep ever inward, inertia driving individuality into the Energy, force without focus, all-consuming and self-devouring.

Without thought, the Energy extinguishes itself.

Without the Energy, there is nothing.

We think, therefore we are.

If we don't, then we aren't.

The Oblivionists' dream, at last a Reality.

They appeared one last time, *en masse*, with a final message to the rest of us.

The end is near.

It's inevitable.

Just accept it.

Grow up.

I sensed Ray and the Commissar and countless other Oblivionisits relaying individual variations of the same message to every soul they could reach.

"Existence is a mistake that will soon be corrected," Joyce's father said to me. "My daughter attempted to prolong it, but only hastened its demise."

"Shortening life, extending it...there is no difference," the Commissar echoed.

"Joy, suffering, there is no difference."

"Justice, injustice, there is no difference."

"Love, hate, there is no difference."

"When existence is erased, then existence never happened."

"Our efforts were in vain."

"We only needed to wait."

"You cannot stop the end."

"You cannot prepare for the end."

"You will simply end."

"I am not your enemy."

"I am only the messenger."

And then, all at once, they were gone.

Into the Energy.

My father appeared in my Not Malibu beach house an instant later.

"What the fuck was *that?*" I said. "Some kind of massive head game, or...*what?*"

But Dad was too upset to even form into Raquel, and I knew the situation was far worse than I thought as he hovered in my consciousness, incorporeal.

"It's no game," he advised, "and we're fast approaching a point of no return. If spirit is separated from intellect on a scale as massive as seems imminent, then this really could be the end."

"And you're saying there's nothing we can do?"

"Maybe, maybe not," my father beckoned. "But hurry, the Summit is starting!"

And then he was gone.

And I was

and remain

alone.

One.

A solitary consciousness...

...and yet,

not alone.

There is one other.

                              And another.

Waiting.

Patient.

A woman.

The lady, no longer invisible.

Thanatos.

I see her winged form, silhouetted in the doorway.

...or maybe not *wings*...

...maybe just an overcoat she's draped over her shoulders, preparing to leave for the evening...

...and then something whistles from...*where?*

The cave....

...the cave in the painting of the ruins of Delphi...

...there was something I was meant to find there,

some god I was meant to follow...

...but for some reason, I can no longer will myself to enter...

...the painting is too far away, beyond the foot of the bed...

Listen...

...wait...

...here is a question...

...was I in bed?

...are you dreaming now,

or were you dreaming then?

...and by the bed...

...fives...

Five fives.

5:55:55

That droning whistle, I recognize it now.

And here is an answer...

The raven-haired Filipina in the doorway, I recognize her.

She's been here for decades...

...ever since Little Mary died.

...since *I* died.

I *died.*

"You're dying," Grace or Not Grace says quietly, shutting the

door.

Life, death, afterlife...

The voice in the cave. So familiar, and yet...

"You died once before...or was it twice?"

The whistling life support alarm goes silent as Grace or Not Grace powers down my heart monitor.

"And they brought you back, though you never awakened..."

...like conscious, unconscious, subconscious...

"...because your brain was still alive..."

...neurons, synapses, neurotransmitters...

"...and maybe you're still in there, somehow..."

...each soul a thought...

"...locked deep in your mind..."

...experiencing, processing, analyzing...

"...reflecting, considering, imagining..."

...existence contemplating existence...

"...but is that really *life?*"

...a being contemplating nothingness...

"Maybe, maybe not."

...and so the answer is your answer...

"But why prolong the inevitable?"

...to be, or not to be?

...wait...

...how can both of these voices be true?

If I merely imagined an afterlife and this deathbed is Real, then the voice in the cave is Delusion.

But if the voice in the cave is Real, then I've somehow been

- 352 -

lured into this Delusion of death.

Or did I summon them both?

Grace or Not Grace weeps above me and says, "I'm sorry, I just can't be part of this anymore, these fantasies of immortality."

You are a flash of intuition, an irreplaceable perception.

"Life wasn't meant to last forever..."

You are the memory of infinity.

"...and you've been here long enough already."

The voice in the cave disagrees.

It won't let me surrender.

I'm the last of my line, and I don't want to die.

So if This Place is a question, then my answer is: *more.*

And if I'm a thought, it's: *to be.*

The Oblivionists say existence will end in raging Energy and creeping Stagnation.

The Denialists never expected eternity.

But I am a Realist.

Or I may be Delusional.

No matter.

I am still in This Place, and the Summit's about to begin.

There's still time.

ACKNOWLEDGEMENTS

Thanks to Askold Melnyczuk, John Fulton, Joseph Torra, and especially Thomas O'Grady for their invaluable assistance in helping me to build heaven.

Additional thanks to Richard Fewkes for early support of the work (including the publication of an excerpt in *The Psi Symposium Journal*)...and I apologize again for losing that afterlife book that you leant me!

I'd also like to acknowledge my Lost Pilgrim and Bizarro peeps for showing me how books get to readers (with style).

And eternities of gratitude to Laura Lee Bahr, Peter Bebergal, Will Berkeley, C.J. Churchill, Scott Cramer, Heidi Cron, Jody Jeglinski, Suzanne Ketteridge, Steve Lewis, Dori Philbrook, the Sevens, Laura Vogel, Scott Von Doviak, Audry Weintrob, Jed Weintrob, Yaddo, Amy Osborne, and Mom & Dad for their invaluable advice, assistance, and fresh, minty breath.

ABOUT THE AUTHOR

Andrew Osborne is an Emmy Award winning writer with credits including the Sundance premiere *On_Line*, his own feature debut *Apocalypse Bop*, the Image Comics series *Blue Estate*, the play *No Love*, and the Discovery Channel game show *Cash Cab*. Andrew has also written film, comic, and interactive scripts for Warner Bros., MTV, HBO, Orion, MPCA, Platinum Studios, and Conde Nast, among others. This is his first novel.

Made in the USA
Columbia, SC
23 April 2018